Heath's Point Suspense

COUNTER POINT
BREAKING POINT
BOILING POINT (Coming soon)
FLASH POINT (Coming soon)

Dallas Duets Clean Billionaire Romance

AIN'T MISBEHAVING
CRY ME A RIVER (Coming soon)
PUTTIN' ON THE RITZ (Coming soon)

Grime Fighter Mysteries

GRIME BEAT
GRIME WAVE
GRIME SPREE
GRIME FAMILY
GRIME & PUNISHMENT

BREAKING POINT

Book 2

Marji Laine

Write Integrity Press
Breaking Point
© 2019 Marji Laine
ISBN: 978-1-944120-88-7

This book is a work of fiction. Names, characters, places, and incidents are either products of the author's imagination or used fictitiously. Any similarity to actual people and/or events is purely coincidental.

Published by Write Integrity Press, PO Box 702852, Dallas, TX 75370
Find out more about the author: *MarjiLaine.com*
Or email her at *AuthorMarjiLaine@gmail.com*
www.WriteIntegrity.com
Printed in the United States of America

BREAKING POINT

Book 2

HEATH'S POINT

Suspense

Marji Laine

Write Integrity Press
Breaking Point
© 2019 Marji Laine
ISBN: 978-1-944120-88-7

Published by Write Integrity Press, PO Box 702852, Dallas, TX 75370
Find out more about the author: *MarjiLaine.com*
Or email her at *AuthorMarjiLaine@gmail.com*
www.WriteIntegrity.com
Printed in the United States of America

Dedication

I dedicate this, my eighth novel
to the eighth member of my family,
my wonderful son-in-love

Matt

with gratitude for the love and kindness that
he pours out on my daughter, Katie.

I'm so delighted that *our* precious redhead chose
such a godly man with whom to share her life.
And I'm grateful to you for exhibiting such
compassion, wisdom, and fun as you do life with us all!

Chapter One

"What do you mean he's missing?" Lt. Jason Danvers set his fishing pole aside. Myra Stone wasn't given to panic. He'd never even noticed the lady flustered. Until this phone call.

"I found a note this morning. I thought he'd taken an early walk, but then I saw that his car was gone and found the note taped to the kitchen faucet that he'd gone to the store for some of his hot chocolate." The older woman's voice broke, though she struggled to lower her volume. "And I called his phone, but it was plugged into the charger in the office."

He pulled a pad out of his jacket pocket and the stub of a pencil. "When did you see him last?"

"I went to bed last night at about eleven. He was watching a baseball game that we'd recorded earlier."

"And you don't know when he left?" Who ventured out in the middle of the night for a silly can of cocoa? Jason jotted the quick details in case he needed to remember them later.

"No. I didn't hear him leave, and didn't … Oh, dear." She was losing control.

"Myra, I'll call Chief Tate, and we'll start a search." He needed to do better than that if he wanted to settle her tension. "He probably ran out of gas or maybe had a flat. With no phone, he couldn't very well call for help."

She stayed silent for a moment. "Yes. I'm sure you're right about that. Please find him for me."

Her plea ripped at a piece of his heart. He ended the call and reeled in his empty line. He'd pack stuff up later. Palming his phone, he jogged to his black Jeep and climbed in.

Pulling onto the gravel road that ran alongside this forgotten branch of Grayson Lake, he called Heath's Point Chief of Police and filled him in on the details. "I'm north of town, but I can swing west a few miles and try some of the back roads from Dallas." That late at night, Ellis would have had to go into the city or at least the suburbs to find his favorite chocolate powder.

"You take that side, and I'll check in town for his car." Chief Dell Tate's normally gruff voice held a tone of worry. "Chances are he came in for donuts or something and just forgot to pick up the note he'd left before going fishing."

Reasonable. But Jason would still feel better when they found the man. He turned onto the county road and tuned in his police radio. He tried to keep the darn thing off on his free days, but this situation warranted his monitoring the feed. Setting it to scan the local agencies, he tried to relax. Ellis Stone would be found. He'd be fine. This would be a non-issue.

But something in his gut argued against all of that.

God, please, calm Myra right now. Help us find Ellis, so she doesn't have to worry.

From her straight-back chair, Alynne Stone kept her eyes trained on the enlarged, black-and-white photograph hanging on the bare wall behind her boss's head. The man's silence unnerved her. She'd half-expected to be congratulated over this morning's casework, but Mr. Fulton appeared more thoughtful than joyful. Almost sullen.

So, the picture was the safer bet. Albeit an unnerving one. The finger of the 1950's deadly tornado that had ripped apart much of South Dallas reached from a bank of boiling clouds to the ground within a mile of downtown. The black funnel kicked up a cloud of debris made up of homes, cars, and businesses that flew from its base. The sight both excited and terrified her at the same time.

Mr. Fulton smacked his palms on the desktop, making her jump. He wiped the wood with his fingertips almost as if he apologized for the earlier offense. Then he leveled a look on Alynne that she'd seen him use countless times in the courtroom. Only he'd never used it on her.

"This sort of sloppiness is not to be tolerated. You made the entire firm look foolish."

Sloppy? Her jaw muscle went slack for a moment, and she brushed an errant strand of hair back into her tight, businesslike bun. "I don't understand."

"Did you think Mr. Brevard would just conjure a beneficial outcome to the lawsuit? Without any evidence or documentation?

What happened to the deposition from the man in France?"

Those papers had been included in the packet she'd given the team. And every one of the sheets was formatted, notarized, signed, whatever they had needed. "Mr. Fulton, I'm sure the paperwork was all in order and included in the packet." Not that she wanted to get Mr. Brevard into any trouble. The man and his wife had been so kind to her—like adopted parents now that her own had moved out to *hicksville*. She wouldn't hurt him for anything.

"What packet?" He pulled his briefcase to the top of his spotless desk. He winced when he set the case down a little roughly, likely leaving dents in the glossy, walnut finish. "This packet?"

She took the flimsy white envelope that had been considerably thicker this morning. "I don't understand," she said again. The collection had the same cover sheet and finance report, but the important documents, the ones she'd discovered a few days ago, the ones the case hinged on, were gone. "I had signed testimonials in here, notarized. And Mr. Razier's deposition ..."

He rounded the desk and snatched the envelope back. "Where?" He withdrew several pages. "This useless notice of concealment?" He held it out, but when she reached for it, he tossed it on the desk. "These bank statements?" He turned, flinging the pages over his shoulder so that they scattered across the wooden surface. Stopping at the opposite corner, he turned the empty envelope upside down.

Well, not quite empty. The receipt from her Starbucks run a few days ago fell out with another page, and both drifted to the

floor near her. Probably got stuck in there as she did her late-night final check. She reached for the receipt on the floor and tucked it into her shoe. No reason to get herself in any deeper with an unintentional reimbursement request.

To cover her movement, she picked up the other page that had slipped out with it and laid it on the desk. "That packet was full, Mr. Fulton. Stuffed. I can't imagine where all those pages went. I personally spoke with the owner of the Hadimon Spa where the other work had broken down. I had pictures and documentation all properly witnessed."

He stared at her, the lines between his eyebrows deepening. "By the time this reached Mr. Brevard, it was exactly as you see it."

How could that be? She looked at her boss's normally pristine desk, covered in a chaos of paperwork and an open briefcase. Mr. Fulton's normally meticulous habits had flown out the window with his outrage.

"I don't know what to say. Everything was there when I put it on the file clerk's desk." Stephanie Carson. A pimple inside her ear couldn't annoy her half as much as that competitive shark. Sure, she'd say anything to make Alynne look bad, especially after losing the executive research assistant promotion to her. But she wouldn't have set up their clients to lose such a huge case just to get rid of Alynne. Would she?

"Ah, so now you're blaming your oversight on Miss Carson?" He gripped one hand with the other as if he cracked his knuckles. "I should think you could be more creative in your excuses, Miss Stone." He leaned over on the wood with his palms stretched wide on the messy surface. Like a panther, he poised before his final attack, unless she did something to offset the knife plunging into her heart. She'd worked way too hard to get where she was to simply sit here and let him lambaste her without a fight.

She stood, her gaze steady on the bridge of the man's nose, a trick she'd learned from her speech teacher in high school. "I'm not blaming anyone, Mr. Fulton. I'm willing to investigate to learn what happened to the file before I start flinging accusations."

"Take care, young lady." His lowered voice sounded like the hiss he used in the courtroom, but she would not be intimidated. He appreciated people with passion, willing to take a stand.

And stand she would. She folded her arms. "Mr. Brevard's case should have been easily won with the extra details I was able to unearth. What's more, I have never let a member of your team down, nor any of the clients they have represented. My reputation here should count for something."

He lowered himself into his seat, his view not wavering from hers. "How long have you been at Fulton Brevard & Sawyer?"

"Seven years." She answered with a strong tone. She'd been hired straight out of college to this firm by Mr. Brevard himself since he was an acquaintance of her father's. But she'd certainly proved herself worthy of the job. Her work had resulted in millions for their clients and handsome commissions and bonuses for the attorneys and their teams. "And in that time, never once has my work been questioned."

"So I recall." He broke eye contact and focused on his messy desk. He picked up some of the scattered papers and stacked them together, popping the edges on the surface.

She braced her hands against her side. He'd used this tactic in court many times, performing some mundane task until the witness was distracted and then hammering home the final deafening blow.

The trick wouldn't work on her. If he was going to fire her, he'd have to look her in the eyes to do so.

He finished repacking the envelope and placed it inside his briefcase. Then the sleek leather case disappeared over the side and landed on the carpet with a muffled thump.

He swiped his hand over the area several times. Several dents and a couple of scratches had appeared where the case had been. Though he'd probably have it buffed and perfect again before Monday, it served him right for wrongly accusing her. Hopefully, he'd figure that out before Monday as well.

How strange to feel embattled against a boss she'd come to appreciate and respect. Even if he didn't fire her, she felt a long, hard cry coming on. The look of disappointment on his face was enough to assure that.

He clasped his hands in front of him and once again looked up at her. "Very well, Miss Stone. We will call this matter closed. I will speak to Brevard and the judge in hopes that a new suit can be filed on behalf of our clients. Of course, another researcher will be placed on the team."

"I understand." He could bet she'd be looking into where the mess-up had occurred in this instance. And if Stephanie had anything to do with it, she wasn't going to back down from that either.

"I suggest that you make your apologies to Mr. Brevard. He's the one who was made to look the fool and had to listen to a tirade from the clients. Of course, if they sue him, we'll have to take responsibility."

She wouldn't apologize, not even to Mr. Brevard. Not if it meant taking responsibility for the error. The envelope, when she'd set it in the organizer, had filled one of the folder gaps on Stephanie's desk. The envelope he'd just put away was less than a third of what it had been. "I will certainly give my regrets to Mr. Brevard."

"You do that."

Dismissal. Finally. Keeping her chin high and her tears at bay, she turned toward his door.

"You know if anything of this sort ever happens again …"

"Yes, sir." She'd likely be booted without discussion. But it wouldn't happen again. It had better not.

Shutting the door behind her, she rushed past the desk of his administrative assistant. The woman was amazingly efficient, and always so nice. And kindness was the last thing she needed right now. The first sign of sympathy would make her erupt in weak blubbering.

With her eyes locked onto the elevator doors, she strode the length of the hallway with purposeful steps, holding her breath and the welling tears that clouded her vision.

Yet even through the blur, determination to learn the source of the sabotage burned in her soul.

The Lord knew where Ellis was. Given a little time, He'd

allow Jason or Dell to find him. And Jason had the time—part of the charm of working for a small-town police department. The fish probably wouldn't even know they'd been stood up.

He traversed one country road after another, each slick and shiny from the overnight rains, but found no little white sedan stopped alongside the asphalt.

"Cruiser 10, single-vehicle accident near Farm-to-Market 457." His gut clenched with the call from the county dispatcher. But there was no reason to assume that Ellis had an accident.

Still, Jason wasn't far from the area. He'd travel that direction if only to get a look at the vehicle and ease his mind that it wasn't Ellis. Jason glanced at his dashboard clock. Almost ten. He'd have been tired of fishing by now anyway.

His cell buzzed from the pocket of his gray-green shirt and gave his normal greeting, "Danvers."

"You hear that call?" His superior's gruff voice barely echoed over the background sounds of his noisy patrol car.

"Yes, sir. I'm already headed in that direction." Thankfully, he hadn't picked up his cruiser. Nothing official. Maybe the deputy he always seemed to butt heads with wouldn't be too hostile toward him since he wasn't in the uniform or the painted car.

"I'll meet you there." Chief Tate snorted. "Those county boys don't like you much."

"I know how to play nice." Too bad the sheriff's office treated every accident and crime as some sort of competition with all the local agencies. "Besides, they don't like you either." Antagonizing them didn't take much.

"That's because they think I'll toss my hat in the ring for

sheriff someday."

Sheriff Beauregard Kindrich had been in charge of the county for almost two decades, and he wasn't about to relinquish his power to anyone. Especially not to Chief Dell Tate, fifteen years younger than Kindrich and exponentially better at his job. Tate had hinted more than once—even within the sheriff's hearing—that he might like to run for the elected position.

The chief scoffed. "But they still don't dare shove me around the way they do you."

Who would shove a rattler with his bare hands? Jason kept the image to himself. After all, he was still the newcomer to the HPPD, only here for a few years. An outsider to many people, even in town but especially to the sheriff and his deputies. "I'll stay out of sight until you arrive, then."

He turned onto County Road 457, a narrow strip of asphalt still glistening in the morning sunlight. This wouldn't have been a direct route to the store that Myra claimed her husband visited, but it might have been his choice to avoid the more direct route, which often flooded in a heavy sprinkle.

After following it for a few miles without spotting anything, he resisted the urge to turn off and head for Myra's place, Sunrise Inn. Maybe Ellis had returned home by now.

Cresting another hill, he sighted a small gathering of county cruisers. Looked like he'd located their accident. He pulled off the road some distance from the other vehicles. No need to poke the brown bears, as the local police tended to call them.

Jason did a quick, three-point turn and found a wide area on the other side where he could park. He jogged back to the curve and stood at the crest of the hill overlooking a sorghum field which was soggy from last night's showers. Sounded like the entire sheriff's department was down there except for one sad lackey on the far side of the curve who'd been stuck with traffic duty.

From his position, Jason couldn't see any accident. The curve jutted out a bit, blocking his view. But he could hear the men talking. Unfortunately, one voice rang out above the others.

Deputy Martin Cain. The man practically worshiped at the feet of the sheriff, probably in hopes of being his successor someday. Cain, one of the senior deputies, had probably taken charge of the scene.

Jason wouldn't get a blade of grass from that guy.

Before the traffic lackey turned toward him, Jason eyed the incline off the side of the road. Steep, but with little flat areas spaced at good intervals. Jason dropped off the edge of the embankment and cut downhill to a grove of leafy cottonwoods on the edge of the sorghum field. If Deputy Cain searched, he might distinguish Jason's pale mossy shirt or his light tan hat in the undergrowth, but Cain missed more than he caught.

Jason had a clear view of a white sedan resting on its roof in the gully at the edge of the field.

A sick feeling punched his gut. He'd held out hope for any other color. But even so, this was East Texas. Every third vehicle was white to reflect the blistering, summer sun.

None of the county people seemed to be moving very fast. He wanted to believe that they'd already transported the injured driver away, but he knew better. This was a new scene. The fact that they weren't moving could only mean one thing. Someone was dead.

No need to hurry. Even after almost a decade of law enforcement, he'd never gotten used to seeing the dead. Especially after what had happened to him in Chicago.

But even without that tragedy, he couldn't fathom how law enforcement professionals were supposed to simply shrug off the ending of a life, callously discarding the dreams and potential of the victim? That went for any victim, but especially for a nice, old man who had made Jason a member of the family, welcoming him with a goodhearted laugh and a firm handshake.

Not that the driver was Ellis. Maybe Chief Tate had found him by now. Jason pulled out his phone and texted in order to keep things quiet. "Found the accident. Deputy Cain's in charge. White car. Tell me you've found Ellis." With nothing to do except wait for his boss's response, he picked a wide leaf from a nearby branch and absently tore it into thin strips while he listened to the discussions from those at the scene.

"Been dead since about midnight, if I had to guess." The county coroner, Dr. Barnes, was a plumpish, middle-aged man with dark hair under his trademark Texas Rangers Baseball cap.

"Don't want *chur* guessing Charlie. I could do that *misself*." Deputy Cain didn't tend to make friends even within his department.

"Medical Examiner'll get closer." The coroner pulled off the cap, scratched his bald spot, and put the cap back on. "Take a while to hear from him."

"*Un-Ax-ceptable.*" Cain's volume rose. "This case'll be wrapped up with a bow by Sunday's paper."

Two days? Cain was dreaming. This was probably a simple

accident, but the county ME, Doc Umbridge, wouldn't even see the data before sometime next week. Maybe the week after if he was busy.

"Like I said ...." The coroner looked meek and amiable, but he had enough gusto to stand up to Deputy Martin Cain. "'Bout midnight. Maybe one. Best guess you'll get for Sunday's paper."

Jason edged to the right, staying in the tree line but hoping to get a view of the driver. He spotted the chief's cruiser coming around the bend.

Good, he'd get some answers.

The county crime scene investigators measured, marked, and photographed every aspect of the scene. Cain stood to one side with his arms folded.

"What you got going on down here, Cain?" The chief made his way down the hill, and his booming voice seemed to fill the entire valley.

"Nothing you LEOs need to worry about." Cain might have jurisdiction over the local Law Enforcement Officers, but he had no sense when it came to talking to the chief.

Jason strode from his camouflage and climbed through the slats of the fence. "I should think after all the help we gave the county a few months ago, during those drug raids, that Deputy Cain would at least extend respect, Chief."

"Great, so the outsider is here, too." Cain glared at Jason.

"The important people show respect, Jason. Others show immaturity." The chief sniffed in Cain's direction as he rounded the car.

Jason joined the county coroner who stood taking notes in a

little booklet. "One occupant?"

The coroner didn't even glance at Cain's thundercloud face before nodding. "Late sixties, maybe earlier seventies."

Not what Jason wanted to hear.

"And that ain't none of their business, Charlie." Cain stepped between the two, bending over the shorter coroner as if chastising an errant youth.

Dell scratched at his whitish beard. "Son, you need to learn how to work and play nice with others."

The coroner snickered.

Dell continued, laying his palm on the deputy's shoulder. "Normal for a cop like Jason to be concerned about something like this."

"He ain't got no jurisdiction here." Cain used that mantra like a business card. "And neither do you."

"Shoot, son. Just because a career officer is hanging around don't mean he wants to take over. Stop getting your shorts in a wad about a fight that ain't even there." Dell's comment raised a rumble of chuckles from the others working the scene and a couple of firemen sent to retrieve the body.

The chief bent over to peer through the shattered back glass. "So. This Ellis Stone's car?"

Jason's gut twisted. He waited, hoped, for someone to say, *No, it belongs to some stranger.*

This time the coroner glanced at Cain. The deputy shook his head, but the older man turned toward Dell. "You recognize the man's car in this condition?"

"Good friend." Dell's tone lowered.

To both of them. The knot in Jason's gut tightened. He squatted, avoiding the view of the man who had been his friend hunched against the passenger window.

"I'm sorry, Chief. Wallet belongs to Ellis Stone. Picture matches." The coroner continued to speak about details to the chief and the deputy. Jason stopped listening.

Victim. Ellis was the victim. And Jason needed to see him in that way to stay detached enough to let his observations connect.

He glanced around the interior of the car. No wires on the accelerator. The car was in gear. The victim wasn't belted into the seat. That was strange. Ellis was always automatic in buckling his seatbelt. His blue jeans were soaking wet in places.

Jason put a knee down in the wet grass.

"Keep your fingerprints to yourself, Danvers." Cain stepped around the car from the other direction.

"Just making observations."

The chief knelt beside him. "Awful way to go."

Jason pointed to a puddle of water that soaked the headliner. "Where did all that water come from?"

"It rained last night, of course." Cain hadn't bothered to get a glimpse of it for himself. He would've seen how unlikely that was.

"Didn't rain that hard last night. Less than a quarter-inch." The chief stood and pointed it out to the coroner.

The man bent down next to Jason. "I'm not an investigator, but it looks strange to me." He turned to Cain. "You should make a note. There's more than an inch of water pooling near the dome light." He stood and looked expectantly at Cain.

"This is a waste of time." But the deputy pulled out his tablet and tapped a few keys.

"Maybe." Jason took another look, particularly scanning the backseat. A smashed Whataburger cup was near the back window. A discarded receipt with a burger wrapper was near it. "Maybe not. You going to collect all of the items in the car?" Jason stood.

"This is an accident scene, Lieutenant." Cain narrowed the gap between them, elbows back like a banty rooster and staring up from the height of Jason's chin. "And this ain't none of your business."

Jason stood firm, looking over the man's head at the chief.

The older man patted Cain on the shoulder. "There's no call for that, son. Procedure says you collect everything from the scene, even of an accident. Insurance, you know." He patted him again, persuading him to turn away from Jason. "And I tell you what, you make sure all of those little details get collected and we get access to them, and we'll go tell the family about their loss."

Cain huffed but released his attitude. "The sheriff will appreciate that, Chief."

"Of course." Dell eyed the junior bear. "Rather it come from me."

"Sorry for your loss." To Cain's credit, he delivered his condolence with a semblance of regret instead of a victory dance. "If it's any comfort, he went quickly."

The coroner chimed in. "Broken neck, head wounds. Didn't have time to even be afraid."

"Probably saw the Lord before he even saw the ground." Leave it to Dell to put things into perspective, but that wouldn't make the loss any easier. He nodded at the two men. "Jason and I will break the news to his wife."

Cain nodded then raised one eyebrow. "But you'll need to contact the sheriff right after you've spoken to her and let him announce it to the media."

So much for Cain's credit. His intention to use Ellis's death to secure voters for the sheriff left a putrid taste in Jason's mouth.

Dell lifted his eyes heavenward but agreed and gestured for Jason to join him on a trek back toward the road.

"Not the way I'd hoped to find Ellis." Jason dug his hiking boots into the soft dirt of the incline.

"Me neither, though I'd never known the man to disappear. Knew something had happened." He fingered his tuft of beard again above his light-blue uniform shirt. "I hate what this is gonna do to Myra."

"Especially with no family around." Though they had a daughter, maybe two, he'd never met them. Myra's closest friend, Cat Alexander, was out of town. "Should we let Cat and Ray know?"

"No. they deserve to finish their honeymoon in ignorant bliss." Dell shot him a look. "And until they get back, we'll make sure Myra has plenty of help and support, starting with you taking her out to Howie-Mem to wait for her husband's body."

Howerton Memorial Hospital served as a temporary morgue until the county could build one of their own. "I'll take care of her." Jason ached for Myra. Losing a soulmate was hard enough without having to go through the loss all alone. He knew the feeling well.

A position he'd vowed to never relive.

BREAKING POINT

Chapter Two

If only she could have some privacy. But no. Several people were already aboard the elevator from businesses on the upper floors. Still, she could have her solitude in her car in the parking complex. Not exactly private, but as close as she would get on a Friday morning. The compartment lowered then slowed to a stop only one floor down. The doors opened to reveal her direct boss, Ms. Oglesby, Supervisor of Research, ready to board.

"Oh, I was just headed to find you, Alynne." Ms. Oglesby backed up a few short steps and ushered Alynne out of the car. "Let's you and I sit down for a little chat." The petite woman put her back to Alynne and clipped down the makeshift hallway between the cubicle walls and various desks.

Great. More tear-suppression. Alynne trotted several steps to catch up with the woman. All four-feet, ten-inches of her remained in constant motion like that battery bunny. But as tiny as she was, she could become a monstrous brick wall if someone ticked her off or did anything to hurt the company or injure her reputation.

Alynne had likely done all three.

Alynne followed Ms. Oglesby through the open room where most of the research assistants and file clerks sat. She focused on her boss's back, but in her peripheral vision, she spotted Stephanie at her desk and could feel her eyes boring into her.

They entered the walled office, Ms. Oglesby's domain. While not an expansive view, she did have a narrow window overlooking the park that spanned a block of Main Street.

"Sit down, Alynne." She motioned to a small couch crammed into the nook of her office. "I've heard you had a rough morning already." She tugged open the door of a refrigerator concealed under an end table and withdrew two miniature bottles of water. Taking her place in the wingback chair on Alynne's left, she offered one of the bottles to Alynne.

"Yes." Alynne cracked open the bottle and took a drink.

"But not as bad as Mr. Brevard's has been." Ms. Oglesby held her bottle unopened and narrowed her expression at Alynne. How could the woman's eyes show such kindness while her tone held such a cold edge?

Alynne took another sip and swallowed slowly. "No, not as bad as Mr. Brevard's has been."

"I'm glad we can agree on that. What can you do to see to it that Mr. Brevard doesn't have another morning like this?"

Alynne hesitated. She didn't want to throw anyone under the bus, even Stephanie, but that file had been full. "From now on, I'll deliver my research files directly to the attorneys in charge."

Ms. Oglesby's brows raised, but she didn't interrupt.

"I have no doubt that we'll end up finding all of the documents that filled the envelope later on today. Maybe on the floor under a desk or accidentally discarded into a trashcan. Had I delivered the file directly to Mr. Brevard, we wouldn't be having this conversation." There, she took responsibility but made it abundantly clear she'd done her job.

There was a knock on the open door, and, of all people, Stephanie poked her head in. "You wanted to know when the court date for the Raffin case was set?"

Ms. Oglesby waved her in and took the file. "Perfect."

Stephanie pulled a straight-backed chair from in front of the desk toward them and sat. "The judge set it for next Thursday and I've done some anticipatory work on the file."

Alynne stiffened. "I thought I was on that case." She could almost hear Stephanie's thoughts. *You snooze, you lose.* And that annoying hum of a chuckle that she used.

"Yes." Ms. Oglesby turned to Stephanie and handed the file back to her. "Since this has fallen into your lap, Stephanie, go ahead and begin the research. If you need help, Alynne can join you."

Wonderful. Even Ms. Oglesby had lost trust in her. Alynne took another drink from her bottle, willing her constricted throat to allow it to go down.

"And about Mr. Brevard." Stephanie settled in her chair as though she were going to stay for a while. "I'm certain that I can assist him with the continuance that he had to ask for in this morning's case."

Now that was an outright frontal attack. And she was only a file clerk. Alynne controlled the grimace that begged to form and

27

willed her facial features to relax as she finished off her water bottle. More and more, she was certain that Stephanie had removed those reports from the file while it was on her desk awaiting trial. But she couldn't prove it. Not even to herself. And Mr. Fulton had already as much as said that the research on the new hearing would be assigned to someone else. Best for Alynne to let Ms. Oglesby make that decision and keep her mouth shut. *Please, God, help her have some faith in me still.*

The supervisor stood and walked to her window. "No, but thank you for your concern, Stephanie. I think Alynne is quite capable of taking care of Mr. Brevard's cases. Besides, the Raffin case should give you some good experience. Maybe a step in the direction of joining the corps of our researchers." She shifted her focus back to the center of the room. "And if you're all right, Alynne, I would like to speak with Stephanie to get her started."

Just as Alynne's concern had begun to ease, her fingers iced up around the empty bottle. She was being invited to leave. Though completely understandable, and it had certainly happened to other people when she'd entered Ms. Oglesby office, it had never happened before to her. "Of course." She rose and tipped the bottle in her boss's direction. "Thanks for the water." She paused at the door and looked back at her supervisor. "And the chat."

Stephanie hummed her stupid giggle, and Alynne pulled the door closed without acknowledging her.

Now to her car.

She wouldn't cry. The tears weren't there anyway. They probably had never been, but she wanted to gather her thoughts and pray a little. The elevator was virtually empty this time. Only a couple of people from one of the upper floors rode to ground level with her.

The bright sunlight of Dallas bled through the two-story windows that opened out onto Elm Street. Her escape. The ringtone of her parents' home phone chimed, and she paused. No, she didn't want to unload on them. Not yet. She silenced her phone.

"Alynne, there you are."

The call of her name echoed against the tile of the entry.

Blayne stood by the security counter. "I was signing in." He scratched his name onto the book.

"I need some air," she said. And though she adored the man, she craved her solitude and hoped he would allow it to her.

"I need to talk to you first."

So much for solitude. "Sure. Is everything okay?" Great. He was going to break up with her. This was just the way her morning was going.

"Yes, well, yes and no." He shifted his weight from his left to his right. "We've only been dating for a few months."

She pressed her lips together and glanced at the security guard. The man was obviously pretending not to hear their amplified voices as he clicked away on a tablet. Like he could help but eavesdrop.

She moved a few steps away. "And?"

"I wanted to talk to you last night, but I was delayed. I've made a decision."

Here it came. "Yes?"

In one graceful motion, Blayne captured her hand and knelt to one knee.

Her neck iced.

"I've got to go to Las Vegas, and I want you to come with me. We can be married today."

The air left her lungs and dried her throat. "Today?" she croaked and coughed.

"I'm asking you to marry me."

"Marriage?" The ice thickened down the back of her neck and spread to her shoulders. Was this really happening? Exactly what she had talked to Pop about on the phone last weekend. The solution to all of her problems. "Of course, I'll marry you." Absolutely. Especially after …

He rose quickly and pressed his lips against hers for a moment. "I've got two tickets for the two o'clock flight."

"Two o'clock?" Her parents. She needed to talk to them, needed to get their blessing. Pop hadn't been all that sure last week, regardless of her arguments. "Wait."

Blayne moved away. She followed, but her feet felt like they'd been glued to the floor.

"Don't worry about a thing. I'll speak to your boss myself." He reached the chrome doors and punched the up button.

"My boss?" She reached out for him.

Blayne was already stepping onto the elevator.

"Wait … no … please." Alynne jumped aboard behind him.

"We need to get her permission so you can leave early. You can leave early, can't you?"

"Well, I don't know." After the morning she'd had, they might just toss her out on the street. "Really, this isn't the best time."

"You're getting married. Of course, they'll let you off."

A chime sounded as they slowed to a stop on the twenty-fifth floor.

"Show me the way." Blayne laced his fingers through hers and urged her forward with a sweet smile.

Well, Mr. Brevard's continuance wasn't scheduled for several weeks. Maybe this could work.

Drawing in a deep breath, she led the way through the main room to Ms. Oglesby's office. The door was open. Apparently, the talk with Stephanie hadn't lasted too long. Alynne tapped on it.

"Come."

Alynne peeked inside. "I was wondering if you had a minute?"

"Of course, Alynne." Her supervisor rose and rounded the desk. "Annnd …" The woman's gaze shifted to Blayne who followed her into the room.

Alynne noticed the question that had formed on her boss's face. "This is Blayne. My … uh … um …"

"Fiancé." Blayne supplied the word and gave her a wink.

Ms. Oglesby grinned and clapped her hands. "Alynne Stone, you never even told me," she chastised and reached to shake Blayne's hands. "Congratulations. You are getting a wonderful girl."

Alynne's faculties were still a little on the stunned side. "It all happened rather quickly."

"I came to ask if you would release Alynne for the rest of the day." Blayne pressed forward with the plan that he'd shared.

Alynne had hoped that he'd let her do the talking. After all, Ms. Oglesby was her boss. This was her job and her responsibility. "As I said, this was all rather sudden. If it isn't convenient, we can certainly schedule another time."

"Nonsense." Blayne spread a charming smile on his face, first for Alynne and then for her supervisor. "Your boss isn't going to stand in the way of true love, are you?" He released Alynne's hand and slipped his arm around her waist, pressing a kiss against her forehead.

"Of course not." Ms. Oglesby said, but her eyebrow arched just a tad. "If this is what you want, Alynne, then you have my blessing. You can have the rest of the day off starting now." She paused. "If this is what you want."

Blayne's smile grew, and he reached to give the woman a side-hug. "Thank you so much. I can't tell you how happy you've made us."

Ms. Oglesby's gaze locked onto Alynne's.

She looked away from her supervisor's searching gaze, but she nodded. "Yes, thank you."

Blayne, once again, laced his fingers around hers. "Let's grab your things."

She reached her desk as her phone chimed, and again it was her parents' number. "I need to take this."

"Oh, no." He pulled the phone from her hand and laid it on her desk. "We're gonna leave this right here." He reached into his back pocket and withdrew his own. "And mine too. We don't want any interruptions this weekend." He grinned at her like a little boy ready for his first trip to Six Flags.

Alynne matched his smile, suppressing her concerns. She was beginning to warm to the idea. After all, wasn't this everything she wanted? The flutter of a giggle rose. What an adventure this would be.

But she still needed to talk to her folks. Needed to gain her father's approval. Blayne didn't even know them.

"Okay, okay, I will, but first I need to take this." She picked up her phone. "Momma?"

"Alynne, precious." Her mom's voice sounded strained.

"Momma, I have some wonderful news to share with you."

"I need … I'm leaving …" Her mom's voice broke. "I'm leaving for Howerton Memorial Hospital."

The hospital? "Let me talk to Pop." Surely, her mom's cancer hadn't returned.

"I can't." Her mom's voice broke again.

"Momma?" It must be her cancer. But she hadn't sounded sick when Alynne spoke to her last weekend.

"I need you to come, Alynne."

"I'll be there, Momma. I'll be there. But let me talk …" The phone clicked in her ear, ending the call.

She pulled the phone from her ear and stared at it for a moment before slipping it back into her purse.

"Wait." Blayne had been watching her through the call and now reached for her phone. "We're leaving these here, remember?"

He reached for her bag, but she held it fast and pulled out the keys. "I'm sorry, Blayne, but I can't go with you."

"What? We have the weekend to ourselves. We're going to be married."

"Not this weekend." She shook her head. The bubble that had drifted upward shrank with the fear for her mom. Three grueling years, her mom had battled cancer into remission. *Oh, Lord, please don't make her go through all of that again.* Thankfully, she had won the fight, and as hard as it was, it was much better than losing her altogether. *But Your will, Lord.*

She straightened. "I have to go home." She pushed past Blayne and made a beeline for the elevator. At this point, she didn't care if he followed her.

"I'll go with you." He joined her in the elevator.

Her throat constricted, and her mouth turned sour. She rode down in silence and crossed the foyer, allowing him to open the door for her. But as she stepped onto the Elm Street sidewalk, she put her hand against his chest. "You have a job to do in Las Vegas."

"I can change my plans," he insisted.

"There's nothing you can do if my mother's cancer is back … except pray."

Shock crossed his face. "She's had cancer."

Didn't he remember? Alynne spoke of her often enough. Particularly how the strong, capable woman she was now was nothing like the invalid she'd been through her chemo years. "If it's back, Pop and I need to make plans. If nothing else, I need to find out what's going on before you and I can do anything drastic."

"I understand." His brows furrowed. "But I wish you'd let me go with you." The muscle near the dimple in his cheek twitched. "I don't like leaving you to deal with this alone."

She kissed the dimple. "I won't be alone. Pop will be with me, and we'll get through this just fine." She brushed a quick kiss on his lips and then turned, calling, "Have a safe trip," over her shoulder.

"You, too." His words followed after her, but she didn't look back as she jogged to her car in the lot.

She climbed into the front seat and rested her hands on the steering wheel. Her gaze fell to her left hand. No ring. But there would be a ring there. Would've been one today, except … She had some things she needed to talk over with Pop.

BREAKING POINT

Chapter Three

Jason paced the hallway outside the chapel at Howerton Memorial. He rubbed his sweaty palms on his jeans. *Breathe. Just breathe.* He paused in front of a landscape painting that interrupted bare walls. An empty rowboat in the middle of a pond. Probably some fancy type of art, but what would he know.

Still, what he wouldn't give to be there. Shoot, he'd be happy to be anywhere other than the antiseptic death palace of this hospital. He continued toward the front of the waiting room. A mom sat in the corner with her kids. Her two boys fought over an iPad. The tired woman leaned against the armrest and stared at the television. And no wonder. Daytime drama actors posed with appropriate shock. Looked like she'd found her own version of that empty rowboat.

He stopped at the windows and gazed into the parking lot. Maybe he should take a walk out there. Get away from the feel of this place. A deep emptiness erupted like a dormant volcano— quiet for five years, now. Since Chicago. He quashed the feeling.

Myra deserved his best right now. A sympathetic friend with a strong shoulder. He'd better not let his own ghosts take over. He scanned the parking lot once more. Nothing new there, but then, Dallas was a pretty far drive.

His eyes rested on the blue Ford that belonged to Pastor Philip Slaughter. He owed the man a big thank you for waiting with Myra in the chapel. Playing chauffeur was easy. Sitting inside that tiny room with piped-in organ music and a thick orchid smell, not so much.

Glancing outside again, he prayed the woman would arrive quickly. Maybe he should try again to persuade Myra to go back home now that the funeral home had taken charge of Ellis's body. He moved back toward the chapel entrance, a bead of sweat breaking out on his upper lip.

He'd faced gun-toting drug addicts, armed gang members, and a driver hyped up on steroids trying to run him down in a truck. None of those situations bothered him nearly as much as entering this over-sized casket.

A heavy, wood-panel door held a small, gold plaque announcing the chapel's wealthy donor. Some couple who had likely died long before Jason ever came to Heath's Point. Had their passing left the sort of hole that Ellis's had?

He took a deep breath and pushed open the door.

The smell of grief pervaded the room. Dim lights filtered through fake stained-glass windows. Reflections of pink, gold, and green splashed on the walls. Jason's eyes adjusted from the brightness of the waiting room. The tone of the chapel was obviously meant to calm and soothe.

Fat chance of that happening.

Philip Slaughter bent his salt and pepper head close to Myra's. Her own hair had a more silver hue, but the confidence she normally showed hid under her lowered chin and slumped shoulders. Though their mouths moved, only the low rumble of his baritone cut through the dreary organ music.

Myra lifted her head and broke the pretense of serenity. "Is she here?"

"No. I'm sorry." He should have stayed in the hall.

She stood and drifted toward the cross at the front of the room.

Philip stretched. "Why don't you call her again, Myra. Let her know you'll meet her at home."

The man practically read Jason's thoughts. "You'll be more comfortable at the inn." All of them would. Sunrise Inn was one of the nicest bed and breakfast inns he'd ever encountered.

She turned, shoulders drooping, and crept back to her seat on the front pew. "You're probably right, Jason, but I think I'd like to wait a little longer." When had Myra become so frail? She'd aged ten years since they had arrived. She shrugged. "I'm not even sure she'll come."

"Of course, she will." Pastor Slaughter reseated himself. "You're her mom. She'll not leave you alone in your grief. She's grieving as well, I'm sure."

Myra pressed her lips together for an instant before she replied. "I couldn't find a way to tell her. About Ellis. She was her pop's little girl." Her voice broke, and she sniffed into a tissue. "At least, she was until we moved out here. We would still see her often enough, visiting at her apartment or meeting for dinners. And she calls regularly, but she hasn't been to the inn in years, and then only one evening during the holidays for a couple of hours."

"You and Ellis tried every way you could to coax her to come." Philip handed her another tissue.

She wiped under her eyes. "I got the feeling that she'd been hurt somehow, but she would never speak of it."

"I know your daughter cares about you, though."

Jason's thoughts exactly. How could she not care about such sweet people? What he wouldn't give to have had parents like hers. She had no idea how blessed she was.

"At least she got to talk with Ellis last weekend." Myra sniffed again and folded her hands in her lap. "But visiting was always out of the question. She would say it was her job, but I'm sure there was more to it."

"What's her job?" Philip's question made for a great distraction at just the right time.

"She works for a law firm."

"She's a lawyer?" If that was the case, no wonder she was too busy to come out here.

"No, no. She was pre-law in college, but she decided she wanted to be a legal assistant. She's part of the firm's research team, and to hear her stories, she's helped the different attorneys win several cases for their clients.

Not quite as key a position for her to never have time for her parents, but for Myra's benefit, he'd accept the excuse.

"She strives for perfection, always. So much like her pop." The lady's face shone for a moment before the words settled in the room. "Like he was." She lifted her head, and worry creased her brow. "I supposed I should contact the rest of the family."

"There's no hurry about that, Myra." Philip patted her hand where it rested on her purse.

The man was right. The woman was remarkably strong, but now wasn't the time for added tension.

Her mouth flattened. "I really should make one more call. Though I'm not sure I'm ready for that conflict, yet." Her hands became fists as they lay in her lap.

"Maybe your daughter can make that call later tonight. Or tomorrow." Philip leaned closer. "Or one of us can."

Jason would be happy to make calls if he didn't have to make them from this tiny, over-perfumed tomb. Whatever it took to ease her stress. "You need to focus on working with your daughter to get through all of this."

"All of this …" She echoed his words and leaned onto Philip as the minister wrapped his arm about her shoulders.

Well, that backfired. "I'll keep an eye out for your daughter." Jason backed out the door. Coward. Regardless of how often he experienced them, a woman's tears undid him. He scanned the waiting room once more and strode to the entrance. He could wait for the daughter as easily outside in the fresh air as he could inside this antibacterial can.

Finally reaching the glass doors, he held one open for a lady entering then escaped into the April sunshine. The smell of rain still clung to the rocks in the cobbled pavement of the drive. Fresh, clean, and not poisoned with cleaners or odd chemicals.

Wait, that woman. He pivoted and rushed back to the door. Surely, that elegant lady wasn't Myra's daughter. She stood beside the information counter waiting for the volunteer to get off the phone.

She looked nothing like Myra, tall instead of petite. But then, Ellis had been on the taller side. The woman's sleeveless navy and beige dress exposed the beginnings of a tan, and her dark hair was wrapped up in some sort of clip at the base of her head.

He paused at the desk to get a look at her face. Her eyes, strikingly blue against her dark hair, had to come from Ellis's side of the family, but her facial structure, sort of a heart-shaped face, definitely mirrored Myra.

The volunteer hung up. "Sorry for the wait. Name?" She beamed up at the visitor.

"I'm looking for Myra Stone."

So, this was Myra's daughter. She did look all business but seemed almost … vulnerable. Not what he expected after their discussion.

The volunteer scanned the computer screen. "The only Stone I see—"

"I can take you to your mother." Jason held out his hand. "Lt. Danvers, Heath's Point PD."

"PD? Why are the police here?" Her deep blue gaze flicked from him back to the volunteer. The phone rang again, taking the volunteer's attention.

The woman ignored his hand but fell into step beside him as he ushered her into the hallway. She stood almost as tall as he, but then she had on platform sandals.

"I'm a friend of your folks. That's all." Well, mostly all. He drew her to the closed chapel door.

Her fingers had whitened around the strap of her tan purse, and she halted a few steps from the door. "Is Momma? Is it the cancer again?" She lifted those beautiful eyes to his, though a crevice formed between her brows.

He shook his head. "Your mom is inside." He pulled the door open and willed the ache expanding within him to cease. Myra's tears had hurt, but the thought of tears filling her daughter's eyes threatened to undo him.

She preceded him into the chapel, one hand still gripping the strap of her purse and the other wrapped around her stomach.

"Oh, Alynne." As her daughter entered, Myra pulled away from Pastor Slaughter and lifted her hands. Alynne grabbed hold of them and sank into the space on the other side of her mom.

Jason concentrated on the cross against the wall behind them. *I know Ellis is fine, Lord. With You. Could You give me a little strength to battle all the tears surrounding me?* How did Philip steel himself against getting sucked into the despair and pain when he had to make these calls?

"It's your dad, dear." Myra pulled back and touched her daughter's face. "He's gone." Her voice faded as her daughter wrapped her arms around her mom, letting the older woman weep against her shoulder.

Jason's throat tightened.

Philip reached across Myra's shoulder and touched Alynne's arm. "I'm sorry, child."

The younger woman clung to her mom, but her face shed all semblance of emotion. Even her eyes seemed to turn into marble, gazing past Jason toward the wooden doors.

He couldn't blame her for wanting to escape. Probably some type of defense mechanism.

"How did it happen?"

"An accident, sometime during the night. County Coroner said he died instantly." Philip's explanation brought a new sob from Myra.

Good thing Philip stayed vague about the incident.

Alynne straightened, barely embracing her mom at this point. "Have you spoken to Phyllis?"

Myra inhaled roughly and swallowed. Her brows knit together in as harsh a look as he'd ever seen her give. "Not in almost fifteen years."

Alynne shut her eyes and stood. "It's all right, Momma. I'll call her."

"Not like she'll care." Myra's voice was barely a whisper.

Who was Phyllis?

Alynne punched in a number on her phone, but only paused for a moment before ending the call. "I'll try again later." She pivoted and turned her crystal blues onto Jason. "Can I see him?"

He cleared his throat. "They've sent him over to Tipkins Funeral Home. You can visit there."

Her eyes widened at the mention of the funeral. "Oh. Yes, of course." Her gaze drifted down to settle somewhere on the carpet behind him. Or maybe she was looking at the door again. "Are there any papers to sign? Anything like that?" Trance-like, she stepped through the exit without looking back at her mom.

Jason glanced at Philip and shrugged.

The older man had put his arm around Myra again. He slid a

clipboard with a small stack of papers across the pew.

"Will you stay with her a moment?" Jason collected the board and joined the daughter near the front entrance.

She stared out one of the windows overlooking the parking lot, flinching as his boot hit the tile floor near her. "The funeral home in Heath's Point will take care of … things." He handed her the clipboard.

The word hung in limbo. Alynne squeezed her eyes shut for a moment, then inhaled deeply as she took the clipboard. "What am I signing?"

He had no idea but glanced over the top form. "Acceptance of temporary shelter for …" He swallowed. "Your dad … until you decide on services."

"I can't even think straight. How could something like this happen?"

Jason shrugged. He'd wondered the same thing, but even a safe driver like Ellis can have trouble during a rain shower. "Thunderstorm. Slick road. Dangerous curve. Could happen to anyone."

"But it happened to my pop." She focused on him, her deep blue eyes brimming with unshed tears. The exact thing he hadn't wanted to see.

He steeled himself against the sight. "Your parents have become very dear to me in the last four years. I'm here to help your mom in any way I can." After all Myra and Ellis had done to make him feel welcome in a new town, he owed them. "You, too, if you need it."

"I want to thank you for your assistance." The clipped,

businesslike tone was followed by a quick sniff. The moisture in her eyes evaporated.

She turned and carried the pages to a lady waiting at an administration desk to the right of the chapel doors. "Do you get these?"

"I do, indeed." The woman licked her fingers and sorted the pages into a stack of boxes against the wall. She'd obviously dealt with the same paperwork for years. "Oh, I need one more signature here and contact information in case we need to reach you."

Alynne filled out the form and returned it to the woman.

"Such pretty handwriting you have. And how do you say your first name."

She pronounced it slowly and glanced toward the still-closed door of the chapel.

The volunteer didn't seem to notice her impatience. "Isn't Allen a boy's name?"

Myra's daughter stiffened. "My name is actually Eudora Lynne, but my pop…" The brisk tone cracked a bit, but she sucked in a breath and kept going. "He took the *A* off of the end of Eudora and stuck it on the Lynne to make Al-Lynne."

"Oh, what a clever man your father is."

Alynne rubbed the center of her forehead. "Was."

"Oh, dear, I'm so sorry."

Jason had to agree. Ellis was one of the most brilliant and godly men Jason had ever met. He retreated toward the chapel. Time to get Myra home. Philip opened the chapel door before he even reached it, and the two of them escorted Myra outside.

Alynne hadn't followed them, however. Jason spotted her

through the windows near the soda machine. She had her phone to her ear and lifted her other hand as she spoke. The brief compassion he'd seen from the woman dissipated as she seemed to be gesturing toward the chapel. Surely, she wasn't complaining about her mother needing her. Although her face held a shallowness to it that Jason didn't fully trust.

"Perhaps I should get my car?" Philip took a step toward the sleek Sonata he'd just gifted to his wife, though she made him take it anytime he was driving further than the church and home. His old junker barely made that short distance and was a constant punchline of jokes and teasing around the congregation.

Before Myra could answer, Alynne joined them—so to speak. More like she walked past them.

"Your mom is ready to leave. Jason and I will be happy to take her to the inn if you don't have the time." Philip's tone was gentle, but his words had to cut. "I know you're very busy." Apparently, he wasn't any more trusting of Alynne Stone than Jason was.

Alynne halted and turned back toward him, lifting finely arched brows and regarding him with wide eyes. "I fully intend to stay, Pastor. I've just spoken to my boss."

Myra straightened her shoulders. "I understand if you need to return home, dear. This has been quite a shock to all of us."

"I'm here to help, Momma." Her voice softened. "The firm gave me off at least two weeks, and I have vacation time I've collected as well."

Is that what she'd been doing? Had Jason misjudged her?

She stepped closer to him and pointed to the next aisle. "My car is over there. The navy Acura." She slipped her hand underneath her mother's elbow, forcing Jason to back away or get stepped on. "I appreciate your help, but I've got it from here."

Myra lifted a hand to her daughter's cheek. "I'm so glad you're able to stay, my dear. We will…" She dragged in a deep breath. "We'll get through this. Together."

Alynne unlocked the door with her key fob, and Philip eased Myra into the seat. "Thanks, gentlemen. Good-bye." She climbed in and started the car.

Dismissed? Just like that?

Philip clapped a hand on his shoulder. "Alynne's not a bad sort, and I'm sure she has her mom's best interests at heart."

"Agreed, but what does she know about Myra or running the inn? She hasn't ever been here." Jason tugged his keys from his pocket. "If Cat were here, I wouldn't worry. She'd take care of the entire inn and Myra's distracting daughter at the same time."

"Distracting?" Philip raised one eyebrow.

"Distract-ed is what I said." Hadn't he? Maybe he should go back to the lake. Fish were easier to get along with. "One minute she seems to be upset and the next she's … marble-ish."

"I see your point. I'm sure she's delightful." He led Jason to where their cars sat side by side. "But our first priority has to be helping Myra through this, with or without her daughter."

"Or that Phyllis person they were talking about."

"Another daughter if I remember correctly. Something strange about her, but Ellis never fully explained."

Great. The two Stone sisters could be matching bookends with about as much heart. "Either way, Myra has been hurt enough. These next few days'll be terrible." Once again, the pang of his own experience stiffened his shoulders.

"Until Dell decides to contact Cat, the three of us are going to need to keep an eye on things. Particularly when it comes to Alynne's treatment of her mom." Philip paused and rubbed the back of his neck.

As much as Jason didn't want to see Myra hurt more, how was he supposed to interfere between her and her daughter? "It's none of our business, Pastor."

"It is our business. She's our sister. And, over the last decade, we've become family, much more so than blood." His brows furrowed. "Until we can be sure the girl truly cares for her mom, I want one of us looking out for Myra's best interests."

If nothing else, she'd need help canceling the reservations that were due in the next few days. "Well, I can cover the rest of today, then."

Philip shook Jason's hand. "Be gentle with Alynne, though. To believe the stories that Ellis told, she's all twisted up inside. Seeking after the things of this world."

He could believe that. A fire roared up his spine as Alynne's car faded into traffic. "I'll take care of things."

And he would. Even if it meant countering Myra's prodigal daughter.

BREAKING POINT

Chapter Four

Alynne plugged pop's folly—Sunrise Inn—into her GPS. It directed her onto a web of back roads that skirted Grayson Reservoir. At the southernmost point of the lake, she turned into the broad gravel lot in front of the blue and white, three-story Victorian that she remembered visiting in her childhood. The last time she'd seen it, several years ago now, it had been dark and bare in the midst of a frigid holiday season.

She crawled toward the white wooden fence that edged the lot and took in the property that had so quickly replaced her in her father's eyes. Coming back to this place, especially with Pop now gone, ripped open all the pain and injury she'd experienced when her parents had abandoned her for this place.

It wasn't like she hadn't seen them. They shared a meal almost every month and talked on the phone at least once a week. They even traveled to Dallas during the holiday season every year except for the one when Pop had hurt his ankle. Even that short visit had been difficult.

Why had Pop left a perfectly good job in Dallas to come out to this wasteland? Why would he think the strain of this enterprise could help Momma after her cancer battle?

But to be honest, Momma had thrived here and was stronger than she'd been in Dallas … when she had been under Alynne's care. From the looks of things, both her parents had been better off without her.

Maybe she should go back home to Dallas after all.

"You can park up by the house." Momma's comment awakened her from the pain she kept stuffed away. She let the car roll to a stop in the center of the lot.

"You've done a beautiful job with the inn." She parked next to her mom's white SUV. "New paint, fencing, gravel. I barely recognize it." A strange warm feeling oozed over this place from her fondest childhood memories. A nostalgia she could almost inhale.

Her resentment of her parents' decision had cost her more than she had realized.

"You're exaggerating." Momma climbed out on her side before Alynne could round the car. "But your dad worked hard. He even removed that rickety old dock and built a new boathouse, oh, and a pool. You can use it if it gets warm enough."

Woof!

Alynne spun in the direction of the bark just as a large golden retriever type bounded around the side of the house.

"No, no!" Alynne lifted her hands in time to catch the muddy paws of the dog across the front of her dress. "Get away, beast."

Pushing off from Alynne, the dog stayed close and began to

shake. Slobber and fishy-smelling water flung into her face, her legs, and all over her dress. "Ugh."

"Go on, Rose. That's a good girl." Momma shoved her back toward the rose bushes that lined the front of the lot.

"What was that?" And why was the thing here?

"*She* is Rose. A sweet, albeit a little clumsy, cast-off that someone left by the road a few months ago." Momma reached back into the car for her purse.

The sound of tires on gravel caught Alynne's attention. A black Jeep pulled into the lot and stopped on the other side of Momma's car. The cop who was at the hospital rounded the end of the vehicle a moment later and halted. "Wow. Looks like Hurricane Rosie took you for a spin."

Great. And there hadn't been an opportunity to pack a bag. Her backseat had a duffel with some workout clothes next to a bag of assorted groceries, but that was all. "Something like that." She'd think about clothes later. All she wanted now was a sink and a clean towel.

The cop stepped alongside Myra as she took the stairs. She waved away his hands. "Haven't needed help getting up these since I moved in, and I don't need your assistance now."

She reached the top, and her lips puckered. "Or maybe I do."

"What is it?" He leaned against the top rail like some model from a boot factory. His were well-worn and dark brown. Not dress boots, but the real horse-riding cowboy type. Did he ride? His jeans didn't look worn in the seat like someone who rode a lot, though the knees of his long legs were a little whiter than the rest of the pant. He wore a mossy green button-down with short sleeves that almost matched the gray of his eyes. And the tan hat he wore perfectly matched the coloring of the hair he'd shown back at the hospital.

Momma touched his arm. "I am going to need your help, dear boy."

"Name it."

"The Cottonwood Classic is next weekend."

"That golf tourney?" He crossed his arms. "You wouldn't want me playing golf, Myra. My stroke would look too much like a fishing reel cast or maybe a batter's swing."

"Silly boy." She swatted at him and moved toward the door. "I have several players coming into town during the week to practice, and we're supposed to be filled to capacity next weekend. We'll have to shut down for both, I guess, to make room for family."

That word, family, sent a shiver down Alynne's spine.

"We'll need to call the guests right away." Momma tilted her head to the side.

"Don't you have a sign that says, *Closed*?" Alynne snatched her purse from beside her seat and held it away from her body to spare it the filth that covered the rest of her.

"I'll take care of it." The cop pushed off the rail and *thunked* across the porch.

"That isn't necessary." Alynne shut the car door.

"I don't mind." He pushed the brass handle, and the heavy door, complete with an oval cut-glass design, swung wide.

"Don't you even lock things around here?" An unlocked door in Dallas meant a break-in at some point.

"Only when necessary, dear." Momma led the cop into the study.

She followed them into the room. This was decidedly Pop, from the fishing calendar to the golf-ball bookends and the sporting news magazines stacked up with Dallas Morning Newspapers. He'd never been much for online browsing.

Momma went around the desk. "The names are listed on the calendar. Phone numbers are in the Rolodex." She pointed to the old-fashioned circle of cards sitting on a paper calendar that covered three-fourths of the desktop.

"I'll take care of letting everyone know that you're closing down for a few weeks." To his credit, the cop seemed to be equally as surprised as Alynne by their outdated method of reservations.

"Oh, dear. I do hate the thought of closing. Putting people out." Momma put a finger to her mouth.

"It won't be a problem, Myra." The cop had a smooth way about him. "Calling them all now will give them plenty of time to find other accommodations in Lackard or maybe the outskirts of the metroplex. People travel that distance every day."

Her mom tapped her bottom lip with her finger. "Suppose you offer them one free night on a future visit."

For pity's sake, her mom's business acumen came from the dark ages. "That's too generous, Momma. They'll understand."

"One free night." She nodded, resolute with her decision.

"Uh…" The cop half-lifted a hand. "How future?"

"He's right. If you give a deadline, they'll be more likely to use the offer." And once the deadline had passed, Momma didn't have to save rooms for non-paying guests.

He turned to Alynne with something of a smirk spread on his lips. "I thought you said the offer was too generous." Was that a dimple that peeked out?

"Well, she's made up her mind. She might as well make the gift something that they'll take advantage of." Her cheeks heated. Why did he look so amused? "Give them three months."

"Six." Momma headed for the kitchen.

Alynne caught up with her. "I think you should lie down."

"I still need to call your sister … and my sisters, come to think of it." Momma might have felt the weight of the responsibilities, but she didn't resist when Alynne urged her through the kitchen to the wing that Uncle Todd and Aunt Pearl had made into a private suite.

"You need to rest first. You'll feel better and more able to speak to all of them."

"Oh, dear. I know you're right, but …"

"I can call them, Momma." She needed to remove that burden, even though speaking to her family, especially Phyllis, rivaled stepping onto a filled pin cushion. Well, before she'd attempt to speak to her sister, she'd call Blayne. She needed his strength and soothing to get through that conversation.

Momma paused outside a door down the narrow, back hallway from the kitchen. "If you're sure you don't mind." She pushed open the door. "I suppose I could simply rest my eyes for a few minutes." She poked her head back out the door and handed Alynne a towel. "And you should use the sink on the back porch to clean up a bit."

Indeed. "After I clean up, I'll take care of the family." And she would. Through her gritted teeth, if necessary.

A paper calendar and a Rolodex? How in this global community had Sunrise Inn continued to thrive? Jason lifted the old-fashioned receiver from its cradle where it sat on the corner of the desk. The phone looked perfectly at home at the edge of the desk blotter. In fact, the only thing out of place was an ancient computer monitor that used up a good square foot of space.

It had to be at least a decade old. He pulled out the narrow, top drawer. Sure enough, a false front flattened and revealed a keyboard with spiraled cords stretching toward the wall bordering the other side of the desk. Could that thing even work with the different programs now?

He sat and picked up the receiver before dialing the first number. Voice mail. Midday on a Friday, leaving messages would likely be the best he could do. "I'm calling from Sunrise Inn. We have experienced an unexpected death within our family and will be closing the inn until further notice. Your reservation for …" He checked the date and rattled it off, explaining the cancellation and the subsequent free night Myra offered. He also left the inn's number in case of further questions.

Alynne wandered in. Her dress still showed some water marks, but the mud design on the tan skirt had disappeared, along with the sprinkling of black freckles she'd had across her legs, arms, and face. "Well, Momma's settled in. I can take over, now."

"You look no worse for the wear."

"Ignorant mutt." She tucked a stray hair behind her ear. "Anyway, there's no need for you to stick around any longer."

He straightened. Her dismissal was plain, but he'd given his word to both Myra and to Philip. "Your mom asked me to contact her guests, and that's what I intend to do."

"I'm perfectly capable of making phone calls."

With her no-nonsense manner and professional tone, he believed her. "I have no doubts, but I gave my word." Why was she so determined to get rid of him anyway? "Besides, I thought she needed you to contact the rest of your family."

"That may be, but there's really no need for you to stay. I can handle this on my own." She was a spitfire. Determined to need no one. What was she trying to prove?

"Thanks, but I'll finish what I've started." He flicked through the Rolodex in search of the next name.

"Look, Officer …"

"Lieutenant." Why did he suddenly care that she know he had ranking? How juvenile.

"Fine. Lieutenant. I don't mean to be rude, but I'd like to take care of things alone." She advanced a few steps and laid her palm on the desk.

He hung up the phone and stood, forcing her to look up at him. Her blue eyes flashed, and a wisp of hair had fallen from her bun, softening her features. That was a face he could get used to.

Where had that crazy thought come from? He knew nothing about her.

She let her gaze lower to the desktop.

"Miss Stone, I'm sure you only have your mother's best

interests in mind, but I'm a man who keeps promises. Once I complete my task, I'll leave. Not before." Though, hopefully, by then, he'd have another task to keep him around.

His declaration, even though he'd kept his voice kind, was wasted. She stared at the narrow keyboard drawer. He followed the direction of her gaze as she lifted a pair of Ellis's reading glasses. Her mouth opened in a perfect O, but nothing came from it. Time froze for a moment before she let the glasses drop, put her hand over her mouth, and fled the room.

Alynne rushed through the front door and down the steps to her car, stifling the tears that threatened. *No crying.* She wasn't a child who needed her mommy. She was the one giving comfort. Just as she'd been the one to care for Momma through her cancer battle. Not that Pop hadn't been there, but he worked a full-time job and a part-time one to make ends meet and pay off the medical debts.

But the image of her sweet father's face behind those readers … more like spectacles … How she had teased him about them.

Somewhere the dog barked. No, not again. She climbed into her car as the floodgates released.

The front door opened, and the cop came out. Why would he think he should follow her? She reached for the ignition to make an escape.

Blast. Where had she left her keys?

The cop came around to her door, but she ignored him, willing her face to cool and the tears to cease. Showing weakness in front of this perfect stranger was unacceptable.

The beastly dog barked again, this time coming at a full run from the south wing. The cop spun and pointed at the dog. "Rose. Sit."

The mutt couldn't exactly slide on gravel, but she seemed to attempt it, coming to a stop next to the cop. He curled the fingers of his palm down hand into a fist. "Rose. Stay." He tapped on her window. "Miss Stone, are you all right?"

"Fine." She shouted the word to impress upon him the need to leave her alone.

He stepped aside and tugged open her door.

She glared up at him. "Don't let that horrible dog in here."

"She's well-trained." He held out his hand. "It helps to talk about it."

He had no idea what would help her. She didn't even know.

"Trust me on this." His hand remained outstretched.

She eyed it. His voice had held compassion, not judgment. Neither of them moved for a moment, then she released the breath she'd been holding and placed her chilly hand in his warm one, allowing him to help her from the car.

But that was all. He released her immediately and shoved his hands into his jean pockets. "Walking a little might help as well, but not in those." He pointed to her dress shoes.

They'd already been murdering her toes, especially when she had to tiptoe through the gravel. "I have another pair." Opening the back door, she pulled her tennis shoes from her duffel. She probably had socks as well, but for a short walk, these would be enough. She slipped them on and set her tan heels on the back floorboard where they wouldn't get crushed.

The cop waited for her at the back of the car, and Rose joined him there after sniffing at all four of her tires. Thankfully, the dog was too distracted to jump on her again.

She met him at the trunk. "I'm not sure I should leave Momma alone."

"She needs to rest." He guided her toward the lake and the woods beside it with the beastly dog bounding ahead of them. "Whether she's willing to admit it or not."

"What about the guests you were calling?" She offered him one more reason to leave, though, at this point, his staying wasn't such a bad thing.

"They'll get called." He gave her a half-smile. "I promised your mom, remember?"

Nice smile. Sincere eyes with little flecks of green in them now that she could see them up close. She looked away, conscious of her staring.

"Your mom said you and Ellis had always been close."

"Had been." Until the great separation. "Hard to stay close with so much distance in between, though."

"I bet it hurt when your parents bought this place and moved away from you."

She glanced at him. How much did he know about her? "They didn't buy it. My father's uncle passed away without any kids. Pop inherited all of the property." And the rest of his assumption didn't deserve her response.

"Still far from Dallas."

"Dallas is home. Always will be. Even if they did move away."

He walked alongside her in silence. Too much quiet. Even Rose had moved far enough down the trail that her steps and sniffs had faded. No traffic. No permanent hum in the surroundings. Just occasional bird calls. Something made the underbrush near her foot rustle, and she flinched and stepped closer to the cop.

He took her hand and led her to his other side. "Probably a skink."

"A skunk?" Surely not.

He chuckled. "No. A little lizard around these parts."

"I call them geckos."

"You're probably more correct. Skinks are usually farther south, but the kids up here have dubbed them skinks, and so the name remains."

Kids? "Do you have children?" No ring, but then that didn't mean much. Not with men anyway. And she had no right to criticize. She glanced again at her bare hand that shouldn't have been missing a ring.

"Me? No. I'm … I'm not married." His voice softened for a moment. "No. I work with the youth at the church in town."

"Good place for a cop."

"They keep me honest."

The lake area was beautiful, with a cleared trail that passed a log cabin ranch house some hundred yards from the inn.

"That's the Kennedale Ranch. I'm not sure why they dub it a ranch, though. Not much land to it. Been empty since I moved here a few years ago." He lapsed into a comfortable silence again.

This time, Alynne felt no awkwardness. Beyond the cabin, the trail wound into the woods away from the lake. This must have been the trail Pop had cleared. Several years back he'd told her about it. Begged her to come walk with him and try out the new fishing spot he'd found. Why hadn't she come then? There was something at work, but likely it wasn't nearly as important as she had made it sound. No, she was mad. Mad and hurt that they had left her without even discussing their move. And her staying away was to make them realize what they had lost when they left her.

Only it hadn't worked out that way. She was the loser. After a few years, it was more like a habit to stay away. She never laid eyes on any of the property since they'd come up to visit Uncle Todd and Aunt Pearl when she was little. Well, except for that one Christmas, but it had been dark and only for a couple of hours.

The dog trotted back toward them through the woods, but this time, thankfully, it ignored Alynne and continued to march toward the water's edge.

"Good dog." The cop continued on the wide trail. "Your dad showed me a great fishing spot over this ridge."

Must have been the one he'd told her about. "He loved to fish. We went to different lakes and creeks all over Dallas."

"You fish?" He slowed his pace and glanced at her.

She stopped. A tear escaped down her cheek, and she whisked it away with the back of her hand. "Not for a long time." And by her own choice, she'd locked herself away from her dear pop until now, when it was too late.

Another tear dripped.

The cop must've noticed that one. He cleared his throat and turned toward the view of the lake. They'd made it beyond the cove. Here, the full width of Lake Grayson spread before them. The distant shore showed speckles of white homes amid the green backdrop. Far to her right, a line spanned the lake, the toll bridge, but it was so far away the cars could hardly be seen and couldn't be heard at all. "Don't people ever use this lake for boating?"

"Wait until this afternoon. Even more tomorrow." He began walking again.

She followed along her pop's path. "You probably think I'm pretty selfish." Though it didn't really matter what he thought. At least it shouldn't. He knew nothing about her life.

"I think you're hurting." He pulled a leaf from a branch as he passed underneath it. "I'm sorry about that." He seemed to really mean what he said.

"I guess I have been selfish, though. This … place … the inn. It stole my parents from me. I've hated it for years."

"That's why I've never seen you out here."

"I didn't come at first, tried to make them sorry for moving out here. Sounds so stupid. I hurt myself more than anyone else."

He peeled apart the leaf he'd collected. "I guess that's how things work when you're trying to punish someone. You're the one who receives the most punishment."

Certainly felt that way. Especially now that she could never apologize to Pop. "Mm-hmm."

He had a quiet way about him that neither approved nor judged her actions. He paused where the trail curved deeper into the woods. "Turns a loop farther on, but down there …" He squatted into a baseball catcher's position and pointed to a narrow cove with some large boulders along one side. "That's the spot where your dad and I have fished together."

"No wonder he liked it here." She would have loved it as well if she'd let go of her anger and pain. If she'd given Pop a chance. "Thanks for showing it to me, but I should get back."

She didn't wait for his leading or response. The trail was plain. And the cop had become too good at reading her. That was the last thing she needed.

Before she did anything else, she wanted to talk to Blayne.

Jason stayed in the squat and watched her retrace the path at a quick pace. That woman was different, all right. And with her emotions all twisted up, as Philip said, she was full of hurt, bitterness, and now regret.

And he could do very little to help her. Still feeling his own pain and regret.

He stood, climbed down to the rocks at Ellis's fishing spot, and whistled for Rose. The dog, soaked from another dip in the lake, ran toward him and halted on the dirt. "Good girl, Rose." She'd probably be better off staying with him while Alynne returned to the house.

Stooping for a small rock, he pitched it into the pool. "I'll do whatever I can for her, Ellis." Though what that was, he had no idea. She certainly intrigued him. More like baffled him.

Lord, help me see her with Your eyes.

Raised with parents like hers, Alynne had to know about Christ. Hopefully, this experience and being around her mom would help her see how the Lord could carry her through this difficult time.

Retracing his steps back to the Victorian, he whistled an old hymn about surrender. Rose trotted in front of him with her tongue lagging out the side of her mouth.

If nothing else, he'd learned that Alynne Stone needed as much help as her mom to get through this. Maybe even more if she didn't have the strong faith that Myra held. He cut right at the house and took the long way, around the south wing and the pool deck beside it. The water danced in the sunlight. Tempting, but deceptive. With the nighttime temperatures they'd had, the water had to be frigid.

Hopping up the side steps to the porch, Jason made his way to the front door. He pushed through the entrance and turned to give Rose a final scratch between the ears. The dog needed a bath—a real one. Probably wouldn't happen tonight. With Alynne around, Rose would likely be spending nights in the barn anyway.

He entered the house and returned to the office area that faced the front windows.

"Don't call me Dora." Alynne's raised voice came from the room next to the office, a large living area that Myra had dubbed the parlor.

Jason hesitated. More was going on with this girl than her father's death, and most of it dramatic. He had no business eavesdropping, but at her volume, he'd had no choice.

Her voice sounded more untethered than angry. A part of him

yearned to go and simply hold her hand through this, but that was a ridiculous thought. Instead, he strode across the entry hall to hang his hat on a rack next to the kitchen entrance and ran his fingers through his hair.

"You mean you're not even going to come to his funeral?" Her voice echoed into the high-ceilinged entry.

A member of the family?

"Momma and Pop always supported you until you got into the drugs."

Was that the woman they'd talked about? Phyllis? She was probably the other daughter that Myra had mentioned.

He was scum to stand there in the entryway listening. He stepped to the opening of the parlor and caught Alynne's eye.

She was staring at the near wall that was covered with old photographs of people and a few landscapes. Alynne was already slightly pink in the cheeks, but a deeper redness crawled up her neck when their eyes met. She lifted her chin for a moment and let her gaze drift to the other side of the room. "I never said you abandoned them, Phyllis, only that you moved so far away. But that doesn't matter. Momma needs us."

Having shown his presence, he returned to the office but couldn't settle his mind to make a call to a guest. Surely, Myra's own daughter would come to her own father's funeral.

But then, who was he to judge. His real dad had been amazing, but he'd be hard-pressed to drop everything and go to his stepdad's funeral. Not after all that man had done.

"Fine. You don't owe me anything, and I don't owe you. But you do owe Momma. You owe her a lot."

Maybe it would be better all-around if this other daughter stayed as far away as she was. Sounded like all she would bring to the table was more drama. Something they definitely didn't need.

"You do that. And while you're at it, you can come up with a way to explain to the media why you couldn't be bothered to come to your own father's funeral."

Media? Was this sister some sort of celeb?

"Yes, I would. In a heartbeat." A tone sounded after her last word. Then she stomped into the office as Jason picked up the rotary phone. "Ugh, that woman."

"I couldn't help but hear." He returned the receiver to its cradle.

"My sister, Phyllis"—Alynne lifted her voice several notes and took on a west coast accent—"can't possibly carve out a moment to come all the way to 'that ungodly place.'"

"I think it's pretty godly." He gave a short nod.

She let her shoulders relax. "Wherever Momma and Pop were, God was there, too." She took a deep breath and let it go. "My sister didn't see it that way. She hated all things family by the time she left. Still does from the sound of it."

"Is she coming?" As much as he hoped against it, her absence would only serve to hurt Myra more.

"I don't know. Her image, well, her husband's image, is all-important. He's running for state senate in Washington."

That was the reason for the media threat. "Do you want her here?"

"Heavens no. She's cruel." She rubbed her forehead with one hand. "But she has to come for Momma's sake. She's not come back since she left, as far as I know."

"I've never heard of her. I heard about you from your dad."

"Pop talked about me?"

He'd said something about introducing them if his daughter would ever visit again. That she was a looker and sweetness itself when she wasn't being all twisted up.

"The fishing, you know." He hated lying, but he wasn't about to share the real conversation. "Why don't I make us all some sandwiches while you finish your calls." He glanced at the clock. It was already past two? No wonder he was hungry.

"I could eat." She turned left and wandered back to the parlor as he strode into the kitchen.

Even with the sister's antagonistic conversation, she seemed more relaxed than she'd been earlier. Hopefully, that trend would last.

BREAKING POINT

Chapter Five

Since Momma was distracted with a variety of visitors, Alynne had a long evening of speaking on the phone with family members. Finally, she'd dragged herself to the south wing suite she'd commandeered.

If only she'd gotten in touch with Blayne. She'd tried to call him several times. All without luck. Her failure delayed her sleep despite her weariness. So much so, that she slept through her alarm the next morning.

She picked up her phone and growled at the illuminated time. After dressing in her workout shorts and T-shirt, she wandered out front and breathed in the freshness.

Something floral and sweet tinted the air. Had to be the roses on the north side of the house.

A police cruiser with HPPD painted on the side was parked by the bank of roses next to the white fence. Just beside the old brass bell that was somehow connected to the Civil War, though Alynne didn't remember the story.

Was this the same cop as yesterday? Why was he here again?

With a happy bark, the tan dog barreled toward her. Not this time. Not with her last clean clothes. "Rose, sit." She pointed her finger at the mutt.

Immediately the dog halted and dropped her haunches.

Alynne's chin dropped, too. "Uh. Good dog." She trotted down the steps and patted the mutt's filthy head. "Don't you ever get a bath?" Rose lifted her nose and gave Alynne's arm a lick.

"I don't need a bath." She giggled and moved away.

Rose trotted toward the asphalt of the road in front of the inn. Alynne followed her toward the mailbox. Only a few letters, mostly business envelopes. She returned to the inn with no other excuses to avoid the cop. Her growling stomach urged her into the kitchen, but not before she failed to reach Blayne one more time.

She sat in the swing outside the front door. Her mom's Bible lay on a small table next to her. Momma had always started her day with the Lord, even through those long months of chemo and recuperation. She always seemed to know God in a way Alynne never understood. Pop had, too. He'd said that the Lord patiently waits for us to want to spend time with Him.

He'd been waiting for Alynne for far too long.

With an ache growing beyond her hunger pangs, she refocused on her need to call Blayne and punched in his number. How many messages had she left? Of course, he'd often failed to return her calls in the past. Annoying, though not worrisome. But after a full day? Even if he'd been overwhelmed with his work in Las Vegas, he should have called. He'd better have had an emergency or …

You've reached Blayne Campbell. I'm currently out of the

office but will return your call promptly if you leave your name, number, and the nature of your business.

She pulled her phone away so the beep wouldn't hurt her ear. "It's me again. I need to speak with you. Call me." Maybe she was being a little too harsh. "Hope you're having a nice trip."

Chances were, he'd found a country club to visit. Vegas was usually sunny, and it wasn't their blistering season yet. Probably wanted to take on a golf game. Or was it hit a golf game? Or shoot? What did people do with golf?

Alynne gave Rose another pat. "Good girl." She went inside and made her way toward a conversation between Momma and a man. After only a few words, she recognized his voice. Strange how she had only known him for a day and yet had that sort of connection with him already.

The cop sat with bowed head at the large, built-in booth by the front window. He looked up and gave her a smile then cut into a thick Belgium waffle sprinkled with blueberries and maple syrup. Alynne's mouth watered.

"Well, there you are. Thought you might stay balled up in that quilt all day." Momma pulled a plate off the warming shelf above the stove. "Sit. I have breakfast ready for you. Got your favorite."

Alynne's stomach growled. "Looks delicious." Her mom set a loaded platter in front of her, complete with waffle, bacon strips, and scrambled eggs. Momma certainly seemed to be handling Pop's death well. Maybe it was an act?

"Have you eaten?" Alynne asked before popping half of a bacon strip in her mouth. Oops. She should have prayed. Too late now. She'd look ridiculous.

Momma took a pitcher of orange juice from the fridge and began to pour it into a glass. The juice jostled in the glass container as her hand shook.

Alynne jumped up and steadied the glass in Momma's hand.

"Thank you, dear." She let her daughter take the glass and set the pitcher back into place in the fridge. "I don't know what's wrong with me."

Pop had died. That's what was wrong. And then there were the dark circles accenting her eyes. "You were too busy talking to all of your visitors yesterday. You didn't get to rest hardly at all."

"And I didn't help you a bit, either. Were you able to reach the family?"

She swallowed down a bite of eggs with a swig of the sweet juice. Fresh-squeezed. Exactly like she would make it. If she had time. Which she didn't and likely never would. "Your sisters will be here tonight or tomorrow. Most of the others will arrive tomorrow or Monday." And who knew about Phyllis?

"Jason, you contacted all of the guests?" Her mom smiled at the cop.

Jason. Nice name. Suited his face. And the uniform suited the rest of him quite nicely as well.

"Two of them made new reservations already. All of them sent their condolences." He wiped his mouth with a yellow napkin and stood. "Thanks for breakfast."

"Wait, I promised you coffee. I'll fill a thermos."

While Momma moved about the kitchen at her task, Alynne avoided the cop's—Jason's—eyes. She took a bite of the crisp waffle and scanned the mail. Advertisement, offer for a new credit card, what looked like bills, and then in a plastic baggie, there was a smaller, card-shaped envelope. And this one had been sent by her pop and returned.

Alynne studied it. The receiver and the address had been smeared badly. Probably due to the abundance of April showers they'd had last month.

The phone in the office rang. "Oh, I'll get that." Momma set down the filled thermos on the table and scooted into the entry hall.

Jason pointed to the letter. "What's that?"

"Came in the mailbox. *Return to sender* from Pop." Alynne held it out. "Should we open it?"

He squinted at the right corner. "It was mailed to Dallas." He held it up to the light. "Looks like only paper, but you never know."

"Pop had a lot of friends there, but I can't make anything out of the smears on the front."

He handed it back to her. "I guess it should go to your mom."

Alynne's curiosity had vaulted. "I'd hate to cause her more distress."

"I don't mess with the US Post Office." He sighed. "But you're his daughter, certainly an heir. And we have no idea where to send it."

"I'm opening it." She picked up her unused butter knife.

"I never said ..."

She peeled back the flap revealing a folded sheet of copy paper. "Too late now." She unfolded the short note. Her father's neat manuscript covered about half the page.

"Who's Mel?" Jason leaned over her shoulder, distracting her.

She paused, breathing in his subtle musky cologne. "An old friend of Pop's from Dallas. He's an attorney. Or at least he was." She began reading one of the last messages Pop had conveyed.

> *Hello, Mel,*
>
> *Myra is unaware of this letter, so please keep your official confidentiality about it. You know of my various family ties. I've become aware of something alarming. I need your professional advice on this matter. Would you have your office make some discreet investigations into my aunt's death? Also, the visitors for the year or so prior to her death, including family members, no matter who they are. I know she was ninety-one, and her death was labeled as natural causes. Still, I have some suspicions. I won't give you any specifics. I'd rather you find out on your own to confirm or deny what I've learned. We'll talk soon, but don't call me with any of this. I don't want to worry Myra. Send me a note when you've learned anything, and we'll meet. My treat.*
> *Blessed to call you friend,*
> *Ellis*

"This is strange." Alynne held the letter steady to allow Jason to finish reading.

"Hmm." Jason leaned against the counter and rubbed his thumb across his chin. The lightest layer of tan stubble graced his jawline. She hadn't noticed that before, but then she hadn't been this close to him.

He stepped back. "Interesting, but random. You have contact information for Mel?"

"Do you want to call him?" Did Jason suspect something strange?

"No." He ambled toward the opening to the foyer. "You should, though. Tell him about your dad. They were friends, right?"

Oh, yeah. She still had to do that. She abandoned the rest of her breakfast and followed him to the front door.

"And when you do," he continued, tugging his hat from the peg on the wall. "You can ask him if your dad had ever asked him to investigate people in your family before."

"Should I tell him about the letter?" Who could Pop have been worried about?

He glanced back toward her. "No reason to. Not at this point." He slipped his hat onto his head and pointed toward the office where Momma's quiet voice resonated as she confirmed to someone on the phone that she was all right. "Tell your mom I said good-bye."

Jason wouldn't let on to Alynne, but the note bothered him. It, along with the niggling suspicion over Ellis's car, tensed the muscles in his neck like an icy claw that wouldn't release.

He pulled his cruiser out of the lot until it was several hundred yards down the narrow, rarely used road. Stopping, he shoved the car into park and pulled out his cellphone. He swiped and punched his way to the number he wanted then held it to his ear.

"This is Charlie." The county coroner was as laid-back as a doctor could afford to be, even answering his own phone.

"Jason Danvers, here, Dr. Barnes. I have a few questions about the death of Ellis Stone."

"I'm not a medical examiner, Lieutenant. I can't believe I know anything that could possibly help you."

"The items in the car. Did they get collected?" Jason was grasping at straws, but his gut was sure there was something he hadn't noticed.

"Yes. I watched one of the deputies bag all the items and photograph where, in the car, each had been found, just as though this had been a crime scene instead of an accident."

That wasn't like the county men. "Does Cain suspect something?"

"I couldn't say, but he did pay more attention to the water on the roof after you mentioned it."

"Could that have just been from the cup?" That would be logical.

"Nope." The doctor's answer came quickly. "Three, maybe four times more water than that cup could have held." He paused. "'Sides, the cup's residue indicated some type of dark soda."

None of this made sense, and the inconsistency bugged him. "Can we get any of the water from the roof tested?"

"Not my department, but I do know one of the men took some samples."

"Is Doc Umbridge doing any more testing?" Surely, the medical examiner would at least check the water samples. That would tell them if it was rainwater, though Jason sincerely doubted it. The car was on the edge of a ditch, but not where any water would've run through it. And the trash wouldn't have remained had that been the case.

The coroner remained silent for a moment. Jason glanced at his phone to make sure the call hadn't dropped. "Are you still there?"

"I'm here. I'm not sure if I should be discussing this with you."

"Did Cain direct him to perform detailed tests?" Maybe the man was more of a cop than Jason gave him credit for.

"No, no. He's pushing for a formal cause of death."

Little bells went off in Jason's head. "You're not satisfied that it was an accident."

"Don't jump to conclusions, Lieutenant. I didn't say anything of the sort."

Jason recognized evasion. "Then why haven't you declared the cause of death."

"A few inconsistencies."

He didn't explain further.

"You gonna tell me what they are?" No way Jason could force the issue. But with the concern of Ellis's letter and now, suspicions from the coroner, this matter deserved more analysis. "If Cain didn't direct you to look into anything, you aren't breaking protocol."

The exhale the man dispelled whistled through the phone

connection. "All right. But not a word of this to anyone."

"Besides the chief." Jason wasn't going to have his hands tied.

"Agreed." The man sighed again. "Did you notice the cuts on the victim's face and hands?"

"No." He hadn't wanted to look at Ellis at all. The victim. Not Ellis Stone … the victim.

"Well, it's normal in a crash like this to have little cuts and nicks from the broken safety glass."

"And?" Jason wasn't usually impatient, but a knot had begun building in his gut. Not sure where to start, but he needed to move.

"I'm getting to it. Had the man died at or near the time of the cuts, there would have been some bleeding. Maybe not too much, but some should have seeped out when the body came to rest."

"And there's not enough?"

"There's not any. And I mean none. A particularly bad cut on his neck should have oozed onto his shirt, but it didn't."

Did that mean what Jason thought? "Ellis was already dead before the accident?"

"Don't know. Could be we're wrong about the rain. Maybe that small area got a downpour and the wounds were washed clean. Doc Umbridge will be able to tell. But I had enough questions to ask him to do the testing."

That lifted a weight. "Thanks for the update. I've learned something here that's given me some questions as well. I'm glad you're looking into things."

"Just understand, Lieutenant, if Umbridge finds out there's reason to believe foul play, I can't tell you anything else. This is a county case."

"Got it. I just want someone looking into it. To get some satisfactory answers." Jason shifted his car back into gear. "Even if you discover that it was an accident." He rang off and tapped in the number for the HPPD then mounted his phone and synced with the Bluetooth app.

"Heath's Point Police Department. Do you have an emergency?"

Jason pulled to the stop sign and took a left down the highway. "Good morning, Mrs. Hawkins." Though his heart rate had doubled since talking to the coroner, he maintained his normal tone and relaxed pace. "Can I speak to the chief, please."

"Of course, Jason. And how is your morning?"

He knew she would ask. "Lovely. And yours?" Hopefully, she would keep her rundown short.

"Well, my silly little beagle ran out the front door this morning. You know Petunia. She gets her nose into something and just goes. I still don't know what carried her away, but I finally caught up to her almost a block away. Can you believe she'd get a scent a block away? Almost had a heart attack before I reached her, and my back is hurting something fierce from all that running, but I took an ibuprofen an hour back, and I have every confidence that it will kick in before long."

The road was smooth and empty as the woman completed her novel. He kept his speech slow and lazy. "Hope so. Can I speak to the chief?"

"Of course." She patched him through.

"Chief Tate." Dell's voice was gruff as always.

"Thank you, Mrs. Hawkins." She always stayed on the line as

long as possible to hear anything newsworthy.

"You're welcome, Jason."

He waited for the click. "You really should speak to her, Dell."

"Soon. What's up?"

"Ellis sent a letter to an attorney in Dallas last week. It was returned as undeliverable."

"Don't tell me you opened that." His boss's voice became a growl.

"I didn't. Couldn't tell who the letter was to, but it was clearly from Ellis." Jason took a little breath. "Alynne opened it."

A growl pushed through the line. "Still not entirely legal."

"No way for her to learn who should get it without opening it. And I didn't touch it."

"Okay, move on."

That could've gone worse. Jason lifted a silent thanks to the Lord and told his boss the contents of the letter. He followed it up with the coroner's questions and request for an autopsy.

Jason flexed and relaxed his grip on the steering wheel as he turned onto another back road. "Where did the deputy send Ellis's car?"

"Probably to Bubba's. I'll give him a call."

"Bubba and I are friends." Jason ran his hand over the steering wheel. "Why don't I go chat with him? We need to keep this under wraps as long as we can to spare Myra."

Dell grew silent.

"Sorry, chief. I didn't mean to tell you how to do your job."

"No sorry necessary. I was thinking that you'd make a pretty good police chief someday."

Jason's jaw slackened. Was the man serious?

"Not that I'm willing to give up the post anytime soon, mind you."

He was serious. High praise. "Uh … Yes, sir." He cleared his throat.

Less than a quarter-hour later, Jason pulled into the crowded lot of Bubba's Repair and Spare, part of a gas station and convenience store all-in-one. Bubba was known all over the county for his re-creations and had something of a junkyard in the lot behind the shop.

The tall black man must've been in his sixties, but only the graying on either side of his head belied his true age. His daily activity gave his arms and legs a natural workout that made him look decades younger. A fact his sweet wife had mentioned she both loved and hated since she, as a high school teacher, had no such opportunity.

He came out of the office as Jason parked and extended a broad smile and a handshake. "Well, Lieutenant. Too early for lunch. Too late for fishing. What can I do for you?"

Jason accepted his hand and leaned in to slap him on the back as well. "Official, today, my friend. That white Acura you got in."

Bubba shook his head. "Sad situation. I didn't know the man very well, but folks had nothing bad to say about him. Godly and kind."

"That he was." And wise and encouraging. Jason swallowed the loss once again. "Have you looked at the car?"

The man frowned and shrugged. "Sheriff didn't seem to suspect nothing. I just loaded it up until I heard something from the next of kin. His wife, right?"

"Yeah, probably in a day or two."

"I figured she'd need to grieve some before I contacted her." He turned toward the yard behind his shop.

Jason fell into step beside him. "Good man. But I wonder if you'll do a little check on the car. Transmission, brakes, steering, tires. Just a quick look to determine if anything's amiss."

"You thinkin' this might not have been an accident?" The man's eyes widened. "Murder?"

Hard to answer that question at this point. "I didn't say anything like that. I only want the car checked. To be sure." He hesitated a step, and the man towering next to him also paused. "Did you notice any blood?"

Bubba shook his head. "Not to speak of." He raised an eyebrow at him. "Exactly what are you getting at, son?"

"Not sure. There were some substantial wounds from the glass and stuff, but no apparent blood. Could you check that?"

"I can do that. Should be some hint of stains somewhere. I'll find them."

Jason fell into step beside him.

"Isn't this a county case?"

"I'm not in competition with the sheriff's department." How did he explain this? "Dell and I ... we've learned something that might throw a shadow over the issue. If we're right, I'm sure Dell will inform the sheriff. If we're wrong, no need to upset anyone. Wouldn't you agree?"

"I agree that Deputy Cain'll be at my throat if he learns that I've done this." Bubba neared Ellis's smashed car.

Jason glanced at the headliner, now hanging down in the middle. "Then we won't let Deputy Cain know about it."

Bubba went to the driver's side where the door had been pulled off the vehicle. He bent down, and a second later, the hood popped up about an inch. "I suppose I need to report anything I find to you?"

"Or to the chief." He started to turn away as Bubba lifted the hood. "On second thought, our office sometimes has ears. We're attempting to spare Mrs. Stone, the widow."

"I gotcha. I'll give you a call on your cell then."

"You're the best, man."

"Now, I'll be happy to take that role if you ever decide to get married." Bubba laughed.

Jason felt a fever creeping up his neck. "Don't hold your breath, my friend. I have no prospects, nor do I want any."

"What about that lady at the diner. The tall one."

"Daisy?" Sweet as all get out since she'd come to know the Lord, but Jason had no interest.

"Yeah, that's the girl." He shined a miniature flashlight into the engine. "Pretty thing. Even with that weird scar."

The S. "That's a long story. I'll tell you about it next time we're fishing."

"Saturday morning. Five o'clock." Bubba lifted his chin just enough to catch his eye. "A. M."

Jason rolled his eyes. "I only set the alarm wrong once. I didn't expect to go fishing at dinnertime."

"I don't know, man. You tend to be a slacker on your days off."

Jason left him chuckling and climbed back into his cruiser. Maybe the field where Ellis lost his life held more information. He shifted into gear and headed that direction. No telling what the accident site might reveal when it was treated as a crime scene.

Chapter Six

Alynne's stress over the morning's mail faded when she'd left for home to pack a suitcase. She'd called Blayne on the way there and then again after she'd packed but still had no contact. Why hadn't he returned any of her calls?

Alarms had started sounding through her head. Had he changed his mind about marrying her? Maybe he was avoiding her calls. Or had something happened to him? *God, please let him be all right.*

Her prayer backfired. Instead of giving her peace, her conscience nagged. Why was it the only time she thought about speaking to God was when her worries overwhelmed her?

Without an answer, she called Blayne's line at his office. He hated her calling him there. He said his bosses tended to notice every personal call that was made, and they mentioned them in staff meetings. The call shifted to the automatic voice mail. He was probably still in Vegas. She called his cell phone once more, leaving another message. Then she attempted to put him out of her mind. She had more important things to do besides worry about that man. Especially with her mom's whole family due at the inn soon.

Momma came out to the porch as she returned. She stood at the top of the steps and waited for Alynne to park and get out. "Oh, sweet girl. I'm so pleased you're back."

A soaking wet Rose shook beside her, and her tail kept up a continuous wag.

"I told you I was going to pack. Were you worried?" The last thing her mom needed was something else to worry about.

"Not really. I think Jason's been, though. He's called at least twice wondering if you had returned." Her mom's head tilted to one side. "Is there something between the two of you?"

Alynne rolled down her car windows to air out the dust that the AC had kicked into her interior and then unlatched her trunk. "We only met yesterday. Why would you think that?"

"Oh … no reason." She tapped on the top of the newel post as though it deserved her rapt concentration.

Alynne reached to give Rose a pat. "Did the dog go swimming?"

"No, I just bathed her." She picked up a thick towel on the wicker chair and began giving Rose a good rub. "He's a wonderful man, though."

"Who?" Alynne pulled her suitcase from the trunk. Her other supplies could wait until later.

"Jason Danvers. Been in town a few years. He'd come out here to help Ellis on his days off."

He seemed like a good guy. "I'm not looking for a new man,

Momma." Of course, Momma had heard about Blayne, but Alynne didn't intend on bringing him up, especially not her engagement, until after she could talk to him again. Probably a good thing she didn't have a ring yet.

"I was just thinking …" Momma led her and the dog into the Victorian and didn't finish her thought. Just as well.

Alynne dragged her suitcase up the steps and into the entry. "Do I need to move to a different room before the rest of the family gets here?"

"No, dear. Until we learn who's coming and when they'll be here, you might as well stay where you are."

Good enough. Momma led the way to the south-wing suite Alynne had claimed. Rose followed behind them, but she darted into the room first when Momma opened the door.

"The dog can't stay in my room."

"She's sweet company, but you don't have to worry. She's happy to sleep under the porch unless someone invites her in." Momma then began a rundown of where they would house the different members of her family when they did arrive.

She had everything planned. Meals, room assignments, and ideas to keep the kids entertained. She and Alynne spent the rest of the day cleaning and restocking each room. By dinner, Alynne might as well have run a 5-K. "You do all this for every guest?"

Her momma nodded. "But I'm used to it. I pray over the rooms as I clean them, asking the Father to bring peace and renewal to those who will stay there. It's a joy to provide a place for folks to reignite their spirits and, hopefully, their faith."

Joy. Alynne let her mind wrap around the word. Had she had

any true joy? Not recently. Not since she'd helped Momma through her cancer battle. Yes, she'd had joy then. Not always happy times, but she'd been where she was needed, doing what she could to help. And she had helped. Had encouraged her mom. Delighted her even, when Momma was at her darkest.

She'd had some happy times since then, like the cruise last Christmas. But it wasn't the same. Wasn't as fulfilling, or lasting. Maybe she needed to take a few lessons at the feet of her momma.

The chief had sent Officer Billings and a cameraman to help Jason analyze the crash site as a crime scene. The ditch itself offered little evidence. Too many people had been through it, not to mention the deep ruts made when the car was dragged back up the slope, probably by Bubba's heavy-duty hauler.

But the road gave a better hint. Not so much by what was there, but by what wasn't there. Deputy Cain should have noticed. On this steep grade and hairpin turn, there was no evidence of brakes, or even an attempt to make a sharp turn.

He called Bubba to tell him to focus on the brakes, but the mechanic had already finished. "Nothing wrong with the line," his friend had said. "And I checked the tires. Nothing strange about them."

"Looks completely like an accident then?"

"I didn't say that. Just that there wasn't any damage to the brakes. Not to the steering either for that matter."

"Why wouldn't a man use the brakes or try to turn the car

when he's going straight into a ditch."

"Oh, he didn't go straight in."

Wait. "What do you mean by that?" He'd just assumed the car had driven straight off the curve.

"No, with the damage on the car, it didn't fly off. It rolled. Your friend didn't drive off the end of the curve. He went off the road and drove on the narrow shoulder long enough to stuff grass up into the crevices of the car, even into the engine. Then it rolled over into the ditch. Didn't even make a full rotation."

Come to think of it, there hadn't been much damage on the driver's side. "Thanks for the report, my friend."

"Don't forget our next trip."

"Gotcha."

Jason called the chief and explained what he'd learned as he made it to his apartment. Thankfully, he wouldn't be the one to make the call to the sheriff, asking him to reopen the investigation.

Alynne found her mom in the kitchen.

"We'll need some groceries for the week. I'd hate to run out of things when all of the family gets here." Momma had filled every line of a long notepad. "Especially, during what will surely be an emotional time."

Doubtless. "Why don't I go out and pick everything up."

"Oh dear, no. I wasn't suggesting that you should take care of this task."

"I know, Momma, but I don't mind. Who knows? Maybe inn-keeping will grow on me." Stranger things had happened.

Momma gave a tight smile. "Well, all right. If you insist." She handed over the list. "Call if you have questions. And I'll get this kitchen in order to receive all of the new items."

With the list in her hand, Alynne spent over an hour inside the store, but she checked off every item. Even collected a hot tea blend that she liked, though she couldn't find the brand of granola she favored. Good thing she'd thought to bring the remains of her bag from Dallas with her. She loved Momma's breakfast this morning, but if she ate like that every day, she'd be a beach ball in no time.

The cashier gave her a strange look as she unloaded the piles of food onto the conveyor belt. "Did you jes move in, ma'am?" The middle-aged lady spoke with a heavy accent and lifted graceful eyebrows over dark, expressive eyes.

Momma had told her before that everybody in this town enjoyed discussing the activities of everybody else, and this store was probably gossip-central. "I'm helping ... out at the inn." No need to explain who she was.

"Oh, that's so good of you." The woman clapped her hands together as if in prayer for a moment. "What a terrible thing to happen to one of the nicest men in this town. Poor Miss Myra. Is she doing all right?" As fast as the woman spoke with her slight Spanish accent, she whipped the grocery items across her scanner and bagged them even quicker.

Alynne nodded, not willing to relay anything her mom might not want to be revealed. "I believe her family will be coming into town soon."

"Ahhh. That explains all of the groceries. I was afraid Miss Myra would try to keep guests coming in. Such a difficult time. So many decisions."

This time, Alynne merely smiled. Enough said on this topic. "Have you lived in Heath's Point long?"

"Seventeen years." She lapsed into silence as she continued to scan.

The quiet was good.

She finally loaded the bags into her cart and thanked the woman as she slipped her credit card back into her purse.

"Please tell Miss Myra that Juanita is praying for her." The cashier handed her the last parcel.

"I will and thank you." Alynne pushed the loaded cart out of the store but jumped as the headlights of an oncoming car flared over her. He was only pulling out of the lot. Why was she so jumpy? But in truth, she was, and for no good reason. She shouldered her purse and shoved the cart over a bump in the concrete.

Another car pulled into the lot behind her. The lights revealed a deep shadow between her car and the brown truck parked beside it. The lights behind her flicked off leaving the area in almost pitch blackness. Was there someone between the vehicles?

Her mind was playing tricks on her. She approached her car. Her finger found the button on her key fob. She parked the cart at the back bumper of her car and reached to open the trunk. Something moved on her right.

She spun around.

Someone came at her.

She swung her purse, catching the runner in the face, but it made little impact. The person shoved her to the ground. Pain shot up her arm.

Jason showered and changed out of his uniform. Chances were, the ladies at the inn might need a little help to get ready for the influx of family that was due. His stomach growled as he climbed into the Jeep. He'd better grab something, but not fast food.

Heading back through town, he spotted the grocery store. An apple and a protein bar would work. He pulled in and spotted Alynne as she pushed an overfilled cart toward her car on the opposite side of the lot. He parked and climbed out. He might as well say hello and help her load her things into her car before he did his own meager shopping.

He looked up, but Alynne was no longer moving toward her car. She lay in a heap at the bumper. "Alynne." He broke into a run.

Something like a shadow whirled over her. Was someone with her? "Stop." He pulled his gun from his holster. The figure disappeared between the cars.

"Alynne." He reached her but scanned the area once more.

"I'm all right. He only pushed me down."

Jason sprinted around the brown truck and into the field beside the store. With no moon and few lights, the whole thing was one big shadow. He might be looking right at the runner and not see him. Or was it a her? He jogged toward the back of the building. Nothing moved around him. He paused at the corner then peeked his head around before jerking back to analyze what he'd seen in the light of a single bulb at the loading dock: a large garbage bin, a high retaining wall from where the store was built into the hill behind it, a couple of broken plastic crates. Everything looked empty.

He peered again, longer this time, but there was no one. No movement. He glanced back at the truck that blocked his view of Alynne. This wasn't the time to chase after phantoms. Abandoning the pursuit, he jogged back over the uneven ground built up with dirt clods and weeds.

Alynne was sitting up by this time. "Did you see him?"

"Was it a man?" All Jason had seen was a shadow.

"I couldn't tell. He wore a mask. And a hood with something like a long coat or maybe a cape."

"You were mugged by a superhero?" He would have laughed if the situation hadn't been so serious.

"Funny. But I couldn't see a bit of skin on him. Gloves, ski mask, long sleeves, and that cape completely covered everything about him."

"Yet, you keep saying him." He reached to help her up.

"What should I say? It?" She took his hand and flinched. "Ouch." She jerked her left hand away and wrapped her other one around her upper arm.

"Did you fall wrong?" He knelt beside her.

She pulled her hand away from her shoulder. Blood covered her palm.

Without a word, he scooped her into his arms and made for his Jeep.

"I'm bleeding." Her voice cracked.

He triggered the automatic door and shouted at Juanita. "Call Dell. There's been a mugging."

"What about my groceries?" Alynne's complaint didn't slow him a bit.

"And take care of the cart." He caught a glimpse of the cashier's wide eyes and nod as he jogged past.

He stowed Alynne in his passenger seat and wrapped the belt around her before racing to his side and climbing in. "What can you remember?" He whipped his steering wheel around and made for the highway.

"How am I bleeding? I didn't think I fell that hard."

"Do you remember the figure knocking you down?"

"He … it rushed at me. Shoved me." She leaned her head against the back of the seat.

He glanced at her. Her eyelids were sagging. "Keep a grip on your arm"

She straightened. "Wait. I remember something hurting, intense. About the time I fell. I thought I'd fallen on a rock, but it …"

There were still a few miles to go. He pressed harder on the accelerator. "It hurt?"

"Yeah. The pain started before I … hit the ground. When he slammed into me."

Keep talking, Alynne. "Did you see a knife?"

"A knife?" She turned her rich blue eyes onto him.

He looked her way for a second, hating the fear that wrinkled her brow and widened her eyes.

"You think he cut me with a knife?"

Not entirely odd for the big city—though most of the muggings he'd ever worked didn't involve weapons—such was a rarity for a little place like Heath's Point. "The doctor will be able to tell. Do you remember anything else?"

"My purse." The bag hung off her right shoulder. She reached for it.

"No, keep gripping your arm." He laid his hand on her shoulder and stroked her collarbone with his thumb. "Your purse is fine."

"Right."

With a reluctance he didn't expect, he released her and placed both hands on the wheel. Not that he needed to. These roads were as much his office as the dusty room at the station.

She faced him, though he could only see her in his periphery. "I swung it at the figure. Caught its face. At least, I thought I did."

"Hard enough to bruise?" That could be a lead.

Her chin drooped. "I don't know. Probably not."

He turned into the ER entrance at Howerton Memorial in record time. "Stay with me, Alynne."

"At least he didn't get my purse."

There was that. He rushed around his Jeep but not before a nurse and an orderly pushing a wheelchair had already helped her out of her seat. He watched with a helpless sensation as they pushed her into that horrible building.

Wait. Why hadn't the mugger taken her purse?

"Ow." Alynne pressed the back of her head into her pillow as the nurse covered her arm with gauze. She could practically hear the pain stabbing with each touch of the woman's fingers.

"There you go. The doctor will need to sign off on your release before you can leave, though." The nurse put another strip of tape across the bandage, once again shooting fire into her arm.

She pushed through the short curtain. "Looks like your visitor is here. Okay if I let him in?"

No. With all that had happened, she probably resembled Rose after a dunk in the lake. But she nodded. Jason had supported her through pretty ugly moments in the forty-eight hours she'd known him.

He stepped through the curtain carrying his hat and with a crooked smile and worry lines between his brow. "The doc says you'll be fine."

Once he'd skewered her. Yeah. "Did you speak to my mom?" As much as she didn't want Momma to know about the attack, Alynne's being so long at the grocery store would worry her sick.

He stepped to the right side of her bed. "I told her you'd fallen and cut your shoulder." His neck turned a light shade of pink. "I'm not much for dishonesty, but I agree that she doesn't need any more stress."

That omission had probably been hard for him. She laid her hand on his arm. "Thank you." She looked up into his soft, gray eyes. "I don't know what I would have done if you hadn't been there."

His smile dropped away, and the lines between his brows deepened. "Glad I was."

Had she said something to make him mad?

"I'll take you home when you're ready." He covered her hand with his own. "And I'm sorry about all this."

He exited through the curtain before she could question his last comment. Sorry? What did he possibly have to be sorry about? He certainly hadn't been the caped creature that sliced into her.

The doctor came in at that point, distracting her with questions and handing her papers for care as well as a pain killer prescription. One she wouldn't use if she could help it. Within the hour, she was loaded back into a wheelchair and pushed into the waiting area.

She scanned the room. Only a few people there: a couple of older ladies, a kid and his parents. Jason wasn't among them. The orderly pushed her through the doors to the lighted driveway.

Jason leaned against the front of his Jeep, his arms folded over his chest, his chin down, and one booted foot crossed over the other.

A swarm of butterflies attacked her insides. He did look the part of the perfect cowboy. He glanced up and lifted his hand. "Over here."

The orderly pushed her down the ramp as Jason moved to open her door.

Once she was settled in her seat, she glanced at the orderly. "I appreciate your help."

She then turned to Jason who was climbing into his seat. How could she thank him? She might be dead had he not been there. Her poor mom … "I'm not sure how to thank you."

"Thank?" He practically spewed out the word then faced her, his mouth drooping. "I'm a cop, Alynne. And I was right there. You should never have been hurt at all."

Was he crazy? "Oh, I didn't realize you had the ability to tell the future. 'Cause that's the talent you would have needed in order to know some monster was going to rush at me in the grocery store parking lot."

His mouth flattened, and he tightened and released his grip on the steering wheel. But he controlled his speed and eased out of his parking space.

"Jason, you're not responsible for my injury any more than you were responsible for Pop's death."

He turned toward her. "I'm not convinced."

"This was just a mugging. They happen even in a little town like Heath's Point. Just like car accidents."

He pressed his lips together again like he was chewing on his inside lip.

"What are you not saying?"

"Not sure your dad had an accident. Some things aren't adding up. And with the letter your dad sent …" He paused, and Alynne let him work through it.

She had to wrap her brain around what he'd said, anyway. If Pop didn't die in an accident … what? Her mind swirled.

"Your dad knew something was wrong. It's why he wrote that letter. And he was asking about family members."

Alynne shook off the brain-fog. "Still, this was just someone after my purse. And it's because of your care that I'm still here."

How could she get him to believe her? She laid her hand on his arm. "I wouldn't be if you hadn't been there. And I'm nothing but grateful."

His grimace relaxed somewhat, and he dipped his head. "You're welcome." He pulled onto the highway heading back toward Momma's inn. "I'm still sorry it happened at all."

"But it's like I said …"

He held up a hand. "I regret that you got hurt." He glanced toward her and gave her a half-smile that ignited her heart.

What was that? She was engaged. To be married. Blayne was a great guy. And she still needed to reach him.

An uncomfortable silence settled on the Jeep's interior. She'd been around Jason enough to know he was a little on the quiet side, but not in an awkward way.

Of course, he was probably acting like normal. She was the one who felt like a pop star had just grinned at her from the stage.

He pulled onto the road that bordered the inn before speaking again. "I'm glad you're here, Alynne. Good for Myra. For you, too, I think."

Yes. Very good for her. "Strange. I've lived in Dallas all my life, but this place feels so comfortable."

"Your mom sure needs you. Won't say it, but she does."

He sure had her momma pegged.

He pulled into her lot. The automatic light at the open gate flicked on as they entered, illuminating the gravel as they drifted to the center of it. "Someone's here."

"Maybe it's another visitor. Momma has had a lot of people stop by."

"I don't think so. The chief brought her the groceries you bought a couple of hours ago. She told him she was turning out the light to dissuade any late visitors."

But the porch light was still on.

"Stay in the car." He shifted into park and pulled out his keys.

She squinted through the windshield. The other vehicle was parked on the other side of her mom's white SUV. Was that … Blayne's car?

Chapter Seven

Jason approached the car from the cover of the SUV. With his back to the white hatch, he peered around the edge to see if someone sat in the driver's seat of the foreign car. All clear, or so it seemed. He did a tour around the Lexus, using the penlight on his key chain to cut through the tinting of the windows to ensure the vehicle's emptiness.

No way Myra had visitors this late. But clearly, someone had arrived. Hopefully, not an unexpected guest for the inn.

He raised his hand to signal Alynne, but she'd already climbed from his car and was crunching over the gravel toward him.

"I know this car." She bypassed him and climbed the steps to the door.

"Friend of yours?" That would explain the late visit.

"There you are." A man rounded the corner of the Victorian with Myra and Rose in his wake. "I was having a lovely chat with your mom."

Sirens slashed through his head. Who was this guy? Jason

bolted up the steps, but Alynne had already grasped the man's hand with her uninjured one and planted a brief kiss on his cheek.

Jason halted. How had he missed that she was in a relationship? But of course, she was. She was beautiful. And smart.

"I was so worried, dear." Myra reached for her daughter. Alynne released the man and embraced her mom in a one-armed hug.

Did the man stiffen as she pulled away? Jason stepped closer. The front porch light illuminated the dark hair of a man. Probably a little taller than Jason, but not very athletic judging from his narrow shoulders. The man settled a blue-eyed glare on him, then stuck on a fake smile. "You must be the policeman." He held out his hand. "I can't thank you enough for taking care of my Alynne."

Jason shook the man's hand, but he didn't miss the implication.

He also didn't miss how Alynne had locked arms with her mom and entered the Victorian in rapt conversation, without glancing back at the man.

"Lieutenant Danvers." He held the man's gaze along with his hand. Surely, he would introduce himself.

A smirk soured his semblance of a smile. "Blayne Campbell." He released the shake. "Alynne's fiancé."

Jason's stomach twisted as much as when he saw the blood on Alynne's forearm. "Nice to meet you." He turned back toward his Jeep. What was with his reaction? Sure, he'd had no idea that she was involved, but why wouldn't she be?

Still … engaged. Wouldn't she have said something about the man? Especially while in the hospital to get a knife wound stitched? Seems like her relationship would have come up on the way to or from the hospital.

Maybe she didn't feel comfortable enough around Jason to say anything personal.

But if they were so serious, why hadn't her precious fiancé come when she'd learned that her father had been killed? Whatever. The man was here, now. And her greeting left little guesswork to her feelings for him.

Jason had a job to do, with or without the presence of Blayne Campbell.

What was Blayne doing there? And why hadn't he called her? She'd left at least a half-dozen messages and as many texts in the last two days.

Heat climbed up her neck as the man followed her and her mom into the kitchen.

"I'm so glad I finally got to meet your young man, Alynne. We had a nice chat, didn't we, Blayne?" Momma filled Rose's food bowl and set it on the mat near the kitchen door. Rose dug in.

Alynne kept her eyes on the feasting dog, but Blayne's smile and nod filtered into her peripheral vision.

"You are the epitome of graciousness, Mrs. Stone. I'm not surprised that Sunset Inn does so well."

Her mom thanked him then filled the large teapot. "Why don't I make us all some nice tea, and you two can go chat in the parlor."

Chat? Alynne wanted to scream.

"Oh, dear, are you feeling okay?" Her mom returned to her and examined her face. "You're reaching tomato status."

"I'm fine." Not fine. Furious.

Blayne neared on her other side. "Babe? Do you need to sit down?"

"No" She ground her teeth and forced her voice to sound as normal as possible. "Only tired." She turned toward the entry hall.

"Let me walk you to your room." He wrapped his arm around her waist. Like he should have been doing as she dealt with Pop's death.

She turned to face them both, pulling away from him. "Please don't. I only need some sleep." She wouldn't look at him. "Momma, will you assign a room to Blayne? Maybe on the upper level?" That would keep him away from her. If nothing else, she'd get the chance to cool off before she said something without calculating the consequences.

Without waiting for any response, she turned and strode to her suite in as calm a manner as she could create. She didn't even allow her hands to ball into fists, and that alone took a lot of effort.

A shower would help. The doctor had sent her home with a plastic sleeve, so she took advantage of the opportunity. The water pouring over helped her relax a little and cooled her face. She'd probably looked feverish before she'd left the entry hall. Hopefully, Momma wouldn't worry about her.

But really. Why hadn't Blayne answered any of her texts or calls? If he dealt with her so callously now, how would he treat her once they were married?

Stifling her anger once again, she dressed and dried her hair, revisiting the memories of the evening. The figure had been faceless, probably wearing something like a ski mask, but the eye holes had been completely black. And that coat, or cape, or whatever it was. Like some ridiculous Phantom of the Opera. A muscle pulsed in her back and sent a shiver to her shoulders.

That phantom thought stuck with her on the fringes of her dreams through a rough night. Her arm ached as well, with sharp pains pulling her from deep sleep over and over. Though she couldn't recall any details of her dreams, she woke with the impression of failure and despair.

And she still wasn't completely over her frustration with Blayne when she awoke the next morning.

Because of the chores she'd be likely to do, she'd brought a selection of her oldest clothes from Dallas. Things she hadn't worn since college, probably. The long-sleeved, denim shirt perfectly covered her bandage. She tugged on a pair of loose jeans and some sneakers that had been her fishing shoes before Pop and Momma moved away from home. Pausing, she glanced at her reflection in the full mirror that stood at the corner of the bureau.

Who was that girl? Her hair hung in long waves, a little tussled, but shining. She hadn't put on any makeup. Not even mascara, but her eyes were luminous bright blue and edged with thick and dark lashes.

She could stand a little blush, though. After applying it and giving in to a little eye shadow and mascara, she made her way to the kitchen, itching to help Momma with breakfast this last morning before the family descended.

"You're up early." Her mom rolled out a mound of dough. A

fruity mixture bubbled in a pan on the stove.

"Is that going to be a cobbler?" Smelled like apples and cinnamon.

"Sort of, only more like a breakfast pastry." Momma cut something like wide fringes on either side of the flattened dough. "If I'm going to stay home from church to prepare for the family, then I should make things really nice for them."

Oh. Church. Guilt whipped her. "Momma, you didn't stay home from church to set up for the family, did you?"

Her mom turned a slight pout toward her. "You needed your rest. And I wasn't about to leave you here alone with your boyfriend. That isn't appropriate." She turned back to cutting her dough. "Besides, I wanted to be the one here helping you if you needed it."

Alynne slipped her good arm around her mom and gave her a squeeze. "That means a lot."

"How is your arm this morning?"

"It hurts a little, but I'd like to cook with you. Your sisters will be here before long."

"And you'll barely be allowed in this room at that point." She chuckled. "I tell you, Billie and Bobbie will never see you as anything but a cute little angel with your halo askew."

"I never put the ants in the sugar bag." Alynne smiled at the memory as she fished out a bottle of ibuprofen from her mom's miscellaneous drawer. "I simply didn't stop them when I saw a line heading in that direction."

"And you never told them about it until after they'd found their dead carcasses in Phyllis's birthday cake."

Good thing they hadn't iced it. "Protein-enriched. I think they should have served that delicacy." She chuckled and sipped some water to urge down the pills. "Put me to work."

Work was the word for it. Like the day before, Momma tended to every task as if for some magical moment. A wedding wouldn't have had more perfection. Though tedious at first, Alynne began to anticipate how Momma would want something prepared, down to the plate on which to serve it and the fruits or herbs added as accents.

By the time Blayne, dressed in slacks and a golf shirt, and made his way into the kitchen they'd completed a braided apple strudel, a variety of cut fruit that could rival a bouquet, and a selection of quiches in personal pie shells. "Something smells amazing." He graced Momma with a big smile, but when he glanced in Alynne's direction, his chin dropped, and his eyes widened. "Uh … what happened to you?"

Okay, so she wasn't office appropriate, but did she really deserve his shocked look? "We're not in Dallas, Blayne."

"Well, I know." He blinked his eyes, and his smile came back in full force. "I'm simply surprised to see my beautiful, put-together lady so …" He held his hands up.

"Messed up?"

He dropped his hands with a sheepish smirk. "I was going to say, countrified." He chuckled. "Been a while since I saw your hair down."

While she'd begun to laugh with him, his remark about her hair brought back the memory of that night about a month ago. Heat rose in her cheeks. She spun and opened the fridge, pretending to look for something inside.

Momma scooted past her. "Do you like eggs? Alynne made some outstanding quiches."

"You've been cooking with your mom?"

With a sigh, Alynne withdrew from the fridge with a pitcher of juice in her hand. "That's right." She set it on the counter.

"We always used to enjoy preparing a meal together. Didn't we, dear?" Momma put the crystal bowl full of fruit along with a matching shot glass full of short skewers on the base of an ancient dumbwaiter in the corner.

"I've missed it." Alynne pulled off her flour-dusted apron and washed the remains of the pie dough from her hands. "Does that thing work?"

"Perfectly." Her mom added the strudel and a basket of assorted muffins then closed a sliding door and pushed a button. "Why don't you two youngsters run on upstairs to the dining hall and set the food on the servers?"

"Sure thing." And she'd get the chance to ensure that Blayne kept her secret. He didn't understand that things were different in her family.

"Actually, I have some work to do." Blayne picked up a filled pie shell and took a bite.

What work could he be doing? "I thought you were in sales."

"I am, but I have some research I need to do for a new region." His eyes lit. "Hey. Research. That's right down your alley."

It was, but she'd left that back in Dallas to help her mom for a while. "I really should be helping Momma."

"That's all right. You both go on ahead." Momma scooted

down through the westside door. Her tennis shoes thumped on the back stairs as she climbed up to the second floor.

Alynne paused to let her get out of hearing. At this point, Blayne was more trouble than treasure. "Why are you here?" She pressed her lips together.

"Why? Well, to comfort you, of course." He came over and put his hands at her waist, but she pulled away.

"Then why didn't you return any of my calls or texts?"

He let his hands drop. "I've come all the way out here. I'd hoped to sweep you off to Vegas after all, but then your mother told me about your father."

"There's no way I can go. Not for a while anyway." Momma needed her. And besides, her mind had twisted in all sorts of directions. She wasn't a big fan of Las Vegas, though the sneaking off to elope had enticed her. Still, did she want to do something as serious as getting married on a whim? Especially without even informing her mom. That would break Momma's heart.

"You're postponing our wedding?" He leaned back in the seat and looked away. "I thought I was important to you, Alynne."

"You are." She took one look at his pout and felt her frustration from the previous night ebb away. "Pop died, Blayne. I have to stay here and help Momma. She needs me."

He lowered his chin. "I can certainly see that, but I can't lie that it disappoints me. Not that you're determined to support your mom. I respect you for that." His shoulders slumped. "I just wish this didn't have to change all of our plans."

This was her father they were talking about. Her mom who needed her during this tragedy. "I think a little delay isn't that big a deal. You don't even have a ring yet." Alynne's frustration and hurt escaped before she could stop the sharp words. Blayne wasn't responsible for Pop's accident. The last thing she needed to do was drive him away during a time when she needed him most.

She laid her hand on his arm. "I'm sorry. I didn't mean to fuss. But we need to put our plans on hold for a while."

He wiped the back of his hand across his forehead. "I understand. I didn't want to tell your mom without you here, but I do want to share it with her."

"We can't." The words came out a little forced. "Surely you can see this isn't the right time to discuss a wedding or even an engagement. It would only make Momma miss Pop more."

He continued, "I don't see why we can't tell your mom our intentions. Bring a bright spot to her grief."

Alynne's breath caught coupled with a wave of panic. "Please, Blayne, no. Momma has been through enough emotions in the last twenty-four hours. With all of her family coming in, she has enough on her mind." What was she doing? Why was she holding back? Shouldn't a newly engaged woman want to shout about the relationship?

Was she afraid? No, not afraid exactly … unsure? Did she need time at this point to think through her decision? Surely not. Barring Pop's tragedy, they'd have been married now. And that's what she needed, that resolution.

He rose and stroked his hand down her good arm, clasping hers in a warm grip. "I'm sorry about your father, Alynne. I should have been here, and I would have been if I'd known about his accident."

"It wasn't an accident." He might as well learn the whole, disastrous truth.

His grip tightened. "What are you talking about? Your mother said he missed a bad turn during a storm."

She shrugged. "I don't know all the details, but the police have reason to believe it was … something else."

"That's terrible" He rubbed his other hand over her upper arm.

Pain that had subsided shot through her shoulder. She winced and Blayne flinched, releasing her arm. "I'm so sorry, darling. I forgot about your bruise."

She shook her head. "Not a bruise. Someone attacked me last night. I was cut by a knife."

He paled and his lips separated. He cupped her cheek and searched her face. "There has to be some mistake."

"I can show you the stitches." His attention was kind, but the counter behind her crowded her in. She slipped to her right, forcing him to release her. She poured a glass of the juice she'd pulled from the refrigerator. "Someone was waiting for me at my car in the grocery store parking lot."

"Random chance. I'll bet things like that happen all the time in poor little towns like this."

"Heath's Point is actually a pretty nice little town. And whoever cut me left my purse behind." She carried her glass to the table and sat down. His concern warmed her, but he'd missed what might be real danger.

"Why would anyone want to hurt you, sweetheart?" He followed her to the table.

His questions tied up her insides. "I don't know." She had no answers for anything. Not why she was attacked. Not why Jason thought Pop's death wasn't an accident. Not even for her strange aversion to Blayne's nearness. She let her forehead drop into her palm.

"I think you're wrong about all of this, Alynne. You, as a researcher, know better than to make assumptions without proof."

"My arm gives plenty of proof." How dare he chastise her? Especially without any firsthand experience at all.

"I still say that was a random attack. Even your mother believes that your father died in a car accident. Aren't you being a little dramatic?"

She wasn't going back over everything. Blayne didn't want to see the truth. Maybe he couldn't deal with the danger. Or his conception of drama. "Never mind." She stood. "If you need to work on something, be my guest. But my mom needs my help to prepare for the family's arrival."

Without awaiting his response, she made her way to the stairs. He needed to work, and she needed to be away from him. Strange, since she'd been wanting to speak to him so badly. But his reaction to Pop's death and her possible danger, not to mention his silence for almost two days, added another layer of tension. Maybe she'd been all wrong about Blayne?

But that only made her original problem that much worse.

Chapter Eight

Jason pulled the sun visor down to deflect some of the glare of the sunset. Between the attack on Alynne and her newly declared fiancé, Jason's sleep had been almost non-existent last night, and the little shut-eye he'd gotten had been full of hideous images. Some of Alynne in tragedy and some of her in the arms of another man.

Why should those even cross into his mind? But they had and rattled him worse than the ridiculous calls he'd had to respond to all day. Even worse than the potholes on the road he took to the Victorian.

Thankfully, after the attack on Alynne last night, the chief had made the inn a focus location for the hourly patrols. Jason turned into the inn's lot where at least a half-dozen cars were parked. He'd hoped to come by in time to help Myra with set up for visitors and her family, but the calls throughout the day kept him hopping.

He met Officer Vasquez on the porch as the middle-age man exited with a plateful of lasagna and salad.

"Just checked in with Myra. Kept it subtle, like the chief said." The man smiled. "I think I'm going to like this new tour." He lifted the plate a bit then straightened and eyed Jason up and down. "You look like a geek during a Star Trek marathon." The man shook his head and whistled. "I'd love to meet her."

Jason released a heavy exhale. "Who's that?"

"Whoever kept you up all night." He chuckled at his innuendo and trotted down the steps.

Great. Now the gossips in town would think he was having some crazy liaison. But then, that wouldn't be new. Some of the grapes on the vine had already married him off to at least three different girls in the past few years.

But he'd not been the least bit interested in any of them. So, what was he doing thinking about this woman—this engaged woman—that he'd only just met?

Ignoring the unanswerable question, he opened the front door and slipped his hat off his head. He hung it on the mounted rack by the kitchen entrance and entered the room. "Myra?"

"Oh, dear boy." Myra set down the large bowl of buttered breadsticks and wiped her hands on her apron. "Aren't you supposed to be off-duty by now?"

"Just. Thought I might check on the wiring in your barn." Ellis had mentioned a possible short just a few days before his death. Jason wanted to stick around—keep an eye on … things. He could do that and help Myra keep things repaired at the same time.

"That's so good of you. I'll fix you a dinner plate."

"Thanks, but no hurry." He smiled and went out the screen door. The garlic and tomato aroma filled the kitchen. The absence of anyone else in the kitchen must mean they were all upstairs at dinner. He should have delayed his arrival by another hour or so. Too late now.

He made his way to the barn, which was quickly filling with shadows. He edged around the large tractor that filled much of the bottom floor and moved to the back edge of the room. Ellis had a bank of battery-powered lights somewhere. He pulled his flashlight from his belt and scanned what must've been a tack room decades ago. The caged light bulbs hung on hooks along one wall. Jason checked a couple of them before finding two that worked. He turned on one of them and trotted up the stairs to the little closet on the side of the old hayloft.

Ellis's ancestors must've had trust issues about electricity. He couldn't think of any other reason why they would put an electrical closet for the entire property in the barn. Let alone way up there.

He was careful to sidestep around the rotted boards that Ellis had warned him about on more than one occasion. He should plan to re-floor the loft before the summer heat set in. Next month would be soon enough, though. He reached the shelves along the opposite wall and found the key to the electrical closet where Ellis had told him it would be, under an ancient metal bucket. After hanging the lights on his belt loops, he carried Ellis's well-filled toolbox back to the doorway and set it down. He unlocked the warped door and tugged it open. Dust and emptiness assaulted his nostrils, but he shoved the toolbox in front of the door and hung the lights on the edge of the rafter.

This might take a while.

He'd disassembled the panel of wires when his stomach

started growling. Part of him wanted to take a break, but the task wasn't going to take as long as he'd feared. These wires didn't look nearly as poorly maintained as he'd imagined, but then, Ellis had been in charge of the place. He was as detail-oriented as they came.

Alynne seemed to take after her father in that attitude.

Wait. He didn't need to be thinking about her. He refocused on his task. He was just here to keep an eye on someone who seemed to need help. That was it. Alynne was in danger. He felt it in his gut, though it made no sense at all.

Telling himself that and being right about it were two different things. This lady stirred up feelings in him that he hadn't felt since his wife … This was crazy. He hardly knew Alynne, and he didn't believe in silly things like love at first sight. Besides, she was engaged. Off-limits. What was happening to him? *Lord, I'm not about to just abandon all that I believe and all that I've learned from You over a pretty face.*

Though Ellis Stone's daughter had already proven to be much more than just a pretty face. Compassionate, clever, strong. And he'd felt she had a knowledge of faith in the Lord even though she hadn't exactly spoken of her beliefs.

None of this mattered. She was unavailable. And he wouldn't disappoint God by pursuing her. He found a loosely attached wire. This had to be the source of the short that Ellis had told him about.

"Sweetheart, we can be back here in a day. Especially after your family arrives, your mother won't even notice that you've gone." The low tenor whined through the floorboards.

The sound startled him. He'd heard nothing from the house, not even a door close. Was that Blayne? He was suggesting that

Alynne leave? Now? Why in the world would he suggest something like that at a time like this?

"Think of how pleased she'll be when we return as husband and wife. And then you and I can share a bedroom without you worrying about what your mother will think."

Jason's stomach turned. The topic wasn't so strange for this generation, but he'd hoped that Alynne was more on the unique side. Maybe her sharing his beliefs was just vain hope with no foundation.

"Stop it. Don't speak of that night. Never." Was that regret in her tone or his imagination?

His conscience seared him from listening, but he had no real choice. Going downstairs and making his presence known would only humiliate Alynne.

"And how can you even think about eloping now? My father just died. I don't want that to be part of the memories of my wedding."

Eloping? His stomach turned sour.

"Alynne, darling. I know you're hurting. But I also recognize the guilt you feel over the night we spent together."

"Don't. The Father has forgiven me for that."

Jason shut his eyes. He didn't want to hear this.

"Still, the guilt. Darling, you won't be able to let go of it until we're married."

Any respect he'd had for this man disappeared along with a little of his admiration for Alynne. After all, she'd accepted the man's proposal, apparently had some type of liaison with him, and had planned to elope with him.

"That's my problem. And it's not going to be solved by some rash action."

"Darling, don't talk like that—"

"Especially not when other things, like my grieving mom, should be taking my attention."

Jason whispered an *amen* at her declaration.

"Of course. You're right." Blayne's voice took a contrite tone. "I simply want to be part of your family as you and your mom go through this. I want her to be my mom, too. You know I lost both of my parents a long time ago."

"I'm sorry. I imagine this brings up bad memories."

Clearly, Blayne was using any tool available to convince Alynne to go with him. Couldn't she see his manipulation?

"I'll get a twenty-four-hour round-trip flight. We can be back tomorrow night. Tuesday at the latest."

"No, Blayne. I'll not even consider it. Let go. You're hurting me."

Jason stiffened. He didn't want to intrude, but he would in a moment if Blayne mistreated Alynne.

"I'm sorry, darling. I'm disappointed. But I want your promise that we'll go through with our plans as soon as the funeral's over. We'll both stay and help your mother through this. Once the funeral is done, we can leave. It's only one day."

"I'll think about it."

"Promise me."

The sick feeling deepened. This guy was pure oil—the over-fried, high-fat kind. Alynne wasn't the girl he'd thought she was if she was actually buying this man's stories.

"I'm not promising anything. Not right now. I don't trust myself to make wise decisions with all that's going on. Frankly, I'm regretting that we'd even considered eloping."

"You're right. Your emotions have you all confused."

Which is why this guy should never have started this conversation.

"We'll get past the funeral, and I know you'll feel better. You'll be ready to take this step with me. I love you, Alynne."

Jason cringed again, thankful that he hadn't gotten any of that lasagna after all. He stayed silent and screwed the panel back over the wires. He'd give the couple a few minutes and then try to make his exit.

Alynne abandoned Blayne on the porch and darted up the stairs to the dining room to lend her hand at cleaning up the remains of the warming dishes. She'd be happier when she could lend both of them, but at least the ache in her arm had subsided somewhat.

The conversation with Blayne unnerved her. Had she been so completely wrong about him? He loved her—that was obvious. He wouldn't insist on marrying her if he didn't. Right? But that very insistence was strange. Why now? The night … ugh. Her memory was terribly blurry about that, but how could she have been so stupid. How could she have abandoned all that she'd believed in?

Still, that had been a month ago. No, almost two months at this point. Why the sudden push, now? She carried the leftovers of the lasagna back down to the bustling kitchen.

"Sweet girl, that's what the dumbwaiter is for." Momma took the casserole from her and pulled out a clean plate. "Those stairs are terribly steep. I'd hate to see you fall."

"I'll remember next time." She turned to go back upstairs.

"Wait, dear." Her mom put a large serving of the lasagna on the plate and added a couple of breadsticks to it. She set it on a tray that already held a water bottle and a bowl of salad. "Would you take this out to the barn? Jason is working out there."

Her neck iced. "Jason?" No. No way. "At the barn?"

"Well, he might be down at the boathouse by now. He's working on something with the electricity."

"Myra, there's a policeman in the parking lot." Aunt Bobbie toddled in from the foyer. "Are you having trouble out here?"

Momma pushed the tray toward her. "Hurry and catch him, Alynne. I promised him dinner, and it completely slipped my mind."

She collected the tray and trotted to the door, though her heart wasn't in it. He couldn't have been in the barn. She would have seen him. Still, she half-hoped he'd be gone before she made it to the porch.

But he wasn't. He climbed into his Jeep then looked up and caught her eye.

"Momma promised you dinner. She's very sorry for the delay." Alynne navigated the steps and avoided Rose's wagging tail to bring it to the driver's side.

Jason got out. "Please tell your mom, thanks, but I'm really not hungry."

"Maybe you could eat a little? Momma feels bad for it being so late."

He shut his eyes a moment gave a slight sigh. Was there meaning behind that or just weariness?

Alynne scratched the furry head that nudged her hand. "Did the electricity give you trouble?"

"No, it was okay." He took the tray from her and circled the car to set it on the hood.

He didn't seem to be interested in talking about it. Was something else bothering him?

"It's a shame you didn't get the chance to meet the rest of the family. Momma's sisters are as kind and friendly as she is, and my cousin Shane is an absolute riot. Aunt Billie's three kids and their families will be here tomorrow. I'm glad you were able to cancel all of the reservations because it looks like every room will be full for the duration."

"Happy to help." At least he gave a pleasant answer, though he still hadn't looked at her.

"Aunt Billie made a marble cake. Would you like a piece?"

He swallowed and shook his head. "No, thanks." He took a swig from the bottle.

"So, what do you do when you aren't … patrolling or whatever a cop does in a place like this."

Putting the lid back on the bottle, Jason lifted the tray and handed it back to her. "I'm sorry, but I need to get back." He wiped his mouth with the cloth napkin and laid it on the tray. "Tell Myra thanks."

Was that it? She stepped back as he got back into his car,

started the engine, and backed away. Taking the tray back to the kitchen, she handed the tray off to her Aunt Bobbie. She, Momma, and Aunt Billie looked to have the clean up on the run.

Rose whimpered and scratched at the screen door. She must've had another bath because she smelled like her name. Alynne let her in and picked up a water bowl from the back porch. She didn't feel much like being alone tonight, though the thought of talking to Blayne again made her a little queasy. She grabbed a few dog snacks from the cookie jar on the counter and stuffed them into her pocket. "Come on, Rose. You can stay with me tonight."

Rose had taken the invitation in stride and made herself at home on half of Alynne's queen-sized bed. She'd also apparently viewed Alynne's new wedges as chew toys.

"You have got to be kidding me. Bad dog." She opened her door, and the dog sprinted out with her tail between her legs. Alynne growled and looked at the damage. The entire back of one of the shoes had been eaten away and part of the other one had been gnawed.

Alynne shut her eyes as the memory returned. The first time she'd worn them, one of her ankles had been so blistered from the new shoes, she'd bled all over the back of it. No wonder the dog had chewed it up. It assuaged her anger but not the chagrin from losing some adorable footwear.

It added to her unsettled nerves about last night. Jason's detachment had stayed with her all night, troubling her sleep with worries over why his attitude toward her had changed. Was it only because of Blayne, or was it … something else?

As she showered and dressed, every conversation she'd had with Jason filtered back through her mind. Had she insulted him? Offended him? Irritated him? But nothing in his responses showed anything like that.

Until last night.

She tied on her running shoes and headed out of the south doors. Seeing or even smelling whatever her mom and her aunts were creating in the kitchen would ruin her resolve. Whatever it was, after the last two days of meals, she had to abstain. The granola she'd snacked on as she drove up here would serve her well. Maybe a walk after breakfast would improve her mood.

Jason pulled his Jeep into the lot as she opened her car door. He shut off the engine and stepped out. "I know this is a small town, but you've seen it isn't always safe."

"I thought everyone left doors unlocked here." Even if he was sort of fussing at her, at least he was speaking to her. Maybe she'd just imagined his standoffish attitude last night.

"Not people who've been attacked. We still don't have any leads on that."

She didn't need that visual in her mind. Maybe his silence from last night would've been better after all. She pressed her lips together in a flat line and clicked the door lock. She shut the door and glanced back at him. "Happy?"

His expression didn't change. "Delighted." Without another word, he stepped toward the front porch.

Oh, this morning was getting better by the second. Alynne

followed him. He paused at the front door and stepped aside to allow her to enter first.

"There you are, darling." Blayne came down the stairs as Jason entered behind her. "I wondered where you went."

Huh? "I was getting my granola from the car."

"Good morning." He eyed Jason. "Officer Dancer, right?"

Jason lifted his chin slightly. "Close enough." He stepped ahead of Alynne and entered the kitchen to hails of greetings from the rest of her family.

Alynne slipped in behind him and poured a little granola into an empty bowl, leaving the box on the counter.

"How did you sleep?" Aunt Billie addressed all of them.

"Well." Blayne put his arm around Alynne's shoulders. "We had a great night."

Aunt Billie's eyes widened, and Aunt Bobbie's jaw dropped. Alynne's whole face heated.

Momma stepped toward her and took her hand. "We have omelets and scones this morning. Interested?"

"Um, no … I think I'll just have cereal." She took a few steps to the screen door with the bowl in hand. "Thanks, though." She needed air. Now.

She practically fled to the lakeside trail that Jason had shown her when she first arrived. There, with shelter from prying eyes, she sat down on a log and let the tears come. Surely, Blayne hadn't meant to mislead people with his declaration. But the looks on her aunts' faces … and what must Jason think after he heard that?

Thoughts of Jason sent her into tears again. His opinion shouldn't matter, but it did. If only she could do something to undo the shame brought on by Blayne's words. But there wasn't anything to do.

She stared at the granola but no longer felt like eating. She left the bowl on the log where she'd been sitting and wandered closer to the water. Pop had fished in this spot. It could have been with her had she not been so full of herself. She picked up a stone and threw it into the lake. "I finally came, Pop."

If only it had been sooner.

"Oh, God, why did I wait so long?" She hadn't spent much time with the Lord lately either. "I've been so wrong ... about so many things." At the moment, she couldn't think of anything she'd actually been right about. Not about staying away from the inn. Not about the night with Blayne. She was probably wrong about accepting Blayne's proposal, too. Maybe she should take some time and pray about this relationship before she went through with anything.

She sat for several minutes just soaking in the peace and praying, but she had to face her family ... and Jason. Putting it off would only make this more difficult.

Turning back toward the house, she wove her way through the forest path. Birds overhead sang and something in the brush moved. She hesitated a bit. Snakes would be coming out of hibernation soon enough. She reached down to retrieve her bowl and found it virtually empty. Looked like Rose had visited her again for a different treat. Then her eye caught a fluff ball that moved in the breeze.

She gasped and squealed. A squirrel lay at the bottom of the tree next to the path. Another one was half-hidden by the undergrowth. Both appeared quite dead.

And a nugget of granola lay between them.

Chapter Nine

Jason resisted breakfast and made his way to the barn. After overhearing the conversation last night, he'd lost all desire to double-check his repairs to the electricity. Hadn't wanted to advertise to Blayne and Alynne that he'd been there, witnessing their conversation. He took the stairs two at a time. The door to the closet still stood open as he'd left it the night before. He went inside and flicked on the breaker.

Nothing sparked. That was a good sign. He jogged back downstairs and tried the switch next to the entrance. The bare bulbs blared immediately. Three of them hung from the ceiling. He went back up the steps and returned the lock, the key, and the tool kit to their places. Back downstairs, he flicked the switch off and pulled the barn door closed to give a little protection from the elements. Heading down to the boathouse, he decided to make sure those lights now worked again before going to the station.

He'd still need to repair the upstairs flooring at some point, but not today. Not until Alynne Stone went back to Dallas if he could help it. Being in her proximity wasn't good for his resolve.

As he neared the lake, he heard something like a muffled scream. Alynne? He shouldn't have let her go walking alone, but it wasn't like he could say anything with her fiancé right there.

He broke into a run, but she shot like a bolt from the trees, almost mowing him down. "Wait." He tried to grab her but missed. She didn't even look back as she sprinted at a dead run.

He followed her to the house and into the kitchen. Gasping for air, she screamed, "Wally!" and jerked the box of cereal out of the boy's hands. "No." She clung to the box and breathed hard.

"I didn't know it was your property." He scowled at her.

"Never mind, Wally." Myra poured a bowl of bite-sized cereal and emptied a glass of milk over it. "Here you go. And I'm happy to make you pancakes if you decide you want them."

Blayne had come downstairs at the shouts. He came closer. "What are you doing?" His voice lowered to a whisper. "It's not like you can't share some of your granola."

She was shaking. Jason wanted to hold her hands and calm her. Stupid sensation. She glanced up at him.

"Alynne." Blayne put his hand on her injured shoulder.

She winced and pulled away.

Idiot. "Careful."

Alynne locked eyes with Jason. "Would you come with me for a moment?"

"Now wait just a minute." Blayne laid a hand on her other arm. "If you need something, darling, I'm quite capable of helping you."

Jason ignored him and nodded at Alynne.

"I'll be back in a moment." She stood and patted Blayne's arm but kept her grip on the box of cereal, and Jason led her to the kitchen door.

"I'll go with you." Blayne raised his volume.

She whirled on him. "No. Stay here. I'll be back."

Whatever was going on, she didn't want Blayne or anyone else involved.

Jason followed her onto the porch and down the steps. "What's happened? What scared you in the woods?"

"I'll show you. I left my bowl of granola on a tree stump while I walked for a bit." She trotted down the hill to the lakeside path and paused just inside the treeline. "When I got back, I found this." She pointed to the empty bowl and then to the ground beside the stump. "And them."

Jason scanned the scene and pulled a pair of gloves from his back pocket. "I need you to move over there." He pointed to a grassy area the way they had come, about twenty yards away from him.

"And I need this." He took the box from her hand using one of the gloves. Setting it on the ground, he withdrew his phone and called the chief.

"We're going to need the coroner out here at the inn."

"Someone's dead?" The chief covered the phone a moment and barked orders at someone else.

"Well, some-*one* isn't exactly right."

"Spill it. What are we looking at?"

"Possibly a double-homicide. Or maybe squirrel-icide would be a more accurate term." Despite the joke, Jason didn't feel like laughing.

"What's happened out there?"

"Seriously, Chief, I think we might be dealing with attempted murder. Poison." If Jason was right, Alynne's trouble hadn't moved on.

An hour later, the chief had set all the teams in motion. The path had been taped off, photos had been taken of the corpses, and the bodies had been taken to the morgue. Seriously. If Alynne wasn't at such risk, the whole thing would've been comical.

Jason left the team to work and went up to the house to check on Alynne. He found her in the parlor.

Blayne cuddled next to her with one arm around her and the other holding her hand. "Darling, you've had a terrible fright. This is the perfect time for you to get away and heal."

"There's still too much to do here." Her commitment to her mom remained, but her voice had weakened.

The last thing Jason wanted was to eavesdrop on another of their conversations. "I'll need to ask you a few questions."

"Go ahead, Officer. We'll be happy to answer anything we can." Blayne didn't move.

"Actually, I need to speak with Miss Stone alone." The *Miss* came out with his professional tone.

"Surely, you can see that she's terribly fragile." Blayne squeezed her tighter to himself.

She cringed slightly but didn't speak.

Blayne didn't seem to notice. "I'm not willing to allow you to speak to her alone."

Oh, right. "That's not the way it works."

"I don't mind speaking to Lieutenant Danvers." She moved to rise, but he held onto her.

"I insist." He pulled her back to her seat.

This time she squirmed. "Ouch. You're hurting me."

Without an apology, he released her, and she moved away from him.

He stood and followed her. "Alynne, I don't approve of this. You should have some protection to be sure this man doesn't take advantage of your vulnerability right now."

She faced him. "Blayne. Stop. I'm not fragile." She pushed past him and through the arch into the entry hall.

The man attempted to follow, but Jason put his hand out to stop him. "Mr. Campbell, you need to remain here."

"I'm staying with my fiancée."

"If you can't follow instructions and stay here, I'll have an officer help you."

"You can't do that—"

"And if you persist, I'll have you arrested for impeding an investigation. Is that very clear?" Jason gave him an unwavering gaze.

Blayne glared back but didn't answer.

It didn't matter. Jason had gotten his point across. He walked with Alynne to the front porch and seated her on the wicker love seat in front of the office window. "I'm sorry. I know you're upset, but I need to hear everything that you saw. Everything you heard or smelled or even thought."

She shut her eyes and a tear escaped from one of them, tracking down her cheek. "I think someone's trying to kill me."

Jason sat down across from her. "Tell me what happened."

"My car was unlocked. Remember? My granola was in the front seat. I snacked on it as I drove out here. Then squirrels ate it this morning and died. Like dead and gone. Just a few minutes. I only left it on the tree stump for a few minutes."

Her hands shook as she tried to brush her hair from her face. Jason pushed the errant strand away and tucked it behind her ear. Then he took her hands in his. "Alynne, I'm not going to let anything happen to you. But you have to stay inside the inn for a while and let us figure out what's going on."

She nodded, though, with her gaze on the floor, he couldn't tell if she fully understood.

"And you have to pay attention. I need to know about anything that seems out of the ordinary."

"I'll try." She looked at him then, her blue eyes puffy with tears but full of trust and hope.

He wouldn't ... he couldn't let her down.

The feeling of Jason's strong hands wrapped around hers warmed her. The compassion and comfort in his eyes added to the heat that suddenly swirled up her neck.

"Lieutenant, the chief is looking for you." An officer had come around the corner of the house.

At the man's call, Jason dropped her hands and stood. "Be right there." He turned back to her. "Remember what I said. Stay inside and stay with people."

Then he was gone.

Alynne breathed in and tried to slow her heartbeat with a long exhale. She went back into the house. Most of the family had dispersed. The boys and their dad had gone hunting on the other side of the lake. Only the promise of a hunting trip had pried the kids from the police activity. Thankfully, the girls hadn't heard about the squirrels. Momma and the aunts swept them into town before the police even got there.

She climbed up to the dining hall and glanced out the windows that overlooked the forest. Jason pointed down the trail as he spoke to a tall man with a grayish beard. She felt his hands holding hers again and relished the sensation of having a protector.

Shame on her for even letting the thoughts pass through her mind. She laid a hand on the window and watched the man in the tan cowboy hat. How dare she even be up here, spying on him. She was engaged, wasn't she? But Blayne had never acted as a protector in any manner. And he kept bringing up her deepest regret.

Turning her back to the windows, she cleaned the spills on the cold bar. Momma had insisted on stocking it amply for lunch. She traced her finger along the icy metal.

Did she want to marry Blayne? She cared about him. They had dated since last summer. She'd even gone on a cruise with him at Christmas, with separate quarters, of course. But this whole engagement had surprised her.

It was the answer to her problem, to the guilt she'd felt. She needed to marry him, and that was the real problem. Should marriage be a need?

Lord, help me see things rightly.

She glanced back down at the group near the forest. Jason had disappeared. Probably gone further down the path. Reality rushed back at her. Someone had tried to kill her this morning. Her granola had been fine on Friday, but it was clearly not fine today.

Thank You, Lord, that Rose wasn't with me on my walk this morning.

She turned away from the windows again and headed downstairs. A tone sounded as the front door opened. Aunt Billie was expecting her family later tonight. Who could this be?

"Hmm, interesting design." A balding man in a business suit seemed to be evaluating the room.

A blonde woman accompanied him through the entrance wearing a Rebekah Taylor design that Alynne had coveted in one of the store windows near her office. "Last century. Ugh, country blue and burgundy? What were they thinking?"

The man caught sight of Alynne. "We'd like one of the finest rooms, please."

Jason must've missed one of the reservations. Alynne looked down at least two inches on the man. "I'm sorry, but we've had to close this week. There's been a death in the family."

"I certainly know all about that. Ronald Surzchenkov and my wife, Sheila. I'm a member of the family. Ellis was my..." He glanced up at Alynne. "It occurs to me that you might be part of our family as well?" He held out his hand.

"Alynne Stone." She shook hands with him. "I'm … I was … his daughter."

"I'm terribly sorry for your loss, my dear. But what is all the activity outside?"

How did she answer that question? "There was an accidental death near the lake. The police shouldn't be much longer."

"Oh, that's terrible." Ronald looked at his wife.

She nodded. Her eyes opened wider, but no other expression showed on her perfectly featured face.

Botox?

"But we're very glad you're here." Alynne did a quick mental calculation. There was one other empty room on the second floor. Phyllis sure wouldn't be using it. "Let me just get you to sign in here." She opened her mom's guest book on the antique credenza and handed him the pen.

"I'll get your key. Room twenty-four is at the top of the stairs and to the left, just across the hall from the men's and ladies' restrooms."

"No bathrooms in our rooms? Are you kidding?" The woman tossed her blond hair over her shoulder. "That's ridiculous."

Alynne shoved down the retort she wanted to give and held out the key to the room. "We have every room spoken for."

"*Spoken for* doesn't mean taken." The woman smirked. "First come, first served. I know you have to have a suite available."

"We have three other families arriving tonight." All had kids, and they couldn't fit well in a room with only a king bed. "But twenty-four is very comfortable."

Ronald held up his hand. "Look, my dear, Sheila is correct. We can't possibly stay in a room where we'll have to use community showers. It's vulgar. I'm afraid I must insist upon a suite. Or must I speak with your mother?"

Oh, it was on.

Alynne put a sweet smile on her face and withdrew the key. "I'm afraid Momma is out right now, but I completely understand Sheila's issue. I'm sure there is a larger room." She went back to the drawer in the credenza that held the keys and returned the one in her hand to its place.

"That's more like it." Ronald chuckled.

Alynne faced him. "The nearest hotel is in McKinney. This side of the metroplex. I'm sure you'll find a number of options there and still be within reasonable driving distance for the viewing and the funeral. If you'll let us know where you've decided to stay and leave an e-mail address or a phone number, I'll be sure to send the information for both." She crossed her arms and leveled a glare at him, allowing her smile to drop off her face.

His eyes became slits. "We're not used to being treated like this."

Alynne wasn't about to back down. "This isn't a business right now. It's a home that my mom has graciously opened to those traveling here for my Pop's funeral. You can be gracious and kind in accepting the gift or you can stay elsewhere."

"Just because you're Ellis's only child doesn't mean you can treat us this way."

Alynne didn't back down. "Actually, I'm one of two."

Ronald flinched. "I didn't hear that. Are you sure?"

Was he kidding? "Do you want the room or not?" She'd be half-willing to pay for his room somewhere else.

Sheila put her hands on her hips. "You have no idea to who you are speaking … to."

Ronald laid a hand on her arm. "Of course, we'd prefer to stay here. Please forgive our misunderstanding. You can imagine the strain we're under right now. I'm sure, you've been feeling it, too."

"Yes, I can understand." Alynne retrieved the key and handed it to him. "As I mentioned, it's the room just past that wall." She pointed up the stairs and to the left balcony. "There are towels in your room along with an extra blanket, and the bathrooms are across the hall. There's a light lunch buffet already set up in the dining hall." She pointed the other direction. "That's at the end of the hall that way. And dinner is at seven in the same place."

"Fine." Sheila spun and clicked her pointed sandals across the tile to the stairs. "Have someone bring up our luggage from the car."

Alynne should've kept her mouth shut but couldn't resist. "*Someone* isn't here." She didn't give them a chance to respond and exited out the front door.

Jason watched as the county cruiser pulled to a stop. Good thing he'd had some warning so he could receive the sheriff and Deputy Cain before they made any trouble for the other investigators.

"Sheriff, Deputy. What brings you over here, this morning?"

"Don't toy with me, Danvers. We know there's been a murder," Cain growled.

The sheriff ignored him.

Murder? Oh, this was priceless. "Yes, sir. We've been

working on the crime scene for the past hour."

Only then did Sheriff Kindrich speak. "I want you to clear your men out of here right now. This entire lake is county property and has nothing to do with Heath's Point."

The man had no clue what was going on, but Jason couldn't let him make such an erroneous claim. "I'm sorry, Sheriff, but the city limits go all the way up to the scout camp on the other side of the cove. But then, surely, you know that."

"I'm not going to stand here and argue with an underling."

Cain moved a few feet down the hill. "Y'all are all no longer needed. Pack up and send your reports to Sheriff Kindrich."

That got Jason's ire up. "You have no jurisdiction here, Cain."

Kindrich moved closer and pointed a finger in his face. "We're taking possession of this crime scene, Officer."

Jason didn't move an inch. "Lieutenant."

"Is there a problem here?" Chief Tate stepped around the white fence and crossed the gravel to their car with Rosie trailing a step behind him. "Good to see you, Beau." He shook hands with the sheriff and ignored Cain. "What's this all about, Jason?"

"The sheriff has declared this area county jurisdiction and demands we turn over the crime scene."

"Oh, you do?"

"Now, Dell." Sheriff Kindrich applied his play-nice voice. "We both know that you don't have the resources you need for a murder investigation."

"I don't know." The chief rubbed his chin. "We did all right last January."

"Don't let your pride get in the way. You need us." Kindrich straightened.

"Well, I can't say that I agree with that either, and this area is definitely within the city limits. Not county jurisdiction at all."

"But—" The sheriff attempted another argument, but the chief cut him off with a raised hand.

"Now, just hold on. You don't have jurisdiction, and you know it, but that doesn't mean we can't turn over the crime scene."

Jason turned toward him. "Really?"

"I don't see why not."

"That's more like it." The sheriff smiled and moved toward the side of the building. "Cain, you get down there and take possession of the body."

Chief Tate walked alongside him. "Actually, they've already been taken to our lab."

"They've? There's more than one?" Cain stopped in mid-stride and came back toward them.

Jason answered, "There are two to be exact."

"What are they doing in a lab? They should be in the morgue." Sheriff Kindrich quickened his pace.

"Actually, there are three." The chief stopped at the top of the hill. "The squirrels are at the lab, but the mouse is still down there if you want to investigate it."

Kindrich froze and slowly turned back.

Jason stifled the laughter that pressed to be released.

"Did you say squirrels?" The sheriff climbed back to the top of the hill and stood toe-to-toe with the chief. "And mice?"

"Just one mouse. We found him a few minutes ago." The chief maintained his position.

"Then why is this going over the county radio as a murder?" The sheriff's face turned a lovely shade of red.

Jason swallowed hard. "I can't imagine. Maybe your grapevine has soured a bit?"

Kindrich turned a withering glare in his direction. Then he glanced at Cain and tilted his head toward the cruiser before returning to it. Cain opened the driver's side door but stopped and pointed at Jason. "This isn't over, Officer."

Really? How Hollywood could he get?

"You need to be more careful, Jason." Dell moved next to him and waved at the pair backing from their parking space. "Sheriff Kindrich is a powerful man."

Jason always thought of him as a lucky idiot. "I imagine the people of this county are smart enough to recognize real police work at some point."

"Well, they haven't yet. And until they do, you need to play nice."

He was right. They could certainly make his job harder if they wanted."

"And we're lucky he didn't press about this situation."

"It doesn't have anything to do with him or his department." How could Dell think it did?

"Ellis died only a few days ago. A day later, his heir is attacked and now her food is poisoned." Dell stuffed his hands into his jean pockets. "I'd say he could lay claim on both of the other issues just from simple proximity."

He turned to look at Jason. "But if he doesn't, you're in charge of seeing that Ellis's daughter has round-the-clock protection until we can figure this all out."

Something he'd already intended.

BREAKING POINT

Chapter Ten

Ugh, those people! It was bad enough that Pop was gone, and she was helping her mom through it. Even harder to be organizing the chaos of a houseful of family that she hadn't laid eyes on in years, but that didn't apply to Ronald Surzchenkov and his little darling, Sheila. Entitled, never-was wannabees.

Alynne stomped off the porch then caught a glimpse of Jason on the side lawn with some other men. She darted to the pool deck and peeked out through the ornate cut-outs in the tall wall that enclosed the limestone surrounding the pool and hot tub.

Jason stood near the old iron bell. Two of the men with him wore tan uniforms. The final was a big man in everyday clothes and a tall, white Stetson. Obviously, they were talking about her and the dead animals.

Rose wagged her tail as the tall man scratched her, then she darted back down the hill to yap at the others and accept more pats. Alynne lifted up another prayer of thanks that the dead creature wasn't Rose. *And thank You that Wally didn't eat any.*

But whatever had killed those squirrels hadn't been meant for Wally. It had been meant for her. And here she was breaking her promise to Jason to stay inside the inn. He'd made it clear that she needed to be around other people, but hanging out with the recent arrivals made her feel a little sick.

"I was wondering where you got off to."

Alynne straightened and whirled around at Blayne's sudden words. He crossed from the far end of the south wing. "I … we have some new guests."

"The place is getting crowded." He eased his arm around her and pulled her close. "But we're alone right now."

She smiled and let him kiss her temple. "There are still some family members who should arrive today, but they all have rooms assigned to them."

He kissed her ear and whispered, "I don't really care." He kissed her neck, directing her hair to fall across her other shoulder.

She tugged his arm from her waist and stepped away. "There are police everywhere. Someone could come in here at any moment."

He pulled her in again. "I don't care about that either." His lips pressed against hers, firm and warm.

His kisses had always ignited her passion and stirred up thoughts of forever. But that was before that night. After that, kissing him was more of a hope. He had to marry her and restore her … What? She could never be a virgin again. But no matter the time and place, or how she was hurting, she felt she had to accept his kisses. Until she sealed this deal, she wasn't fully … well, okay … un-dirty.

His kiss deepened and his arms around her waist tightened, pinning her against him. She pushed against his biceps and tried in vain to back away from him. She turned her head a little. "Please, Blayne."

"Darling, I love you." He kept her close and spoke into her ear.

"I love you, too." It was a habit to repeat it, and she whispered with less conviction than she'd ever felt before. "But this isn't the time." Or place. Or situation. She'd almost died for pity sake.

"This isn't a safe place for you." His breath tickled her ear. "Let me take you away from here, protect you, and make you my wife."

She shut her eyes. He didn't understand how hard that would be for her mom. He was only trying to make things better and, like he said, protect her. But her mom needed Alynne's attention. And she needed her mom's approval of any marriage before she took that step. Regardless of what had gone on before, a surprise elopement was no longer an option. "I can't, Blayne."

"Of course, you can. You know you want to." He scratched her back and started kissing her neck again.

She pulled away. "No … no, I really don't."

Blayne released her at that point. "You don't? Are you … have you changed your mind?" Shock crossed his face for a moment and then changed to pain. His blue eyes opened wide with a sad droop at each corner, and even his dimples seemed to sag.

She shut her eyes for a moment. "No … I mean, well, it's only … I need to be with my mom. I want her approval. I don't want to elope, Blayne. It was a crazy, exciting thought, but then reality stepped in." She looked away.

He captured her hand and kissed her palm. "An elopement would make things so much easier on your mom. If we planned a wedding, she would insist on doing everything. I've only known her a couple of days, and I can see that."

He wasn't wrong. "I know, but something is telling me that it's the wrong choice." She couldn't explain it. She was still convinced that marrying him was the right thing for her to do, the only real choice that she had. But the thought of keeping another secret sickened her. How could she ever look her mom in the face again? "I can't explain it any better than that. We can make it a small ceremony, maybe in a few weeks, but I want to talk to my mom about it first, and I want her to be there."

His chin lowered. "That disappoints me a great deal."

Ugh, that word.

"I had hoped …" He tugged a folded sheet of paper from the back pocket of his jeans and handed it to her. "I really thought you might … now that your mother has plenty of family around her, you might agree to come with me tonight. I'd have you back by tomorrow evening."

She unfolded the paper and looked at yet another flight reservation. Blayne had already wasted so much money.

"We could leave in an hour. Your family would barely miss you. And when we came back, we'd be a family ourselves." His eyes took on a hopeful gleam.

Oh, he was such a sweet man. Alynne didn't deserve his kindness, not when her own guilt and insecurities continued to disappoint him. She set the paper down on the table beside her and took his hands into hers. "Blayne, you have been so patient with me. With all of this tragedy, having you here with me means so much, but I can't even consider leaving right now."

"Darling, I'm worried about you."

"I know. Me, too. But leaving isn't an option. I would feel like I was abandoning my mom, no matter how many other people are here with her."

He bowed his head and kissed her hands again. "I understand. I won't mention it again, then." He squeezed her hands and then released them. Then he kissed her forehead and left around the south end of the wing the way he'd come onto the deck.

Alynne watched him walk away. He didn't look back, and the tilt of his head threatened to break her heart. Was she right to refuse him again? But how could she even consider his request at such a time?

Oh, God, please help me know what to do.

Jason slipped off his hat and wiped his forehead. Not so much because of sweat in the mild weather as due to the unwelcome officials that had just pulled away. The chief was amazing when it came to showing grace and having patience with the county boys.

A piece of paper flitted from the pool deck, drifting toward him. Why would there be trash coming from the enclosure? Surely no one had used the pool anytime recently.

He strolled over and stepped on the slip, bent down and picked it up. An airline ticket? He glanced through the opening to the pool deck. Alynne came into view as he entered.

Great. He'd asked her to stay inside for a good reason. "So, are you challenged by the difference between inside and outside, or are you just opposed to taking wise counsel?"

She jumped and spun around. Good. She should be startled.

"Oh, yes, I mean no. I left because of the new guests who arrived. I didn't want to say anything I would regret. I didn't think about what you'd asked me until I came in here."

"And you've been alone?" He could probably find a way to justify the question with all that had happened, but his curiosity was more personal than anything else. She was taken, engaged. The mantra kept playing over and over in his mind. He certainly needed the constant reminder.

"Yes, I'm alone. But Blayne only just left."

"I expected as much." He held out the airline ticket and pressed his lips together. He wasn't fooling himself. He'd admired Alynne Stone, but his growing affection was for the woman he'd thought she was.

She caught his gaze as she took the ticket. "I'm not planning on going."

"That's none of my business." His task completed, he started to turn away.

Laying a hand on his arm, she stepped closer. "But I'm not. I wouldn't leave Momma at a time like this."

"I'm glad to hear it. But it looks like your boy … your fiancé doesn't have the same commitment to helping your mom through all of this."

"How do you know that?" Her voice pitch went up several

notes. "I mean, who told you he was my fiancé?"

"He did. That first night when you and your mom went into the house." He tucked a thumb into his front pocket. "Is it a secret?"

"Yes. I mean …" Her gaze moved across the ground in front of her. "I thought it was. It's supposed to be." She looked back up at Jason. "Momma doesn't need any other emotional milestone moments."

"I can see that. I won't mention anything to her." At least, Alynne had a good reason to keep the secret. "I wish the man could understand the weight this week holds on your mom."

"Blayne's worried about me. The pain of losing my father. And then there's the attack on me the other night. And now this."

Hmm. Blayne might not be so bad after all, but Jason was still skeptical. "He should be worried. Someone attacked you the other night and might've killed you. And this situation was certainly no accident." As much as he hated the thought of her being attached with the smooth-talking dude, going away made her safer. "Maybe you should reconsider your trip after all." He pointed at the ticket she held.

She gave the ticket a long look and sank into a deck chair. "You really think I'm in some kind of danger?"

He moved to a chair on the opposite side of the deck table and wrapped his hands around the wrought-iron back. "Enough to schedule security for this place until we can figure out what's going on."

Her gaze lifted to his and something akin to horror crossed her face. "None of this makes any sense. Why would someone want to hurt me? Especially someone here? No one even knows me here."

She had a point, but it didn't change the facts. "No one?"

She shook her head. "There's only the family here, and besides Momma, I haven't laid eyes on any of them for years or longer."

"Any trouble between you and your family members?" If she didn't know anyone in Heath's Point, her attacker had to be an outsider.

She shook her head slowly, thoughtfully. "No one who's actually here."

A horn sounded from the lot. Cruisers had begun leaving, so Jason hadn't paid much attention to the sounds of tires on the gravel. He moved toward the pool deck entrance.

Alynne followed as the horn honked again, longer this time. "Is that one of your men?"

"No one I know." He spotted a tall woman with reddish-brown hair and a painted-on tan standing next to the driver's side of a black BMW. She reached through the open window, where the driver still sat, and laid on the horn.

"May I help you?" Alynne shouted over the noise as she pushed past him. Then she halted. "Phyllis?"

What was her sister doing here?

Alynne shook off her annoyance and advanced on the BMW that had come to rest in the middle of the lot. She held out her good arm. "Phyllis, I'm so glad you were able to come." She took a quick glance over her shoulder, but Jason had made a quick exit. Probably best.

Her sister moved around to the passenger side and tossed a reddish ball of fur onto the seat before giving Alynne a firm hug. "Dora, precious, I'm so sorry for my insensitive remarks. Of course, we're here. We need to honor Father and stand by Mother at such a stressful time."

She sounded sincere, and her hug was warm, even if she did use Alynne's hated nickname. "Momma will be so happy to see you." She backed away a step. Her sister wore a crimson double-breasted jacket over a full skirt covered with a floral paisley that matched the jacket perfectly. Had to be something designer, though Alynne couldn't place it. "Can I help you with your luggage?" She caught the attention of the driver, a tall man with peppered-colored hair. The two made a perfect pair, both slender and elegant, similar strong jaws and light blue eyes. This must be the husband she'd never met.

"No, no. Carl can take care of them." She gestured to the man. "Oh, my goodness. How thoughtless of me. Dora, precious, meet your brother-in-law, the soon-to-be Washington state senator Carl Henderson."

He had circled around the car in perfect time during his introduction to take Alynne's hand in both of his at the moment his wife completed her presentation.

"Alynne." She shook his hand.

"So nice to meet you, Alynne. Phyllis has told me so much about you, I feel like we're old friends."

And just like that, he'd made her a fan. "I'm so sorry we have to meet for the first time under such circumstances."

"And that's entirely my fault." Phyllis put an arm around both of them. "When I left so many years ago, I was so mixed up. And then purely embarrassed to return."

Fourteen years was still a long time to stay away. But then, Alynne had no room to criticize. Momma and Pop had lived at the Sunrise Inn for over ten years and she'd only come here once, though they'd met in other places. "Well, you're here now."

"And this place is still charming. Remember the fun we used to have here?"

With over fifteen years between their ages, *they* hadn't really had any fun when they had visited Uncle Todd. Not together, anyway. Pop had been her ever-present playmate the two or three times they'd visited when Alynne had been a child. Phyllis had always had her nose in a book or complained because the TV didn't have all the channels she wanted.

But Alynne smiled and nodded. "Uncle Todd certainly made the place fun, and Pop kept it all up—even put in a pool and hot tub." He'd told her some other things he'd done, but she had glazed over during Pop's discussions about electricity and wall studs.

Rose's yapping started in the distance, but the dog rounded the side of the house at a full run.

Phyllis gasped. "Keep that creature away." She held out both hands in front of her.

"Rose, sit." Alynne gave her best authoritative voice.

Again, the dog stopped on a dime and looked up with a goofy smile on her face.

"Good dog."

"It's a beast." Phyllis reached into the car and withdrew the little fluffy ball.

"I know you all must be tired after your trip." Alynne led the way to the front door as it occurred to her that she'd not set aside a room for them. She paused with her hand on the knob.

"Actually, I'm famished. Do you think we can scrape up some lunch?" Phyllis hadn't seemed to notice her hesitation.

Food was something they had. And lots of it. "Yes, of course. Momma set up a spread on the cold bins in the upstairs dining room—sandwich fixings, chips, fruit, and there's some cold stew that you can microwave if you're interested."

"That sounds delicious. Is the dining room still on the second floor? I hate that Mother has to climb those stairs carrying food. That's dangerous."

Alynne walked them into the kitchen pointing out some of the renovations Pop had made, including the repairs to the dumbwaiter. She even dug out a bowl of Rose's kibble for her sister's Pomeranian.

"Oh, the trouble we could've gotten into had we known that was there." Phyllis laughed, but Alynne had the distinct impression that her childhood self probably wouldn't have enjoyed the *trouble* nearly as much as Phyllis.

She directed them up the stairs and then backed off, giving the excuse of collecting their keys and moving their luggage for them. She had to insist to get them to leave her to it, but she needed a few minutes to empty the room of her possessions.

Bolting to the suite, she thanked the Lord that she hadn't completely unpacked yet. She moved through the sitting room where she'd left nothing and into the bedroom. There she hoisted her suitcase onto the coverlet of her bed. She trotted to the bathroom and collected her assorted toiletries then shoved them into the pocket on top of the suitcase. She double-checked the drawers and found them empty, as she expected, then grabbed the towel she'd used off the rack. There were still three others. That would have to do.

She rolled her suitcase into the hallway. Where to stash it? There were suites on either side of the hall in this wing, but a stairwell at the end of it. That would have to do. In fact, there was a little storage space under the stairs. It held a couple of folded tables and some stacked chairs, but Alynne's luggage fit easily in the space.

After moving her sister's luggage into the suite, she glanced around once more. Things looked good. As nice as any five-star. She palmed the key and returned to the kitchen to find another ibuprofen for her arm.

Chapter Eleven

After spending most of the morning at the inn, Jason had taken a quick trip to the office to write up the report for the chief. But his thoughts kept straying to the dark-haired beauty with the crystal blue eyes that someone had tried to kill.

One of the other officers, Gene Billings, elbowed him as he refilled his thermos at the coffee machine. "That was some looker, that daughter of Ellis Stone." He chuckled. "Don't tell me you didn't notice."

"I shouldn't think you would have noticed." Jason screwed on the cap. "How long you been married?"

"Fourteen years next weekend. But this ring just cuts off my circulation. It doesn't make me blind." He picked up a mug and filled it with the dark liquid. "Besides, my Mavis has been stewing over which of her friends' daughters and nieces she should introduce to you. She's determined to get you happily married off."

Been there. Done that. Not gonna happen again. "I think Mavis would have more fun and a better chance of success going fishing with you next weekend."

"Nice try, Romeo, but I've got duty next Saturday."

Jason patted the side of his shoulder. "Not anymore. I'm free and happy to take your shift."

The man's joking demeanor fell off, and his chin dropped. "You serious about that?"

Popping an almost fresh donut hole into his mouth, he spoke around it. "Sure am. Go. Celebrate your anniversary." He waved off Billings' thanks and headed back to his desk. Maybe he'd bought himself a little more freedom before Mavis Billings sent the beautiful girl pageant to parade through town.

Not like there could be anyone prettier than Alynne Stone.

Ugh. Where had that thought come from? She had a boyfriend. No, a fiancé. She was almost as taken as she could get. Besides, he wasn't the least bit interested in women. Never again. He sat and slammed his thermos onto his desk a little too hard.

A half-dozen faces turned toward him at the loud noise.

"Sorry." He glanced around and gave a half-smile. His coworkers only stared for a nanosecond before returning to their work.

He pulled out a stack of files: a burglary, a hit and run, several instances of vandalism, which were typical nearing the end of every school year. Then his eyes fell on the file on the assault from Saturday night.

Regardless of her beauty, her fiancé, or Jason's determination to remain a bachelor, she needed protection. At least, until he could find out why someone had attacked her. Could that have been the same someone who had put the poison—okay, suspected poison—

into the squirrel-bait? They'd had a fine laugh about it at the sheriff's expense, but truth be told, Alynne could be in serious danger.

With his laptop and his thermos in hand, he climbed into his patrol cruiser and headed back to the inn. Mike Evans sat in his own cruiser on the outer edge of the parking lot.

Jason rolled down his window. "Everything okay?"

"Yep. Most everyone's gone. Got two new couples in and one o'them left, too. Prolly for dinner. I don't think Myra is back yet."

It had to be hard on Myra to leave Alynne here to deal with the morning's issue. The little kids would keep her distracted. Good thing her sisters had insisted. "Anyone out and about?" With so many people staying at the inn, better for them to be inside so that strangers could be easily identified.

"Only her." Mike pointed to the porch where Alynne stroked Rose while sitting on a broad wicker chair that overlooked the woods to the north of the property. "She came out about an hour ago."

Of all of the pea-brained ... What was wrong with her? Couldn't she follow simple directions? He swallowed hard, willing the heat around his collar to subside. "I'll take over."

"You sure? I was planning to be here until eight. I thought you had the o-dark-thirty shift tomorrow morning."

"Yeah. I'll sleep in between." If he'd be able to sleep at all. He stepped out of his car and pocketed his keys. "Go ahead. And do me a favor. Back at the station, there's a file on the assault last Friday night at the grocery mart. Go visit the witnesses again and see if they remember anything new."

"Yes, sir. Gotcha covered." Evans pointed a finger at him and clicked out of the side of his mouth before shifting gears and pulling out of the lot.

"And I'm gonna have me a little talk with a stubborn woman."

Another car crunched across the gravel as he neared the house. He glanced back. That boyfriend—no, fiancé. Jason ignored the man and walked around the large iron bell that had probably guarded the house for a century or more.

"Miss Stone." He crossed his arms and looked up at her where she sat on the porch above him.

She straightened and a pucker formed between her eyebrows. "Am I in trouble? I feel like I'm in the principal's office all of a sudden."

"I'm just wondering why you're outside. Again. After I asked you to stay inside. At least twice."

She shut her eyes and exhaled what sounded almost like a growl. "I know. I'm sorry."

"I don't want you to be sorry. I want you to be alive."

"Look. I stayed on the porch. Your man was right there."

"You'll have a guard here that can monitor the property a lot easier if you stay in one place. Inside. Better yet, stay in your room. Keep the curtains closed and chill until we can work out the details of what's going on."

She rolled her gaze to the eaves as he was speaking. "I can't," she said when he finished. "I don't have a room anymore. My uncle, or maybe he's a cousin, anyway, he showed up. Then my sister came in."

"Uh-uh, the sister that wasn't coming." He'd thought the

woman's name was Phyllis.

She gave him a knowing look. "Exactly. The one I was talking to that first day I was here. She and her husband now have my room, and I'm at a loss of where to go."

"Well, that's simple, sweetheart." The fiancé strolled around the corner of the house and joined Jason in the yard. He glanced up at Alynne. "You can stay with me in my room. I know you wanted to give the look of propriety and all that old-fashioned stuff, but your mom will understand. Surely, she would expect us to already—" The man's phone chimed as he spoke, and he glanced at it. "Gotta take this."

Good thing. Had he gone much further Jason might have forgotten his dedication to being a peace officer. He glanced at Alynne.

She'd shut her eyes, but tears had already streaked down her cheeks.

The heat in his neck increased by several degrees. He shut his own eyes and lifted his chin. *Okay, God. Why is this woman affecting me like this?*

That wasn't the right question. It didn't matter what his emotions were doing. Maybe he was just missing Dawn. But this was a real problem. *Help me help her, Lord.* Beyond it being his job, he had the gut feeling that the Lord had brought him to this situation for a reason.

Sighing, he opened his eyes. The blue of the sky above him was beginning to deepen, and a splay of yellow painted the windows of the third-floor suite. Cat's suite. Wait, had she thought about that? "What about Cat's suite?" He took the steps at the end of the porch.

"Momma has a cat?"

"No." He crossed closer to her. "Cat McPherson ... I mean Alexander."

"Alexander McPherson?"

"No, Cat Alexander. She just got married, but she lived here with your mom and dad, helping them with the inn because it's quite a job for folks their age." Wait. He hadn't meant to sound judgmental.

It struck her though. He was sure he saw regret flash through her eyes. "Oh. Of course, Momma has mentioned her. I might have met her when I came a few years back."

He continued, "She lived on the third floor."

Her eyes lit. "I completely forgot about the attic. It was always a storage room when I was a little girl. But it's a suite now?"

He opened the door to the kitchen. "It's probably pretty dusty, but from what I saw of it, it looked like the best room in the house."

She paused and gave him her full attention with one raised eyebrow. "Really."

It wasn't a question, and the insinuation stopped him cold. He swallowed his need to explain and preceded her across the room to the stairs. "I'm not sure they had the chance to fix the bullet hole in the window up there, but I'm sure it's been patched." There, that should answer the question in her eyes.

"Bullet hole?"

"Cat was the target of a hitman. So, you see, I've kept this place under surveillance before." Not very successfully, but this time would be different. "All I ask is that you keep the drapes closed when the lights are on and stay away from the windows."

They had reached the top of the steps. "Oh, that's all?" Sarcasm dripped from her tone.

He grimaced. "You're right. That will be too difficult for you. We had to put Cat in a jail cell to finally keep her safe. Maybe we should just try that with you up front?"

She had the grace to gasp. "I'll be sure to stay away from the windows." She pushed open the door and stepped inside.

He followed but left the door ajar. "Bathroom's in there." He swiped his hand across the edge of a tall bureau decorated with a cream-colored doily. No dust to speak of. "Looks like Myra kept the room ready for guests."

She moved to the corner and looked down through the windows to her left. "We're awfully high up here."

Did she have a fear of heights?

"Should give a pretty view of both sunrise and sunset." She turned and smiled at him. "Thanks. I wasn't sure what I was going to do."

He couldn't help but smile back. Then he nodded and took control of his stupid emotions.

"I mean … well … I was waiting for Momma. I was planning to ask her to let me share her suite."

"Oh, yeah. That would've worked, too."

"I … just didn't want you…" She moved back toward the uncovered window, being mindful to stand to the side. "I don't know why Blayne suggested that."

"It's none of my business." That was true. Entirely true.

Her gaze sought his. "I know. But … I guess I didn't want you thinking the worst of me."

What had possessed her to say that to him? Alynne turned away from his tender gaze and searched the trees on the north side of the house for answers.

Jason should think the worst of her. And she couldn't blame Blayne for offering to share his room, not after what she'd already done.

She felt a hand at her elbow and turned to look into those warm gray eyes once more.

"You should stay away from the windows."

Oh yeah. She'd already messed up again.

A loud crack resounded somewhere outside.

"Get down," Jason shouted. His arm encircled her as he stepped between her and the window and pressed her to her knees. He joined her on the floor.

"Was that a shot?"

He didn't take the time to answer. "Downstairs. Go."

She stayed low and darted for the open doorway.

"Wait."

She was halfway down, but she paused at his call. He dashed in front of her and peered around the edge of the steps into the dining room. Pulling out his cell phone, he dialed a number, then motioned with his hand for her to follow.

"Nine-one-one. What is your emergency?" Obviously, he'd placed the phone on speaker.

"Mrs. Hawkins, this is Jason. We have gunfire at Sunrise Inn. Require backup." He held up his hand and moved to the edge of the windows that banked most of the northern wall and looked out onto the forest beside the lake.

"Sunrise Inn, 10-4." The phone had the rumble of conversation in the background for a moment before it went silent.

He glanced at her. His eyes taking on a blacker tone than the soft gray they had shown upstairs. "Okay, come."

She darted toward him and whirled around the corner. Going halfway down the stairs again, she stopped, this time without his help, and let him take the lead.

"Coulda been hunters … poachers." He slipped past her. "Somehow, I don't think so."

She'd caught that drift.

He paused again at the bottom before waving her closer. "We're going the back way to the south wing," he whispered and took her hand.

There was a back way? She followed him down the narrow corridor that led to her mom's suite. She hadn't been in it since it had belonged to Uncle Todd and Aunt Pearl but remembered the huge bank of windows looking off a wide patio, down the hill to the lake. At the end of the corridor was an opening that looked a little like a pantry.

"I think this used to be a mudroom." He wasn't quite whispering anymore but kept his voice low.

And his hand felt warm and supportive.

Another turn and he paused again near a brightly lit hallway. He peeked to the right then to the left. Then he stepped to the right and ushered her ahead of him. She matched his moves and found herself in a tiny alcove where the main house met the south wing. A large glass door behind Jason illuminated him in the dazzling sunset.

"Get to the hallway."

She mimicked what he had done, peeking around the corners first before stepping into the hall and putting her back to the wall. "Why are we here?"

"I wanted to keep you away from the main rooms. Too common for you to be there and too many windows."

Another blast rang out. Glass broke somewhere, and a tight scream followed. She knew that scream. "That was Phyllis."

Jason had already started moving, pulling a gun from the holster at the hip of his blue uniform. "Which room?"

"That one." Alynne pointed to the door next to him but stayed in her place.

He tried the knob, but the door didn't open. He pounded on it. "Open the door, Phyllis."

"Help … help me!" Phyllis's plaintive cry tore at Alynne's heart. She knew another key must be in the drawer in the office, but Jason didn't want her near the windows or in the common rooms.

He tucked his gun under his jacket from where it had come, backed up to the opposite doorway, took a giant step forward, and kicked the door next to the knob. It bowed considerably, but it didn't open. Jason repeated the move, and the second time, the facing broke and the door swung wide. Jason tucked and rolled into the room.

"Oh, help me." Phyllis whimpered.

She could almost hear Jason screaming at her to stay where she was, but her sister was hurt. Maybe even shot. She dashed to the open door and crouched before peeking around the corner.

Phyllis sat with her back against the bed. A glass lamp from the bedside table was shattered a few feet away from her. She'd changed into a burgundy maxi dress with a long pink sweater, and she clung to the Pomeranian furball. "Someone's trying to kill me."

"Are you hurt?" Jason had crawled next to her. The dog growled and snapped when he reached his hand toward her.

She gave the ball a tiny shake that sent a shiver over her shoulders. "Or they're attempting to assassinate my husband."

"Phyllis, were you hit by anything?" Alynne stayed next to the doorway, only seeing her sister at the edge of the bed.

Phyllis's gaze fixed on Alynne's face. "This place is monstrous. How could Mother and Father think of living out here? We must get rid of it immediately."

Shock. She had to be in shock.

Jason didn't bother asking her again if she was hurt. Clearly, there was no blood, but the dog wouldn't let him even help her move.

Sirens sounded in the distance. Good.

"The shooter is probably gone by now. Will you follow me out into the hallway?" Jason turned and crawled a few feet toward the doorway. "Put your dog down. He'll be okay."

"Rufus, follow Mommy." She put the furball down and crawled a few inches before pulling her skirt from under her knees.

Then she moved quicker and joined Alynne in the hallway.

"Where's Carl?" Maybe her husband could help her calm down.

Her gaze hit the ceiling as she collected the dog into her arms again. "He wanted to muse."

She didn't make air-quotes but with her tone, she might as well have.

"He likes to walk at sunset and think on the day."

Alynne glanced at Jason. Carl had been out there with someone shooting a weapon. Could he have been hurt? Obviously, Jason connected with her thoughts. He shot down the hallway to the south side exit. He cracked the door and checked in both directions before darting out.

And the sirens were so close at this point, if the cops weren't in the lot, they would be in seconds.

"What possessed you to let Mother and Father stay in this awful place?" She stood, careful to avoid the opening to her room. "People shooting at other people. Crazy dogs trying to eat my poor Rufus. And all of the money Father must've sunk in this black hole. Good grief, Dora, didn't you have any concern?"

"Of course." And her name was Alynne. But this wasn't the time.

"Poor Mother. She has no one, now. And she has nothing to sustain her."

Alynne hadn't thought through what Momma would do now. She assumed that the inn would continue, but of course, Momma couldn't keep it going all by herself.

"There's no other question except to sell this place." They'd reached the main building where the south wing joined at the opening to the left of the staircase.

Alynne remembered how Jason hadn't wanted her in the common areas of the house. But then, no one was trying to shoot her. They were trying to shoot Phyllis. Or rather, her husband. Still, she pulled Phyllis back when she would've continued into the entry hall. "Let's wait here. Jason didn't want us in the common rooms."

"And who is this man with you? This Jason?"

"He's a police lieutenant. It's a long story, but they're keeping an eye on the inn."

"He's police?" Her color faded. "Why … why is he here?"

At least he was here, or she and Phyllis would've been alone. Strange that so many people were staying in the house, but none of them were actually present.

The front door chime sounded. "Alynne?" Jason's voice echoed through the entry hall.

"We're here." She led Phyllis to the edge of the stairs. "Did you find anyone?"

"It's all right." He leveled a meaningful gaze at her. "Officer Evans has everything under control out there."

It was all right? Then he'd found the person who had shot at Phyllis? Had it really been some kind of plot to assassinate Carl before he was voted into office? That was crazy. She glanced at Phyllis. The gravity of the situation must've hit her hard. Her face looked ashen against the pink of her sweater and the orange of her dog.

"Let me get you some tea." Alynne took her hand and led her

into the kitchen. "Can we go in here now?"

Jason followed her and pulled down the shades on the windows. "You still need to keep the windows covered at night. And stay away from them."

"The window in their suite will need to be fixed. We don't have another room."

"I can't stay in that room. Someone tried to shoot me in there." Phyllis flounced into one of the chairs around the small breakfast table, but her tone had lost the insistent intensity it had carried a few minutes before.

Reality kicked in. The family would be descending any moment into this circus sideshow of police running around like ants again. Just like they were this morning when everyone had left to protect the kids from this nightmare. "Jason … we … none of us can stay here."

Where else could they go? She pulled her cell phone from her pocket. "I have to find a hotel nearby. Something."

He stepped closer and put his hand over hers. "No, you don't. Things are all right." Jason cleared his throat and glanced at Phyllis. "Actually, none of the shots hit the inn. Someone was shooting out toward the lake. Practice."

Was that all? She stared into his eyes. Gray again, and calm. He gave a hint of a nod. Was she supposed to understand something? Maybe she was just supposed to trust him. She slipped her phone back into her pocket and glanced at her sister.

Phyllis looked positively sick, but her eyes were riveted to Jason's face. "So my husband…?"

"Will be back soon, I imagine."

The front door chimed, breaking the strange moment.

"Alynne?" Her mom's voice shook. "Alynne?"

"I'm in here, Momma."

"Oh, sweet girl." Her mom rushed in with her arms open wide. "It was bad enough leaving you here this morning, even though Jason promised he'd look after you. But then coming back to find more police. The front lot looks like a carnival midway."

"Things are all right, Myra." Jason nodded to her, then made his way out the front door.

The fact that he kept saying the same phrase over and over unhinged her a bit, but she didn't want to ask in front of Momma. "I'm sorry, Momma. I completely forgot to get out the casseroles." A last-minute plan when her mom and aunts left. If they didn't get back, she was to pop the pre-made backup plan into the ovens for a couple of hours.

This was why she'd make a terrible innkeeper.

"No worries, child. I have the pizza place on speed dial." She turned toward the office and halted.

Alynne had completely forgotten that Momma hadn't seen Phyllis yet. It must've been a shock after such a long time.

Phyllis let Rufus down and rose from her seat. She straightened her back. Her eyes didn't waver from Momma's face, almost as if they held a challenge. "Hello. Mother." The title seemed an afterthought.

"I'm so sorry, Momma. I should have called you about Phyllis's arrival …"

"It wouldn't have mattered. My phone died." She continued to stare at Phyllis. "Were you able to find room for her?"

"I gave them my room and moved up to the attic suite." Strange that she didn't even greet Phyllis. "Are you …?"

"Them?" Momma turned to look at Alynne.

"My husband, Carl, is with me." Phyllis lifted her chin. "He should be back soon."

Momma glanced back Phyllis. "I see. Very well." She moved further into the kitchen.

"We also have other guests." Alynne might as well tell her about all the surprises. "Ronald and his wife Sheila. I don't remember the last name."

Momma whirled to face her. "Surzchenkov?"

"That's it." Her mom looked positively stricken. "I don't remember ever meeting them before, though."

"I know them." She set her gaze on the tile near Alynne's feet. "Your father's … side of the family."

"Yeah, that's what Ronald said." How strange that Alynne had never met them. And she hadn't; she was sure. She definitely would have remembered them.

"It's been a long day. Think I'll turn in." Momma hesitated and looked back over her shoulder. "Alynne, would you see to dinner?"

Her strange look shot all sorts of alarms through Alynne. "Of course, Momma. Is everything …?" She glanced at Phyllis. Her sister had turned stony-faced. "I mean, can I do anything?"

"No, sweet girl. I just need to rest. I'll see you in the morning." Her mom went through the back corridor toward her suite.

Phyllis sank back into her chair, and Rufus leaped into her lap.

"What was that about?" Alynne pointed toward her mom's

exit but advanced on Phyllis. Maybe she shouldn't have allowed her sister to stay here after all.

Phyllis faced the entry hall where more of the family drifted inside. "That was Mother hating me all over again. I found a successful, wealthy man, and Mother has hated me ever since." She cut her eyes toward Alynne. "Just be sure, if you ever find a man, that he isn't a businessman, especially not a successful one. She'll hate you, too."

BREAKING POINT

Chapter Twelve

Successful? Wealthy?

Jason didn't know much about Carl Henderson's business or politics, but he was lucky he wasn't jailed. Seems his wife had the brilliant idea that attempts on his life would be a newsworthy event. Dell had mentioned locking him up just for the stupidity of it all, but he wouldn't actually do it.

At least Jason didn't think he would. But the chief spewed gravel with his cruiser as he spun the car toward the exit. Henderson was going to get the ride of his life to the station and might even chill in a cell for a few minutes before this was all over.

Jason followed Alynne into the office, standing between her and the closed blinds over the windows facing the parking lot.

"You kept saying everything was okay. What is it you aren't saying?"

Jason shrugged.

"The lamp was busted, but not from a gunshot."

"You noticed that." He was impressed.

"Clearly Phyllis broke the lamp. Are you suspecting this was all some sort of game?"

He shrugged again. "It doesn't really matter at this point."

She pulled out her phone and dialed to order the pizza.

There was always a lot going on under the surface of Alynne Stone. Jason had rarely met anyone truly sincere. Pastor Slaughter was one. Ellis Stone was another. He would've aligned Myra there as well before seeing her reaction to her daughter's arrival. Phyllis, not Alynne. And he'd like to add Alynne to that small group, but he couldn't even consider it. Clearly, she had issues with her sister, her mom and dad, even her boy … fiancé.

Where was that guy anyway?

Alynne finished ordering and hung up, her hand resting on the receiver for a moment.

"Obviously there's animosity between your mom and your sister. Can you tell me about it?"

She bowed her head and sank into the desk chair. "Not really." She looked up at him. "Phyllis left home when I was little. We still saw her from time to time, but I only remember her arguing with Pop about money. I haven't laid eyes on her since I was in middle school."

"She didn't sound like she was coming for the funeral, right?"

Alynne shook her head. "When I called her, she was full of venom. Didn't seem to care about Pop's death. And wasn't even interested in seeing Momma." She shrugged. "I was shocked to see her. And more surprised to see Momma's reaction to her being here."

"What do you know about her husband."

"Is this an interrogation, Lieutenant?" She narrowed her eyes and pressed her lips together.

He'd pressed too hard. "No. I'm just trying to understand some things."

"Like what things?" Her gaze didn't waver.

"Like ..." He hesitated, but she'd already suspected what they'd learned. "Like why we found Carl Henderson out in the woods with a .22 rifle."

"Do you think he set up a publicity stunt?"

"I didn't say that."

"Then he was trying to kill his wife and is just that bad of a shot?"

"I didn't say that either."

"Well, ask him. Where is he, now?"

"Now, that's a question I would expect to hear, but what I'd like to know is why your sister hasn't asked it."

"Why I haven't asked what?" Phyllis carried Rufus into the room and put him down on the desk. He immediately hopped down and began to lift his leg.

"Phyllis ..." Alynne shouted, but her sister was already ahead of her. Apparently, Rufus was inclined to use anything standing upright, including Ellis's office desk, as his own personal tree. At least his mistress had caught him before he could actually wet the wood floor.

As she rushed the dog out the front door, Alynne's clear gaze fell back on him. "Do you have Carl in custody?"

Jason felt put upon to nod. "He's only being questioned."

"You don't really think he might have shot at her?"

He shook his head. "I can't comment on an ongoing investigation. Still, there were others here in the house. Why didn't they appear with the gunshots?" He couldn't help wondering what had happened to Blayne. And where was the other couple that Alynne had mentioned?

"I guess they're all in their rooms." She lifted her chin. Yeah, she knew he was considering Blayne.

"Specifically, I'm wondering about the people who just checked in." He let her relax for half a second. "And then there's your fiancé."

"But you can't really suspect any of them having anything to do with this. Blayne doesn't even know my sister, and he wouldn't hurt a fly. And nobody knows my uncle."

"I thought he was a cousin." He'd need to get more details about all of her family members to complete the file.

She looked at the ceiling. "I don't know. Momma said he was part of Pop's side of the family. I assumed he was an uncle, but he's a lot younger than Pop. I've never met him, but I guess if he's Pop's cousin, he's mine, too. Second or third or something like that. Momma would probably know. Like I said, she recognized his name."

The front door chime rang out, and a noisy group entered. Alynne was pulled away into hostess mode as the final expected members of her family hustled in with several youngsters in tow. From the looks of it, Alynne was one of the youngest of her cousins, though this new guest carried an infant. And clearly, Alynne was the only one who wasn't married.

She had lively interaction with the kids as well as the adults.

While Phyllis reentered and seemed to drift into a sulk in the kitchen, Alynne engaged all who had arrived. She showed the newcomers to their rooms, checked on her aunts as they worked on breakfast preparations, joked with her cousins and their spouses, and still listened to the stories of the boys who had been hunting and the girls who had visited the Dallas zoo.

The lady would make a dynamite innkeeper. The perfect helper for her mom. And she'd make a great mom herself someday.

Enough. The officers outside were wrapping up their investigation. After finding the likely gunman, they wouldn't stick around much longer. He caught Alynne's eye as she headed for the steps to the dining hall, and she smiled at him, altered her course, and came his direction.

"I'm heading out." He moved into the entry hall, and she followed.

Her smile vanished. "Oh, I … the pizza should be here any minute. You're welcome to stay for dinner. There'll be plenty."

He glanced at her troubled look and put his hand lightly on her uninjured shoulder. "You're going to be fine, Alynne. There's a cop in the lot keeping an eye out all night. I'll be taking the shift at four tomorrow morning myself."

She'd been looking down, a little sheepishly until he mentioned his shift. He shoulda kept that to himself.

"Four? In the morning? I'm causing you all so much trouble."

He rubbed her shoulders. "No, no. *You're* not causing anything. The person who attacked you, who poisoned your cereal, he or she is causing trouble."

"Good-night, then." She was immediately distracted by the

children, and he made his way to his car. Vasquez was sitting in his cruiser next to it. He wished the man a quiet evening and drove to pick up his Jeep at the station. His thoughts whirled. There were too many pieces to this puzzle. And some simply didn't fit.

Alynne watched the taillights of Jason's cruiser pull out of the parking lot. She liked his Jeep better. The man was nothing if not formidable, and his protection warmed her all over, like a thick cotton blanket on a chilly night.

She pressed her lips into a grimace, her conscience stabbing at her. She had no business contemplating the protection or even the kindness of another man. Much less the way his hair perfectly matched the tan of his cowboy hat. How his broad and muscular shoulders accentuated his narrow waist. Or the way his eyes crinkled in the corner when he smiled, full of honesty and compassion.

No. She mustered her discipline and turned her back on the glass panel in the door. He'd wanted her to stay away from windows anyway. Ugh. Getting him out of her mind wasn't going to be easy. She wandered through the kitchen.

Please help me, Lord. She'd already messed things up royally in her love life. Surely, she could be faithful to the one man she'd already committed to, although, more and more, she wondered if she should have.

Where was Blayne anyway? His car had been out front for most of the day. Had it been out there just now? She hadn't noticed.

Just as she reached the stairs to the dining hall, the front door chimed. Had Jason changed his mind? She whirled and scooted to the entry hall.

"Anyone here?" Blayne almost ran into her as he approached the kitchen.

"I noticed you weren't here." Alynne eyed him. He hadn't been simply walking around, or he would've seen all the police. "Where were you?"

He winked and took her hand, coming close for a light brush of his lips on her cheek. "You almost sound like a jealous wife. I like it." He pulled her across the room. "Is the crowd all here?"

"Mostly. I haven't seen my … I'm not sure what he is." Her store of energy ebbed, and her arm ached again.

"New family that you don't know?" Maybe Blayne was interested in her family after all.

"The guy is related to Pop somehow, but I don't remember how. Ronald Surzchenkov and his wife, Sheila."

Blayne stiffened. "Huh, we don't have a big family, but I just assumed that anyone on your dad's side of the family would have Stone as the last name."

"Like I said, I don't know how he fits in, but I expect they'll be back soon. We have pizza upstairs in the dining hall."

"That sounds delicious, but I confess, I'm exhausted. Would you bring me a plate?"

"Are you feeling all right?"

"And a salad, ranch dressing."

Really? "Yeah, okay."

"And a diet cola."

She straightened and glared at him. Was the man helpless? Did he not remember that she only had one good arm right now?

He pulled her in around her shoulders. "Thanks, you're the best." He kissed her forehead and then released her without even noticing her grimace of pain. He trotted up the steps and darted for his room, nearest to the dining hall. For pity's sake, it was less than twenty steps for him to serve himself.

She'd bring him his dinner all right, but he'd be waiting until it was good and cold before he got it. She made her way into the kitchen to make sure nothing was left out downstairs and then went up the back steps.

Someone, probably one of her aunts, had made a point to neatly stack the empty pizza boxes on the dumbwaiter. The leftovers were warming under the heating lamps. Alynne slapped a couple of warm slices onto her paper plate and chose a diet soda from the cold bin before heading to a table where her aunts chatted with their respective sons. "May I join you?" she asked Aunt Billie.

"Of course, dear child. We haven't had a good chat, yet."

"Aunt Bobbie was telling us about the inn." Wyatt, Aunt Billie's youngest son, was still a good decade older than Alynne, and he sported a goatee several shades darker than his blond hair. "I can't believe you have a treasure somewhere on this property, Alynne."

Oh, that silly treasure story. She'd forgotten all about Uncle Todd's stories.

Aunt Bobbie waved a hand in her direction. "I'm only going by what Myra's told me. I bet you know more about it than I do."

Alynne shook her head. "Oh, no. I was only a little girl when my uncle filled my mind with talk about the confederate treasure."

"*Confederate* treasure?" Wyatt's wife chuckled. "It can't be worth all that much if it was from the losing side."

"Oh, but it might be." Aunt Bobbie took over again. "Myra told me that when Texas embraced the confederacy, Ellis's ancestors, at least the female side, were none too pleased about it. Said authorities would come by requiring special payments to keep their house safe. After two or three of these visits, the great-great-whatever packed up everything they had of value and buried it somewhere on the property. Then when the ancestor died, his son took over the property without knowing anything about the treasure."

She left out some key parts.

"If no one knew about it, then how does Myra know about it?" This from Wyatt's very astute oldest son, Daryl, probably about twelve years old.

"Mother heard about it from Uncle Todd, same as me and Dora." Phyllis chimed in.

"Alynne." She spoke loudly enough for the room to hear so there could be no confusion. "I go by Alynne, now." Always have, but then Phyllis didn't call her Dora as an endearment.

Phyllis lifted her chin before regarding the boy. "The oldest son didn't know about the treasure, but his little brother did. He didn't know where it was, though. Uncle Todd always teased Eudora…" She leveled her challenging gaze on Alynne. "He said that the boy grew up digging everywhere on the property and his digging is what created Lake Grayson." She nodded her punctuation as chuckles filled the room.

"That didn't happen." One of William's girls exploded in a fit of giggles.

Aunt Bobbie reclaimed the story. "Maybe not, but the boy searched for it all his life and so did his son. His grandson didn't care about it all that much. He was the one who started doing all of the renovations on the old farmhouse. I think Myra said the man's name was Alfred."

"Uncle Todd's father." Alynne knew that much. "And his sister, Uncle Todd's Aunt Tally, was treasure crazy. Uncle Todd said she made his dad dig up every inch of ground before he made any changes to the old house."

"The only aunt I remember knowing is Aunt Pearl." Phyllis squinted her eyes. "Whatever happened to her?"

"Myra said she moved in with her sister, who was very well-to-do, after your Uncle Todd died." Aunt Billie added her two cents. "I think Myra mentioned that she finally died last summer somewhere south of here."

"New Orleans," Aunt Bobbie chimed in.

A strange sadness fell over Alynne for the loss of her aunt. She hadn't seen her since before she finished elementary school. Another connection with Pop was gone.

"But that still doesn't tell us where the treasure is." Daryl wasn't about to let that part of the story go.

"You'll have to ask Aunt Myra about that," his father told him and stood. "Long day."

His wife picked up her youngest. "Please excuse us."

"We'll see y'all in the morning." Aunt Billie kissed her granddaughter, their oldest, as the little girl followed her parents to the south wing where they had a second-floor suite.

"I hope we can hear more about the treasure." The girl obviously wanted to stay, but her tired eyes made it just as obvious that she needed some rest.

"I 'spect you will." Aunt Billie gave good-night hugs to each of William's girls.

Alynne glanced at her watch. Oh, her aunts had to be exhausted after such a long day chasing after the little ones. "I'll clean up."

"Oh dear, no." Aunt Bobbie stood and reached for a paper plate.

"It's all going in the trash anyway. I can do that." She waved her good arm toward her aunts and started stacking up the used plates.

The family called their goodnights to one another as they made their way to their wing. Alynne picked up a clean plate and filled it with several slices of pizza and the remains of the salad. There weren't any more colas. She set down the plate, snagged a bottle of water, and tucked it under her good arm before picking up the plate again.

"Glad to see you didn't completely forget me." Blayne entered and glanced around the dining room.

There went her last nerve. "Oh, dear, you took a whole sixteen paces out of your room. Do you need to sit down and rest?"

"Sarcasm doesn't become you, Alynne."

"Laziness doesn't become you." She carried the plate to him, then let the bottle drop at his feet.

He picked up the bottle, wandered to the cleaned end of the

table, and sat down. "So why have you kept this treasure thing a secret from me?"

Alynne turned and stared at him. "You were listening in?" But he couldn't be bothered to join them?

"I'm hurt." He didn't answer her question. "Didn't you think you could trust me with the story?" He dug into one of the slices.

"I was a kid." She could ignore his questions as easily as he ignored hers. "I haven't thought about the story for decades." She moved to the dumbwaiter and unloaded her arm of trash. She was tempted to take one of the pain killers the doctor had prescribed.

Blayne finished his pizza and went to the window, raising the blinds. He hadn't been here when the shots were fired and didn't know to keep the windows covered. "I guess I understand."

Alynne pushed the button to send the dumbwaiter down and loaded a bin with drinking glasses.

"Shame you can't see the lake very well from here." Blayne leaned closer to the pane and peered hard to his left. "I think those stairs should be moved to give this room the lake view it deserves. What's on the other side of those stairs?" He pointed to the wall where the stairs went down to the kitchen on the right and up to her suite on the left.

Why did he care? "I'm not sure." A wall, probably the attic over her mom's suite. She closed the lid on the large cooler and turned off the warming lights before plopping the leftover box of the pizza on top of the bin full of dirty glasses. She shot Blayne a sour look … couldn't he see she could use some help?

"Even if there isn't treasure on this property, this place could be quite lucrative if placed in the right hands."

"I think Momma and Pop did pretty well." Alynne hoisted the heavy bin with her one arm and set it on one of the side tables. Then she grabbed a couple of napkins off the server. "You should have seen how many reservations had to be canceled to get the family housed this week." She wiped down the tables then shoved the chairs back in place so they would be ready for tomorrow.

"*Pretty well* doesn't come close to the vision I have. This place should be a resort. The forest is part of the property, right?"

"Some of it." There was the big house to the north that marked the line. "And it goes to the south and west all the way to the road and the scout camp on the hill over on the other side of the cove." Such a beautiful place. No wonder her parents had loved it so much.

She scanned the room once more then hoisted the bin again. "I'm going down. Would you lower the blinds?"

"I think when we get married, maybe we should consider moving out here."

What? She set the bin right back down. "Why?"

"Make this into a showplace. A little influence from the right people could make us millions."

"It's not ours, Blayne."

He turned his head to stare at her as though unaware that she'd been in the room.

"Would you get those?" She pointed at the window blinds.

"What?"

Wow, he really had been in his own little fantasy. "The blinds. Would you close them?"

He glanced at the window again. "Why?"

She picked up the bin and balanced it on one hip. "Because I asked you to." Did she really need to explain to him? No. "I want them all closed." And that should be enough reason.

He rolled his gaze to the ceiling then turned to work the blinds.

She didn't wait for him to finish. Anger fueled her steps to a trot as she descended the stairs to the slightly dark kitchen. At least, the windows down here were all covered. She put the leftover pizza in a storage box and set it in the fridge. Then she began loading the dirty glasses and a few cups into the industrial dishwasher, one of the renovations Pop had made.

Blayne came down the steps. "I'm going back to bed." He slipped his arm around her and pulled her close. "Wanna join me?"

"Ow." She pushed away, repulsed by his lack of compassion for her. She clamped her teeth shut for a moment to eliminate the growl that was forming in the pit of her throat. "No, Blayne. I don't. And I don't want to hear you speak of that again. Especially not in front of anyone else." The heat rose in her cheeks as she put space between them then turned to face him. "I know you don't get it, but that night we spent together is a huge shame for me. It won't happen again before we're married, I promise."

"Ah, sweetheart, I love your old-fashioned streak, but this is the twenty-first century."

"Uh, you don't think this same thing happened in the last century and the one before that?" The Bible story of the woman caught in adultery flashed through her mind. That was her. "Women have been making idiots of themselves over men since the beginning of time. But that doesn't mean I have to enjoy the reminders of my poor judgment or that I'm doomed to repeat the behavior."

"That's harsh, Alynne. I thought you loved me."

She sighed. She did. Didn't she? "This isn't a reflection on you, Blayne. But that night was a horrible mistake, a sin. I know that's an old-fashioned word, but it is what it is. And I don't care if everyone and their dog laughs at my conviction, I know it was wrong, I regret it, and I'll likely feel the guilt from it for the rest of my life."

"No, no. Now, this is just the thing, exactly the reason why we need to get married right away. See, I haven't been feeling comfortable about that night either."

"You haven't?" Could the Lord have been convicting him as well? Alynne cringed. She didn't even know if Blayne was a believer.

"Why do you think I've been trying to settle this matter and get us married? I didn't know you felt so strongly about it, or I would have insisted."

Still, flying off to Vegas and getting married the week Pop died didn't feel right. And leaving Momma here, especially after her reaction to Phyllis, was out of the question. "So, you understand how I feel?"

"Absolutely. I can get us a flight out of Dallas first thing in the morning."

Grrr. He just didn't get it. She slammed the empty bin onto the counter. "I'm not going anywhere with you, Blayne. Not now. Not this week. Not even next weekend. After that … I'll think about it." She wiped her hands on a towel hanging on the oven door and practically sprinted up the steps to the now darkened dining room.

Shoot. The blinds were still opened. What was his problem? She marched over but halted as she neared the window. Was that a light out in the woods? She sank to her knees and crawled to the opposite side where the cords for the blinds hung. There was a light. Over at the house next door, but Jason said it had been empty for years.

She ducked under the sill, pulled the release cord, then darted up the steps to her room.

Jason worked his wrist back and forth to let the weight of the rod find its rhythm. When the movement reached an apex, he thumbed the button releasing his lure to fly some thirty or so yards, tucking it into a deep crevice near the edge of the dam.

The chief had insisted on assigning Sanchez to the early morning shift since Jason had worked all day. He'd argued, but Dell wouldn't back down.

After a sleepless night of worry over Alynne, he'd forced himself to come here. Well, after he'd dropped by the lot to check with the officer on duty. Sanchez confirmed everything had been quiet all night.

She didn't need him there. And he didn't need to be there. Didn't need to be so close to her or the distractions she created simply by being in close proximity.

"This is crazy, God." He reeled in his line slowly. Five years he'd been without Dawn. Sixty-one months of constantly thinking of her, missing her. No, not all of that time. The pain had ebbed just as he'd been told it would. Leaving Chicago a few years ago had helped.

"But I barely know this woman. How come I'm so attracted to her?" Beautiful women had always been around him, even as pretty as Alynne. As striking as she was, it wasn't her looks that drew him. What was it? With all the women who had been placed in his path, some who had literally been flung at him by his well-meaning friends both in Chicago and here, why was this girl impacting him so much? Why her? Why now?

He drew the lure in the rest of the way. He should cast again, but his heart wasn't in it. After attaching the hook to his pole, he picked up his tackle box. This hadn't been exactly a dumb idea, but he didn't feel any the better for the trip. Tucking his gear into the backseat, he climbed in and started the engine.

Was this a case of him getting attached to a helpless female? Maybe his desire to protect her masqueraded as attraction. Sounded right in his head, but there was a fatal flaw there. Alynne wasn't some hapless waif.

Helpless couldn't be used to describe her in any way. Strength poured out in the control she used with her sister and in the hospital with her mom. And the way she was with her mom, so gentle, with genuine love and concern. And yet, she could laugh, even at herself. She'd made friends with Rose, despite a fragile beginning.

He refocused on the road. Thinking so deeply about Alynne Stone did nothing but make his minimal attraction deeper and more meaningful than he'd originally thought.

A siren sang out, jarring him from his thoughts, and he caught lights approaching in this rear-view mirror. "Oh, what is this?" He had to drive another mile before he found a shoulder wide enough for parking. But he stayed in his car, rolled down his window and watched Deputy Cain approach in his side mirror.

"License and proof of insurance." Cain's eyes were hidden by mirror sunglasses, but the smirk on his mouth showed exactly what his intentions were.

Jason didn't respond, simply tugged his cards from his wallet and handed them to the deputy.

Cain stood, studying the cards. Jason used the opportunity to pull his phone from his back pocket and turn on the video camera to catch the conversation.

"Seems to me like your insurance is expired."

"Next month. That's what the June means by the words expiration date."

"Don't get smart with me, boy." The man was such a cliché, it hurt. He'd have been a perfect supporting antagonist for the movie *Smokey and the Bandit*.

"Is there a reason why you stopped me, Deputy Cain?" Might as well get this over with.

Cain sauntered down the side of his Jeep. "Yep. One of your brake lights is busted."

No, they weren't. "The brake lights are fine." He picked up his phone and got out of the car.

"They were fine." Cain reared back and smashed one of them with the heel of his boot. "Not anymore."

Had Jason's phone picked up all of that? It was turned the right way. He left it where it was, hanging nonchalantly at his side, but the lens had the correct view.

"Hefty fine for a broken taillight." He pulled his notebook from his back pocket. "I'll have to write up a violation for that."

This wasn't the time for a fight. The words kept repeating in his brain like a mantra. Somehow, they had the chief's voice behind them. "Fine. I'll take the ticket." Jason started to climb in when the car jerked with another smashing sound.

"What a shame." Cain regained his balance after kicking in the other brake light. "They're both damaged." He clicked his tongue and shook his head as he began writing in the book. "Two different violations in one stop. You know, if you get three within a month, you have to go on mandatory desk duty while your record is reviewed."

"I can't imagine that the judge would accept three infractions on only one stop. Besides, I'm out of brake lights."

He moved to the front of the car. "I can fix that." He kicked at the driver side headlamp, but it didn't give. A minivan drove past and slowed down. The middle-aged mom and two young boys stared at Cain. Clearly, they'd spotted him kicking at the headlight.

"That might be trouble." Jason made sure Cain could hear him, then climbed back into the driver's seat. Surely, after having witnesses to his obvious harassment, he'd let Jason go. And he needed to let him go if he wanted to keep his nose in place.

Cain watched the van drive on then turned to glare at Jason. He stood where he was, writing the tickets. Then he advanced, ripped out the two tickets, and threw them with his ID and insurance card through Jason's window. "Get off my roads."

Gladly. "Have a nice day." He kept his response on the quiet side. Just in case.

BREAKING POINT

Chapter Thirteen

Alynne slept poorly, but staying in bed wasn't an option with Pop's funeral to plan. Momma needed her.

She showered quickly, wanting to get downstairs before the family converged so she could have some time to talk with her mom alone. After blowing her hair dry, she applied some cover-up and mascara to her eyes and a hint of blush to her cheeks. Then she slipped on some blue Capri pants and a sleeveless sweater and jogged down the steps pausing in the dining room.

"Good morning, Alynne." Aunt Billie bustled over and wrapped her in a warm hug. "How was your night?"

They didn't need to know the details of her lousy sleep. "Good enough." Alynne turned to wave at Aunt Bobbie who had her hands full with a pan of sausage casserole. "And yours?"

"Can't complain." Aunt Billie went back to the cold unit where she was transferring chunks of fruit from a plastic bowl into a crystal one. "Coffee's on downstairs, and we're about to make some orange pancakes."

One of Alynne's favorites. "Yum. Sounds great to me." She refused to think again of her waistline while the memory of those dead squirrels was still so vivid. Granola was definitely out.

She crossed to the next level of stairs and skipped to the kitchen, meeting the early light as it streamed through the east-facing windows.

As the sunlight caught her attention, so did a new guest. Her long orange hair caught every glance of the morning beams and almost reflected them. She sat facing Alynne in the large built-in booth that Pop had added beside the bay window that looked out on the front porch. With her face buried in her hands, she shook with labored breathing interspersed with sobs. Momma also sat on the bench with her arms wrapped around her, gently rocking back and forth and stroking her arm.

Alynne tiptoed to the coffeepot and poured herself a mugful with hardly a sound, but her mom noticed and looked up with an apologetic smile. Alynne warmed her hands around the mug and prayed peace on the woman and Momma.

The woman raised her head and took a tissue from the box on the table. She sniffled slightly and Momma murmured something to her. Alynne looked away and sipped her coffee. Was it the fact that her mom clearly doted on this woman that bothered her or was it because the needy woman was stealing the comfort that Momma should've been receiving? She set her mug down, whispered a prayer for guidance and gentleness, then turned back toward the pair at the table.

Momma rose and came toward her. "Good morning, sweet girl." She reached out with both hands on Alynne's shoulders and gave her a brief kiss on the cheek. "Today is going to be a much better day than yesterday." She assured her, though how she could say such a thing on the verge of going to plan her own husband's funeral, Alynne couldn't imagine.

"And I have a precious friend to introduce you to." She took Alynne's elbow and guided her toward the table. The woman scooted from the bench as they approached. "Cat, this is my daughter, Alynne."

The much shorter woman tossed a strand of red hair over her shoulder and reached up to give Alynne a hug. "I am so glad to officially meet you," she said. "I think we waved at one another several Christmases ago, but I've heard so much about you from your mom and dad. I know you're hurting and probably feeling a little unsteady right now." She sniffed into her tissue again. "I recently lost my own dad and those feelings still visit far too often."

Momma gestured that they should both sit. "Cat's father passed away last winter. He owned the diner in town."

"I see." Alynne let Cat have the bench while she settled into a lightweight chair that faced the window. She turned to the redhead. "I'm sorry for your loss."

"And I'm sorry for yours." Cat looked down at her hands on the table. "My dad was pretty amazing and left quite a legacy for me of kindness, compassion, and evangelism."

That was a legacy?

"I only hope that I can live up to his example," Cat continued without looking up.

Alynne thought of her own pop. Kindness and compassion,

absolutely. There hadn't been a mean bone in Pop's body or a hard attitude that she'd ever seen. And generous—incredibly generous—paying for part of her college and offering to move her out to the inn when she finished. When that wouldn't work after she got her job, he insisted on paying for the first year of her apartment to help her earn a little nest egg.

And all of that after he'd had to deal with Momma's cancer and those medical payments.

"I'm whipping up some Orange Jacks. Do those sound good to you ladies?" Momma moved around the wide serving counter.

"Delicious." The redhead wiped at her nose once more and turned on a dazzling smile. "The perfect thing for strength and the encouragement we need to face this morning with the funeral director."

Alynne had looked forward to this delicacy since the aunts mentioned them. Wait. Cat was going with them to the funeral home? She glanced at the redhead who was looking expectantly at her.

"Oh, yeah. That sounds fine." She stood and wandered back to the counter, picking up her coffee mug. Her emotions whirled from annoyance to guilt to gratitude and back again. She mentally brushed them away and set her mug at her place on the table before turning back toward her mom. "Can I help you?"

"Zest those and then you can use them to make some fresh juice." Her mom pointed to a short basket of oranges.

Alynne hadn't zested anything in years, but she'd been schooled in all of those techniques under Momma's watchful eye until she'd gotten sick. And during those years, Alynne had done most of the cooking for them all since Phyllis had already moved away. But none of her training mattered if she couldn't find the zester. She opened the third drawer down from the sink to find an assortment of wraps and aluminum foil.

"It's over here." Cat had joined them in the kitchen and held up the zester. Apparently, it went in the drawer next to the stove. She handed it to Alynne and then, without being told or directed, proceeded to pull eggs from the fridge and began breaking them one at a time into a bowl. She and mom kept up a happy banter as they both worked.

Alynne went on with her zesting on the other side of the kitchen island. For the most part, since Momma and Cat were both near the stove, they kept their backs to her. At least most of the zest got into the bowl she'd found. And she'd only had to look in two cabinets before she'd found that. Meanwhile, Cat was moving to and fro through the kitchen with ease, grabbing a skillet from a deep drawer under the stove and a large spatula from out of a tool bin on the opposite counter. She even knew where Momma hid her spices and helped herself to a couple that Alynne wouldn't have considered using for eggs.

Who was she kidding? If it wasn't plain salt and pepper, she wouldn't have considered using it on eggs.

Having completed the zesting, she took a knife to the remaining peel. Cat gave her a worried look more than once and traded glances with Momma, but thankfully, neither of them said anything. She wasn't sure what she was doing wrong, but she knew Momma had a juicer. That's all that mattered. And it was something she could locate since she'd spotted it in the pantry a couple of days ago. She pulled it out and plugged it in, but that's where what little know-how she had left her. "The fruit goes in here, right?" She pointed to an opening in the lid.

Laughter spilled out of Cat. "I can help you." She set the spatula on the spoon rest and turned down the flame under her pan. "This way." She latched the top in place and put a heavy glass under what must have been the spigot. "Put the fruit in here." She pointed to a wide cylinder and then handed her a plastic block. "Use this to press the fruit all the way in if it gets stuck. And you turn it on here." She pointed to the on/off button.

That much Alynne could have figured out.

"You'll need to dump that glass every so often." She turned and pulled open a low cabinet door. "This will work." She set a large plastic pitcher on the counter. Its putty brown color reminded Alynne more of burnt coffee residue than orange juice.

"Not that one, dear." Momma had turned around to face them, her nose wrinkled. "Get the two crystal ones."

"Sure thing." Cat stuck the plastic one back under the counter and went directly to the china cabinet against the interior wall.

Alynne hadn't even noticed the cabinet over there. Her neck muscles tightened. She sighed and began juicing the oranges as Cat returned and set down the cut-glass, footed pitchers. Obviously, this woman had been part of Momma's life for some time.

Regret mingled with jealousy as she finished the juicing. Her aunts joined them in both the work and the banter. Alynne let them talk. She had little that she wanted to say anyway, and the machine whirred loudly with every piece of orange she inserted. After juicing the first few, she turned it off and began peeling new ones.

"Didn't you, Alynne?"

Alynne was brought out of her deep thoughts as her mom drew her into the conversation. She nodded absently, having no idea with what she was agreeing. Her mom wasn't one to make jokes at someone else's expense. Even her mom's banter, though lighthearted, was honest and direct.

Cat smiled in her direction. "That must've been exciting," she commented. "Going all the way to the Ivory Coast. I've only been outside Texas once. Well, twice after the last two weeks."

Oh, that was what Momma was talking about. "Yes." Alynne set down the cleaned fruit and picked up another to peel. This was a topic she could warm up to. "I was stationed in Niakara. Well, the name was a lot longer, but that's what we called the town. The people there were so warm and generous."

"Did they speak English?" Cat layered a tray with a thick paper towel and began transferring the freshly cooked bacon slices to it.

"No, I spent the first two months there learning French."

"Months? I was thinking this was just a little short trip, a week or two."

Not unlike some of the younger missionaries who had grown too homesick to stay before even completing their training period. "This was considered a short-term mission, but it lasted fourteen months." Months she wouldn't trade for anything. A break between her sophomore and junior years. Her thoughts drifted back to the wonderful faces of the saints she wouldn't see again this side of heaven. Even to Stephan and Heidi, her German partners.

For a little over a year, she'd known what it was like to have a sister-type who really cared about her and a brother from another mother. They'd been so close. How strange that they only occasionally texted or e-mailed anymore. And how different her life's focus had become.

"I remember going to Disney World when I was like three or four, but Mom and Dad opened the diner the next summer and there wasn't any time to travel. When they were finally able to hire some folks to start taking some of the burden, Mom got sick. I guess the desire to travel sort of left Dad at that point." Cat had reloaded the heavy skillet with bacon pieces and touched each of them in turn with her tongs.

"That might change now, though." Momma laid a towel over a tall stack of pancakes on a china plate. "Ray said something about speaking to others wanting to start and fund local homeless missions?"

Cat turned to straighten the tray on the counter. Enough that Alynne caught her smile and the pinkish tone to her cheeks as she answered. "Yes, my husband has done a wonderful job with Sunset Mission. Especially with the funding. And the men who stay there are purposeful in giving back to the community."

Alynne wasn't sure what Sunset Mission was about, but Cat clearly championed the project and adored her husband.

"While we were in the mountains, Grady had them renovating Mrs. Chisolm's back porch and painting the siding on the church. Today, Ray's got them working on repairs at the diner."

"I still think that whole situation was so sad." Aunt Bobbie cut fresh fruit near the sink with Billie. "I'm so very glad you were not hurt, dear."

What was she talking about?

Cat turned to the older woman. "Thank you. On the bright side, I don't have nightmares about the fire anymore."

Alynne couldn't conceal her curiosity. "Did something happen to your dad's diner?"

"Well, it's mine now. Mine and Ray's."

"Didn't I tell you about that, Alynne?" Her mom turned off the griddle and turned to face her, wiping her hands on her apron. "About the man who was trying to …" She glanced at the redhead. "Maybe I shouldn't talk about this if it bothers you."

Cat shook her head. "I'm finding ways to cope with the fear. I can't pretend it didn't happen." She glanced over her shoulder at Alynne before going back to her bacon. "A man tried to kill me earlier this year. And he set fire to the diner. It was pretty much gutted."

Connections started linking. Jason had said something about that when he showed her the third-floor suite. "Oh no. I'm so sorry. But you're repairing your diner?"

"More like rebuilding it from the foundation up." Momma picked up her platter of pancakes and toddled toward the dumbwaiter. "I wouldn't have thought it possible to see it after the fire, but it's actually beginning to look rather nice again."

They continued to another conversation as Alynne turned on the roaring juicer again. There was more to this redhead than she'd suspected. And she didn't seem to have any ulterior motives where Momma was concerned. She could be a good ally when it came to helping Momma get used to not having Pop around.

At least those were the kind thoughts she'd had before they ventured out the front door, ready to take Momma into town. Cat decided to drive her husband's truck, and Momma was delighted to climb in on the bench seat next to her. Alynne wasn't the fan of old trucks like her mom was, but she'd certainly go with them.

Then, Phyllis came down the steps bemoaning the fact that she wanted to accompany them but couldn't drive her rental the extra miles to get to town and back.

Fine. Alynne didn't mind driving her sister and meeting Momma there. She pulled out her keys and unlocked her door. Maybe she and Phyllis could continue the positive feelings they'd had with a good chat on the way to the funeral home. She climbed in and snapped her seatbelt into place.

"We'll see you there." Her sister waved at her as she climbed into the final seat of the old blue truck.

Or Alynne could simply drive by herself. With her own whirling thoughts attacking her. She puffed out an exhale. This would be fine too. A good day, even, with friends and family and pleasant surroundings.

A drop splattered on her windshield. Followed by another.

Chapter Fourteen

Jason slipped the screwdriver into his pocket and closed his Jeep's hatch door. "Easily fixed." His video had only gotten glimpses of Cain kicking at his taillight, but the sound was clear enough.

"That's the guy." The young voice floated up as a couple of kids came out of the convenience store attached to Bubba's Repair and Spare.

He glanced at the towhead kid, about nine, and his smaller brother.

"Mister, did you get a ticket from that cop?" The younger boy looked up at him with wide blue eyes.

They'd seen Cain stop him? "As a matter of fact, I did."

"Come along, boys," a woman called. She had to be their mom, with the same round eyes though hers had dark circles under them. He knew those eyes. And the van she ushered the boys into.

He stepped to the back of it. "Ma'am, do you have a moment?"

"I'm sorry if the boys bothered you." She slid the side door into place and then faced him. "They've been cooped up in the car for a couple of hours. Never a good thing on a spring day."

"No." He wouldn't ask why they weren't in school. "But your son mentioned me getting a ticket?"

Her eyebrows lifted. "Oh, I do recognize you. That deputy kicked your headlight. Did he break it?"

"Not the headlights, but he smashed both of my brake lights."

"You're on the wrong side of the law." She tilted her head and took a step back.

He pulled out his wallet. "Actually, I'm not." He showed her his badge. "That was just a little squabble between departments, but his false tickets can put a mark on my reputation."

"I don't know how I can help you. I didn't see him bust your brake lights."

He pulled out his phone. "No, but you did see him kick at the headlights. That would be enough to support my efforts to fight the tickets."

"I'm not sure I want to get involved in this battle." She shook her head slowly as she spoke.

"It's only a traffic ticket. No intrigue or anything like that. And all I need is your say-so over the phone. Basically, leaving a voice mail message for my boss. That's all." He held out his phone. "I just need your name and phone number."

She pressed her lips together and audibly exhaled. "I guess." She took the phone and typed for a moment. "I won't be able to come back this way, though."

"Not an issue." Jason smiled and accepted the phone back from her. "Like I said, it's just traffic court. I can't thank you enough."

She cocked up one eyebrow. "Yes, you probably can. I've been trying to find Ryerson Drive. It's supposed to be in a new development to the south of town, but my map app can't find it and I've had no luck following the laughable directions I've been given. Can you help me?"

In his sleep. "Absolutely." He asked for her phone and opened the app. "Yeah, Ryerson Drive is the other half of Miller Road." He showed her the map. "Your road isn't on the map, but I've plugged in Miller where it intersects FM 4770. You'll see the new construction at the intersection."

She lifted her gaze upward before settling it on him again. "Thank you so much." She took her phone back and smiled her good-bye as she climbed into the driver's seat.

Jason took a look at his phone after she'd driven away. Lorenda Snyder. Cain was about to have his cup overflowing with trouble. He smiled and turned to go back to his car. Two women emerged from the funeral home across the highway. They stood talking at the corner and looking around. He'd recognize the dark-haired one anywhere.

"Alynne." He waved and jogged across the empty roadway.

She turned her stunning eyes toward him. "Ja- … Uh … Lieutenant." Was that a little blush growing on her cheeks? "You remember my sister."

Phyllis stuck her hand in his. "Always support our boys in the trenches."

He slid his hand from hers. "I'm sure they appreciate that." Alynne had been pacing during the exchange, her gaze searching in all directions. "Is something wrong?"

"What's right?" Alynne's sister grimaced. "This tiny town of yours is forcing us to put off the funeral until Saturday. The viewing is Thursday, but apparently, the whole town is shutting down on Friday for some strange reason."

"Oh yeah. That's senior day. Activities all day for the high school seniors, all over town."

Alynne turned an incredulous look on him? "Like a senior-skip day?"

"More like a field trip. Merchants and community groups have all sorts of plans for visiting seniors during the day. The department is giving out HPPD *Back the Blue* stickers and sunglasses and the church is having a huge lunch and afternoon concert."

Phyllis shot her gaze upward. "And that ridiculous practice is why we can't do the funeral on Friday. I still don't understand why we can't just have it at the funeral home."

"Momma wants it at the church." Alynne glared at her sister for a moment before turning back to him. "Have you seen her, by the way? We sort of lost track of her."

"Myra doesn't need babysitting. She's been a staple in this town since I've been here."

"I know that." She shook her head. "She got a little overwhelmed in there." She tilted her head toward the funeral home. "Cat took her out to help her calm down."

"Positively left us to finish all the planning without any help at all." Phyllis had the voice of a circus ringmaster. And the attitude of one of its animals.

"It wasn't …" Alynne sighed and looked back at Jason. "I'd like to take Momma back home. I don't suppose you saw them."

"Sorry." He'd been focused on his brake lights. Now he focused on the woman in front of him. The one without a police escort. "Why are you here alone?"

She pinked. "I'm not exactly alone." She looked down. "I'm sorry. I'm not used to having a bodyguard. I guess I left the inn when he was checking the property or something."

"Or something." He would check on the duty list. "As far as your mom goes, she and Cat like to walk in the park. It's just around the corner over there and up the hill." He pointed across the road in the direction past Bubba's Repair and Spare.

"Oh. Really," Phyllis puffed out. "That's most inconsiderate. I'm not even wearing walking shoes."

Jason glanced at Phyllis's feet. Truth was, she wasn't wearing anything that would be considered appropriate for Heath's Point, Texas. Not the short pencil skirt, the black halter, the sheer duster that covered both of them, nor the pointy-toed stilts she referred to as shoes.

"Here." Alynne withdrew her car keys from her purse. "We'll just drive over there."

"I'll go with you." And then follow her back to the inn.

Alynne struggled to keep her tone even. Phyllis had made one suggestion after another at the planning meeting. Most of them dealt with lighting and staging for photo ops and reporters.

Momma had paled more than once during the discussion. So much that Alynne had been about ready to belt her sister.

Thankfully, Cat had stepped in and pulled Momma away. With her gone, Alynne let Phyllis set up her little production with the director. As soon as she got Momma home, she'd call the director and cancel her sister's ridiculous plans.

And, though she couldn't admit it, Jason's presence at just this moment was incredibly soothing to her rankled nerves.

They paused at the corner while a compact crawled past. Though this was a highway, the road speed dwindled to an in-town limit.

He ushered them in front of him as they stepped into the roadway toward the downtown lot across the street. An engine roared from somewhere on her right.

"Go!" Jason yelled from behind her.

He shoved her forward, launching her into her sister, and they both tumbled onto the sidewalk on the other side of the road.

Phyllis screamed.

Pain shot across Alynne's injured shoulder. She looked back in time to see Jason leap onto the hood of a speeding black SUV, his back slamming against the glass with a crashing sound. Somehow, he hung onto the car and jammed the screwdriver through the glass on the passenger side. It stuck. For a moment, she thought he was going to hang onto it like a handle, but the car swerved.

He flew off into the other side of the intersection.

Alynne raced toward him as the car roared away. Phyllis followed her and stood guard in the middle of the street, stopping traffic while Alynne checked on Jason.

A man from the convenience store sprinted toward them. "I called 9-1-1."

Jason groaned.

"Don't move." She told him and put a hand on his back. She didn't see any blood, but he'd had a bad fall at the bare minimum.

"I'm all right." He went to his knees but laid flat again.

"EMTs are on their way." She put more pressure on his back hoping to get him to stay still.

"I know how to take a hit." He pushed up again. "I was a patrol officer in Chicago." He put his hand around the back of his neck. "We kept tallies of the number of cars who aimed at us." He chuckled.

Unbelievable. "You'll still need to get checked out." Surely, he wouldn't question that.

"Not necessary." He waved his hand, but he looked a little drunk.

"Danvers?" A lean officer dashed toward them.

"I'm okay." Jason waved his hand again.

"Good, but you're still getting a ride to the hospital." The officer put his hand on Jason's shoulder as he tried to rise.

"I don't need an ambulance, Evans."

"What happened?" The tall man in the cowboy hat, who had been at the inn talking with Jason the day before, rushed over.

"Chief." Evans tipped his head at the man.

Alynne stood and backed away. Phyllis put her arm around her sister's shoulders. "He'll be okay."

She nodded but felt some strange paralysis on her vocal cords.

The chief knelt and talked with Jason in low tones while a siren sounded. The high pitch cut off as an ambulance turned onto the highway and pulled ahead of where Jason was lying. Two EMTs climbed out both carrying a bag.

A tear slipped over Alynne's lashes and tracked down her cheek. This man hardly knew her. Why in the world would he risk his life for her?

"We need to go find Mother." Phyllis tugged her back toward the parking lot.

Momma needed her, but she had Cat right now. "You go." She held out her keys that had remained gripped in her hand. "I need to …" What? Stay? How could she explain her need to stay with this man?

Thankfully, Phyllis didn't insist on further explanation.

Alynne watched as the responders loaded Jason into the ambulance. Several officers had gathered, giving encouragement and laughing with their friend.

As the ambulance pulled away, she didn't know what to do next. She wanted to go to the hospital, but … she glanced into the lot. Phyllis was long gone. Probably already found Momma and was halfway to the inn.

The man in the hat approached her. "We haven't met, Miss Stone." He held out his hand. "I'm Chief Dell Tate."

She shook his hand. "How do you know who I am?" She'd only seen him as she looked down from the upper window.

"Detective Danvers, there…" He nodded at the departing vehicle. "He has excellent description skills. I coulda picked you out of a football stadium crowd." He smiled. "Can you tell me what happened?"

"He couldn't tell you?" Oh no. That wasn't a good sign.

"I want to hear your impression of what happened." He put his hand at her elbow. "Maybe I can give you a lift somewhere?"

"I'd like to go to the hospital, but my sister took my car." She looked around. The man had come from wherever the police station was further downtown. Not like he could easily give her a ride.

"I've got Jason's keys." He pointed her in the direction of Jason's Jeep.

Alynne glanced behind her, but no SUVs roared up the road.

"Frankly, Miss, we don't want you to be alone." He opened the passenger door. "I'd be obliged if you'd let me take you back to the inn."

"No, not the inn." She couldn't go back there, not knowing what was going on with Jason. "The hospital, please. I don't want to be trouble, but I …" How could she explain this? "He saved my life … again. I can't abandon him."

"He's got lots of friends. He won't be alone."

She shook her head. He didn't understand. "That's not the point."

"Okay, okay." He put up his hands and then started the engine. "If I take you to the hospital, do you promise to let me take you back to the inn?"

She cut her gaze in his direction. "I can't really promise that, Chief. Not until I know what's going on."

He heaved a sigh. "All right. I give. But I need to know what you saw. Everything you saw."

She recounted her view as best she could. She hadn't noticed even the impression of the driver behind the heavily shaded glass. She didn't think about the license plate, only knew it was an SUV and was black.

She remembered hearing an engine roar but couldn't even answer where the car had come from because she only saw it when Jason had been hit. She was able to tell him about the screwdriver.

"He marked the car." Well, yeah. "He almost went through the windshield. Of course, he marked the car."

"Glass can be fixed pretty quickly, but that screwdriver that went through would have punctured or at least scratched the dashboard."

He was right. Not something that could be easily repaired.

He voice-dialed his phone as he laid it on the dash. A woman's voice filled the car with a curt greeting.

"I'll be there in a bit, but I need an APB out on a black SUV with a broken windshield. Check for a separate hole on the passenger side, a small one. And scratches on the dashboard of any car that's been repaired anytime today."

The woman agreed and shared that Danvers had just arrived and was in with the doctor before she signed off.

Alynne's neck stiffened. How much farther did they have to go?

Alynne sat near the door that led back to the triage area and watched as Jason's friends came and went. A female officer had been in the waiting room when they'd arrived and stayed close to the chief. He even put his arm around her at one point.

Looked like the chief had a belle. Pretty one, too, about forty-five with a trim figure and darker skin that hinted of Hispanic heritage. Alynne spied on their interaction and facial expressions, analyzing everything she saw. Anything to keep her mind off Jason lying on the pavement after being struck by a car aiming for her.

The couple stood near the entrance, and each officer who entered went directly to them. The group swelled in size for only a few minutes before the shift change demanded others leave.

Looked like the chief's lady friend wasn't part of the working shift. Chief Tate clasped her hand and bent to whisper in her ear.

Alynne's pastime engaged her better than watching television, but her face heated when the woman looked up and spotted her stare. The woman's smile helped a little, but Alynne still felt rather foolish.

She approached and held out her hands as she came near. "My dear Miss Stone. Please accept my condolences on the death of your father."

How did she know who she was? Alynne summoned a faint smile. "Thank you." Should she recognize this woman?

"I'm Officer Estrella. Chief Tate pointed you out to me. Could I ask you a few questions while we're all waiting?"

That could distract her as well. "Sure." She followed the officer to a cushioned bench and sat on one end.

"Please think back over what happened today. Before you went into the funeral home, did you notice an SUV anywhere nearby?"

She'd expected to have to rehash the situation, but the woman's question surprised her. She stared at the corner of a coffee table and forced herself to recreate the morning. "I don't think so."

"What were you thinking about?"

This would be embarrassing. She glanced at the woman, hoping she'd misheard her question. "What was *I* thinking? How will that help matters?"

"I want to define your level of distraction. Going into a funeral home, you couldn't have been happy and relaxed, but it would help to discern whether you were reflective. In that case, you probably would have seen the car had it been there. Not so much if you were upset or irritated."

Okay, that made sense. "I was a little on the irritated side."

The officer smiled. "Well, at that time of day, here in Heath's Point, I'm believing that the traffic had not upset you." She chuckled.

Alynne joined her. "No, I was upset with my sister a little. And with the lady who has apparently been helping my mom. She decided to join us as we planned Pop's funeral. And mom rode with her. Then my sister came out at the last minute and took the last seat in the woman's truck."

Her irritation sounded ridiculous to her own ears. "I guess, I was just annoyed because I ended up having to drive to this terribly emotional situation by myself." A frustration, indeed, if she'd actually been emotional about it. Momma had been, but the loss of Pop hadn't really connected with Alynne yet. She knew it would at some point. Probably over and over again. "So, I'm not really sure if I would've noticed any big SUV."

"Okay, so what did you notice? Any other people around?"

Were there? "There were a couple of cars at the convenience store. Someone pumped gas into a truck." She shut her eyes and relived crossing the street alone after she'd parked her car in the lot. "It should've occurred to me to be aware of my surroundings. After all that has happened."

"That's all right. Just relax and let your mind wander back there." The officer's slight accent gave her voice a musical lilt. Very soothing.

There wasn't any traffic. Not really, except for the cars parked at the convenience store next to the repair shop. "I think there were three cars parked there: two sedans and a minivan."

"And the truck at the pump?"

"Yeah. I saw a little girl go in the side door of the minivan. Dark gray, the van, not the little girl."

"I figured that out."

"She had a bag, but I couldn't tell much more about her. Wearing a long-sleeved pink T-shirt and dark pants. Her dark hair was in a ponytail."

"See. You were paying better attention than you gave yourself credit for. What else?"

The van had driven away, but Alynne didn't have a view of the driver. No one else came out of the store. She kept her eyes closed and tried to visualize the scene again. "There might have been people sitting in one of the cars. I never saw them get out."

"How many people?"

"Hmm. Maybe two."

"Were they moving around in the car like kids or dogs or were they still?"

Alynne tried to picture the car with the shadows moving. Nah, that didn't seem right. "They were still, at least two people, but there could have been more. I didn't notice them getting out of the car, and they didn't drive off before I went inside."

"What kind of car?"

"It was hard to see, the bushes at the edge of the lot blocked part of it, but I think it was red. And the truck got in the way of the back of it." Unless it was a short car.

"Now think about when you were coming out. Did you exit with your mom and sister and Cat?"

Well, that part she remembered. "No. My sister had some strong opinions. Momma got upset, and Cat took her outside. We were about to go look for them when ..." She hesitated as the image of Jason flying through the air and landing in a heap on the asphalt jarred her. She opened her eyes. "Has there been any word yet?"

Officer Estrella shook her head. The chief stood behind her with his hand resting on her shoulder. How long had he been there? She took in the rest of the room. The other cops had left. Only an old man sat on a chair near the window.

Officer Estrella touched her hand. "So, you were looking around for your mom and Cat when you came out?"

"Yes, again there were people at the store. A couple of folks pumped gas."

"Any SUVs?"

Alynne hadn't noticed, and her head hurt, but she shut her eyes again to block out distraction and concentrated on the scene she'd experienced. "There was an old-fashioned Suburban over there, but it was cream-colored. The one that h-hit …" The terrifying image played again. Jason flying. The sunlight glaring off the back end of that shiny black vehicle … "Wait, there was something white or maybe silver on the back glass of that SUV." She described it as best she could, "Sort of oval, wider side to side. Everything had shined on the car."

"It was really clean?"

"I'd say so." Her own car rarely shined that much even after a wash, but then she didn't have the contrast of the black paint job in the sunlit glare. She opened her eyes.

Officer Estrella tapped something into her phone and then held it out for Alynne to see. A flat oval with a letter U in the center. "Was this what you saw?"

"It could have been." She'd been more focused on Jason than the car. "Maybe my sister got a glimpse of it."

"I'll check."

"What is that?"

Officer Estrella traded looks with the chief. He straightened. "Might be that your car was from Union Rental. If so, we should have a good chance of finding it and the person who rented it."

A woman in a white lab coat came through the triage doors at that point and headed for the chief. "You have a lucky boy, there, Dell."

"I know that. He gonna be okay then?"

"Okay and throwing a fit that he's here. I'm going to discharge him against my better judgment, but he's been pretty clear that he'll leave one way or the other."

"Sounds like Danvers." Chief Tate shook his head slightly. "What do we need to do?"

The doctor put her hand on the back of a cushioned chair and shifted her weight. "He needs watching. I don't trust that if he starts experiencing symptoms of concussion that he would come back in."

"Wise woman." Officer Estrella chuckled.

"I swear I tried to find something that would require him to stay, but I couldn't. No broken bones. No head wound that I can find. The worst he has is scrapes on his palms that require nothing more than a large bandage, not a hospital stay."

"No indication of a concussion?" Chief Tate furrowed his brows.

"Not that I can tell. I'll analyze the tests we did. I don't expect any complications unless he starts exhibiting signs of one like a growing headache, vomiting, dizziness, or ringing in his ears."

Officer Estrella looked up at the chief. "We'll need to find some people who can keep an eye on him through the night." The doctor smiled and went back into the triage unit.

The chief nodded in Alynne's direction. "We'll need to put a solid guard on you as well."

That would put a strain on any department. "What if you did two at a time?"

The two older people stared at her.

"One officer could guard us both outside Jason's home, and I could keep an eye on him." That would certainly solve the problem, yet as she spoke the words, she realized how ludicrous they sounded. She barely knew Jason. He might have a girlfriend who would be decidedly opposed to such a setup. "Unless he's got family or other close friends around."

"He's got a lot of friends…" At least, Officer Estrella hadn't given her a suspicious look. "But few that could stay the night with him. What about your mom?"

"The whole family's with her. Both of her sisters and Phyllis, that's my sister." She'd be fine. "And the visitation isn't until tomorrow night."

"Not gonna lie, Dell." Officer Estrella looked up at him again. "I like the idea of no one knowing where she is for the night. Gives us a chance to watch those who might be trying to spy on the house or search for her."

"Can you turn your phone off and keep it off?" Chief Tate furrowed his eyebrows in her direction. "I'll let Myra know you're all right, and you speak to no one for the night."

Wait, what had she gotten herself into? She couldn't spend an entire night in Jason's home. She was an engaged woman. Even if Blayne was really beginning to irritate her, she couldn't just ignore the fact that she'd made a commitment to covenant with him.

But then, Jason was in this situation because of her. "Yes. I can keep it off. If you'll let Momma know I'm all right. And she can tell the family?"

"Only that you're all right. Nothing more." The chief tugged on one ear lobe and glanced at the other officer.

She nodded. "Miss Stone, why don't you go in and see him while the chief and I get his paperwork in order. Then we'll pull his Jeep around to the loading area."

The chief stepped over to collect his cowboy hat from where it rested upside down on a table near the door. "Sounds like a plan."

Officer Estrella smiled at her once more. "You did very well. Gave us some details to track down. We will find out who hurt Jason. Of that, you can be sure." She winked and followed her boss to the discharge desk.

Chapter Fifteen

Jason felt, rather than heard, a presence enter his room. He cracked open one eye and felt an immediate stab of pain as the bright lights assaulted his vision. But he pasted a pleasant look on his face and greeted the beautiful woman.

"Hey, Alynne. Glad to see you're all right." Though in his estimation, she looked paler than she should.

"And I'm glad to see you are." She stepped fully into the room and let the door slowly swing closed.

"I suppose Dell gave you the third degree?"

She moved to the side of his bed. "It wasn't so bad, though I don't know that I was able to help very much." She picked up his empty cup and began refilling it with ice chips from the pitcher beside it. "Your chief and Officer Estrella will come visit in a short while. They're taking care of your account here and bringing your car around."

They were going to let him drive? He hadn't expected that, but he could probably swing it if he went slow. Especially if no one used their bright lights in his direction. "What's Dell saying about all of this."

"Nothing besides the fact that you need someone to keep an eye on you tonight."

"I need someone? That's ridiculous. You're the one in danger. Does he have any plan about keeping you safe?" If he didn't, Jason could just as easily sit in his Jeep in the inn's parking lot as he could sit on his couch at his apartment.

"Actually, he's killing two birds with one stone, though that probably isn't an appropriate metaphor for this situation." She cracked a smile that lit up her whole face.

He chuckled, but it hurt too much for him to fully engage. "So, you're the Stone he's using?" Was she beginning to blush?

She fingered the side rail of his bed. "Your chief would like for me to be out of the way tonight. Give them a chance to watch those who might be looking for me. So, I volunteered to keep an eye on you."

Both of his eyes flew open causing instant regret, but he pushed through the pain. "You did what?"

She bit her lower lip and looked to one side for a moment. "The department didn't have enough people to guard me *and* watch over you."

"I don't need watching."

"The doctor says you do." She leaned over the side rail with a fierce expression. "I haven't known you that long, but I've noticed your flinching and squinting. You've got a headache, don't you?"

So much for trying to cover up his pain. "The doc gave me pain meds, but they haven't kicked in yet."

"If they don't take away your headache, you need to come right back here."

"Is that what you're supposed to do, be my headache police?" The conversation was wearying.

"Something like that." She lifted her chin. "And while I'm keeping an eye on you, there'll be an officer outside your apartment guarding me. Bird number two."

The nurse breezed in with a form for him to sign. She spouted all sorts of "watch out fors" that he didn't pay attention to. Alynne looked like she was hanging on every word and even asked a couple of questions. Jason just wanted to get home. The nurse was leaving when Dell came back in, followed by Juanita Estrella.

"Looks like you're all set to go." Dell's booming voice should be outlawed within the echoing walls of a hospital.

"Yeah." He watched the women duck out the door and pushed off the bed in search of his clothes. His head spun, but only for a second before settling, though it screamed its disapproval. "You tell Alynne to stay at my place tonight?"

"Technically, it was her idea, but yeah. We'd be hard-pressed to find others who could stay with you while we're also guarding her and doing regular patrols."

"That's what she said." He tucked the front of his shirt into his jeans. "You know she's engaged." Or did Dell know that?

The big man shrugged. "This ain't no romantic liaison, Danvers. You're hurt. We're down a man. And we're stretched past our abilities. This will allow us to do everything that must be done and let tomorrow's shift get a few hours' sleep. Simple as that."

"Not sure I like it." That wasn't true of course. He was beginning to enjoy Alynne's company. Probably more than he should. But he didn't want to see the possibilities of her future be destroyed over some non-existent scandal.

"Not sure I care." Dell smirked at him. "Oh, but ..." He handed Jason his cowboy hat. "This thing probably saved your skull."

Not hardly. He'd lost it when he pushed the women to the other side of the street, but contemplating a debate with Dell, even over something stupid, made his head hurt worse. He laid the hat gingerly on his hair. His head already felt like a C-clamp tightened over it. The last thing he needed was another tight thing pressing on his brain.

He followed Dell into the hallway where the chief handed the keys to his Jeep over to Alynne.

"You sure you want to do this?" He gave her a sidelong look. Blayne was likely to throw a fit when he found out. And Jason had already seen hints of how self-absorbed and unfeeling Blayne could be when it came to Alynne.

"Absolutely." She had an expression of all business. "This is best for everyone. And I'm not sorry to keep any potential danger away from my mom and family. If I'm not at the inn, there's no good reason for crazy drivers, gunfire, or muggings."

Yep, she'd been through a lot in less than a week.

The nurse brought over a wheelchair and began fussing that he couldn't walk out under his own power. He looked at the ceiling and sat, pulling his boots onto the footrests. "This is humiliating."

"Ha." The chief had no mercy and his laughter boomed as loud as his greeting. "Serves you right for playing in the middle of a busy street. What were you thinking?"

Jason didn't even try to answer but shook his head slightly. Once the pounding slowed its tempo, he'd be able to think of clever comebacks again.

Alynne didn't talk much as she drove Jason through town. Dell had given her Jason's apartment address with instructions to go directly there. When her stomach growl filled the interior of the Jeep, she altered course to a drive-thru on the highway and ordered a submarine sandwich. Jason would need to eat, too.

When they got it to his apartment, though, he wasn't interested in eating. She persuaded him to take his medicine but convincing him to go to bed was out of the question. He insisted that he was fine and had work to do.

She turned on the Texas Rangers baseball game and lured him to the couch. Once there and partly relaxed, he finished off his half of the sandwich. Then she propped a pillow on one side of him. By the time she'd finished her part of the sandwich, he'd fallen asleep.

She turned the volume down. No reason to wake him at this point. He didn't need to take another dose of meds for four hours. Going into his bedroom, she dragged the man's comforter into the living room and gently covered him with it. Though it wasn't terribly cool, there was a slight chill to the air, even this late in the spring.

He almost looked boyish lying there, with a sandy fringe of

lashes on his closed eyes and his relaxed jaw. *God, please bless this man. Pour out Your blessings on him, Your servant, and reward him for the good that he does for Your loved ones.* She wasn't talking about herself, more about her mom. Jason had been such a help to her since Pop had passed. Momma brightened every time she saw him.

It would completely crush Momma to have seen that horrible moment when the car struck him. She shut her eyes against the image in her mind. It would revisit her tonight, she was sure. *Thank You for protecting him.*

She couldn't have meant the gratitude more if the man had been a member of her own family. He'd saved her life twice now. At least two times that she knew about. And he'd put his own life in danger to do so. What kind of man does that for someone he barely knows?

Would Blayne have done that for a stranger? She wasn't even sure Blayne would do such for her. She didn't like to contemplate it and even less to judge, but she needed to analyze Blayne. If she was serious about marrying him, she needed to be sure she loved him.

But no, Blayne had trouble letting cars into his lane when they'd found themselves stuck behind a stalled vehicle. Self-abandonment wasn't his style, especially not if there was a chance of pain in the action.

No way Blayne would have put himself in harm's way had he been in Jason's position. How could she marry a man who clearly loved himself more than anything else? A man who still hadn't explained who he worked for or what he did beyond something in sales. And who never spoke of his past or his family. How could she marry him?

But considering her past weakness, how could she not?

She took an afghan from the recliner and curled up on the love seat, determined not to look at Jason again except when she had to awaken him to take his medication.

Jason slept hard and woke up sore sometime in the wee hours of the morning. Sleeping on the couch hadn't helped since he didn't fit on it by a good half-foot. He rolled off soundlessly and made his way to his bed to get a few more hours of sleep before dawn.

When it finally did arrive, he felt more like himself. His disorientation was gone and so was his headache. A hot shower helped the pain in his back and neck. Halfway through it, he remembered about Alynne. He tugged on some jeans and a HPPD T-shirt.

He'd not heard a sound from the front room, so he quietly edged open his bedroom door. Alynne lay curled up on the love seat, wearing his Dallas Cowboys hoodie and wrapped in an afghan. Poor thing. He hadn't even been conscious enough to turn up his heat. Spring temperatures hopped all over the place in May, and there was a definite chill in the air this morning.

Making every effort to help her stay asleep, he went into the kitchen and made a pot of coffee. The refrigerator was pretty bare. A leftover baked potato from a barbecue place on the freeway, a half-eaten bowl of cereal that looked more like cat kibble, and a dried-up orange. Well, there was a jar of Mrs. Paulson's berry preserves on the door rack. Mrs. Paulson usually brought him a new jar every month—blueberry, strawberry, this time a jar of blackberry. Delicious.

He pulled it out and moved to his cabinet, withdrawing a loaf of bread and his jar of peanut butter. Not a breakfast of champions, but unless he was blessed to be near the inn, it was his normal fare in the morning.

With the coffee brewed and several slices of toast with PB&J already slathered on them, Jason returned to the living room to awaken Alynne. She'd beaten him to it and was just pushing herself from the pillow on his couch.

"Oh, I didn't hear you get up." She rose with a pained expression. "Do you need anything. Are you feeling okay?"

"Not gonna lie. My back and neck are both pretty sore. I'm gonna assume they were just stretched wrong for a few days before I talk to any doctor, though."

"Stubborn." She folded the afghan and grimaced. "But I'm glad you're fine."

"Looks like you're in a little pain." As much as he wanted to check on her shoulder, he leaned against the doorframe, keeping his distance from the beautiful and very engaged woman.

She lowered herself back onto the seat with care. "I knew I had fallen on my injured arm. I hadn't realized that I'd fallen so hard."

"Lemme guess. You didn't have a doctor look at it yesterday."

She gingerly rubbed her arm and shrugged.

"And you're calling me stubborn." He shook his head. "Maybe I should take a look to make sure the bleeding hasn't started up again."

"I already checked. It's okay, only sore." She slowly stood again. "Like the rest of me." She straightened. "Wow, really stiff."

He knew the feeling. "I've got coffee and some peanut butter and jelly toast until we can get to a real breakfast at your mom's."

"Peanut butter on toast?" She tilted her head and ruffled her delicate eyebrows.

"Of course. Was my go-to before every game. Sorta like a peanut butter and jelly sandwich with a crunch."

"Football?"

He'd played football, but not for long. Didn't want to ruin his knees for his real sport. "Nah. Baseball. I even got a scholarship to OU, but once I graduated, I had my heart set on law enforcement." Why was he spilling his life story? All she'd asked was what sport he'd played. "And I'll tell you, the protein and carbs are a great balance in peanut butter toast. I started adding the jelly when Mrs. Paulson started bringing me monthly jars."

"Wait, a little old lady here in town brings you jam every month? That's so sweet."

He'd hardly call Mrs. Paulson a little old lady. A widow and only a few years older than him, she wore leather and rode out to her job at the aluminum factory on a Harley. "She's ... yeah, *sweet* works." And had been trying to get romantic attention from him since he'd arrived in Heath's Point. "And she makes great preserves."

"Um. Dish-is-de-icious." She held a hand over her mouth as

she chewed.

Jason drank a cup of coffee and ate a couple of pieces of toast while she finished hers. But having finished the prelude to their real breakfast, he grabbed his keys from the coffee table and opened the front door. "You ready to get back?"

She followed him into the room. "Yes, but …"

As he opened the front door, she snatched the keys from his hand. "I'm not ready to let you drive." She stepped onto the second-floor walkway.

Great. This wasn't a fight he wanted to have. He reached back to lock his door.

"Oh." A new voice, a very familiar one. "Hi. You're a friend of Jason's?"

Of all the times they could have left, they'd chosen this one. He stepped out the door. "Hi, Donna." Donna Culver was high on the Heath's Point rumor tree, working at her mom's hair salon since she was in high school and getting the skinny from Mrs. Hawkins, their 9-1-1 dispatcher, almost daily. She and Cat had been besties for years, but Cat didn't go in much for the gossip mill.

Alynne's face was a bright shade of pink. "He was in a car accident yesterday … the chief, he asked me to stay with him last night." The pink shade darkened.

"They thought I had a concussion. Doc said someone needed to be on watch, give me meds, you know what I mean." If only Donna would lower her eyebrow and wipe that knowing look off her face.

"A concussion. Can't play around with that." Clearly, the

woman didn't believe them. Or at least, she didn't look like she believed them.

"He was hit by a car."

"Was you hurted, Uncle Jason?" Molly, Donna's four-year-old daughter wandered out of her apartment, dragging a Snoopy backpack.

He squatted in front of Molly as her mom trotted down the breezeway to close their door. "I'm just a little sore. But cars aren't something to mess around with, right?"

"Look both ways." The angel with the dark, curly pigtails tilted her head looking to the right and then to the left. "And hold mommy's hand." Her mom rejoined her, and Molly exampled her statement.

"I'm Donna Culver." She reached to shake Alynne's hand.

Jason stood there helpless as Alynne continued to redden and give Donna more fodder to share around town. Her name. How she was helping her mom with her dad's funeral. How she wasn't the only daughter, but her sister wasn't very close to their mom.

At that point, Jason could see embarrassment was causing her to ramble. "I'm sure you and Molly are on your way somewhere?"

"I was going to take her to Whataburger for some pancakes before we head over to the Beauty Barn." She glanced at Alynne. "That's the downtown hair salon."

"Oh, you're a stylist?" Alynne put on a smile and an interested look.

Donna just nodded instead of telling the long story. Seems both he and Alynne could take lessons from her on how to keep from pouring out the novel versions of the details of their lives.

She led her daughter downstairs. Jason traded a look with Alynne and lifted his shoulders. They had nothing to be ashamed of, but the story of her coming out of his apartment so early, having spent the night there, was bound to be all over town before lunchtime.

Chapter Sixteen

Alynne tugged her phone from her purse as Jason rounded the car to the passenger side. She'd kept it off as instructed but turned it back on now, wondering what types of messages she had.

If the reaction from that perfect stranger was any indication, Alynne was in trouble when she got back to the inn.

To think there'd been anything going on was ridiculous, but it wasn't going to be easy to persuade anyone who wanted to believe otherwise. She'd already heard about the way folks in this town had been trying to set Jason up with different ladies, Momma and Pop included.

She started the engine and followed Jason's directions out of town. He probably could have driven, but she wanted to be sure he was fully recovered before putting her life in his hands.

Shields up. She thought of the way Pop had talked about visiting Grandma Klein who had suffered from dementia before she died. After driving to southern Kansas and praying most of the way there, Pop said they would agree to keep their shields up just like the captain's orders in *Star Trek* and put Alynne and Phyllis in front of them as they arrived.

She felt something of the same heading back to her family, especially Phyllis. As she pulled into the lot, she sent up a prayer for understanding and peace.

"You ready to face the dragon?" Jason gave her a sheepish smile.

"Dragon? Who's the dragon?" She couldn't help the raised tone in her voice.

"Not who, what. It's going to take some patience to keep peace and balance when people are going to make bad assumptions and even make insinuations."

His pep talk wasn't helping.

"Look…" He turned in his seat to face her. "You and I both know that nothing inappropriate happened last night. Heck, I barely even remember getting to my room, let alone crawling into bed."

"You didn't. You fell asleep on the couch in front of the baseball game after you finished eating."

His eyebrows ruffled. "What did I eat?"

"A six-inch Subway Italian sandwich." She glanced at him. "Does that stir up any memories?"

"Not at all." He laid his hand on the dash. "Then how did I get into my room?"

"I think you moved there after I gave you your meds at three o'clock." She looked in the rearview mirror and noticed an HPPD cruiser had pulled into the lot behind them. She hadn't even seen him following.

"I don't even remember taking them."

He'd been pretty out of it. "I guess there's no use hoping that my family won't assume the worst?" She shut off the engine.

"Those who know you, who really care about you, will know better. Your mom and your aunts. Your sister. And, of course, your fiancé." He fingered the latch and pushed the door open. "See if I'm not right."

She opened her door and stepped out, catching his eye over the hood of the Jeep. "You really believe that?"

"Your family cares about you, Alynne. Those who want to believe the worst about people will. But your family won't want to assume such because they love you."

For a man who was a little on the quiet side, he certainly knew how to convey truth. She clamped her jaw tight. The way he said the word *love* ignited sparks she shouldn't be feeling. Or maybe she should? She had barely given Blayne a thought last night and not at all this morning until just now. Pulling her phone from her purse she glanced at the messages as she followed Jason toward the house.

Momma had sent a note urging her to be careful, but that was the only message. Really? Not even a *where are you* or a *goodnight* from her fiancé? She tucked her phone into the pocket of the pants she'd put on the morning before and trotted up the light blue steps to the matching porch. Maybe Blayne hadn't thought about her either, and she wouldn't hear anything about last night at all?

Jason opened the door for her and let her go in first. A hum of conversations drifted down from above. Jason closed the door behind them and hung his hat on the rack. "I guess they've already started breakfast."

She glanced at her watch. It was a little later than she thought. "Probably." She led the way up the main staircase and along the balcony until they entered the dining hall. Sure enough, the family had assembled, having shoved the tables together to make one long enough to seat them all.

"Good morning, sweet girl." Momma left her seat at one end and came around to embrace her. "I'm so glad you were all right last night." After she hugged Alynne, she moved her attention to the man beside her.

"We're both fine," Jason assured her, bending over a bit to receive her embrace.

"I'm so grateful you were there for my girl." Momma stepped back grinning. "For both of them." She claimed Jason's arm and tugged him to a few open chairs near hers. "I hope you're hungry."

He glanced back at Alynne. "Starved."

"Me, too." She took in the room. Blayne didn't seem to be there. "Have you seen Blayne?" She sat in the chair next to Jason, across from her mom.

"Not this morning." Momma filled Alynne's mug with coffee from a carafe then leaned over to fill Jason's.

Alynne took a sip of her coffee. Jason's hadn't been bad by any means, but Momma made the best coffee. The perfect balance of bitterness and acidity. She let it ease down her throat.

"And he didn't come in for dinner last night." Momma set a plate with eggs, bacon, and a Belgium waffle in front of her and another in front of Jason. "I knocked on his door, but he didn't answer."

Little alarms rang in the back of Alynne's head. "You haven't seen him at all?" She rose and moved to the east-facing windows that showed the gravel lot in front of the house. Blayne's car wasn't there. She hadn't even noticed. "Has he been gone all night?" She pulled out her phone and dialed his number, but it went straight to voice mail.

"You seem anxious?" Pop's cousin, Ronald, was nearby, refilling his empty plate with grits and sprinkling them with sugar.

"Oh," Alynne responded, turning toward the heated buffet and pasting a pleasant look on her face. "It's nothing. I was just wondering where my ... uh, boyfriend might be."

She glanced at her mom. The words fiancé and engagement hadn't been used around her to Alynne's knowledge, and with all that was going on, she didn't want to add anything to Momma's brain right now. Enough emotional turmoil was going.

"I might have seen him yesterday morning." He rubbed his left eye. "Sheila and I were reading on the porch for several hours after breakfast. We came in about the time your mother and your sister returned from town." He stabbed at a sausage link with a skewer and his left eye twitched. "The temperature was rising about then, you know."

"Did he say anything to you?" Like where he might have been going?

Setting the utensil down, he rubbed his eye again. Must've had some type of allergy. "No. He seemed to be on-task and focused. I don't often engage perfect strangers anyway, but especially not when they have a fiercely determined look about them."

She murmured a thanks as he strode back to the table and took his seat next to his wife.

Alynne picked up her napkin from her chair and reseated herself.

Momma had a kind look on her face. "Sweet girl, I know you're concerned about him, but maybe this is all a bit much for your boyfriend. I mean, the seriousness of the situation, the crowded circumstances, and a big, noisy family to boot."

On cue, one of her cousins gave a punchline that had the other half of the table erupting in laughter.

"You think he just needed some time away?" That seemed plausible, but wouldn't he tell her about it or at least send a text to check on her?

"He's a young, independent man. Men don't think about sharing their plans or schedules with the women in their lives. Wouldn't you agree, Jason?" Momma draped her napkin in her lap then took a bite of waffle.

"Oh, no." He shook his head. "I'm not getting into this."

From what she'd noticed, Jason was rather particular about when he spoke and what he said.

"I'm sorry. I forgot that you haven't really had a woman in your life, not recently anyway." Momma showed her mischievous twinkle.

Jason looked from the ceiling to Momma. "I've had women in my life. You know that. But I have learned to avoid flat-out disagreeing with you, Myra."

"That's right. Memory lets me down sometimes." She wasn't fooling Alynne, and from the look of his face, she wasn't fooling Jason either.

But her words stimulated Alynne's curiosity. *So, who were the women he'd had in his life?*

"So, you disagree?" Momma continued.

He clamped his mouth shut for a moment and glanced down the length of the table. "I don't mind sharing my schedule or plans with someone I want to spend my time with."

A judicious answer. But Alynne's mind kept turning back to him having women in his life.

Momma pushed again. "I would so like to see that happen, Jason. I have a friend whose daughter is a teacher in Dallas."

He had focused on the food on his plate, and the hum of the room subsided as the family moved downstairs and out of the house.

The awkward silence begged her to come to the man's rescue. "Great pancakes, Momma."

"Thank you, dear, but it's really Billie and Bobbie who should be thanked. They've done the lion's share of the work since they arrived." Momma proceeded to share the details of all that Alynne's aunts had done.

Jason shot her a grateful gaze and the semblance of a smile.

"I think your gentleman friend is back, Alynne." Ronald had moved back to the hot bin for yet another sausage link. He strolled across the room to where his wife stood near the kitchen stairs. "If he drives a gray Lexus."

"Gray Lexus. That's Blayne."

Sheila took his hand. "If you need us, we'll be at the lake."

Jason turned back to his plate, swiped a bite of waffle around in the syrup, and shoved it into his mouth. Alynne noted the tightening around his jawline. "As usual, Myra, delicious." He stood, taking his plate and coffee cup with him. "I'll drop these off in the kitchen on my way out."

"Wait a minute." Alynne put her fork down. He couldn't drive off like that.

"Are you sure you're up to driving, Jason?" Momma half rose.

"I'm still a little sore, but we do have a case to solve." He hesitated.

Alynne moved to stand in front of him. "You need to let your body heal. You could've died yesterday."

He lowered his voice and stared hard into her eyes. "That may be, but it wasn't me someone was trying to kill. You seem to have a target on your back, and I'm not relaxing until I find a way to remove it."

Her gaze was riveted to his. A fierceness poured out from him—determination, dedication, passion. He held her gaze for a prolonged moment before dropping his for a second. Was he looking at her lips? Then he turned away and left through the back stairs to the kitchen.

Alynne's heart pounded with every boot step, leaving her breathing hard. She closed her mouth and swallowed, returning to her place at the table.

Momma eyed her as Alynne toyed with her food. What she'd eaten already seemed to harden in her stomach. Then Momma's eyes lifted beyond her. "Blayne, dear. Come and have some breakfast."

"Is everyone gone?"

Alynne twisted in her chair as Blayne glanced to the left and right.

"There seemed to be a great exodus out the front doors. No wonder this room is so empty." He sat beside Alynne as Aunt Billie picked up the empty plates from in front of them.

She coughed and took a sip of water.

"Are you hungry?" Momma had hopped up and was loading up a plate for him.

"Not really. I had a business meeting." He lifted an eyebrow as Momma laid the plate in front of him, but he smiled and thanked her. Did he know nothing of what happened yesterday?

Alynne had no hint of recollection about a business meeting. But questioning him about it in front of Momma wasn't the best idea. Alynne always tensed when the two of them got around each other anyway, sure that he would say something at some point about their engagement or intent to elope or worse.

Aunt Billie returned to the table. "You should see those kids. I wonder that you'll have any grass left, Myra."

Blayne looked up with a quizzical look.

"The treasure, remember?" Alynne stood and wandered to the windows. Wyatt's kids were organizing all of the others and passing out shovels, garden trowels, and hoes.

"I remember hearing something about that." Blayne picked at his food while Aunt Billie recanted what she'd shared a couple of nights before.

"You really believe there's a treasure buried here?" Blayne's blue eyes sparkled at Momma as he asked.

"Ellis sure did."

"And the only thing you know is that it's buried somewhere

on the property? This is a big place." He shrugged. "Why even try?"

Momma smiled. "Because of the adventure of the hunt. Have you forgotten what it's like to be a little boy?" She took a sip from her water glass. "Ellis actually said there were directions to the site somewhere."

"Like a map?"

"No, I think just a description of what was buried and where it was put, but Ellis mentioned it more than once. He didn't spend time looking for it. Said he'd wait until things around the house were finished." She chuckled. "But he always had another dream for this place."

"Pop was like that." Alynne took after him. She had kept thinking she'd end up spending time with him and Momma when her job settled down and her relationship was more established. It was pure procrastination.

Yes, she'd resented their move. She and Momma had become so close during her recovery from the cancer treatments. And then, after she had finally won the battle, they left. Sure, Alynne had gone to school, but she'd chosen a local one, expecting to come home on weekends.

Seeing this place, though, the beauty and the tender care they'd put into it, she'd been so wrong in staying away. She was the one who had been hurt by her actions, and now she could never make it up to Pop.

She could, however, make it up to her mom.

Momma picked up the plate of food that Blayne had toyed with. Alynne followed suit, collecting a few of the empties that the kids had left behind and transporting them to the bin on the dumb waiter.

Blayne caught her hand on the way back to the table. "Feel like taking a walk?"

She still needed to tell him what had happened yesterday. Letting him hear rumors that she'd spent the night at Jason's apartment would make her look even guiltier than she already felt. "Sure, but let's clean up first."

He lowered his tone. "Your mom and your aunts can do that." He lifted his hand in their direction. "They already are. And, frankly, they need something to take up their time. What else would they do?"

What was that supposed to mean? Clearly, Momma and Pop hadn't sat around for the last ten years.

Momma carried another small load to the dumbwaiter. "It's a lovely day, Alynne. Why don't the two of you enjoy it? Sisters and I will tend to this."

Blayne smirked.

Alynne sighed. "I'll be back to help with dinner."

"No worries." Momma waved at her.

She left the dish she held on the table and let Blayne draw her out down the main stairs and out the front door. Kids were shouting and squealing. And Rose bounded across the parking lot from a group using garden spades on the far side of the south wing all the way to the forest on the north side where two of the boys wielded actual shovels. This place was going to be so pockmarked by the time the family left, but what great memories they would have.

Jason's Jeep sat at the edge of the lot, near the cruiser that had followed them. Looked like they were chatting. Then the cruiser pulled out of the gate. Alynne lifted her gaze to the cloudless sky. The man clearly didn't know the meaning of rest or recuperation.

"I bet you did this with your dad." Blayne's voice shook her back to his presence. His gaze traveled all across the front of the property. Then he steered her to the left, turning around the porch wrap.

"Yes, several times we came to visit Uncle Todd. He would fill our heads with his treasure talk."

"Did he look for the treasure, too?" Blayne laced his fingers through hers as they wandered down the hill toward the lake.

"Momma said he used to, but I never noticed. I think he viewed it like Santa Claus. A fun story for the kids." Blayne's hand felt warm in hers, but it held none of the spark that they had enjoyed before this trip. "Pop always had a place to search and a reason to search there."

"Like where?" Blayne hesitated then veered toward the barn. He reached up and tucked a stray hair behind Alynne's ear.

Her breath quickened, but knots formed in her stomach. They really needed to talk. She'd already determined that she had no business eloping with Blayne. But she'd keep things light for the time being. "See that big cottonwood over there? We dug all the way around it on one summer trip. Uncle Todd kept fussing that we would ruin the roots, but I don't see that we affected it much."

Blayne chuckled and stroked her hand with his free one.

She was a skunk. Clearly, he adored her. But she was all twisted up with doubts.

"Then one weekend, we dug around the old well-house." She

pointed toward the barn. "On the other side of the barn."

A couple of kids were running toward Momma's herb garden on the west-facing hill behind the kitchen door. "Hang on, y'all. It won't be in either of the gardens or on the fence line where the roses are. They were all dug up when they were originally planted by Uncle Todd."

The kids halted and looked at each other, though Alynne couldn't hear what they were saying. One pointed toward the barn, and they both took off, going around the backside of the big, red structure.

"Hope they don't find a bunch of poison ivy back there." She and Pop had sure gotten a bad case when they'd dug around the well-house.

"So, you dug there and by that tree, and then the gardens have been dug. Anywhere else?"

His eyes had a sparkle to them. His fondness for her was clear, but she found it more and more difficult to face him. She shook her head.

"And the Stone property goes all the way up to the camp on the other side of the cove?" He tugged her toward the field beyond the barn.

This was going to be a long walk.

BREAKING POINT

Chapter Seventeen

The last thing Jason needed was to sit around watching Alynne and her boyfriend. He watched them head for the back of the Victorian. Several minutes later, they strolled around the newest wing and headed for the south path that paralleled the county road. Rose had joined them for a moment but then came bolting around the front of the house yapping at the groups as she passed them.

He could take a lesson from that dog and keep his eyes open to everything around Alynne instead of on her. She wasn't alone, and he could view the entire area better from where he was. Besides, he'd sent Evans to the scout camp and back to do more recon. He would be able to see the couple as he traveled along the road.

She was fine. Completely protected. Didn't need him. And his headache was coming back. He needed more rest. Yet he couldn't force himself to leave. Something in his gut demanded he remain.

He was really beginning to dislike that Blayne guy. Nah, he'd already arrived there. *Lord, please let Alynne realize that man's true character before she makes a stupid, lifelong mistake.* Not that marriage was lifelong anymore, but for someone like Alynne, he felt it would be.

Rose yapped at something. He looked up and found her about thirty yards north of the house, propped up against the trunk of a dead tree and barking her head off. Something flashed as the breeze rustled the leaves. Was there someone over there?

He glanced toward the polished log cabin that the trees almost hid. The Kennedale Ranch bordered the Stone's property, though he'd never known anyone to live there and there wasn't any cleared land for cattle. It was a beautiful house though.

Had someone moved in?

Rose still threw a fit. He could see the squirrel just a few feet above her chattering away. But nothing shiny. He climbed out of the Jeep and took a step toward the pair. Wait, was that …?

The squirrel scampered up the tree and Rose bolted back to him. He scratched her ears. "Good girl, Rose." He picked up his phone and called Evans to come back into the lot. Then he dialed the chief.

Ten minutes passed before the first cruiser crawled past the gate—no lights or sirens this time. He'd slowly walked down the hill toward what appeared to be a vehicle, black or some dark color that didn't show up in the shadows and covered with brush. Purposely covered with brush, for that matter. Someone had taken great pains to hide it.

"You touch anything?" Tate had parked in the short drive of the Ranch.

"Only my phone." He scratched Rose. "And the dog."

A photographer passed them and began collecting photos of the scene as it was found while a couple of other officers stood back waiting for her to finish.

"You think it's the car that ran you down?" Dell joined him.

"We'll know in a minute." Jason knew it was. His gut told him so. But why would it be stowed here?

The photographer finished her initial work and stepped aside while the officers began to uncover the car with a few calls of *clear* that started the process. The SUV hatch was closest to him and he crossed closer.

"Notice that?" Dell pointed to the rental sticker on the back window. "Alynne described that sticker on the SUV that struck you. I'll get Juanita to start searching recent rentals for a familiar name."

"Just what do you all think you're doing?" Sheriff Kindrich speed-walked the path while his much shorter deputy, Cain, followed.

Dell put his phone back into his pocket. "Why good morning to you, Beauregard." He touched the front of his hat. "Been listening to our radio bans again?"

"This is a county matter, and your officers are disturbing the scene of a crime."

Jason wanted to laugh out loud, probably from the tension he'd been storing up. But Dell was right about keeping on as good a side as possible with the county people. "Who said anything about a crime?"

"There's a body in that vehicle. Don't say there isn't." The man straightened and put his hands on his hips like he was daring them to deny it.

Was he kidding? Had he actually been told that by someone?

The sheriff must've read the surprise on Jason's face. He stepped back and loosened his stance a bit. "At least, that's the skinny that I've learned." He glanced at Cain.

Uh-oh. Jason could see the whole scene that played out. Cain had picked up their dispatch and assumed there had been some sort of crime like auto theft or murder to draw Kindrich in.

"Boys, any sign of a body in that SUV?" The chief didn't lift his eyes from Kindrich's face, though the sheriff had trouble keeping his gaze steady.

"No, chief. Busted windshield," Billings called from the other side.

Now that was information that Jason wanted, but he wasn't about to show any interest until the county people had left.

"I'm pleased to say that you were misinformed, Beau. Now I know we're standing feet from the city limits, but since this is part of the land that belongs to the Kennedale place and the house is clearly on city property, we've always taken care of the woods as well, for fires and things like that. If you want to add the possibility of a dumped vehicle and perhaps a simple trespass to your repertoire, we'll step aside and let the county take care of the woods from here on out."

The sheriff glared at the chief with one eye a slit and the other eyebrow arched and ruffled like an angry cat. "I want to know about anything you learn." He turned and marched back up the trail.

Cain remained. "Some woman made a claim about our

department. Said she'd witnessed a deputy kicking at the headlights of a motorist. You wouldn't know anything about that, would you, Danvers?"

The chief rocked back on his heels, his gaze shifting from Jason to Cain and back again. Jason had always believed Cain to be a competent officer, but now he wasn't so sure, bringing this up in front of a witness like Dell. "That's interesting. Someone stopped me when I was fixing those brake lights you helped me realize where broken. She and her kids described what you were doing to my car quite well. I wonder if it's the same lady."

"You set me up." He practically spat the words.

"And how did I do that? By driving on a road between Lake Grayson and Heath's Point? Or was it by pulling over when you came up behind me with your lights flashing? Maybe when I stood by while you kicked out the taillights and tried to do the same to the headlights?"

"That's enough, boy." Dell's growl silenced Jason. Good timing. Recounting his experience with Cain was ticking him off something fierce.

Dell turned to Cain and reached over to straighten his collar. "Seems to me you would be wise to let whatever you have against Lieutenant Danvers drop. Completely." Then his hand curled around the edge of the collar and pulled Cain a little closer, lowering his voice. "But I don't expect you to be wise. So, I'm warning you. Once. You like your job? You like life on this side of the bars? Leave. It. Be." He straightened the collar once again and pierced the man with a wicked stare while half a smile grew across his face. "We good?"

Cain, to his credit, gave the chief respect. Maybe he wasn't as stupid as he'd seemed to be. He nodded at the chief then nodded at Jason. Didn't even have the challenge in his eyes that he usually had around him. He turned and followed his boss's path.

"He expected to get your job." Dell continued to watch the retreating figure. "Was pretty ruffled that I had the gall to hire an outsider. I did him a favor and mentioned to Beau that I had a hot new prospect I was about to hire, accidentally dropping Cain's name." He turned a devilish smile on Jason. "You have to admit that they deserve one another."

Jason couldn't argue. He worked his way uphill through the brush to the front of the SUV. Sure enough, the windshield sported a break that looked like a giant, egg-shaped spiderweb.

"Looks about the size that a man's back might make." Billings eyed Jason across the hood.

Seriously. Seeing the damage gave him wonder and awe that he'd not had more injuries. That was truly a God-gift.

Jason rounded the front, pointing at a hole at the base of the windshield on the passenger side. "Bet you find a flathead screwdriver with a taped-up red handle in there."

Blayne had gotten a call during their walk and disappeared again to places unknown. Alynne had wandered alone for a little while, staying close to the house. She noticed the activity near the woods, but she preferred watching the kids digging until the heat set in, and they all scampered to the pool. Now, *that* was a rollicking spot. Thankfully, the police hadn't filled the inn's lot yet again.

She neared the large porch and settled on one of the cushioned chairs in front of the breakfast booth window. Momma probably brought these fancy chairs inside anytime there was rough weather.

Phyllis came out the front door with two glasses. Rufus trotted after her with his tongue lagging. With no effort, he leaped onto a wide chair and made himself at home on the cushion.

"I've got lemonade."

Lemonade? For her? "Uh, thank you." She took the offered glass and made a conscious effort to wipe the amazement from her eyes.

"I've been waiting for you. Thought you'd come into the kitchen first."

"Oh." Alynne braced herself as she sipped from the glass. "Did you need something?"

Her sister gave a sharp sigh. "This is all foolishness, you know. Mother can't possibly run this place alone. She needs to sell it, now, while the inn is in such good condition. I'll give Dad that much credit."

She supposed they should work out the details of what came next, but Momma wasn't a dimwitted old crow. And this place, by all rights, was hers. "I think Momma is wise enough to make her own decisions."

"Then you're as batty as she is." The harsh tone that Alynne had grown up with filled the porch. "Mother has the ridiculous notion of hiring on that witchy redhead to help her run the place. Maybe even have that cop that you're so fond of live here free of charge to be a sort of guard."

The fact that Alynne had little regard for Cat wouldn't influence her response. She wasn't a child that Phyllis could manipulate and utilize. "Sounds like Momma's making her own plan."

"She's delusional, and I'll testify to that in court when I move to have guardianship over her."

Say what? "You're outta your ever-lovin' mind!" Alynne stood. "There is nothing wrong with Momma, and I'm not the only one who'll have the judge laughing you out of court. As for courts, I have a feeling Momma can press charges for your husband firing a weapon on the property." She hoped her knowing about that didn't end up getting Jason in trouble, but Phyllis had to be stopped.

Her sister's eyes widened. Alynne had obviously hit a nerve. "And as to that, I happen to know that any hint of ulterior motives in cases like these can result in a lawsuit that would most certainly rip your sweetie-pie right out of his cushy career. You really want to pursue this and ruin his political aspirations?" As she spoke, her shaking splashed her lemonade all over the porch.

"Are you threatening me, Dora?" Phyllis rose to her full height, towering over Alynne.

"I don't need to. You're the one committing political homicide." Phyllis's candy-coating didn't fool Alynne. She would never move down here to take care of Momma.

And she didn't need taking care of anyway.

Lifting her chin, Phyllis moved toward the railing. "I have a friend, a connection, who would pick this place up in a second for the right price."

Ahh, so that was it. "And how much of a finder's fee would you receive?"

She turned toward her. "You know as well as I do that this place is too big for her. Better to set her up with financial stability for when she needs more care. That can't be too far down the road. I'm trying to help her."

"You're trying to help yourself. Though why you're trying to persuade me to go along with you I'll never know. As far as I'm concerned, this is Momma's home, her property, her responsibility, and her business for as long as she wants it." Alynne's volume rose with each statement. What a horrible thing to even consider. "And I'll fight you tooth and nail if you're serious about having your own mother committed."

Phyllis stomped back toward the front door. "*Your* mother."

Momma came up from behind Alynne. "What was that all about?"

"Oh." Well, she couldn't tell Momma that her own daughter wanted to take away all of her rights. "I didn't see you there."

"I was in the herb garden, and I thought I heard some raised voices over here." She glanced past Alynne toward the pool area. "Well, besides those." She sat on Phyllis's vacated chair and motioned Alynne back into her own.

"It wasn't anything. Just a difference of opinion. And, well, Phyllis doesn't like it when I don't agree with her."

"She always had to have a sidekick. When you stopped letting her sway you, she always had a friend or two who would have her back." Momma described Phyllis perfectly. "So, what does she want this time?"

"She said she has a buyer for the house. I think she wants the commission or something." Alynne wouldn't divulge the measures Phyllis seemed willing to take to have her own way.

"Ah. Yes, she's broached the subject with me as well. Sell it and split the profits between the three of us."

And collect the commission. Sounded like Phyllis. "That's crazy. You're the owner. If you sold this place, you should get all of the profit. I sure don't deserve any of it." Her regret continued to build. "I didn't even come visit, remember?" Alynne dropped her chin, avoiding the tender gaze that she knew Momma's eyes held.

Momma sighed. "I know, honey. And I know it hurt you when we moved here. But this was our dream. Your dad and Uncle Todd had talked about sharing the business for years, but my cancer put the whole plan on hold. You know, insurance and medical costs. It just about destroyed your dad. Then Todd died and left your dad as his only heir. I couldn't, I wouldn't even consider staying in Dallas. You were already standing on your own. I didn't think another forty miles would've made such a difference."

"Except that I was full of myself and resentment that you'd left me after you were finally better." Alynne shook her head as a tear spilled over onto her cheek. "I can't believe I was so foolish, Momma. There were times early on when I wanted to come out here, but stupid pride held me back. And then more recently, it was easier not to come because I always had something to do for work."

Momma put her hand on Alynne's cheek and wiped away the tear. "I forgive you, baby. I'm just glad you're here now. And I hope, when this … this reunion is over, it will mean a new beginning for you and me. One where you might come and relax in this, your father's dream."

Alynne chuckled and put her hand over Momma's. "Yes. This place. It's everything you said it was. I can see why you love it so."

"And I see your dad in every inch of it. My roses that he tended for me." She pointed to the bushes that circled the old iron bell. "That hanging philodendron. And the boathouse, he rebuilt that thing from the ground up."

"Or from the water up." Alynne smirked.

Her mom laughed. "That, too." She stood and pulled Alynne to her feet. "Don't let Phyllis's schemes bother you." She patted Alynne's cheek and walked into the house.

Alynne took a bracing breath. Once again, her mom was the one doling out the encouragement and comfort. It would be so hard for her when everyone left her here without Pop. Alynne would need to be more accessible. Maybe come down on weekends for a while.

She'd have to think about it a little more.

BREAKING POINT

Chapter Eighteen

Jason had tried to persuade the chief to let him have the duty of guarding Alynne and her family for the evening, but Dell was having none of it.

"Go home. Rest. That's an order."

He wouldn't even let him do the research on the rental car. But then again, Juanita was the queen of research. And the chief had been right again. Jason had even allowed himself to sleep late into the morning before getting ready for the visitation.

Oh, he'd tried to get assigned the guard duty for the event. Dell wouldn't hear of it. "You need to grieve over the loss of Ellis Stone as much as anyone."

Probably so, but until he could be sure the man's daughter was safe, he couldn't consider focusing on his own feelings about her dad. He scanned the room. Alynne sat between her mom and one of her aunts. Cat was on Myra's other side with Ray next to her.

Alynne had plenty of support and didn't need Jason crowding her. He headed for a table of light snacks and coffee. Myra probably set up all of this with her sisters. She was a born hostess.

That was a good thing, too. The place was still rather full after almost three hours of guests coming and going and eating. A lot of eating. Looked to him as though the entire town had come to pay their respects to the man.

Jason poured himself a cup of coffee and glanced back at the little group where they accepted condolences from one member of the multitude after another. Where was Alynne's fiancé? Had the man even shown up? He scanned the room. No Blayne.

Alynne looked sad, though. Seemed to Jason that a man should be comforting and supporting the woman he was going to marry, but he probably wasn't being fair to Blayne. He had no idea what the man did for a living or what sacrifices he'd made to even be in town.

Funny that Myra's other daughter was nowhere to be seen either.

Cat and Ray moved away as the guests thinned out. Jason poured two glasses of ice water for Alynne and her mom. He brought them over when the mayor and his wife stepped away. "Thought you two might want something cool." Both ladies gave him gracious smiles that looked remarkably alike.

"I can always count on you, Jason." Myra smiled and sipped her water.

"You had a good turnout." Jason moved to Myra's left where Cat and Ray had left an open seat. "Ellis was dearly loved."

"Oh, you are too kind, dear boy." Myra shifted around in her seat to face him and then seemed to freeze.

"Momma?" Alynne set her glass down and took the one out

of her mom's hands. She hopped up and snatched a plate from the table, filling it with a sandwich and some cookies. She brought it over. "Momma, do you think you can eat something."

The woman stared ahead of her. Jason turned. The crowd had become sparse, opening up the view to Ellis's closed casket and his picture in front of it. Jason stood and moved to be directly between Myra and the coffin.

She continued to stare at his stomach for another moment. "Ellis wouldn't like being in the dark like that." Myra aged ten years in a matter of seconds. Her shoulders slumped and her face looked drawn.

Alynne moved to stand next to Jason then knelt to be on her mom's level. "He's not there, Momma. Pop's not in that dark place. Not at all." Her voice broke.

Jason stroked Alynne's shoulder.

Myra's eyes refocused on her daughter. "Of course, you're right, sweet girl." Her lips pressed together for a moment. "This …" She pressed them together again. "This is a little … harder"—her tone grew husky and she bowed her head—"than I thought it would be."

Alynne stood and embraced her mom. Cat must've seen something was going on because she returned. She and Myra's sisters surrounded the two along with Jason.

Alynne looked up at him. "Will you help me get her home?"

Myra didn't argue. Alynne took one of her arms. Jason took the other and could see that weariness had set in. She'd been spending so much time making sure everyone was comfortable and well-fed, she hadn't prepared herself for this. She cried softly as he and Alynne assisted her toward the door. Thankfully, most of the visitors had left. The family members seemed to catch what was going on and began cleaning up the food and gathering the children.

They exited into the sunlight and headed for Alynne's car. Blayne stood near it at the edge of the lot, schmoozing Mr. and Mrs. Heath from the looks of it. He shook the man's hand, smiling and laughing, then kissed the woman's hand.

Oily, but she seemed to enjoy the attention.

As he neared with Alynne and Myra, Blayne caught sight of them and moved toward them. "I'll take it from here, buddy." He stepped in front of Jason and tried to take Myra's arm.

How ridiculous. Like she was some sort of toy.

"My mom isn't luggage or schoolbooks, Blayne." Alynne shot him pure venom. She didn't tell him to back off, but he got the message.

Myra quieted, but Jason practically carried her the last several yards to Alynne's car. "You gonna be okay to get her back to the inn?"

Alynne paused as she opened her door. "I think so."

"I'll follow you and help you get her inside." Jason's Jeep was at the station, but if he ran, he could catch up to them on the highway.

"She's my fiancée. If anyone will help her with her mother, I will." Blayne had his keys in his hand. Strange that the couple hadn't come together.

"Oh, stop your silly arguing." One of Myra's sisters shooed her hands at Blayne and climbed into the back seat of Alynne's car.

"We won't be needing either of you." The other sister chimed in and climbed into the other side of the back seat.

True enough, the family trudged out a few at a time and climbed into vehicles. Blayne gave him a brief glare before whipping his head around and climbing into the sedan parked nearby. He gunned the motor and roared away from the funeral home.

Alynne was delaying for some reason. She waved him over after Blayne exited the lot, rolling down the passenger window. Myra peered out at him, looking surprisingly vital after having such a weak spell inside. She pointed at her daughter. "Tell her that I can stay here tonight."

"You want to stay here at the funeral home?"

"Yes, a wake. That's a thing."

"Momma, it isn't a slumber party."

She nodded. "I suppose you're right."

Cat joined him on Myra's open passenger window. "He's with the Lord, Myra. And he couldn't be happier." Cat's whole face glowed and tears shown on her cheeks.

Alynne put her head down as Cat began talking Myra through her pain.

Jason backed up and rounded the car to the driver's side. "You okay?"

"I think this is all starting to get to me, too. If I could take a walk or a drive to get away a little bit, I think I'd do a lot better, but between my less than peaceful family, the weight of losing ..." She took a prolonged breath. "The weight of losing Pop, and some crazy person lying in wait to do me in …"

"You're right. You do need some time out." Cat had left Ray chatting with Myra and her sisters and joined him at Alynne's window. "There's a ladies' Bible study tonight. I want you to come with me."

"Oh, I'm not sure." Alynne chewed on her bottom lip.

"I know you don't know me very well, but there's something so peaceful being with other women who share the same Spirit and speak the same language of God's love. Please say you'll go with me."

Myra chimed in from the other seat. "Absolutely, sweet girl, you must go. I'm going to let Billie and Bobbie take care of things tonight and hermit in my bedroom for a while. You need to refresh your spirit as well."

Alynne glanced at Jason. "Am I allowed?"

At least she was taking her protection seriously. "We'll have someone follow you there and back. Cat, will you drive?"

"I can do that."

Cat could be counted on, and he'd take the duty himself if the chief allowed. He nodded.

"Shall I come pick you up in a couple of hours?" Cat waited for Alynne's decision. Good thing. He had a feeling that Alynne was the type who would avoid commitment, but once giving it, wouldn't renege.

"Okay. It's probably just what I need." Her words didn't match the doubt that painted her face.

No matter, as long as she was careful and followed his instructions, she'd be okay. He'd make sure.

Torn. Yeah, that was it.

As much as she adored Momma, Alynne needed to recharge … somewhere where her sister wasn't. And then there was the houseful of people. She liked them, but still … so many people.

But going to a ladies' Bible study with a roomful of strangers? This was not the recharging she intended. She just needed a long drive or a walk around the lake, but Jason had nixed both of those ideas.

So, Bible study it was.

By the time they'd finished their in-depth discussion of Philippians 4:1-9, Alynne was beginning to feel renewed and had been generously encouraged by the Holy Spirit and by twenty or so ladies she'd never before laid eyes on. So gracious and so kind.

She'd even begun to like Cat. "These ladies certainly made me feel welcome."

"Well, they love your mom. Loved your daddy, too."

"It's crazy. They were only here for a little over ten years. How did they get so close to so many people?"

Cat smiled as she maneuvered Alynne through the hallways of the church's educational wing toward the rear parking lot. "Your folks made an impact from the moment they moved in. We used to have our Bible studies at the inn until our leader needed to move it to a different night. Myra would normally be hosting the local scout group tonight. She and Ellis made every effort to get involved in church activities and community events."

"In the same ten years …" Alynne shook her head. She was pathetic. "My roommate is the only person I speak with regularly. And we only live together. We don't socialize. She and her best friends travel every weekend."

"But there's Blayne."

Oh, yeah. Alynne trailed as Cat turned down a darkened hallway.

"You having trouble defining your relationship with your boyfriend?" Cat slowed for her to catch up. "I'm not trying to pry, but if it helps for you to talk it out …"

"I'm not sure about him … about us." Alynne slowed to a stop and leaned against the wall. "I was, at least I thought I was sure. He asked me to marry him the day I found out about Pop." Had it really been a week already? "I was sure then, but he keeps pressing me to elope."

Cat shifted her weight to one leg. "Now? I mean with your mom and all?"

"Yeah, I know, right?" She shook her head. "I don't know what got into him. One day he's pressing me to fly to Vegas, even bought us tickets. The next day, he's disappeared. I don't even think he knows about the car that tried to run me down."

"You didn't talk to him about taking care of Jason the other night?"

Wide-eyed, Alynne turned to look at her. Did the whole town know about it?

"It is a small town."

Alynne crossed her arms. "Blayne and I took a walk yesterday, but he kept asking questions about the inn and the property and the history and stuff. I wouldn't be surprised if he tried to buy it from Momma."

"You think that's why he … well not why he wants to marry you, but maybe why he's been in such a hurry about it?"

Could that be it? Alynne's mouth dropped open. She thought back through the days. "It has been strange. I mean, we've been dating for almost a year. Then suddenly he asks me to marry him and presses it again and again. He even wanted me to fly out and back in one day, promising to return in time for the funeral."

"What was he thinking?"

"Maybe he felt Momma would be more inclined to sell to him if we were married?" Could that be the case? "Do you think he was serious when he proposed? I mean, surely, this wasn't purely a financial matter?" No. Blayne cared about her. He did.

Cat tilted her head. "What do you think?"

Didn't he? "I thought he loved me. Now I'm not …" Shame flooded and heated her face.

"Do you love him?"

That was a good question.

Cat continued, "I mean. The life-long kind of love that always protects and hopes and trusts."

Alynne smirked. "You forgot perseveres."

"Yeah. So, do you love him with that forever kind of love?" The question in Cat's eyes demanded her attention and pierced deep into her soul.

With a slight groan, she bowed her head, shaking it gently. "Sometimes, I don't even …" She couldn't say it out loud. Not even to herself.

"Are you really preparing to marry a man you can't imagine loving for the rest of your life? And even now, you're not sure you love him or even like him?" She propped her hands on her hips.

Alynne shut her eyes. She wasn't going to tell this virtual stranger her darkest secret. "It's complicated."

"Is there a child?"

"No!" Alynne pushed off the wall and stormed farther down the hallway.

"Well you have to admit, that *would* be complicated." Cat's voice didn't seem to follow her. She called after her a little louder, "And you're going the wrong way."

How humiliating. Alynne did an about-face. "This isn't your business," she spat as she passed Cat.

"I know." The woman fell into step beside her. "But Myra is one of my closest friends. I owe her so much for taking me in and giving me a sense of family after Daddy died."

Alynne halted. Could she trust this woman? "Would you not say anything to Momma about the engagement?"

"Is that why you're not wearing a ring?" Cat turned.

Alynne hadn't allowed herself to even think about the ring again. "I don't have a ring yet."

"Okay, that's troubling. Why did the man want to hurry you off to get married, but he didn't even offer you a ring to display his commitment?"

"What are you getting at?" She didn't want to hear Cat's assessment, fearing it would be too close to her own concerns.

"It all just seems rather spur of the moment. No fancy

wedding. No ring."

Heat rose along her shoulders and flooded her face. "I'm through talking about this." She turned away.

Cat laid a hand on her arm. "You're right. This is none of my business. But don't marry this man because you think you're supposed to for whatever the reason. Pray about it and ask God to put a passion in your heart for Blayne if He wants you two together. If you don't get that passion, you have your answer."

It wasn't like she hadn't prayed about it, but she hadn't asked God what He wanted. "Okay." She could do that much. If only she could ask Blayne to pray with her, but he didn't go in for anything having to do with faith.

"I'm sorry if I've overstepped." Cat pushed open the door into the dark church parking lot. One light on the far side provided the only illumination. At least their car wasn't far. Alynne could barely make out the bushes that marked the end of the lot. They resembled a blob with Cat's truck nose-in to them.

She concentrated on her feet for a moment to step over a parking chock then looked back at the truck. Was there someone … no that was just the bush. But for a moment, it looked like a cowboy leaning against the truck, head down and boots crossed at the ankle like one of those cutouts that people put in their yards.

Then the head rose.

Cat must've noticed the shadows as well because she halted at the same time Alynne stopped. She reached out and gripped Alynne's arm, shoving her to the right. "Whoever you are, I have a weapon, and I'm prepared to use it."

What weapon? Unless she was talking about her Bible as the Sword of the Spirit.

"Well, now, that was just dumb." The shadow stood to its full height and turned to face them. A subtle light caught Jason's face. "You just told a would-be attacker to prepare to fight against a weapon. Better to let him think you're unarmed and surprise him."

"With what?" Alynne couldn't hold back her question any longer.

Cat gave a sheepish shrug. "I have mace in my car."

"Even worse." Jason reached them. "Now your attacker is prepared, and his adrenaline is pumping to battle against a weapon that you don't even have. And I'm not even gonna start on how you parked in a dark, empty lot."

"It wasn't empty when we got here, but the smaller lot on the other side was totally full." Cat's excuse sounded weak, even to Alynne's ears.

"Yeah, yeah." Jason ushered them toward the truck. "Cat, your husband is waiting for you here in town. I can take Alynne back to the inn."

Cat unlocked her door. "You sure you don't mind?"

He nodded and pointed to his Jeep parked on the street. "No problem."

Alynne gave Cat a hug. "Thanks for bringing me tonight. It was exactly what I needed."

"You're more than welcome."

"And thanks for helping me … well … think through things." Alynne added with a whisper.

Cat straightened and climbed into the cab of the truck. "If

you're around, we do this every week."

"I'll keep it in mind." She joined Jason on the trek across the gravel as Cat's truck roared to life and crawled out of the lot.

Following Jason, she committed to think long and hard about what Cat said.

"You have a nice time?" Jason gave a quick sidelong glance at Alynne as he set his hat in the back seat. She'd been so vulnerable this afternoon after the viewing, the sight of her had tugged at his heart.

"It was revealing." She wiped her fingertips across her forehead. "I hadn't even realized some of the attitudes that have been holding me back."

He didn't want to pry, but he wanted to hear more. "Yeah?"

She hesitated. "So, you really liked my pop?"

"Everyone loved Ellis. Kindest, most generous man I've ever known." Jason turned right onto Farm-to-Market Road that led out of town.

"In what way?" She tugged at something on the knee of her jeans.

While Jason preferred to listen rather than speak, Alynne looked like she needed to work through her thoughts. He did something completely unnatural for him to give her that chance. "When I moved here, he came into the station with Pastor Slaughter to welcome me. He and Myra invited me out to the inn for dinner that first night. We found out we both like fishing. From then on, I spent at least a few hours with him on every day off. We'd fish, do odd jobs around the inn, volunteer for the church or events in the town." He paused, trying to think of something else to add.

"Pop really made an impact on this town, didn't he?" She kept her chin down, but her question came out clear enough.

"Yeah." That's all he wanted to say, but this wasn't the time to think about himself. "From what I hear, they jumped into town life from the moment they arrived."

"I don't know anyone back in Dallas like the ladies I met tonight."

"Life moves faster in a big city."

She turned toward him. "How would you know that?"

He chuckled. "I grew up in Austin then worked in Chicago before I moved here."

"When was that?"

This wasn't a can he wanted to open. "Several years ago."

Silence invaded.

"Why?"

He released a breath he hadn't realized he'd been holding. *Lord, I don't want to go into this right now.* "I needed to get away from the big city."

"What's wrong with the big city? I love living in Dallas. So many things to do and places to go." She seemed to relax a little.

"Like what?" This might be a good avenue for discussion that would get him off the hook.

"Well ..." Her chin lowered again. "I mean, there are all sorts of sports teams: Rangers, Cowboys, Mavericks, Stars. Seems like there's always some game on."

The word *on* revealed a lot. "Which is your favorite?"

"Baseball. I like all of the sports, but baseball is my favorite."

"Oh, yeah. I'm a Cubs fan, myself. Nothing like a night at the ballpark, right?"

"Yeah. Well, I mean, I do like watching the games after work."

She was nothing if not honest. "But you've been to a game, right?"

"Well…"

Seemed that was her go-to word when she didn't want to answer. "You've never been to a game?"

"I have a lot of responsibility at my job."

"Sure, I can get that. But there's a great art environment downtown. Do you ever go there?"

"Our offices are in One Main Place, so yeah, I go downtown every day."

Wow, that was quite an address. "Do you ever do theatre or concerts?"

"No." She began answering even before he finished the question. "I work a lot. Usually late into the evening until I'm starving enough that I have to force myself to stop. I grab something at a drive-thru and then work some more at home, usually with a baseball game going on in the background."

"Wait, you love Dallas because there's so much to do, but the only thing you do is work?"

She leaned her head back. "That's about the size of it." She rocked her head back and forth. "Except for a mission trip I took while I was in college, in the same ten years that Momma and Pop have lived here becoming important to almost all of the people of this place, I've stayed in my hometown, and even my roommate and I don't talk very often."

"What do you do?" he asked. She worked for some attorney according to Myra. But if she was an admin, couldn't she leave her work at work?

"I'm a research assistant. I find out things like the details of a business involved in a lawsuit—the financial background, the existing networking lines, people connected to the company, anything I can learn."

"And that helps?" He could see the financial details as being important.

"You can never tell how seemingly unimportant details can make the difference between the client's win or loss."

That was certainly true in crime. "I guess I can see that." But that didn't explain why she was so sold on living in a big town. "Sounds like Dallas is just comfortable and familiar." He slowed to take a curve. "You don't go to church?"

"I watch a couple of online services, usually."

Jason would never have taken Alynne to be a hermit, but between her work and the wall she'd built around her emotions, that's exactly what she seemed to be. "No wonder the ladies at the study surprised you."

"I'm so pathetic." She put her head into her hands. "The only people I talk to, besides Blayne, are the people I work with. And if I hadn't come here to help Momma, I'd not even realize what a closed-off workaholic I've become."

Jason parked the car in the lot. Shutting off the engine, he turned to face her. "And now?"

She didn't look at him but climbed from the car. She stood leaning against the door as he came around the front of the car.

"Now, do you want to go back to the life you had, or do you want a change?"

"Change what? I can't very well leave my job."

"Why not? Or better, why can't you do the work remotely. Sounds like it's all on the computer anyway."

"Mostly." She looked up at him. "You think I should move here? Maybe help Momma with the inn?"

The thought had occurred to him, but he hadn't planned to ever mention it. "Is that what you want to do?" He took a step closer and lowered his voice. Her feelings about her mom or the inn weren't anyone else's business.

The woman's blue eyes remained steady. "I haven't really allowed myself to consider it." She moved away from the Jeep, coming closer to him. His arms ached to surround her, easing her pain and loneliness.

The front door of the inn opened, and Jason took an automatic step back, wiping his hand over his face. The heat surely meant his cheeks were reddening. "Same as before. Stay in the house. I'll be out here for the next few hours." He glanced up to the porch and caught a hate-filled glare from Blayne. He would be the one who just happened to come outside.

"Thanks. And thanks for the ride." She took another step away from the Jeep and stood staring at him as he climbed in.

He gave her a nod and put the vehicle into reverse. What had he been thinking? She was taken, thoroughly taken. If he'd been in Blayne's position, he'd have been furious and with good reason. He rolled down the windows needing to get some cool, fresh air and put his Jeep into park at the end of the lot. His job was to protect this woman. Not fall for her.

That was a crazy thought. He'd not been in love since Dawn. His jaw clamped shut. He would not go there. Not now. And the last thing he needed to do was compare Alynne to the woman who had been his wife.

His cell phone rang. Perfect timing to put uncomfortable thoughts from his mind. "This is Danvers."

The lilting Hispanic tone of Juanita Estrella drifted over the line. "I thought you'd want to know that I tracked down the agent at the car rental."

"Got a name?"

"Not a real one. Got a copy of the license, but it's a fake too. Not even a good one."

"I guess making those copies is just routine." How often would an agent need to actually pay attention to the card?

"But I do have some good news. If we can put a name to this situation, the rental agent is fairly sure she can identify the man who rented it."

"Male?" That was something. Narrowed down half the planet, but most of his suspects were men anyway.

"Ten-four." Juanita ended the call.

Not exactly the news he'd hoped for, but at least there was still a lead to pursue.

Chapter Nineteen

Alynne followed Blayne into the inn. Reaching the door, she glanced back at Jason. He gripped the steering wheel and stared at his hands for a moment, looking almost angry. Or maybe only intense.

But she couldn't watch him. Blayne had opened the door for her and made an impatient sound. She entered and turned to face him. "Where is everyone?" The silence was deafening.

"Down by the lake when I last looked. Doing s'mores, I think. Except for your mom. Your aunts stayed with her in her suite." His face was unreadable. "I thought you were at a meeting of some sort with that redheaded lady."

"Cat, yeah, we went to a ladies' Bible study at her church."

He pointed his thumb over his shoulder at the front door. "That wasn't a redheaded woman." His eyes didn't hold the mirth that his comment might have stirred up.

She'd need to choose her words carefully, at least until she could thoroughly evaluate their relationship. "The lieutenant was on duty outside the church. Since Cat lives in town and he's staying on duty a while longer, he volunteered to bring me back, saving Cat the trip."

Wait a minute. Why did she feel like she should apologize to him? She hadn't required him to tell her where he'd been the other day, nor had she questioned him about his whereabouts during the visitation. "And I don't have to explain myself to you, Blayne Campbell." She turned toward the main staircase.

"Hold it." Blayne's voice was low and hiss like. He clamped a hand around her injured arm.

"Ow." She struggled to pull away, but his grip tightened. "You're hurting me." Tears formed in the corners of her eyes.

He pulled her close enough to whisper. "You love me, Alynne. You know you do. You've proved it. And no extra Bible study or piling up on goodness or kindness is going to erase that." He took a quick glance at the opening of the kitchen behind him.

"You let me go right now." She stared him down, quite ready to release an earsplitting shriek if she had to.

He caressed her face with his other hand and eased his grip. "I don't want you to feel this guilt for the rest of your life."

He was right. Her guilt had only grown since that night. Was marrying Blayne her only option, though? "If I do, it's nothing I don't deserve."

"I can't help but think this Bible stuff is making you feel even worse." He released her fully and stepped back. "Get some sleep, darling. Things will be clearer in the morning, and we can talk again.

Tomorrow. The day before Pop's funeral. She didn't answer

and didn't look back at him as she headed up the staircase and into the dining room. With her tearing eyes, the narrow entrance to her room created a strange kaleidoscope. She entered and left the lights off as she moved to the western windows. The fire at the edge of the lake glowed, and her family made shadows against the flames.

The scene reminded Alynne of an old church camp song. Something about a flame or a spark. Neither the tune nor the words fully connected with her brain, but it was about spreading God's love. Her tears spilled over her eyelashes.

She regretted that she wasn't able to go down there. But her regret went well beyond feeling sorry for herself.

How had she ever shared God's love? At work, she usually focused on doing her best but never engaged with anyone beyond the needs of her job. Not even for lunch.

She leaned her cheek against the cool glass pane. She'd been invited by several of the other admins but … what? She couldn't be bothered with socializing. She had work to finish. Then she could … do more work.

God, I've wasted so much time. Please don't let me ignore others. After all, according to the leader at tonight's study, part of her job and purpose here on earth was to show love to others that they could see God's love through her.

Had she even been conscious these past ten years? The loss of Pop had forced her to stop and look back over the decade. She didn't like the pride and futility that stared back at her. Moving away from the window, she left the lights off. She felt her way around the room, changed into her pajama short set, and climbed into her bed. Taking out her cell phone, she opened an audiobook

Bible app she'd been using and prayed the Lord would soothe and speak to her heart.

She fell asleep reading through Ephesians but felt purpose when she woke the next morning at dawn's first light. And no wonder since she'd gone to sleep so early. Today stretched in front of her with no plan and nothing pressing. She wanted to make an impact on the members of her family. Let them know she really did care even though she hadn't been around for their outings.

Hurrying through her shower, she decided to leave a simple braid in her hair to fix it quickly and keep it out of her face. She pulled a Texas Rangers ball cap over her bangs and slipped into some jean shorts and a T-shirt. After tying on her shoes, she trotted down to the empty kitchen. Hmm. She expected her aunts, at least, would be here. They had likely already made a plan for breakfast that she didn't want to alter. What else might Momma do first thing in the morning?

Rose. She needed feeding. Momma kept her bowl in the pantry. Alynne filled it with kibble and took it out the side door. "You out here, Rose?" She walked around the wide, rounded corner of the porch to the front side of the house. "Here Rose." She smacked her pucker together several times to make kissing sounds.

The dog came out from under the steps and stretched as she climbed onto the porch. "Aren't you a good baby?"

"Very good." Momma rounded the corner behind her. "She's even a good guard dog."

"Morning, Momma." Alynne gave her a half hug. "I imagine Rose muddies or slobbers anyone foolish enough to wander onto the property?"

Her mom laughed. "There's that. But once the porch light is off, she won't let anyone come near the steps. She's better than one of those newfangled doorbells that give you video and let you talk through them."

"Rings?"

"I suppose they do that too." Momma completely missed Alynne's meaning and patted Rose as the dog wolfed down her food. "It was kind of you to feed her."

"We've come to an understanding." Alynne clasped her hands in front of her. "What can I do this morning?"

"Well." She looked around the porch. "I need to go start breakfast with Billie and Bobbie. Breakfast burritos this morning. But you could water the hanging plants out here. And then the cushions on these chairs need some airing. Sort of like the old-fashioned rug beating. I usually hit each of them on the top rail several times to get most of the dust out."

"I can do that." Sounded like a productive way of getting out her irritations.

Her mom left her to the jobs. Alynne had purple thumbs, even killed a cactus one time, but surely, she could water the flowering plants. She duplicated what she'd seen her mom do a few days ago in hardly any time at all. Then she pulled the cushions off, one at a time. When she reached the farthest chair which faced the pool, she found a large black wreath with a card. Momma's name was on the front of the envelope.

Rose sniffed around her ankles and sat in front of her.

"Are you wanting a scratch, girl?" she ruffled the puppy-soft fur between her ears. "Let's go give this to Momma." She pushed through the main door, noticing that the chime didn't sound yet. Good thing. She hadn't wanted to awaken the others.

Momma and her sisters chatted as they each worked their own tasks.

"I found this on the porch." Alynne handed her mom the card and held up the black wreath. The thick circle was covered with virtual petals made of lightweight plastic and had an ornate, matching bow hanging from the bottom of it.

Momma opened the envelope and drew out a card. "Oh, this is from that nice Mrs. Doleson who lives on the other side of the cove just beyond the scout camp."

"That's so kind of her, but why wouldn't she deliver it in person?"

"Oh, she probably didn't want to intrude with all of the family around." She handed the typed card to Alynne. "She says that it's tradition for a family member, usually the youngest child of the deceased, to hang this on the lakeside of the boathouse."

"Guess that's me, huh."

"I like the tradition. I've noticed the lake people all have special traditions. Like at Christmas, everyone decorates and lights up their boathouses right along with their regular houses." Her mom's smile wavered. "Guess I'm gonna need someone to help me with that this year."

This wasn't the type of impact Alynne had wanted to make. "I can't do much about that right now, but I can take care of this task. Can you direct me to a hammer and nails?"

The question seemed to draw Momma out of her troubled thoughts. "Oh, no need. There are hooks all over that building for ropes, fishing poles, nets, and all those lights at Christmas."

"Great, I'll finish the cushions when I hang this baby." She scooted out the side door and called for Rose. The dog expected a walk down the trails and took off through the trees. Alynne whistled, and she came bolting back, taking her guard duty seriously. Alynne glanced to the parking lot. Yep, an HPPD cruiser sat at the edge of the lot. That should have made her feel safe, but a shiver wriggled its way down her back. She was ignoring Jason's instructions again. Well, as soon as she finished the cushions, she'd go inside and stay there. "Come on, Rose."

The dog stopped at the ramp leading up to the pier Pop had built. Alynne couldn't blame her with the way the walkway bobbed a bit under her weight. She squatted and held out her hand. "Here, Rose." It was no use, and she gave up. Even as well-built as this was, it was a little on the unsteady side by its very nature.

Alynne crossed onto the boathouse and moved to the far corner. The wreath knocked into a net that clattered onto the deck. Alynne bent to scoop it up. A shot rang out. Wood somewhere above her splintered.

What? Someone … She flattened against the deck. Another shot landed near her. Rose started barking and tore off into the trees. Another shot came way too close. She'd never be able to get back to the safety of the house. Whoever the shooter was almost had her in his sights. She only had one outlet of escape. Staying flat, she spun around and slithered into the lake headfirst.

The cold water shocked her, but she clung to one of the pontoons at the end of the jetty. Someone screamed. Oh, no. Momma would've heard the shots. A dog's yelp and whine echoed from the woods. Heavy footfalls clomped up the gangway. "Miss Stone." The man's voice was tense. "It's Officer Evans. If you're hiding, stay where you are but call out."

"I'm here. In the water."

"I have backup coming."

A sudden rumbling engine started up somewhere in the distance then trailed away. More, lighter, footsteps sounded on the pier. "Alynne, where are you?" Momma cried.

"She's all right, Mrs. Stone." Evan's gentle tone held a firmness. "I need you to stay on the land."

"You're sure she's okay?"

"I'm okay, Momma."

"Stay silent." Evan hissed. "Please stay on the shore, and don't let anyone know you heard from her."

"You want the others to think she's dead?"

"If the shooter is still around, I don't want to advertise that he failed." Evans was practically whispering at this point. Alynne could barely hear him over her chattering teeth.

"I'll do as you say." Momma's sharp steps receded on the gangplank.

"I'm pretending to search for you," he whispered. "Stay as concealed as you can."

Well, that would be tough. Anyone on the other side of the cove could see her, but she hadn't noticed anyone in that direction. But wait, was that movement in the underbrush to her left? She wouldn't chance it.

Filling her lungs, she ducked under the water and followed the edge of the pontoon to where the water was the darkest. She rose slowly, enough to get a breath, but she was in a good place, just inside the closed door of the boathouse, she still had the pontoon on one side of her and nothing but Pop's fishing boat in front of her. Still, she stayed close to the pontoon, clinging to it with freezing fingers. *God, please keep all of us safe. Even Rose.*

Had the dog an inkling of the danger? She'd sure run into the woods fast enough. Hopefully, she'd be fine.

There hadn't been any other shots after what had sounded like a motorcycle leaving, but a siren sounded in the distance. Alynne looped her fingers through the coiled ropes that were tied high up on the pontoons. She twisted her frozen fingers around them and then allowed herself to relax. Yes, the coils would keep her from going underwater, even if her fingers relaxed. She began to kick her legs in rapid motion as hard as she could to try to work up some heat.

"Evans, where is she?" That was Jason's voice. Terror-filled. Was something else happening? She drifted to her right, breathing hard.

"In the water. I didn't want to show the shooter had failed until we had more backup."

Jason's feet clomped on the deck. "Good thinking."

More clomping and more voices.

Alynne's teeth began to chatter.

"Alynne, where are you?"

"I …" Her throat constricted and her jaw wouldn't stop spasming. She pulled up on her hands and kicked at the bottom of the garage covering.

The main door rattled. "How do you get in here, Myra?"

Her mom's voice called out, but Alynne couldn't make out what she said.

I'm okay. But she probably wasn't. After all, she couldn't talk, and she could no longer feel her fingers.

Then Jason was there. "Oh, honey." He rushed onto the platform that surrounded Pop's boat.

Momma popped in, then went back out and called for someone to get blankets.

Jason slipped into the water, holding her with one hand and untangling her fingers from the cords on the pontoon. "You're a pretty smart cookie, Alynne Stone."

She shivered in response.

An EMT arrived carrying a large black case. "She needs to get out of the water, now." He lay down on the dock with his face and arms extended down to her.

Alynne felt like a rag doll as Jason handed her over to the other man. He held onto both of her arms, keeping her face out of the water, while Jason climbed out.

Good thing, too. Alynne couldn't even kick her legs at this point.

Another officer rushed in and the three of them hauled her soggy self onto the deck. It took three strong men? That was humiliating. Maybe they should've used a crane.

The EMT laid her on the deck and opened the case. "My name's Mark. What's yours?"

The smile he offered was utterly charming, enough to kick her spunk into gear. "Ch-ch-cheesy p-pickup line."

He chuckled. "Strange name, but we'll go with it." He pulled out a plastic package and tore into it.

"What can I do?" Momma came close and laid a hand on her forehead.

Mark unfolded a thin blanket and laid it over her. "Warm apple cider? Not hot."

"I can do that." She scurried out.

He reached back into the box and withdrew a large silver plastic bag that looked like an ice pack. Surely that wasn't for her. He squeezed it in the middle, then shook it slightly before lifting a corner of the blanket and laying the bag on her chest.

Ohhhh. Not ice. Warm like a mug of hot chocolate.

Another EMT came in carrying a gurney. "What's the status?"

"I don't think we need to take her to the hospital." He flashed a light into her eyes. "She's completely responsive and even has her humor still intact. I'm happy to see you didn't freeze it off." He smiled again.

She tried to smile back, but another spasm shook it out of her.

"Let's get her up to the house," Mark said when the other guy laid the gurney next to her.

"How can I help?" Jason took a step into her line of vision.

"We got it." Mark took her shoulders while the other man lifted her feet.

She wondered if they should get the crane they seemed to have needed before, but they lifted her quickly and smoothly this time. The breeze on her back sent shivers throughout her body, but the warmth laying on her chest seeped deeper into her being.

Mark strapped the pack and her to the gurney and then tightened a belt around her hips. The two of them hoisted her into the air, giving her a sense of weightlessness. Surreal. They trotted her up the hill and into a side door of the inn. Momma directed them into the parlor next to the main staircase. Her aunts stood by the counter as they passed, wringing their hands, but thankfully, they were the only other ones around at this hour.

She wanted to set their minds at ease, but words were still difficult. "F-f-fine." She forced out.

Jason had apparently followed. Momma put a large quilt on one of the chairs and made him sit down, then she covered him with another quilt. Aunt Billie came in with a tray of mugs. Momma handed him one and ordered him to drink it. Poor guy. Somewhere he'd even lost his hat in all of the chaos.

The EMTs unbuckled Alynne from the gurney. "Can you sit up?" Mark asked, taking hold of one of her arms.

"I-I …" Alynne didn't finish the thought. Mark pulled her to a sitting position. The pack slid off, but her shivering had subsided. "Let's get you to the couch."

Momma scurried to lay a thick quilt onto the sofa and held it there. The other EMT braced her on one side while Mark helped her on the other. They lifted her up, and her feet tingled. Gently, they lowered her onto the quilt, helping her recline against the arm of the couch. Mark picked up the warming bag and put it on her back, pushing her against the cushions.

"Ohh."

"I hope that's a good sound." Mark smiled.

"Oh, yeah."

"Do you have another blanket?" he asked her mom.

Of course, Momma did. Probably hundreds. She moved to

Alynne's right and lifted the cushion of a wide window seat. A third of the section opened. Momma extracted a thick blue comforter and handed it to Mark. He unfolded it and covered her up to her chin. "There now. Are you feeling better?"

She nodded. The warmth was finally starting to travel down her arms and legs.

He slipped her right hand out from under the blanket. "Can you move your fingers?" He held her hand up a little.

She concentrated. They still weren't behaving, but they moved a little.

He nodded. "That's better." Then he tucked her hand back under the cover. "You're going to be fine." He folded up the blanket she'd been using. It had to be a thermal one since it was so lightweight and yet so thoroughly warmed her. He took a thermometer out of his case. "Under your tongue."

She opened her mouth and positioned the plastic-covered tube as instructed.

Jason set his mug on the glass cover of the table beside him. "You want to tell me what happened? Why you were out of the house?" His words pierced.

"That was my fault." Momma's chin dropped. "I wasn't thinking." Her voice broke. "I almost got you killed." She began to cry.

"N-no. Momma." Shivers ran through her arms and legs.

Jason must've felt like a heel. He stood and put his arm around Momma. "I'm sorry, Myra. I didn't mean to upset you. Can you tell me what happened?"

Momma sniffed. "Alynne came in from the porch with a

funeral wreath that Mrs. Doleson had brought over."

"Did you see Mrs. Doleson?"

"No, she just left it on one of the chairs on the porch."

"How do you know it was her," he asked.

"There was a card."

"May I see it?"

Momma mumbled something and left the room. Mark had jotted something onto an iPad and then uncovered her enough to wrap a cuff around her wrist. He pressed the edge of the cuff and the band began to tighten as it filled with air. Once it automatically took the reading, he removed it.

Momma and Aunt Bobbie brought in a few pillows from Momma's bed, placing them behind her against the arm of the chair so she could sit up a little.

"Here." Aunt Billie held a mug of apple cider up to Alynne's lips. "It's not hot. Only warm. Let me help you."

Alynne nodded and took a sip as her aunt held the mug to her lips. Good thing. Her hands would never have been able to hold it steady—if they had been able to grip the mug at all.

The liquid floated down her throat, warming her all the way to her belly. Oh, how she appreciated her family. Her purpose today had been to make an impact for the benefit of her family. This hadn't been what she'd intended. In fact, quite the opposite.

Mark waited until she took several drinks before pumping up the blood pressure cuff again.

Momma came back with the card and handed it to Jason. He opened it.

"See," she said. "Perfectly normal, and quite a kind gesture."

"Then why is it all typed?" he asked as he pulled a baggie from his back pocket and slipped the card into it. He pulled a pen from the same pocket and wrote a note on the bag.

"Surely you don't suspect Mrs. Doleson of being involved in anything wrong."

He didn't answer Momma but turned toward Alynne. Mark pulled the velcro that released the cuff and moved away to write on his iPad again. The other EMT had carried the gurney into the main hall and folded it into a little case.

Jason stepped closer. "Can you talk now?"

"Y-yes," she said. "I'm feeling warmer." Though the words were still a little difficult to get out.

"Tell me exactly where you found this wreath."

"I f-found it on the porch. In the chair n-n-next to the door."

"And the card?"

She nodded. "It had M-momma's name typed on the envelope."

"Anything else?"

"N-no."

"Anything on the porch at all?"

She smirked. "The dog. Under the s-stairs."

He didn't seem amused.

"Rose would've barked." Momma looked from Alynne to Jason. "If Mrs. Doleson had tried to get onto the porch, even just to leave the wreath. Rose would have barked her head off."

Rose had a loud yap. Alynne certainly would have heard it. In fact, most of the house would have heard it.

Jason hesitated. "Even for someone she knows?"

"Absolutely. She sleeps under the steps when she's outside. And nobody, not even Ellis or I, got up the steps after dark without enduring a noisy greeting."

Jason nodded and turned back to Alynne. "What did you do after you found it?"

"I took it to Momma." She wrapped her arms around herself and gripped the blanket. Ooo, it felt good to have control of her hands and fingers again.

"And?"

"She read it out loud, and I said I'd take care of it since I'm the youngest child."

He tilted his head. "That's a strange request."

"Well, it said it was tradition," Momma chimed in. "There are all kinds of traditions like that."

He scrutinized Alynne's face. "Myra, have you ever seen funeral wreaths on the boathouses around here?"

"Well, no, but I'm not sure I would have noticed. I didn't do much at the lake. The boat was Ellis's thing." Momma seemed to be able to speak about Pop without hurting today. That was a good thing. She kept her gaze steady on Jason. "You think that someone sent that funeral wreath specifically to get Alynne alone on the lake?"

Jason glanced between the two women. "I don't want to commit to anything yet." He refocused on Alynne. "What happened when you went to the boathouse? Did you hear anything."

"Just the c-crashing of Rose as she chased s-something in the woods, but I called to her, and she came back."

"You called the dog?"

"Yes." Was that special?

"Did you whistle?"

"I think I m-might have?" Why was that important?

"And she came running back."

"Yes." Alynne struggled for the details. "But she wouldn't go onto the g-gangplank even though I t-tried to coax her.

"So, you stood on the gangplank for a few minutes?"

"More like squatted with my hand out t-trying to lure her to follow."

"But she wouldn't." He pointed to Aunt Billie and made a writing motion. She tugged open the drawer of one of the end tables and brought him a pen and paper.

"No, s-so I gave up. I walked to the end of the d-decking around the boathouse."

"And you heard the gunfire?" he prompted.

"Not then." She'd been on her knees when the first shot sounded. Why had she been down there? "I knocked something down. The fishing n-net from the wall. And I heard the shot and the bullet ricochet. I don't know if it hit the b-boathouse or the railing or what."

"Did you hear it hit something or ricochet?" he asked.

She stared at him and blinked. Was there a difference? "I'm n-not sure I know the difference."

"You used the word *ricochet*. I'm curious as to why you chose that word." He shifted to one foot.

Mark had finished taking his notes and slipped the thermometer back into her mouth. So much for her answering more questions. He slipped the cuff back into place and went through the entire routine again like he hadn't done it only ten minutes before. This time, he even uncovered her toes and stroked the bottoms. Whatever he learned, he must've been satisfied.

He jotted a couple of notes into his iPad and removed the thermometer. "There now. That's the temperature I wanted to see." He tucked the rest of his tools into his case. He reached over her and took the warming bag. "I'll take care of this." It joined the rest of his supplies in his case which he closed. Then he moved back toward Alynne and squatted in front of her, his blue eyes twinkling. "Are you feeling better?"

"Much." Alynne smiled at him.

"A warm shower will help once all the tingling goes away. Not hot. And not a bath until you're feeling completely normal."

Sounded incredible to her. "I can't thank you enough."

He stood and hoisted the large case and smirked. "Stay safe, Cheesy." He and his partner clomped through the entrance hall. The door chime proclaimed their exit.

"We were talking about a ricochet." Jason had the memory of an elephant.

"I'm not sure why I used that word. Is it important?"

Jason tugged the quilt from around him, folded it over his arms, and put it back on the chair in which he had been sitting. "If it hit something, we might be able to get information from the leftover bullet. If it ricocheted, it's unlikely that we'd be able to find it."

She closed her eyes for a moment and tried to relive the event. She'd bent down to pick up the net and … "Wood splintered.

Somewhere above me when I bent down. That's why I thought of it as a ricochet."

"That's all?"

She couldn't think of anything else. She sat up with more ease than she expected and rumpled the blankets. "Look I heard shots and ducked. Then I sort of slid into the lake."

"And you heard nothing else?" Jason continued to prod.

She shut her eyes again. Was there anything else? "The motorcycle revving. It drove away, but I couldn't tell from where it came."

"How many shots?"

She focused her thoughts. "I know there were two before I went into the lake. I don't think more than that. And maybe one other." What else had she heard? "And a whimper. Wait, I heard Rosie yelp. Is she okay?"

Momma tensed. "Oh, dear. Was she shot?"

Jason hit a button on his radio. "Anyone have eyes on the dog that belongs to Myra Stone?"

A voice crackled over the device, but she couldn't make out what it said.

Jason clicked the button again. "Thanks." He turned to Alynne. "That was the chief. She's been hurt."

"Oh no." Alynne tried to stand up, but Jason stepped in front of her.

"I'll go. Don't worry. We'll take good care of her," he said then looked at Momma.

"You need to get changed dear. I'll go with you, just in case you need help." Momma and Aunt Billie helped her stand.

"I'll be fine." She wobbled even as she spoke.

"Just in case," her mom repeated and guided her into the main hall.

Chapter Twenty

Stupid girl.

The words rushed through Jason's head as he stepped onto the porch, but he didn't mean them. If anything, she was one of the smartest women he knew. If only she'd think about her own safety.

He went out to his Jeep and exchanged his soaked shirt for a dry T-shirt and a jacket. Then he moved toward the tree line where the majority of the activity was going on. The two paramedics carried their gurney toward him.

"Another injury?" Jason couldn't get a good look at what they carried.

"The dog's not dead," Mark Bannister assured him. "Though she's been hit with something. We're going to take her over to Dr. Harpavat."

He wasn't the only vet in town, but he was a good man. And new enough to be willing to see patients at odd hours. Once in a while, he'd even been known to take off some time to go fishing with him and Ellis, so he already knew Rose.

"Is she knocked out?"

Harris, Bannister's partner, replied. "She was when they found her. Now only groggy."

"Poor thing." Jason watched as the two men worked to make the dog's ride smooth. "I promised Alynne I'd take care of her."

Bannister laughed. "Well, if you promised Alynne ..." He lifted an eyebrow. "Don't worry, man. We've got her."

Harris chuckled. "You got her. I have no idea what to do with a dog. I only had turtles when I was growing up."

The doc would keep her until she had fully recovered. Knowing he could report that Rose was in good hands, he moved toward the tree line again.

"I'm going to want a cast of that tire print. Any footprints at all?" The chief was shouting at Evans, keeping his distance from the crime scene tape that already encircled a large portion of the wooded area.

"And you're way out here, why?" Jason watched the photographer click shots of some odd indentations near the base of a large live oak.

"Still hard to say where the forest ends, and the crime scene begins. I can direct things out here just as well. The fewer people in that area, the better the chances of finding small details."

"Like the motorcycle tire track."

"Yeah. The back tire spun out it seems. But the front one has a print that's still intact."

Fishtail. He'd seen that before. "Anything else?"

The chief took off his cowboy hat and wiped his forehead before putting it back on. Jason felt a twinge of jealousy. His had gone in the lake. Even if he could fish it out, he'd never want to wear it again.

"Looks like someone was here for a while. More than a half-hour, but probably less than an hour."

Dell was as observant as they came, but this was a lot of detail, even for him. "And you know that how?"

"They found a smoldering cigarette in the dirt under that tree and some marks there near it. Coulda been a rifle stand."

"A rifle stand?" That took some planning.

"Like I said, they'd been here a while."

"How did they pack it up so fast?" Evans had called in the shots, but it hadn't been five minutes before he'd heard the retreating motorcycle.

"No answer for that. That's exactly what our unidentified subject did, though." The chief picked a piece of bark from the tree next to him. "The gun stand makes this an attempted murder. No two ways about it."

Jason breathed deep and held it a moment. "You think this has something to do with her dad?"

"It has to."

He concurred. "She hasn't said anything about accidents that happened in Dallas."

"I think you need to take a closer look at the family members." Dell threw down the wood chip. "And what's all this talk of treasure? I heard about it from Todd a couple times. And I know Ellis used the stories to add to the mystique of this place. But why is it coming up now?"

Jason had wondered the same thing. "I get the impression that it's only a distraction for Myra. Have you heard buzz around the town, though?"

"Some guy was in the library the other day. He was looking up the history of the inn. When it was built, renovation documents. There wasn't a lot."

"And how did you find out about that?" Jason asked him, eyeing the team as they prepared the plaster to make the tire-print cast. Another investigator took measurements.

"Juanita was looking into things. She's nosy like that," Chief Tate told him. A siren sounded in the lot and wailed a good five seconds before it was finally turned off. Dell grimaced. "Too early in the morning for that nonsense."

Couldn't be one of HPPD officers. They're downright threatened to use the sirens sparingly. Before he could voice his suspicions, Sheriff Beauregard Kindrich arrived with Deputy Cain in his wake like a loyal puppy.

"I don't mean to be rude, Beau, but aren't you getting a little tired of coming to all of my crime scenes." The chief leaned against one of the trees.

"I have county CSI men on their way here now." The sheriff raised his voice. "You men, move out of the area."

Most of the officers didn't pay attention to him. Those who did looked up for a moment then went right back to their tasks.

"You're in violation of county law, Dell. And I'll thank you to get your officers out of my crime scene."

The chief turned to face the man. Beau Kindrich was probably the only man in Permian County that the chief would look up to, physically anyway. And even at that, he barely paid enough attention to him to look him in the eyes. But he did this time. His gaze unwavering. "Now listen up, Beau. You know you're standing south of the city limit line. I'm not going to waste your time proving it to you. But if you show up at my crime scene just one more time. Any of them, I'll make sure the voters of Permian County know you can't read a map when I run against you for sheriff."

"You are not." Kindrich flinched. "You haven't filed to run against me."

"Prior to the deadline. Check the record." Dell still didn't move, though the sheriff backed up a step, almost tumbling over Cain.

"This isn't over, Dell." He pointed his finger at them then turned back to the lot.

"Better be the end of me finding you at my crime scenes," Dell called after them. "And we'll find out in a couple of weeks about the rest of it."

"You really running for sheriff?" Jason studied the man. He'd certainly make a good one.

He shrugged. "Nothing ventured, as they say." He gave Jason a half-grin. "And we got a good man in the HPPD who can take over for me. More than I can say for our county department."

Well, Jason sure wasn't going to vote for him. No sir. Dell needed to stay right where he was and keep Jason from having to do all of the tedious administrative work.

"Back to where we were, though." Dell wiped his hand over his face. "Juanita caught a vibe that maybe not everyone here loved Ellis as much as it seems."

"You're talking about Alynne's sister."

The chief nodded then pushed the button on his radio. "Make sure the photographer gets a picture of the tracks and the indentions by the tree before they make the casts. And while he's at it, get photos of the tree itself. Maybe our unsub leaned the gun against it."

Jason reflected on what he'd seen in Phyllis. "She's not very nice. And yes, I think Phyllis is hiding something. I don't know much about her husband except that he's running for office."

The chief chuckled. "And you can't trust anyone who's running for office, right?"

Jason didn't dare agree. "I think he's an all right guy. Ambitious."

"Look into his background anyway." The chief pulled a toothpick from his pocket and tucked it into his teeth.

"Yeah, since he was the one shooting the gun several days ago." Jason stroked his fingers through his hair, finger-combing the tangles that had dried there. He must look like a half-eaten haystack.

The chief turned to look at him. "He had a pretty stupid reason if I remember. And we know she was all involved in that, so check them both."

"Anyone else?" Jason had the feeling they were missing something.

"Everyone else."

The chief didn't need to say it. Whoever their unknown subject was, he was getting bolder. And that spelled danger for Alynne and her mom.

Alynne woke up even earlier the next morning. Well, of course, she did. She'd done little but sleep all day and take warm baths. Cat even brought her meals up to her. Thankfully, she'd been with her when Blayne came up to her room. The redhead was really beginning to grow on her. Cat had shooed Blayne off with a sweet smile and a spine of steel.

She gave her head a shake. The last thing Alynne needed to do was spend any mind time on Blayne. Pop's funeral started in just a few hours. She needed to be ready for it, but more importantly, she needed Momma to be ready for it.

By the light of a bright moon filtering through her windows, she fluffed her hair and put on a pair of clean pants and a T-shirt. If she stayed much longer, she'd need to bring more clothes in from Dallas. She shrugged on a jacket and slipped on some shoes. Jason would probably fuss at her for stepping outside without bodyguards and protective clothing, but she needed his help to complete this morning's plan.

She opened her door. A white card sat on the top step with her name on it. She recognized Blayne's handwriting and a pang of guilt washed over her. Had he been worried about her? She should have at least taken some time to talk with him. If nothing else but to assure him that she was fine. Unfolding the card, she read the short note.

I know I'm letting you down, but it can't be helped. I have an important meeting in Dallas tomorrow. Yes, on a Saturday. And another one first thing Monday morning. I'll return Monday evening and hope that we can have some time for only us. No drama or interruptions. Sorry I can't be at your dad's funeral, but I bet it will be very nice. Funerals aren't really my thing anyway.

Thanks for understanding.

Blayne

Understanding? There was no understanding here. She stomped down the steps, across the kitchen, and out the front door. This is a funeral, not a baseball game. Though he'd never taken her to one of those either. Life stopped when the people in one's life needed consoling. Even if it meant going to something that wasn't his thing.

Her irritation grew as she crossed the moonlit gravel parking lot. Truth be told, she really didn't care that he wasn't coming. And that in itself was telling.

Jason climbed out of his cruiser. "Do you have trouble understanding the concept of staying inside? It means remaining within the confines of that house." He pointed. "*In* doesn't even include the porch and certainly not the parking lot."

"I need a donut run." If he was forcing her to deal with bodyguards, then the least he could do was help her feed her family, so Momma didn't have to.

His jaw sagged open. "Are you kidding?"

The silent walk across the lot also reminded her of the missing beast. She swung the passenger door wide and slumped into the seat.

He climbed into the driver's side. "Ah, so you can be a bear in the morning." He only looked at her once and then circled the cruiser in the gravel toward the exit.

"I am not. I'm downright chipper in the mornings." She glared at him. "Most mornings."

"I can see that." A pasted smile appeared on his face. "And you want donuts."

She shut her eyes and willed the heat behind them to go away. "Yes. Donuts." She took a deep breath and lowered her voice to normal levels. "I don't want Momma to be cooking today unless she really wants to."

A tear squeezed out of the corner of her eye. This was the last thing she needed this morning, but she had to know. "Have … have you heard anything about Rose?"

"Last night, doc said he'd keep her under observation for a couple of days."

"Is she okay?" Why Alynne should care about that beast was beyond her, but she did.

"I think she'll be fine."

They rode in silence for a few moments before Jason gave her a look of genuine concern. "What's got you so riled up this morning?"

Besides his tirade? "It's my boyfriend."

"Blayne? I thought he was your fiancé."

"Yeah. And … I don't know what he is." Her head was beginning to hurt. "But he's not coming to Pop's funeral. Has a conflict. A business meeting." She shook the card in front of her.

"And besides, funerals aren't really his thing." She slapped the card into her lap.

"And he left you a card to tell you all of that?"

"Right." It could have been worse. He could have blown her off without a card, a call, or even a text.

"I'm sorry."

He might've said it, but his tone didn't sound like he was sorry about Blayne. "I suppose you're on duty."

"Sort of. Chief has us all on special duty during the services."

"I see. So, are you expecting trouble, Officer?" Her voice had gone icy. But she wasn't mad at Jason.

"Not in the least. Just hoping to support the family in their time of grief."

A half-hour later, she delivered the donuts to the warmer in the dining hall with Jason's help. Then he went back on duty in the lot, and she returned to the kitchen just in time to find the three sisters chatting as they washed their hands.

"We already have breakfast. I didn't want you to have to cook this morning of all mornings."

Her mom hugged her. "Oh, thank you, sweet girl."

The way Momma oohed and ahhed about the different types of donuts, one would think Alynne went all the way to Paris, France, for the pastries. But at least those treats gave her and the aunts the chance to simply enjoy the meal. It became a party as each family member entered.

Phyllis came in dressed to the nines in some designer pencil dress, black stilettos, and a little hat with a black mesh veil.

"Wow." That must've cost her husband quite a bit. And he

was no slouch either in a dark Armani suit. "I love the outfit, Phyllis, but I think you might be a little overdressed for this small-town affair."

She smirked. "Things aren't always what they seem, little sister. You might want to doll up a little extra unless you want to be a national embarrassment."

Alynne went cold. "What have you done?"

"Why nothing." She sniffed at the donuts and poured a mug of coffee. "Nothing more than allowing the news outlets to know of our deep grief." She turned fully toward Alynne. "After all, Carl is a celebrity. And the voters back home want to see this heartbreaking scene. You can bet this will be worth at least five percentage points. And the timing is perfect for the upcoming election."

"I'm so glad Pop's death was so convenient for you." An icy tone filled her voice, and she didn't care. Her sister was actually planning to exploit the death of her own father. How could she do that?

But what could Alynne possibly do about it?

Who would've thought something as private and serious as a funeral would become such a circus? Jason had heard of instances of picket lines and riots, but he'd never seen any at a funeral. And he'd never seen such a thick cloud of paparazzi hovering at such a reverent time. He lifted off his back-up cowboy hat and wiped the sweat off his forehead. Not as lightweight as the one he'd left in the lake, this one made him sweat even before the summer heat set in.

He stationed an officer at the door and made it his own responsibility to ensure no reporters or photographers set foot on the church's property until the service was over and the mourners had left. Thankfully, they'd gotten word of the media early enough to put up police line tape. Jason monitored the only entrance left unblocked. He had a clipboard, but it was only for show. As long as the people in the cars gave him their names, he pretended to check them off and assumed they were honoring Ellis instead of exploiting the situation.

It had worked so far. Until Carl and Phyllis Henderson turned into the lot.

"What is all this?" Phyllis shouted across her husband through the open window.

Jason had assumed that the reporters had been brought in because of Carl Henderson and his candidacy. "If they aren't here to get a story about your husband, I'm not sure, ma'am."

"I know why the reporters are here. What's all the police line lunacy? Why isn't the media inside the church where they can hear the service?"

Was she serious? "The family doesn't want media attention at such a time."

"*I'm* the family. I say they must come in immediately." Fire shot out of her eyes.

"With all due respect ma'am ..." Or at least the thimbleful of respect he could muster for her. "Your mom is the one who has the say here. She doesn't want your dad's funeral to become a media event." At least, he'd gleaned that much from her when she'd arrived with a shocked look on her face.

"This is reprehensible. You will do as I say at once, you hear?" The woman almost popped her husband in the nose as she shook a fist at Jason.

"Sweetheart, the reporters can hear you." Carl Henderson's patient smile never ebbed.

Phyllis straightened and put her hand to her forehead under a short layer of filmy, black material. "I'm sorry. I'm so desperately distraught." She paused and looked out the passenger-side window where a videographer took it all in.

Distraught, indeed. Carl Henderson continued on, pulling into a nearby parking space though there were dozens of others much closer to the church. He jogged around the car and made a show of opening the door for his wife. Then he waved to the photographers with a sad look on his face and turned his attention to his wife who sniffled into a lace handkerchief.

Whatever. Jason left an officer on duty at the church lot while he collected Officer Evans. The two of them drove to the Thompson Cemetery on the east side of town and parked across the street in an empty lot.

The graveyard was already buzzing with media. A news team had set up near the newly dug grave. Several other teams and single reporters were finding just the right places to catch the tears of grief that would sell this story.

Evans gave him a surprised look. "You don't think they expect to stay here, do you?"

"Who knows." He motioned him to the left while Jason struck

out to the right.

He approached the most prominent team near the mourners' tent. "I'm sorry, but this is private property. You must leave immediately."

A woman about his age stood and gave him a sultry glance. "We were called in by the family to do a story here."

"No, ma'am. You were called in by a member of the extended family to get free publicity." Jason halted his explanation, noticing the camera was rolling. No way would he be responsible for names leaking out. "If you want to continue to be used as puppets, you must do so from outside the fence. Maybe next to the sign that clearly notes this is private property? Huh?"

The next few reporters had already heard the interchange and were heading to the entrance. No doubt to gain the best view. They would still be working to get the most heartrending images of the poor, pathetic widow and her family. But he'd had enough notice to make a plan.

Evans had already made it back to the open gate. Jason only had to speak to two other reporters. Both argued, but in the end, they complied. Thankfully, the news team had moved as well. They glared at him from their spot opposite the mourner's tent. With the right angle, they probably thought they'd have a great shot over the casket and right into Myra's face.

Let them think that.

Cat and Ray arrived a few minutes later, lugging large boxes from their car.

Ray helped his wife put two boxes on each side of the gate opening, then moved to Jason. "The tip you got was a good one. I don't think we had this many cameras at the Easter Kiddy Carnival."

Jason laughed. "Maybe not so many fancy ones." But there'd been hundreds of moms and dads getting shots of their kids in the field of bluebonnets in a roped-off area of Memorial Park. "You get the supplies all right?"

"Yup." Ray grinned. "The manager at the store even said if we bring them back with the tags on, they'll return your money."

"Nice of him." Jason hadn't expected that when he'd contrived this little plan. "Did the minister make an announcement?"

"We didn't stay for the end, but I don't think so. His assistant stuffed the program with these." Ray handed him a quarter sheet of paper.

Please help us protect the private pain of our dear sister, Myra Stone. Collect an umbrella at the cemetery gate. Open and use it to create a barrier to keep the family members from unwanted exposure of their grief.

That would do it.

"Looks like the procession has arrived." Cat pointed up the street where a solo motorcycle cop had stopped in one of the town's busiest intersections to allow no less than thirty cars to move without interruption. The hearse and the limousine carrying the family pulled into the graveyard and parked at the side while the other cars in the procession parked along the street. The funeral director and his assistant moved to the back of the hearse and were joined there by six pallbearers. Jason had been asked to be one of the team, but he had declined, believing he'd better serve the family in this capacity.

The chief stood tall at the head of the group. Carl Henderson was opposite him, acting as the new patriarch of the family, which he was, sort of. Phyllis, being the oldest, held the old-fashioned rank in the family over Alynne. It galled Jason. Especially when Alynne cared a great deal for both of her parents while Phyllis didn't seem to give a hoot about either of them. Maybe she had a different way of expressing her sorrow.

One of the church elders and Ellis's Bible Fellowship teacher were also in the group. At the back was an older gentleman whom Jason didn't recognize. Opposite him was another member of the family, Ellis's cousin maybe. Jason couldn't remember the name. He kept looking over his shoulder and scanning the crowd. The director's assistant followed with his head appropriately bowed.

A few mourners arrived and opened their umbrellas. They walked alongside the casket to prevent more photos as it reached its final resting place. More people moved to the other side. When the small group finally reached the grave, the area had been completely surrounded by open umbrellas. Even Jason couldn't see more than the top side of the green tent that covered the space.

A couple of minutes passed as more and more people filled the path. The funeral director stood at the door of the limo, watching the sea of black umbrellas ebb and flow in the brilliant sunlight. Good thing he was tall, or Jason wouldn't have been able to see him at all. He could only guess that the man was opening the limo's door and helping the family members out of the car. Phyllis must've been inside since she hadn't been with her husband. Friends surrounded the vehicle, successfully ruining every shot that was attempted.

"It's Jason, isn't it?"

He'd been so engaged in the human drama that he hadn't scanned the rest of the crowd and had missed Carl Henderson's approach from the area of the tent. The cameras flashed away.

Carl took Jason's arm and turned his back to the media, dropping his voice to a fraction of a whisper. "Your plan to spare Myra was brilliant."

What? Really? Jason awaited the dropping of the other shoe.

"I only wanted to thank you for protecting her ... well, from me, I guess. Phyllis can't help it. The prestige and influence are like a drug to her. But I was sick when I learned of her plans. I know I'll have to smile for the cameras, but I'm terribly glad that poor Myra doesn't have to."

"Uh ... your welcome." Jason shook the hand that was offered and then stared after the man as he strode to the walkway and inserted himself into the black covering. It moved like an amoeba to the green tent. The service only lasted a half-hour or so. A song of God's sovereignty rose up unaccompanied. The mourners began drifting away, lining the path once more.

Once Myra, her sisters, and Alynne had been seated again in the limo, it backed out of its place and then led the hearse back through town to a luncheon that awaited them at the church.

The people returned their umbrellas to Cat and Ray at one side of the gate. Jason helped lift the boxes into the bed of the pickup. He turned to go to his own car and caught the flashes of a dozen cameras still on sight. A tearful Phyllis was being consoled by her husband for the expressed purpose of reaching the national television audience.

They'd probably do an interview before all was said and done, but Jason wasn't going to force himself to watch that.

Chapter Twenty-One

Was it simple gratitude?

Alynne didn't know. She wasn't sure she even cared. What she did recognize was the hop her heart made when Jason Danvers walked into the church's family life center and removed his cowboy hat. No, she hadn't been waiting for him. Not really. But she had moved around the table to put her back against the windows so she could have a clear view of the entrance.

Momma sat on her right and gave the man a wave. "You can sit with us, dear boy."

"I heard the service was moving." He set the hat upside-down on the table.

"And blessed." Alynne gave him a smile. "I'm sorry you couldn't be there, but I appreciate all that you did."

Momma's face clouded for a moment. "I just can't see what got into that girl. How could she justify inviting all those journalists?"

Alynne put an arm around her mom. Ostracizing Phyllis

wasn't the answer. "I think she was simply trying to make the best of this sad situation. Letting the media in on her grief would help Carl look heroic for his election."

"I don't think she has any grief. That girl's as shallow as a snake's belly. And after all that Ellis did for her." Momma had gotten ticked at Phyllis plenty, especially during her ugly teenage years, but she'd never spoken about her like that.

"I know Phyllis loves you and Pop as much as I do. As much as any daughter would. Maybe she has trouble showing her true emotions."

Momma turned toward her and stared for a moment.

"Well, finally." Aunt Bobbie was sitting on the other side of Momma and gave a loud harrumph.

Phyllis preceded Carl into the room.

"I'd about decided that we were going to need to deliver their lunch out to the parking lot so the reporters could get some realistic shots of them eating ribs and corn on the cob." Aunt Bobbie laughed.

Aunt Billie chimed in with a laugh of her own. "Wouldn't those have been glamorous shots. And the burps afterward would have made some newsworthy sound bites." A tremor of giggles erupted from both of them.

Momma gave an unladylike snort and shook her head.

As much as Alynne felt she needed to defend her sister for Momma's sake, she wanted to kick her pencil-thin skirt right back to Seattle or Portland or wherever she lived. At least it was far away.

Phyllis moved to their table and put her hand on the chair

across from Alynne. The one that Jason was standing by. "You don't mind, of course. After all, this is a family table." She glared at him openly.

"Jason is family." Momma stood and raised her voice so that a hush fell on the room. "You either mind your manners, Phyllis, or you can jolly-well go right back out to the parking lot and all those photographers that you love so much."

Jason moved to the end of the table. "I can sit down here. No problem."

He was two seats away from Momma now and three away from Alynne, but then that wasn't important. And the fact that she had Phyllis right across the table from her wasn't all that big a deal in the grand scheme of things either.

After the minister prayed, several people moved to the food tables. Alynne's aunts kept everyone at the table engaged while she went to fill a plate with some of Momma's favorites. She hadn't been eating much this week. Alynne thought she'd been imagining it until Aunt Billie brought up her concern about it. Momma would eat at this meal. With a full plate, Alynne made her way back to the table and set it before Momma.

"Oh, my. So much."

"You don't have to eat it all. But I wanted you to have a sample of all the dishes from your friends and neighbors."

"They are such kind people." Momma picked up her fork.

"So, about the inn." Phyllis laced her fingers together and rested them on the table.

"This isn't the time." Alynne gave her a pointed look. How could she even think about discussing that here?

"I'm only wondering about Mother's plans."

Phyllis's use of the word *mother* grated on Alynne's nerves. Momma never liked that term.

Alynne prepared to answer her, but Momma beat her to it. "My plans for the inn are none of your concern, Phyllis, and frankly, none of your business."

"But as a member of this family …"

"That is enough." Momma only slightly raised her voice this time.

Carl returned to the table with two loaded plates and set one in front of Phyllis. "Sweetheart, let's enjoy this gathering. After I take office, it might be some time before we can return."

"Humph. Probably not until someone else dies." Her eyes flashed.

Alynne leaped to her feet and shouted at her, "You won't be invited." Once again, the room quieted.

Jason stood and put a calming hand out. "Look. Times like these are full of emotion. Let's not let it get the best of us."

Alynne leveled Phyllis with her glare, but her sister didn't flinch from the challenge.

Momma stood in the silence and pinned Phyllis with a calm and steady look of her own. "I want you to leave. Now."

Phyllis shifted her stare and dropped her jaw. "You can't be serious."

Momma didn't answer. Alynne studied her profile, the unwavering gaze and the set of her shoulders. Not raised in anxiety. And her jaw wasn't tight as though angry. She seemed completely assured and full of peace, as though the words she'd said couldn't have come out of her mouth.

Jason hated the drama he witnessed. Myra loved her family, and it must've taken quite a lot for her to speak such a final word to her oldest daughter.

And Phyllis's response had been confusing at best. "All right, dear Mother. For now."

She turned and sashayed out of the room leaving her husband to apologize for her rudeness. Again. Didn't the man get tired of cleaning up after her?

Jason took the opportunity to move down to the seat in front of Alynne. He shoved the two filled plates aside and sat. "I hope you don't mind." He took a forkful of brisket.

"Oh, course not." She smiled and took a delicate bite from her sandwich.

"Officer." He turned as Ellis's cousin stood close behind him. His voice all but a whisper. "I have a problem."

Jason stood again and put his napkin in his chair. "Excuse me, ladies." He got the feeling that the bite of brisket was all he was going to get and carried his hat away with him.

The man, Ronald, led him outside under the covered drive. Happily, the media had moved on to other areas of interest. "It's my wife."

Jason waited for the man to continue, hoping he wasn't about to get knee-deep in a new bit of family drama.

"She didn't come." He gave the impression that his statement was the extent of his complaint.

"Maybe she wasn't feeling well or had something else to do?" Was this guy really complaining to him about his wife's attendance at the funeral?

"No. You don't understand. She didn't come home last night. She … had an errand to run."

"I see." Jason pointed left toward the downtown square. "You'll want to go down to the police station and file a missing person's report." Though being gone for one night wasn't really a big deal.

"Something's happened to her. I know something's happened to her." He grabbed Jason's arm with a death grip.

"Okay." Jason detached the man's hand and tugged out his notepad and pen. "When was the last time you saw her?"

"Yesterday. In the morning. She had an errand."

"You told me that. Where was she going?" Could her car have had trouble?

"She … uh … I'm …" The man's worry turned into agitation. "You're probably right. I'm probably making too much of this."

Something wasn't right. "Well, since I'm already taking notes about it, you might as well go ahead and tell me the rest."

Jason extracted what little information the man was willing to give as they walked toward the station. He jotted down the basic information about his wife, Sheila, as well as the details of the red car she drove. When he escorted Ronald inside, the man's face paled, and he began to sweat.

Noting the strange behavior, Jason took the man to Juanita Estrella's office. "I think we have a missing person," he told her as he ushered in Ronald. Juanita was easily the most intuitive person he'd ever met. "His wife, Sheila, ran some errands yesterday and never returned."

"Oh dear." She offered him a chair and caught Jason's eye. He lifted his chin, a sign that something was up, and she nodded. "I'll take care of completing the report."

"Thanks. She was last seen at the inn, so I'll head out there. And I'll drop off a BOLO on her car."

It was the best he could do for the man with what little he'd been willing to share. But Jason had no doubt Juanita would be able to extract deeper information. She had a way about her.

Jason set his GPS to document his movements and started for the inn. Reaching the road that ran along the front of the inn, he didn't stop but took that oil-topped road around past the turn-in to the Kennedale ranch. It turned into a gravel road at that point, but Jason had been down it before. It joined up with County Road 2817 prior to where the county road crossed the dam at the other end of Lake Grayson. He finished the circuit by turning left on Arron Road that went up to the scout camp on Arron Point. Then he returned to the inn. No luck, but that was only the first ring.

Jason spent the rest of his time off on Saturday doing slow circles. He spent part of the night in the inn's parking lot then caught a few hours' sleep before church started. He couldn't fathom that Alynne and her mom would actually be there, but Officer Evans was staying by them at the inn and would accompany them if they did come.

On his way to the service, he heard a call on his radio. "HPPD zero-seven-zero, reporting a 187 at FM 8817, one mile south of

Junction 523."

Jason slowed and pulled into the empty spaces in front of the hardware store to turn around. A murder didn't happen often in this little town, though Heath's Point had been on a bit of a spree. But his thoughts immediately went to the missing woman.

"Be advised, this is a 10-71."

A shooting didn't automatically spell murder. Not in this hunting mecca of East Texas. But Sanchez knew his stuff. If he said it was a murder, it was murder.

"Victim resembles 10-57."

That's why he'd been listening: the missing person code. Jason picked up his magnetic light and attached it to his roof. He turned on his siren for the trip. It would take a bit. His arrival at Farm-to-Market Road 8817 coincided with a county cruiser coming from the other direction.

Great. Sheriff Kindrich had been monitoring the HPPD radio again. And from the looks of things, Chief Tate hadn't come, probably still at church. Jason put in a quick call to Mrs. Hawkins to get the chief on site, and he then climbed from his Jeep.

"You might as well just hop on back in that vehicle, boy." Cain, aka Deputy Puppy, glared at him as he approached the yellow tape that Officer Billings had already attached to trees around a red Smart car and a dirt bike.

The sheriff barely looked at him as though he regarded him as nothing more than an insect bite. "Thank you for preserving our sight. You can move along now," he said to the older cop.

Billings was a little on the short, dumpy side, but that didn't keep him from standing up to the taller, higher-ranking man.

"Sorry, Sheriff. The victim resembles a woman reported as missing to our department." He put his hand on the weapon at his hip. "I'm sure our departments can work together, but I can't let you take a step onto this crime scene unless I'm instructed to do so by Chief Tate."

Jason had to hand it to the man. He'd not known he had such gumption. "Sheriff, so good of you to come. I'm sure we'll be sharing information with your department soon, as, clearly, we are in your jurisdiction, but Billings is correct. Since we received the missing person report and found the scene, we can't turn it over to you without direction from our authority. You're welcome to wait, though. I've already contacted the chief, and he's on his way." Jason ducked under the tape but stayed near the other officer, a good ten yards from the car and cycle. He donned some latex gloves.

The sheriff turned a death look on Jason.

"Look, boy. You can't talk to the sheriff that way." Cain took a step toward the tape.

Jason stood his ground, stretching his hand slightly in front of him. First, to urge the man to stop, though he doubted that would work. Second, to put him in a good position to draw his weapon, though he prayed it wouldn't come to that. He'd only had to do that a handful of times and never came away from the event unscarred. "I'm asking you, Deputy, to follow protocol." Might as well feed his ego, tossing around the titles. "You know this is procedure for a fresh crime scene. Please, back away." He didn't raise his voice or make any motion that would give a hint of a dare. No bravado or arrogance to his tone. Nothing condescending.

Heck, he'd even used the magic word.

Cain chuckled and shook his head. "If you aren't the …"

"That's enough, Deputy." The sheriff spoke to Cain but locked his gaze with Jason. "We'll wait for your supervisor, Lieutenant." He nodded and edged away, grabbing Deputy Puppy's uniform and spinning him around as well.

Jason could swear he heard the sheriff hiss, "Bad dog."

They would have to turn this scene over. No question about that, but he intended to learn everything he could before that happened. He turned and scanned the scene. The car faced them, having pulled onto a turn-off, little more than a tractor road that led to an empty cattle range. The dirt bike was on its side in the mud in a slight culvert to the right of the car. A female was face-down on the side of the culvert. Almost looked like she died trying to climb up to the car from the ditch. A hunting rifle lay in the mud next to her. Jason couldn't see her face or any other details at this distance. "So, what does it look like?"

He approached the vehicle from the side opposite where the woman lay.

"Shot twice in the back as far as I could see, though I didn't look too close." Billings stepped alongside him.

"Is it the right woman, the one who's missing."

"Looked like it to me." The officer's tone went down. "Can't imagine what errand she'd have way out here."

Jason glanced through the back window. A sweater was in the backseat. On the floorboard, near the open driver's door, was what looked like a broken frame. Glass shards filled the mat. "Any other details? Anything besides that rifle?"

"Yeah, I figured you'd see that." Billings smiled. "Great hunting weapon. She looked to be carrying it over her shoulder."

"How do you figure?"

"Well, the strap's still over her left elbow." He turned to Jason and gestured toward the dirt bike with a tilt of his head. "Think she was the one shooting at Alynne Stone?"

The thought had occurred to him. "Chief thought the shooter used a stand of some sort. See anything like that?"

"Maybe." Billings shifted his weight and barely gestured with is head to the right. "Dirt bike looks to be laying on a bag. Duffle or something like that. Could be a mobile stand."

Jason took a casual look in that direction, but he couldn't tell anything from this distance. "Keys?" They weren't in the woman's hands.

"On the ground near the open door."

Jason backed away and circled the car, keeping a good distance. Strange that the door was open. "Looks to me like she was trying to climb up to the car."

"I'd say so. Body position would back that up."

"But she didn't make it." He looked at the keys under the open door. "So, who unlocked the door?"

"And why?" Billings joined him. "Had to have taken something from the car. It's the only thing that makes sense."

Jason had to agree.

Billings paused and responded something on his radio. "We'll make sure the keys and all get dusted for prints."

"I want copies." Jason looked across at the woman. Billings was right, the strap could very well have been over her shoulder.

"Couldn't she have been carrying the gun in her left hand instead of over her shoulder?" It probably wouldn't matter, but it completed the picture.

"No, sir. Her left hand was pretty mangled."

"Was she also shot in the hand?"

"I don't think so." He turned toward Jason, one eyebrow cocked. "Looked to me like a bad dog bite."

Alynne had begged her mom to lie down for a bit after church. All of the greeting and assuring that she was fine had taken quite a toll on Momma, if she was any judge. Finally, Alynne had walked her back to her suite and convinced her that she could cook a simple meal for the small group that was still left. Then, the front door chimed.

"More guests." Momma had to be exhausted but showed a brilliant smile for the chief and Lieutenant Danvers. "I haven't been able to put lunch together yet, but I've got some chicken salad in the fridge. Shall I make you a sandwich?"

"We're here on official business, Myra." Jason didn't glance at Alynne, keeping his attention on Momma. "Is Ronald Surzchenkov here?"

"I guess he's upstairs." She pointed to the room across from the bathrooms.

"Is something wrong?" Alynne took a step forward, hoping to distract her mom.

Jason leveled a gaze at her. "We need to talk with Ronald."

"So, talk, Officer." Ronald came from the dining hall, taking the landing span in two strides and trotting down the steps as though he owned the place.

Jason's eyebrow arched, but it was the chief who answered him. "Perhaps we'd better go into the parlor?" He glanced at Momma, and she nodded.

"This is unnecessary drama. Simply answer me. Is my wife with you? Where has she been?" The man crossed his arms as though to ward off whatever answer the chief had.

Clearly, the woman wasn't with them, or she would have come in. Unless she'd left Ronald. Maybe that was what this was all about.

One of the cousins came in then with her husband toting a sleeping infant, Momma's youngest niece.

The chief watched them go into the south wing hallway, then returned his attention to Ronald. "I'm afraid I'm gonna hafta insist." He held out his hand to usher the man in the right direction.

Ronald harrumphed but uncrossed his arms and preceded the chief into the parlor.

Jason looked at Momma. "Can you bring some tea?"

She nodded. "And a sandwich for you."

He smiled as Momma retraced her steps back to the kitchen. Alynne turned to join her, but he touched her hand. "You may or may not want to hear this."

"Why?"

"We believe the woman's disappearance might have something to do with the shooting on Friday."

A bolt of ice chilled the back of Alynne's neck. "Oh, no." She followed Jason into the room where the chief had requested her cousin to sit.

"I'd rather stand and get this over with. Obviously, my wife has decided not to return to this place, and I can't say as I blame her." He directed his disgusted look at Alynne as she sank into the armchair nearest the door.

"No, because she's dead," the chief blurted out.

The man froze for a moment, his gaze riveted to the coffee table in front of him. Then he lowered himself onto the sofa along the opposite wall.

He could have been a little gentler in his announcement.

The man lifted his eyes to the chief.

"Do you own a gun, Mr. Surzchenkov?"

"What?" The man's voice broke.

"A rifle to be exact." The chief pulled out his phone and scrolled for a second before pointing at the screen and turning it toward Ronald. "This Beanfield Sniper Remington Sendero. You own one of those?"

The man glanced at the screen and raised his eyebrows. "I don't particularly like guns."

"That didn't answer my question." Chief Tate tucked the phone back into his pocket. "Don't you own that weapon and several other hunting rifles of various styles?"

"Not being a man of arms, I couldn't tell you."

The chief pressed. "Let me make this easier. Is there a hunting rifle that has been registered to you?"

"Possibly." The man lifted his chin.

The smile that spread across the chief's face should have shot terror through the man. It sure creeped-out Alynne. "See there. That wasn't so hard." The chief sat on the chair next to the sofa. "Would you say you have more or less than five such weapons registered to you?"

"I don't see what this has to do with my poor wife."

"More or less?" He leaned forward, putting his elbows on his knees.

Ronald sighed dramatically. "We own seven rifles. My wife is something of an expert."

"*Was* something of an expert. Yeah, I heard about that." The chief kept his tone downright conversational. Unnerving, but thankfully, Alynne wasn't on the other side of it. "Your wife was particularly good with a hunting rifle, wasn't she? Had all sorts of awards."

"Is that a crime?" Was the man incapable of simply answering a question?

"It is if she's shooting at people."

"Don't be ridiculous. She would never …" He turned on the waterworks. "She was the gentlest, kindest person …" His voice trailed off.

That wasn't the Sheila that Alynne had met, but maybe she was gentle and kind to him. Unlikely, but Alynne chose to give the woman the benefit of the doubt.

"Mr. Surzchenkov, do you have a dog?"

He recovered quickly enough. "No. Sheila hates them … hated them. Are you sure she's dead?" His face clouded.

The chief didn't answer him. "Did you know that Myra's pet, Rose, was hit in the head yesterday? Apparently, someone was shooting at Miss Stone there …" He glanced at Alynne. "And the dog attacked the would-be shooter."

"I can't see what that has to do with my wife." The man's voice wiggled.

Alynne didn't like the turn this conversation had taken. She'd only barely met Sheila Surzchenkov. What was the chief not saying?

"I only ask, because your wife has a nasty bite on her hand. Dog bite as far as we could tell, and from the amount of blood on the sleeve of her denim shirt, it happened before she died." He took a breath. "Where did your wife go yesterday morning, so early?"

The man shot a glance at Alynne and then at Jason standing on her right. "She said she had errands to complete. I assumed they had to do with the funeral. Maybe she needed new shoes or a dress?"

"And you didn't think it strange that she carried her rifle with her when she left to go shopping?"

"Well, I didn't know where she was going." His voice cracked. "Maybe she wanted to do a little hunting out here? Squirrels and rabbit are all over the place."

Alynne couldn't argue with that.

The chief nodded in silence. The pause grew to awkwardness. For a few seconds, Ronald kept his eyes on the chief, but then he fidgeted with the couch cushion. "When can I see my wife?"

Chief Tate didn't answer. "Mr. Surzchenkov, I'm terribly sorry for your loss. But I can't help but wonder, sir, why you haven't asked how your wife died?" The chief paused, and the hammer pound resounded.

He was right. That had been Alynne's first question about Pop. Would be for anyone.

Ronald lowered his chin. *Oh my gosh!* Had he killed his own wife? And for what? For shooting at Alynne? None of this made sense.

"I think, sir, that you and I need to go down to the station and talk a little more." The chief raised his volume. "Billings, you want to come in?" The uniformed cop who had been waiting in the foyer entered the room and helped Ronald to his feet.

Tate continued, "You're not under arrest, Mr. Surzchenkov. We're just transporting you to the station for questioning. You may refuse all questions or request your attorney's presence at any time. If you don't have an attorney, one may be provided for you at your request. Do you understand?"

The man mumbled something and then turned to stare at Alynne. Hatred shot from his eyes. "Aren't you the perfect little princess?"

A chill, like a cold clammy hand on her back, ran down her spine.

The officer left with the man.

Alynne caught sight of her mom coming in from the kitchen with a silver tray. "Let me take that for you." Alynne jumped up and hoisted it as Ronald was led through the entry hall. Momma dropped her hands and paled.

"Jason," Alynne called as he followed the men.

Momma's chin sagged.

Alynne set down the tray on the floor as Jason caught her Momma. He hoisted her into his arms.

"She all right?" The chief met them at the parlor door and helped Jason take Momma to the recently vacated sofa.

"Momma?" Alynne looked down at her mom's slackened face. "Do something," she shouted at Jason then looked at the chief.

Jason had felt for a pulse and put his ear to her face. "She has a pulse, and she's breathing. She only fainted."

Not surprising, considering all the emotion that had passed through her house over the last week and more. But what about the arrest of Pop's cousin, or nephew or whatever he was, triggered her fainting spell? Surely, there had been more intense issues in all that had occurred. Not the least of which was Pop's death.

She began to moan slightly.

"Momma, are you all right?"

She moaned again, and her eyes fluttered open. "I ... I was ..."

"Getting tea." Alynne dashed out to the forgotten tray and brought it into the room, setting it on the coffee table. "Here." She poured a cup for her mom. Jason lifted her slightly while Alynne held the liquid to her mom's lips.

Myra took a sip and thanked them. She moved her legs to the floor and sat straighter as Alynne settled in next to her and put her arm around her shoulders.

"I'm sorry. I ... don't know ..." Momma stopped and stared at the chief. "What happened to Ronald?

"I sent him to the station with another officer. We're holding him for questioning." Chief Tate came into the room and squatted near where her mom sat as Jason sat beside her. "I don't want to alarm you, either of you …" He included Alynne in his gaze. "We think his wife Sheila was the one who shot at Alynne yesterday."

Alynne had concluded that from the chief's questions, but she watched Momma. Her face wore a veiled look which seemed to cover her eyes.

The chief put his hand on Momma's. "Can you offer any information that might explain why she would do that?"

Momma blinked and pursed her lips together. "My family is beginning to leave, Chief. You and Jason should come back for lunch tomorrow." She stood.

In chorus, Alynne and the two men stood, each with their own urging. "Momma, you need to rest a bit."

"Myra, please sit back down," Jason said.

"I need an answer." The chief's louder response won the verbal tug-of-war. "I have another dead body and evidence that the victim was, in fact, trying to kill your daughter. This can't wait."

Momma looked almost straight up for her gaze to reach the chief's face. "Dell, you were a good friend to Ellis, and you have been to me as well. I will have the answers to your questions tomorrow." She moved past the men and greeted the cousins coming down the stairs.

The chief scratched the back of his head. "I swear that woman's a wizard."

BREAKING POINT

Chapter Twenty-Two

Jason hung around the parking lot for part of the evening, until he couldn't keep his eyes open. If Rose had been around, he would at least have had a companion or something to watch. Instead, he made his way home for the night. The chief had suspended the guard duty. Alynne should be safe. The rifle that they found with Sheila's body matched the bullet they had taken from the rail of the boathouse. There wasn't anything to tie her to the attack in the grocery store parking lot or to the poison in the granola, but Juanita was digging away at Sheila's history. At Ronald's too, for that matter. Now that they had a direction to look, she'd find out if the rental car that tried to run Alynne down had been rented to him.

After a restless sleep, he had arrived at the inn late in the morning, hoping to learn more from Myra.

The widow called to him from the kitchen as he hung his hat on the rack. "I'm so glad you're here. I've been so worried about Rose, but I haven't remembered to check on her during office hours. Have you heard anything?"

He nodded. "Doc said he was pleased with her behavior. Dell talked to him yesterday. I'm sure you'll hear something about her return soon."

After that, she chatted nonchalantly with him as she and her sisters stirred the steaming pots and tasted the contents, but not about Ronald or anything important.

Jason helped them load up the dumbwaiter then sprinted up the steps to unload it.

Alynne was there, setting a gorgeous formal table full of china.

"Whoa. What's all this?"

She shrugged. "Momma has only used her china a couple of times that I know about. Both for fancy dinners. When they informed me they were moving here, and before that, the night she told me she had cancer." She pulled the paper from her pocket. "Looks like several courses."

"Courses?" Even his own wedding hadn't been a formal affair. Just a couple of friends at the local church and some barbecue at his neighbor's house.

She put crystal water goblets at each place. "I'm probably making more out of it than I should. It's just a special meal in honor of Pop."

"What's happening in here?" the chief boomed as he entered from the upstairs landing. "I thought this was a simple lunch and discussion with your mom."

Alynne shook her head. "I think she's invited everyone who's still here: my aunts, my sister and her husband, and I guess Ronald, though I haven't seen him. Is he still in jail?"

The chief set his jaw the way he did when he didn't like something. "He is for the time being, under suspicion of accessory to attempted murder. That's all I could hold him on, and I have flimsy evidence at best with that. If yesterday hadn't been Sunday, he'd already be out."

Jason kept his eyes on the chief's face. The man's jaw twitched, and he shifted his look from Alynne to Jason and then somewhere behind him. Plainly, he wanted to tell Jason something away from the ears of others. In this case, that obviously included Alynne.

"I'll go get some ice." Alynne must've sensed Dell's need to talk.

He hesitated until she turned the corner. "I don't know why Myra is keeping this a secret, but we're all here because Ellis's attorney is reading the will today."

"That's ridiculous. I couldn't be involved in that." Sure, he and Ellis had enjoyed fishing together, but that was the extent of it. "This is a family matter." Besides, why would Myra promise to answer their questions today with that going on?

"I get the feeling there's more to it than we realize." Dell checked behind him where the landing from the main stairs joined the dining hall. "Ronald's no cousin."

That would explain a little more. Jason didn't have time to ask anything as Billie and Bobbie ventured into the room with hot pads and serving utensils.

"This is going to be a grand meal," Bobbie said.

"I'm so glad you could join us." Her sister tucked her hands into the mitts of a long hot pad that looked more like a short blanket. "Having you here this week has been such a comfort to Myra." She opened the dumbwaiter and started to lift out a large dish before Dell rushed to help her.

"Let us unload that for you." He took the hot pads and tossed them to Jason. Bobbie handed another set to Dell and followed her sister back downstairs.

"Ellis's Uncle Todd was his only uncle. He and his wife never had any children." Dell hoisted a large chafing dish. "And Todd didn't have any sisters. Not according to census files. Just Ellis's dad and then Todd much later." Jason pointed to the heated bins, and Dell carried his burden over.

He picked up a dish of his own and followed suit. "So, who is Ronald? Myra said she knew him." And what was he doing here if he wasn't family?

Dell brought over the last one. "Not sure. Still working on that."

"Juanita's been working her magic again." How that woman got the details that she did was beyond him.

He and Dell unloaded a slew of cold platters that came up the dumbwaiter next. By the time they'd finished, Cat and Ray had arrived and stood chatting with Myra and her sisters.

Myra didn't wear her typical grin when she greeted them. In fact, she was rather subdued. So was Alynne, and she stood away from the others on the opposite side of the table.

Phyllis marched into the room followed by Rufus and took the seat at the head of the table. The dog hopped up into her lap and put his front paws on the table. Carl followed at a much slower pace and stopped to greet Myra and her sisters before he wandered over to join Phyllis.

"That's gonna be trouble." Jason sidled closer to Alynne who stood mid-table with her back to the windows. She'd obviously spotted Phyllis's entrance, and her reddening face proved she wasn't pleased about it, though Myra seemed to take it in stride. He nudged Alynne with his elbow. "You okay?"

"I hoped she would leave yesterday with the rest of the family but no luck." She put her back to Phyllis's end of the table. "After everything she did at the funeral, she should never have come back here."

Jason faced Alynne and caught Phyllis's open glare at her sister's back.

Myra turned to take the seat across from where Alynne stood. "I asked her to stay." It was plain that she wasn't afraid of Phyllis hearing her. "This is a special meal, and I told her that it would be to her advantage to remain."

Her advantage? Jason could almost visualize dollar signs over the obnoxious woman's eyes. She wasn't here to honor or even care about family. She was here because she expected to get some type of payment.

Cat rounded the table to stand on the other side of Alynne. "You holding up all right?"

Alynne nodded with a semblance of a smile. "I'm glad Momma invited you two today to help honor Pop."

The doorbell chimed as Billie and Bobbie sat in the seats on either side of Myra.

"Did you invite someone else, Momma?" Alynne sat in the chair she'd been standing behind.

Jason took the one between her and Carl Henderson.

Myra turned to greet the final guest. "Thank you for coming, Tom."

Tom Norton of the Norton-Hughes law firm sauntered to the table. Myra introduced him to her sisters then to Alynne, Phyllis, and Carl. She ushered him to the seat between Phyllis and Billie.

Yep, Dell had nailed this one.

She asked Ray, who sat at the other head of the table, to say grace. Ray Alexander had such a way about him when he spoke with the Father, like a conversation that he might have with anyone, but with a reverence that only the Lord deserved.

When he finished, Myra sniffed, then rang a little bell that she'd placed next to her plate. Three young people from the church came from the kitchen stairs and pounced on the assorted fruit in one dish on the cold bin, serving it in miniature bowls all around the table. And with polite conversation, the meal began, one course at a time. Soup, bread, and salad were courses he could identify. They had fish of some sort followed by a tiny scoop of lime sherbet. Then a large plate of roast beef and vegetables was served. A few other dishes followed, but Jason stopped paying attention. Stuffed after eating the first courses, he could barely taste the other dishes.

Myra tapped her tea glass once slices of Magnolia Pie had been served. "We've had a few assistants here this afternoon. It was important that all of us could focus on the purpose of this event, to honor Ellis's memory as his beloved family and friends. I'd like it if we could go around the table here and share something about Ellis.

After a slight pause, Dell spoke up. "He made a huge impact on this little town in only a decade. He will be terribly missed."

"I was honored to call him friend." Ray nodded his head. "He showed me all over the lake area. And I look forward to having Ellis be my tour guide when I get to heaven."

That elicited a sniffle from Myra.

"I will miss him so much." Cat's voice wavered slightly. "He had such a way of making people feel welcome, like they belonged."

Alynne stared at her plate in front of her. "I treasured our talks when he and Momma would visit me in Dallas. Pop was the wisest man I've ever known." She dipped her head.

"I'd agree with that."

She'd pinpointed exactly what Jason had wanted to share. "Ellis's knowledge of Scripture and love for the Lord has made a huge difference in my life. I'll be forever grateful."

Carl spread out a sad-looking smile. "Hearing you all speak of him makes me wish I'd made it a priority to meet him. He must have been quite a godly man."

He'd never met his wife's father? Wow. Hadn't even spoken with him from the sound of it.

Phyllis glanced at her husband then lifted her pointed chin. "Strange. Hearing you speak of the man makes me wonder if we're thinking of the same self-centered, stingy dictator I was forced to grow up with."

Alynne leaped to her feet. "How dare you." She lunged at her sister, but Jason reached his arm around her waist. "Pop was a great man. You couldn't even be bothered to come home when Momma got cancer so what do you know about anything?"

"Stop." Myra stood. "Phyllis, you were invited here out of respect for Ellis's wishes, but if you cannot honor him and respect those around you with your mouth, then keep it closed."

Phyllis leaned her head back and then tilted her chin toward her mom with something of a pointed, hateful look in her eyes. Jason would swear he was watching the interaction between a parent and teenager and kept having to remind himself that Phyllis was on the north side of forty.

"I do want to thank you all for being here today. This isn't the way wills are generally read, but I thought the formality was worth it."

Jason glanced at Alynne and confirmed from the look on her face that she'd not known about this either.

His will? Why would they need to go through that? Momma should get everything since she was his wife. She had certainly proved that she could take care of an inn full of guests this week. This had to be some sort of legal formality.

Momma was saying something about Mr. Norton. His presence made sense now, and Momma asked him to go through each portion of the will.

Alynne glazed over with the first part, the legalese droned, threatening to put her to sleep. Until Dell's name was mentioned.

"My good friend would never tell me how much he likes the baseball card collection of my childhood, but I can see it in his eyes every time we use the file to check some detail we're arguing about. I want Dell Tate to have that collection in its entirety." Mr. Norton looked up at Dell.

The chief grinned and tears shined in his eyes. "That was too good of him."

Mr. Norton read on, including Jason in his conversation. Apparently, a really nice fishing rod and reel went to him with the suggestion that he receive any other fishing gear that she, Alynne, didn't wish to keep. *Oh!* He wanted her to have his fishing gear. That would certainly stir up some memories.

Next, Mr. Norton announced that Pop donated shares from three different stocks to the Sunset Mission under the direction of Ray Alexander and shares from the same three stocks to Kathryn McPherson for the support of Macs Diner. The stocks were to be sold or retained at the sole discretion of Ray and Cat. The two of them beamed, and so did Momma.

The attorney was moving on to another long list of stocks and investments. Out of these, from the firm managing them, a lifetime monthly income was to be paid to Momma. She was to retain all property purchased during their lives together.

That was a strange way of putting things. Why hadn't he just put her last with the rest of his property going to her? She glanced at Momma and saw dark circles under her eyes. "Wait a minute, Mr. Norton."

Aunt Billie turned toward her sister while Aunt Bobbie handed her a glass of water. "Here, honey. Take a drink of something."

Looked like the fainting spell she'd had yesterday wasn't the end of it, but it had been an intense two weeks. For all of them, but especially for Momma. "I think she needs to go lie down."

"I concur." Aunt Billie stood and urged her sister to her feet.

"I'm fine. Just a little tired." Momma let her sisters lead her to the stairs. "Please continue, Mr. Norton. This needs to be finalized now."

"Well?" Phyllis turned a scoff in the man's direction.

The man didn't even look in her direction. "For my two children…" Mr. Norton raised his eyes toward Alynne. "They alone may inherit the Sunrise Inn and all of its property as it is to remain in the Stone family in perpetuity if at all possible."

He stopped reading and leveled a look on Alynne. "There are all sorts of legal stipulations in this document, but the bottom line is that either or both children may work the inn and thereby inherit it. If only one child wishes to work the inn, then that one child inherits the entire property with a small monetary gift to the heir who doesn't wish to manage the property."

Phyllis burst into laughter. "He would do something so mean. Ha, you get nothing, Dora. After all this."

Alynne's face heated. Phyllis didn't need to know that she'd already thought about staying. Alynne wasn't her mom and never would be, but she'd so enjoyed meeting Momma's friends, baking with her, and slowing down to take a walk and sit on the front porch.

Besides, it was Phyllis who wouldn't be getting anything. No way would she want to stay here.

Mr. Norton gave her a smile. "You don't have to make any decisions right now. But to fully inherit, the heir or heirs must remain living and working on the property from the time of this reading until ten years after this date, allowing no more than thirty nights per year spent away from the inn, and that no more than a week at a time. If neither of the children wants to or are physically capable of staying and working the property, they may together agree to sell it, with each heir receiving an equal portion of the sale."

That would mean Momma received nothing from the sale. If Alynne didn't stay, her sister would get what she wanted once the property sold.

He began reading again. "And as for my stepdaughter, Phyllis Henderson, nee Stone . . .."

Wait. What? Stepdaughter? Phyllis wasn't Pop's daughter. Alynne glanced down the table at the smirk on the woman's face.

Of course, she knew. She'd known all along. She'd tried to ingratiate herself with Alynne to sell the property, but it was so she could get that finder's fee or commission for it. When that didn't work, she didn't care what Alynne thought of her and let her true colors show. Like she'd done at the funeral. Like she was doing now.

Mr. Norton hadn't paused. Alynne's tumultuous thoughts almost made her miss her sister's … no, stepsister's inheritance. "I bequeath one special gift. When and if she is physically present, Phyllis will receive this gift from Myra."

Mr. Norton continued with some concluding statements.

This didn't sit right. Was that what had Momma so upset about this meeting? She'd had a daughter with someone else? Alynne had never thought to put Phyllis's age with Pop and Momma's wedding date.

"I'm ready to leave this barn. How much is this gift I'm supposed to get?" Phyllis ignored her husband's hand on her arm.

"Oh, I'm afraid I don't have any information on that. Your mother will have to give you that herself."

"Myra is not my mother." Phyllis stood, her eyes flashing.

Alynne stared at her then focused on closing her mouth. If she wasn't Pop's daughter or Momma's daughter, who was she?

Phyllis snorted as her gaze hit Alynne's. "I'm sick of pretending for the sake of my poor, pitiful Dora."

"Okay." Alynne straightened her shoulders to take the attack. "So, let all the truth come out then. The will says that Pop was your stepfather." That in of itself wasn't so hard to believe. Phyllis was nothing like Pop, not in looks or in manner.

"He adopted me when my mom cut out." Phyllis gave a cat grin at Alynne. "Ellis's first wife."

She willed her mouth to stay shut this time. Pop and Momma had been married so long, more than thirty years. He'd been married before that?

"Mom took off less than a year after they were married. She couldn't stand the man either or his better-than-you ways." Phyllis stood. "I didn't have a say in the matter. I think I would've been better off in foster care."

Or the pound.

But this certainly explained how Phyllis could be so openly obnoxious with Momma and Pop. How she didn't seem to have a grateful bone in her body for these two people who exuded gratitude to all who were around them and to the Lord. She hadn't belonged to the family at all.

"Your mother couldn't even be bothered to adopt me. She only wanted to keep me around as her little slave, baking your cookies and washing your dishes and cleaning your bedroom."

"I was a baby." She saw her sister ... her stepsister ... with new eyes. The grown woman was still living with all the pain and injury of being abandoned by both her father and her mother.

And suddenly, Phyllis's rants didn't touch her anymore.

But the secrets Momma had kept certainly did.

BREAKING POINT

Chapter Twenty-Three

As Phyllis's face reddened and the slander spewed from her mouth, Jason felt, rather than saw, Alynne's strength wane. "Let's get some air."

He left Phyllis in the care of her husband and the chief. If they couldn't calm her down, he'd suggest a dunk in the lake to chill her out.

Cat followed them out. "I know this is difficult for you."

"I feel so stupid." Alynne paused in the kitchen and walked a worried circle. "Why wouldn't they tell me? Especially after she had moved away?"

Ray joined them and put his arm around his wife. "I know your dad had to have had a good reason to hide this."

Mr. Norton patted her on the shoulder. "I don't think I'm wrong in revealing that the secret they kept was for Phyllis's benefit, not yours. Your father told me that they tried everything they could to help your stepsister feel she was an important part of the family."

Alynne shrugged. Then a pucker formed between her eyebrows. "If Phyllis isn't Pop's other child, then who is?"

The man lifted his chin. "I wish your mother was able to discuss this with you."

"Myra, come back to your room." Aunt Bobbie followed Myra down the hallway.

"I thought I heard your voice, Mr. Norton." Myra moved to sit at the booth. "Please, go ahead."

Bobbie stood on one side of her while Billie took her stance on the other side.

"You might as well," Billie said. "She's not going back to bed until all of the truth comes out."

"I already know about Phyllis, Momma." Alynne had to be hurt by the deception, but her voice was kind and full of compassion.

"The other heir, then…" Mr. Norton cleared his throat. "It's Ronald Ellis Surzchenkov."

Alynne tilted her head. "Pop's cousin? I don't get it."

"Ronald isn't his cousin, sweet girl." Myra kept her voice steady and her eyes held Alynne's gaze. "He was Ellis's son by another woman when they were in college. Ellis didn't even know about Ronald until last summer, just after the man's mother passed away. Ronald is the reason your father redrafted his will a few months ago."

Alynne hadn't moved. Myra lowered her chin as though every ounce of energy had left her. Her sisters once again urged her down the hallway to her suite.

Jason didn't wait for anything else. He ushered Alynne out the kitchen door and into the late afternoon sunshine. Cat and Ray followed them.

"Family secrets are hard to swallow." Cat touched her shoulder. "Believe me."

"It does explain why Ronald would want you out of the way." Jason steered her toward the rose bushes.

Alynne hesitated and looked at him. "I've learned I have a brother, and oh, by the way, he wants me dead."

He should have continued to listen to them instead of chiming in. "This is a shock, but I can guarantee you that Ronald is very glad you're alive at this point."

"Danvers…" Cat eyed him. "Go back to being the strong, silent type."

"He's not wrong." Ray chimed in. "If he does get charged, it won't be for murder."

Jason nodded. That's what he meant. "And what we learned about your sister does explain some of her behaviors."

The group rounded the end of the white fence and aimed for the front of the house.

"I'll say. She has the quickest temper of anyone I've ever met. Momma hardly ever loses her temper and usually only with Phyllis. And I don't think Pop ever even had a temper."

They said good-bye to the Alexanders at the bottom of the steps, and Alynne headed to the swing that hung from the rafters. Jason sat beside her. He caught himself and scooted away. "I guess you've got a lot to share with your fiancé."

She shook her head. "I can't."

"You can't tell him?" Why not. If the guy was serious about

her, he'd want to know about her family, even the warts.

"That's not what I meant." She dropped her chin. "I … he's not what I thought."

Jason loved hearing the words but felt he had to stay objective. "Sometimes people miss things they shouldn't. None of us are perfect."

"No, I'm not going to fool myself this time." She paused. He let her collect her thoughts. "It's not his fault. It's mine. I'd decided he was someone that he simply isn't. I'm the one who made the mistake … all the mistakes."

"You're in one of the most traumatic times of your life." If not *the* most. "Cut yourself some slack." He rubbed her shoulder.

She turned to look at him. "You have been so kind this week. Pop's not here to thank you for being my guard and helping my mom, but you've proved yourself to be a good friend to him in taking care of us." A single tear tracked down her cheek.

"Your dad was very important to me. He and your mom became something of a family for me at a time I'd thought I'd lost everything. My own mom died in an accident with my stepfather drunk at the wheel." He swallowed his emotion. The bitterness he'd felt for so long for that man had given way to pity. "And then my new family, my wife, was killed."

Alynne's face contorted and her eyes shown with unshed tears. "I'm so sorry."

"She was a cop as well, off-duty, and happened upon a robbery in progress. Startled the thief, and he shot her." He'd never before been able to explain what happened to Dawn without breaking down. At the very least tearing up. "It's going on six years, but I finally believe that I'm healing."

She reached for his hand. "I'm glad the Lord brought you here. Looks like He blessed you as much as you have blessed my family."

He squeezed her fingers. "He certainly has."

Her eyes held questions that he couldn't answer. Not yet. But she held his gaze. He leaned in slightly, transfixed on her lovely face. She reciprocated the move and glanced from his eyes to his lips and back again.

She felt the same connection. A smile welled up from within him, and he reached to stroke her hair, leaning closer to capture her lips.

The sound of a car on the oil-top road jerked him back to reality. He stood and moved several steps away.

Alynne rose as well. "That will be Blayne." She moved to the porch rail. "I need to speak with him."

Jason could appreciate that. And her hesitation kept him from kissing the fiancée or girlfriend or whatever she was of another man. "I'll check in with Dell."

Going back inside was the right thing to do, but he couldn't ignore the feeling that he should have stayed.

The afternoon discussion with Blayne had lasted until dinnertime. At first, Alynne had let him talk. He'd gone on and on about the beauty of Sunrise Inn and things he'd like to see change. For more than an hour, he droned on as they sat on the porch swing.

Alynne barely listened. And more than once she looked around to see what Rose was up to, only to remember about the dog's absence. Blayne didn't capture her attention until he mentioned quitting his job and moving out here.

"It occurs to me, that I don't even know exactly what you do or who you work for," Alynne finally interrupted him.

"Well, none of that is really important now." Blayne stroked her cheek and gave her the charming look that used to curl her toes. "I think we'll be quite happy out here."

That struck a chord. How did he know she was the heir? By all rights, the owner should be Momma. "Strange of you to assume that I'll own it."

"Well, you certainly will someday." The man had reddened. Feverishly reddened all the way up to his dimples.

What was he hiding?

He gave her his sultry look. "Let's talk about us. Funeral's over. Your mom's fine. Let's go. Right now."

No. Stinking. Way. "Blayne I can't elope with you."

"I have been so patient through all of this. I want to make this official now, tonight."

"I know. You have been patient, but I think the Lord delayed this wedding for a reason."

"What's the Lord got to do with anything?"

Yet another confirmation that they weren't right for each other. "I agreed to marry you for the wrong reasons." She glanced over her shoulder, but they were alone. Momma was in her suite with her sisters. Dell and Jason had left shortly after Blayne had arrived. As for Phyllis, she was likely in her room pouting and waiting for her gift from Momma.

Blayne's face hardened. "Oh no. You are not going to blow this off again. There's no reason why we can't go."

"You're not listening. I won't elope with you tonight or at all."

"Alynne, I'm not the fancy wedding type. I want to marry you and that should be enough."

"Why?" As much as she wanted desperately to go hide in her room, this conversation needed to be had.

"I don't like weddings any more than I like funerals. If it were up to me, I'd simply ask you to move in with me, but certain things have to be done officially."

Certain things? Officially? He really had none of the values that she'd carried with her all her life. "I meant, why do you want to marry me?" Maybe if she got him talking, he'd realize that they were wrong for one another.

"I told you. I love you."

"Yes, and you said that a month ago, too. But you didn't want to marry me then."

"I … don't know what you want. Are you mad that I didn't give you a ring? Because I thought we could pick that out together when we get to Vegas."

"I'm not mad at all, but I won't be going to Vegas with you."

"Okay. Then let's get through with whatever documents we need and go to the justice of the peace. Surely this county has one of those."

He still wasn't getting it. "Blayne, I don't think I'm right for you. We don't have the same opinions or values. I'm wanting to focus on my faith in the Lord, and you…"

He snorted. "Is that what this is all about. I wasn't raised to be ashamed of my actions, but if you want to call the deepest part of our relationship *sin*..." He used air-quotes. "Then fine, I'll jump into a confessional or dance down some aisle so you can have your slate clean." His tone was getting ugly. Maybe she should've asked Jason or even Dell to stay.

She shook her head. "That isn't necessary. My slate's already clean. But I can't marry you, Blayne. Not now. Not at all." She kept her voice steady and low.

He froze. Then his eyes began to squint together. "This is about that cop, isn't it?"

"No." She had a clear conscience about that. While she might've been developing feelings for Jason, they in no way influenced her doubts about Blayne. "I don't believe you would be happy with me as your wife, and I'm certain I would not be happy with you as my husband."

"Just like that, you're blowing me off." He put on his puppy dog eyes. "And all this time, through all of this waiting, I believed you were a woman of your word. That you would eventually follow through on the promises you made."

Alynne could see through his act now. It had no effect at all. "If that's what you'd like to think, you are welcome to. I know that my decision is best for the both of us. But regardless of the motivation, the result will stand. I will not marry you. Ever."

"Is this because I couldn't go to the funeral? You're making me pay for an appointment I couldn't cancel?"

He just wasn't getting the concept. The conversation continued for another hour, with Blayne alternating between anger, charm, and finally tears. They didn't touch her any more than the anger or charm had, and she was nothing but relieved when he finally left.

She'd made herself a sandwich, checked on her mom, said goodnight to her aunts, and headed to her suite. As far as she knew, both Phyllis and Carl were in the inn for one more night. And she didn't want to happen upon either of them if she could help it.

Maybe she'd get lucky, and they would leave without saying good-bye.

The next morning, Alynne trudged down the steps to the kitchen. Something about the air out here, or maybe the quiet, thoroughly rested her. This morning, she hadn't bothered with makeup or even matching socks. Since there was a nip in the air, she tugged on her most comfortable blue jeans and matched them with a thin sweater, enough to keep her warm, but not so much that she'd get sweaty if the sun came out.

Her insides, though, were much like her socks, not quite connecting. But unlike her socks, she felt a real need to connect to something today, make a decision. Although, she wasn't really sure what that decision should be.

She'd been happy at Fulton Brevard & Sawyer, and she'd been successful there, too. She'd come to terms with the fact that she'd never become a lawyer, and that was fine with her. She enjoyed helping their clients with the information they needed to succeed, even if she didn't get star billing.

But the thought of moving to Heath's Point, of helping Momma with the inn and meeting all sorts of new people each week, excited her. Yes, and being closer to Jason intrigued her as well. There was something there. She couldn't deny it, but she wasn't sure she was ready for anything new in that realm of her life.

At least Blayne was out of her life.

She wasn't fooling herself, though. She could never make up for her weakness, her lack of resistance. No, she was as guilty as he was. But that's exactly what Christ had made up for when He died on the cross, and she needed to let it go. She needed to forgive herself as He had forgiven her, with her whole heart. Though she wondered if she'd actually ever be able to release the guilt she felt.

Blayne had left last night, but she peeked out the front windows, confirming that his car was still gone. Momma and her sisters sat on the other side of the window, sipping coffee from Momma's good china.

Wait, she was using her china?

Alynne poured herself a mug of coffee and went out to the porch to join them.

"Good morning, sweet girl." Momma set down her cup and took both of Alynne's hands. I was just talking with Bobbie and Billie about what the future might hold for us."

Alynne glanced down at their breakfast laid out on the wicker table. "You're using your wedding china."

Momma beamed. "Yes, seeing it last night made me regret not using it very often. So what if a dish gets broken? That's not the end of the world, nor does it signify carelessness. It just means that these dishes are well-loved. And they are, so I want to put them to use more often.

Aunt Billie chimed in, "Yes, if nothing else, they make your mom smile."

Aunt Bobbie slipped a breakfast sandwich onto an empty plate and set it in front of her. "I hope you like provolone cheese." Aunt Bobbie was always so attentive to everyone around her.

"Thank you," Alynne mumbled and nibbled at the moist biscuit.

"I know the decision is up to you, sweet girl." Momma laid her hands in her lap. "And I will be happy with whatever decision you make, I assure you. But I wanted to let you know that your aunts and I have decided that we want to run a bed and breakfast together."

Aunt Billie smiled. "Your mom already knows how to do everything, so Bobbie and I only have to take orders. Even though your mom is the youngest, we've been doing that all of her life." She chuckled, and Aunt Bobbie joined in.

"Oh, you." Momma picked up her linen napkin and threw it into Aunt Billie's lap.

"With my investments and the income Ellis has given …"

"And Billie and I have money we can invest as well …"

Aunt Billie took over. "That's right. We feel we can hire people for any work we can't do ourselves, but the day-to-day needs—the cooking and cleaning and decorating and greeting guests—are the things we love to do most."

"And after spending the week together, we've realized just how much we've missed each other." Aunt Bobbie slipped her hand into Momma's.

"We belong together." Aunt Billie put her arm around Aunt Bobbie's shoulders. "And between us, we have quite enough to purchase a rather nice facility."

"Something old, but not run-down," Aunt Bobbie added.

Momma's eyes sparkled. "Something exactly like this beautiful place. So …" She took a breath. "If you decide you want to sell it, Alynne, we'd like to offer a bid."

Alynne reeled. Now she had two viable options for her own future—stay and help Momma with the inn or sell it to her and return to her life in Dallas. Did she really want to do that? "Oh … wow. I need to contemplate this. And then there's Ronald's opinion to consider."

"If they let him out of jail," Momma commented. "But even if they do, he won't want to stay here. He'd rather have the money. That's all he ever asked for from Ellis. Your dad told me several things that he'd learned about Ronald just before he died. His mom must've given him your dad's name at some point. Ronald apparently did all sorts of research on the family. Learned about Uncle Todd and went to visit Aunt Pearl. She lived down in New Orleans until she died last summer."

"I remember her, though she was mostly off traveling when we would come to visit."

"She was a flight attendant. So yes, she traveled often." Momma chuckled. "Anyway, I guess he felt he had enough dirt on your father. He contacted your father over a year ago. His mom had died, but Ronald wanted his portion. Your dad was willing to help him, but I guess, not the full measure to which Ronald felt entitled."

"Could he have had something to do with Pop's death?"

"I can't imagine why he would. After all, Ellis sent him money

every month from the time he was able to confirm his paternity."
Momma's face clouded. "I was hoping the police would go back
to thinking it was an accident?"

She shook her head. "Jason's positive."

Momma squeezed her hand and released it. "I think he's sweet
on you, and he's quite a catch."

"I barely know him." She didn't want to admit the growing
interest she had in the man.

"Then there's that Blayne fellow." Her mom shook her head.
"I probably haven't seen the best side of him."

"And you won't. I have a lot of regrets with him, Momma."
She wouldn't be so vulgar to detail them. "But I told him last night
that we were through. He's gone for good."

BREAKING POINT

Chapter Twenty-Four

Jason hadn't waited to talk to the chief about Ronald Surzchenkov's place in the family. Or rather, his possible motive for conspiracy and attempted murder. And Dell had been quick to pass it along to the DA.

Even though they had bite marks on his wife's hand that matched Rose's mouth, and the bullets fired at Alynne were from the gun found with his wife's body, they couldn't connect the man to either the shots at the lake or to his own wife's death.

The rental agent did identify him as the man renting the car, but they couldn't even hold him for trying to run Alynne down since no one saw the driver.

Jason's gut told him that he'd also poisoned Alynne's cereal in her unlocked car and attacked her when she'd first arrived in Heath's Point. He'd never prove it, though. Those crimes had little to no evidence to help him.

He pulled into the virtually empty lot at the inn. He was only there to warn them of the man's imminent release and to guard in the lot until Dell could reset the rotation. He left his Jeep at the far end of the gravel and jogged across it to the porch.

Voices led him into the kitchen, per usual. Alynne, Myra, and her sisters were each on task. A buttery aroma wafted through the kitchen as Myra kneaded bread, her sisters worked some dough into shapes, and Alynne sliced strawberries into a bowl of salad.

"Oh, you're just in time for lunch, dear boy." Myra's face didn't show a hint of the distress and weariness that it had for the last several days.

"Sounds delicious, but I can't stay." He glanced at Alynne where she was coring and slicing apples. "I needed to let you know, though, that Ellis's son, Ronald Surzchenkov, will likely be released today."

Worry troubled Alynne's brow. "I thought…"

He nodded. "So did we, but speculation is too flimsy for a case. We would have enough to hold his late wife, but a good lawyer would likely even get her off. There simply isn't enough to connect to Ronald."

"That is troubling." Myra opened the oven door and pulled out a baking sheet full of croissant rolls. "Do you really think he's dangerous?"

"I do. I think he and his wife were in this together. I don't know if she was trying to kill you, Alynne, or simply to scare you so that you wouldn't consider staying." He wanted to believe the latter option, but his gut wouldn't let him.

"Could he have had something to do with Pop's death?"

"That's a question for your mom." He looked at the older woman, but she was staring at the wall in contemplation. "What about it, Myra?"

Her jaw worked for a moment. "He spent some time down in New Orleans with Uncle Todd's widow."

Learning everything he could, most likely.

"I can't say. I'd only met him the one time when he first introduced himself to Ellis. And then it was only for dinner. He and Ellis went off walking afterward." She gave a single shake of her head. "No, sir. I don't know enough about the man to make that judgment."

"That's all right. I appreciate your honesty. And I need you all to be alert. I'll be in the lot for a little while, and then we'll be back on rotation."

"Oh, but wait." Alynne snatched a large platter from the cabinet and piled on fruit, lunchmeat, cheese, and several fresh croissants. "We wouldn't want you to have to skip lunch."

He gave her a grin and sidled back out the way he'd come in. He set the plate down on the porch table and reached for his keys.

The front door burst open, and Phyllis stomped out with her little furball in her arms. "You're a fool, Dora."

Alynne followed with vigor in her steps. "I would be to listen to you."

Her sister turned on her. "You know I deserve half of this place. You don't want it. I don't want it. Sell it and split it with me."

Alynne stood her ground and leaned into her sister's tirade. "You forget, stepsister. You're not an heir. You have no horse in this race."

Her sister teetered on her tall heels but ducked to Alynne's height in her sneakers. "I hope this darling new brother of yours buries you!"

With that, she turned and stomped down the steps. She opened the passenger door and tossed the furball into the backseat before getting in and slamming the door shut.

Carl came around from the kitchen door, dragging and carrying their luggage, probably hoping to avoid the argument altogether. Jason couldn't fault him for it. After all, he had to live with the woman.

He stopped and piled the bags on the lawn then moved to the porch. Myra had followed them out. She crossed to the rail and took his raised hand. "I'm so glad to have finally met you, Carl. I pray that the Lord will bless you for the kindness you bring into Phyllis's life."

The man smiled. "I know she's … well, relived unpleasant times being with you all. Certainly nothing against you. It's only the way she sees it."

Myra nodded.

"But we really do have a happy life in Washington. She's a kind person, creative and energetic."

"I'm so glad to know she's happy there." Myra squeezed the man's hand. "If you would delay her just a moment, I'll get the gift that Ellis set aside for her."

He chuckled. "No problem there." He went back to his pile of luggage.

Jason trotted down the steps. No need to let the man struggle all alone. "Let me get that one." He picked up a hanging bag and grabbed the handle of one of the rolling cases.

"Thanks. It was nice to meet you, Lieutenant. And I appreciate the way you handled … well, that little mistake I made."

Jason lifted his chin and gave a half-smile.

Carl closed his mouth and eyes and shook his head. "Phyllis thought it would make for positive news. Get my name in the headline again. I didn't realize at the time that there was a chance Ellis's death could have been murder. And I had no idea that Alynne was at any risk."

"Not a problem." At least, not now.

Having slid all of the luggage into the trunk, Carl held out his hand. "I'm sorry for the confusion, though."

He shook it.

Myra bounded out of the front door with a box wrapped in her arms. Jason hurried over and braced her elbow as she descended the stairs. "Here it is. Ellis always kept it in the safe under the floorboards, but I got it out yesterday." She brought it to the passenger side of the car as the window lowered into the door. "This is what your dad set aside for you, Phyllis. He wasn't your biological father, but for good or bad, he was the only dad you had. And he loved you truly and deeply."

The woman's painted face seemed to crack and a tear … an actual tear … tripped over her thick eyelashes and made a track through the color on her cheek.

She pulled open the metal lid and the soft look she'd shown a nanosecond before disintegrated. She glanced up at Myra. "Really?" She looked down again at the contents of the box. "A Bible? You think I would want a Bible? This is useless." She tossed the box onto the gravel. The car began to move, and she flipped the lid out the window as well before the glass closed.

Alynne bolted down the steps. "Momma? She didn't hit you, did she?"

"No. I'm fine." She stooped and picked up the lid while Alynne lifted the old Bible from the now-broken metal box. "This was so kind of Pop."

"More than kind." Her mother turned her back on the retreating car and moved to the stairs. "The one thing Phyllis wanted all her life was family, a history. And his gift would have given her that. Not only a place in God's family ..." She pointed for Alynne to set the book down and opened it carefully to the first few pages. "This is Ellis's family tree. Over a century of Stones listed here. And many of them have left letters in this book for their future generations."

"She made it pretty clear that she didn't want our family." A little crinkle formed between Alynne's brows.

"Everything always had to be on her terms, and this was no different." She closed the book and gave it a pat. "It's yours now." She stroked her daughter's face and made her way into the house.

Alynne hated the look on Momma's face. She hadn't failed Phyllis. Phyllis failed Phyllis, again and again, with decisions meant to lash out at her parents. Ultimately, those decisions usually ended up hurting her. Like her decision to toss away her inheritance.

She stroked her hand across the cover. "Wanna find some

treasure?" She glanced up at Jason as a hint of joy welled inside her. This was treasure. Not only God's word, but generations of her family and their thoughts, hopes, and dreams.

"Sure." He sat on the love seat and helped himself to his plate. She sat next to him with the Bible spread across her lap.

She opened the book to the middle, and a number of papers and envelopes shifted, threatening to fall out. "This is going to be harder than I thought. I want to be sure to return each item back to its original place." She closed the book again and then opened the front cover. She glanced through the first few pages that Momma had pointed out. Dates of births, marriages, and deaths were noted beside each name.

"This truly is a treasure." Jason set the platter back on the table. "All these people are connected to you."

She wanted to wrap her mind around it all slowly and began flipping through a handful of pages at a time until she found an envelope, brown with age, tucked into the middle of Exodus. The name on the envelope proved to be the wife of the oldest ancestor on the chart. The Bible must have been hers.

Alynne carefully unfolded the two pages and laid them out. The paper was thin, almost translucent, but the ink was still readable. The woman wrote of her hope that her children's children could grow up in a land of peace. Where people didn't have to fear each cloud of dust that grew and moved toward them. She hoped that her grandchildren could learn true forgiveness and that her actions wouldn't be held against them.

"That's a strange thing to hope for." Alynne set aside the first page.

"This was around the time of the Civil War, maybe she owned slaves."

"A lot of people in Texas owned slaves. Maybe she helped them escape. That would be an action that could have been held against her if the South had won the war."

He stared off at the trees for a moment. "I suspect she's written this before the end, maybe even before it began."

Alynne focused on the second page. "I think she's a lot older here. Look how spidery her handwriting is."

"Looks like it had some damage."

He was right. The first couple of lines had a long smudge as though someone had brushed the ink before it dried. She skipped them and began reading aloud.

Make no mistake, son. Your father learned of my treachery, but my actions saved our farm. I simply could not fund a cause that I believed, and still believe, is the exact opposite of our Lord's teaching. When Jarvis instructed me to sell my jewelry to be paid for in Confederate currency, I could not. Instead, I buried the jewelry and the silver, and a box of gold coins that my father had given to us. I would not donate one thing to the Confederacy. Though your father had to endure disgust from his friends, and though I had to listen to significant lectures from him, our minister, and acquaintances, (which I should never have considered friends and will never after the way they treated you and your brother through those years) I am not sorry for my action. As the aforesaid people lost their businesses and homes and were forced to leave the area, we were able to stay in this paradise. We were able to pay our taxes with money I had not exchanged. Because we neither owned slaves nor financially supported the Confederacy, Jarvis enjoyed honor after the war that was withheld during those hard years.

How happy am I that he did not insist that I retrieve my valuables. How blessed that we had little need for them. As I reach the end of my days, dear Joseph, I should not like your endurance during your adolescence to go without reward. I hope you will open this wonderful book to the story you used to love so much and find this letter for you. Your sisters did not suffer the trials that you had to suffer, but you, as their only older brother now, are given the rights and responsibilities for their care. Especially Mary and Hannah who must live as widows.

I urge you, my son, do not let this land that has cost us so much sift through your fingers. Keep it intact. Keep it within our family and let your son do likewise after you, as we have often discussed. Should you or your sisters experience trials, the jewelry and valuables that I hid so long ago are yours to use as you see fit. Mark twelve paces due north from the iron dinner bell that always sang your call to home.

*I love you, my son. I pray that your heart will
return to the God of your father and mother.*

Jason held a half-smile. "The treasure is real."

"Sounds like it." She folded the pages and tucked them back
into their envelope. Setting the Bible onto the wicker table, she
stood and eyed the iron bell that stood within the roses at the white-
board fence marking the edge of the lot. "Twelve paces due
north?"

Bracing a hand on the rail, Jason threw his legs over it and
landed on the lower level. He jogged over to the bell as Alynne
scurried down the steps and over to the north side of the house.

"Someone's been digging around this thing." He got down on
one knee and put his weight against the stone podium that held the
iron structure. It lifted slightly off the ground.

"The kids certainly didn't do that." Maybe one of her cousins
had helped? "At least they didn't dig up Momma's roses." The
white-plank fence that marked the edge of the parking lot was
entwined with several rose bushes of various shades.

Jason lined up with the north side of the bell and marched off
twelve paces across the gravel path that led to the boathouse and a
few feet down the hill toward the woods. "But we have the benefit
of the notes in the Bible." He cut his boot heel across the grass.
"Got a shovel?"

"There is no way that my great-great-whatever had your long
paces." She counted twelve off, finding herself several feet closer
to the bell than he was. "This is a better place."

"Are you sure?"

No. She wasn't sure about anything. For all she knew, her son

Joseph had found the letter and taken the treasure after his mother's death. But then why leave the letter? "You don't think her son found it, do you?"

"I think her son might well have been like Phyllis. At least, that's the implication from his mother's words. What possible value could the Bible have for him?"

Alynne strode back to the bell. "Okay, let me do this again, then."

"This time keep in mind that likely your ancestor wasn't as tall as you are."

"Oh, yeah." She shortened her stride somewhat and ended up about ten yards from the bell, in the center of the gravel drive. She kicked aside the gravel to get to the dirt underneath it. "According to the photo in the parlor, this would have been the cattle pasture."

"I guess that makes sense." He started to go around the back of the house. "I'll be back with shovels."

The sun hit his hair just right and made it light up. She shouldn't be noticing, but she'd noticed quite a lot of things about Jason Danvers in the last couple of weeks. Noticed his kindness and compassion to her mom, the way he played with her cousin's kids, how he was willing to do grunt jobs like sit in a parking lot all night and unload the dumbwaiter. And she couldn't lie. She'd noticed how attractive he was, how his shoulders filled his shirts and his muscles seemed so well-toned.

Blayne was out of her life, but she didn't need to even entertain thoughts of replacing him. She had way too much growing to do, regardless of her age. She knew nothing of life except what she'd experience at the law office. And while that was plenty, it didn't touch her. It was like a movie playing in the background.

Jason could certainly fit well into her life, though. Kind and considerate, he was solid. Should he ever care for her, she could be sure he'd never hurt or manipulate her to get what he wanted. But no. He had the attention of every unmarried female in this town according to her mom. Probably even some of the married ones. The man had enough fish to choose from.

He returned carrying two shovels.

"You don't really think that I should dirty my sensitive little hands with this ugly old tool, now do you?" She applied a thick Southern accent with a little hint of helpless into her voice.

He handed her one of the shovels. "That a good enough answer for you?"

"You heartless creature." She laughed and attempted to break through the hard soil.

The driveway had been hard-packed long ago. After several minutes of getting nowhere, Jason ran back around the side of the house for a pick. Alynne went inside for some bottled water. Her mom came from upstairs with an armful of linens as she exited the kitchen.

"Can I help you?" Alynne set the bottles down on the table.

"Oh, no, dear. We send all of this out to be laundered and pressed." Momma paused at the kitchen entrance. "Did you get to look through the Bible any?"

Alynne grinned and scooped up her bottles. "We might have found the place to dig."

Momma dropped the bundle near the kitchen door and then

moved to look out the side window. "Oh, sweetheart, I'm sorry, but it's not there."

"Are you sure?" It had to be there.

"Well, I'm sure it wasn't there when Uncle Todd made that road down to the dock. That area was a little hill. You can still see it in the old photo of the place. We came out here when the parking lot was brand new, and Uncle Todd shared how he had scalped that hill."

"If any treasure had been there, he would have found it I guess."

"Definitely. The dirt was used to level off other areas of the lot. The workers would've noticed a big box or ..."

"Even a bag."

"Yes." Her mother tilted her head. "Anything like that. I'm so sorry."

Alynne turned back toward the window where Jason was wielding a pickax to loosen the dirt. She'd better tell him to save his energy. Upon opening the kitchen door, she paused. The man had laid the ax down and pulled off the three-button shirt he'd been wearing. His arms bulged as he swung the ax, and his narrow waist proved a commitment to his training.

She shook herself. *Go. Stop him.*

What a bummer that the letter in the Bible hadn't been helpful after all. Not that Jason expected to actually find the treasure ... Okay, he thought there was a chance. But he wasn't sorry to stop chipping away at the ground under the lot. It barely gave an inch with all of his work.

Thankfully, a shift change showed up at the same time. He allowed himself a little relaxation under a steamy shower. After his workout with the pickax, he should've chosen cooler water, but the hot sure felt good. Until it got stuffy.

An hour later, he parked his car on the street and hopped out. He still had a bit before his shift began and wandered down the block to the activity around the shell of Mac's Diner. They'd had to rebuild it, basically from the slab, but the walls and the roof were standing. "Looks good." He waved at Ray Alexander, who worked with a level on one of the windowsills.

"Slow but coming." Ray laid the tool aside and came toward him, taking off the hard hat he wore. He laid the hat aside and sat at the top of the stairs. "Something on your mind? Maybe a girl with dark hair?"

Jason gave a half-smile. "You don't know me well enough to read me like this."

"Yeah, well, my mom's the gossip queen around here. Not me. That is, if you did have something or someone on your mind. Make no mistake, I never tell my mom anything about anyone other than myself."

Violet Alexander was Mrs. Hawkins' best friend for a good reason. "Good to know, since your mom has set me up on not one, not two, but five blind dates in the few years I've been here."

"I think she's fearful of losing her touch. You might want to rethink this single life before she gets plain desperate."

All Jason could do was hope that Violet lost her interest in playing matchmaker for him, but that didn't seem likely.

Ray rubbed his hands together. "It's simple. Show some interest in a woman and the Yentas will back off."

"It's not that easy."

Ray chuckled. "I didn't say it was easy. I said it was simple. It is. Choose a lady, a lady like Alynne Stone, maybe. That's the simple part."

"I think I understand."

"No, I don't think you do. All kidding aside, that daughter of Myra's seems to have been through a lot. Cat doesn't tell tales, but she implied that there was a lot more there. Some pain. Some guilt and regret. I'm hoping she broke up with that Blayne guy …"

"I'm pretty sure that's the case." Seemed that she was going that way, and Blayne was gone.

"The guy was poison from what Cat shared. She's been praying for Alynne." The man smiled the smile of a newlywed. Jason had seen it before on his own face.

He met Jason's eyes again. "If you're interested in Alynne Stone, tell her. For all you know, she's planning to return to Dallas."

Jason shook his head. "I don't know." Yeah, he was interested, but could he allow himself to go down that path again?

"Don't expect a romance right away, is all I'm saying. A friendship might be what she needs right now to give her a chance to heal."

Jason nodded. He could probably give it that much.

BREAKING POINT

Chapter Twenty-Five

Alynne bid Momma and her aunts good-bye. A movie would be a perfect getaway for the three of them. She waved at the officer in the cruiser at the edge of the lot, and he touched the brim of his hat. Hard to say which of the men it was, though she'd met all of them at least once.

The fluffy white wisps that hung around the sky all day were beginning to collect into a cloud party. Thunder rumbled in the distance, but the sky was still blue overhead. Alynne had lived in Texas all her life and knew what to expect from Spring storms. She'd get her shower right away before the lightning got too close.

As she trotted up her stairs, her cell phone rang out with her generic ringtone. Likely a scammer, but she glanced at the screen. Mrs. Oglesby. Guilt swept across her. Her two weeks weren't quite up, but she hadn't given anyone at the firm a thought since she'd left. She swiped the receiver icon.

"This is Alynne Stone." Her business greeting felt strange after so long. She hadn't received a half-dozen calls since she'd been gone. Something else to thank the Lord about.

"Good morning, Alynne." An echo proved she was on speaker. Whom else might be in the room? "Mr. Brevard was able to receive that continuance last week from the judge, though he's on his last leg with Judge Hubner. I know you're in the midst of a family situation, but I wanted … well, the truth is, I believe you need to repair this situation."

She did if she ever wanted the firm to believe in her again. "I'll be back in the office next Monday, Ms. Oglesby, but is there anything I can do to help you now?"

"I hope so. I checked the Dropbox account."

Alynne would have thought of that had she not be so emotional about it all.

"There is a record of transmission the morning of the case, but none of the files are still there."

Purged? "That would have been noted. A timestamp?" She opened her computer and clicked through to the program.

"Yes." The woman's voice was troubled. "But people are adding and removing files from the account all the time. That morning, there were at least a dozen files removed by users."

Alynne scanned the file section. Mrs. Oglesby was right. Files were uploaded and downloaded all the time. And as a file clerk, Stephanie Carson's username was all over the system. "Well, I have no way of proving that I had placed them in the file for Mr. Brevard, but I have all of the documents on my own computer."

Rain began to splatter against her windows. Once she completed this call, she'd head back to the safety of downstairs and take her shower later. She opened her own files and uploaded them to the program. "At least, you can have access to the documentation that I gathered. It should be enough for Mr. Brevard to prevail in the case."

"I see them." Clicking came from the other end of the line. "But you're correct. Just because you had the data on your computer doesn't confirm that you turned it … wait … Alynne?" The woman sounded funny.

"Is something wrong?"

"I've downloaded Mr. Razier's deposition."

"And …?" The man had given his deposition at an attorney's office in Paris, and his assistant had translated it and sent it to Alynne over a month ago. "Is something wrong with it?"

"There's a misspelled word in the first paragraph. Missippi. I assume it was intended to be Mississippi?"

"Yes, one of the contractors had done work for the Mississippi Wildlife Preservation Commission."

"And your name is in the box as the sole receiver of this deposition. Did it go anywhere else?"

She was the research assistant in charge. "No. That would be a breach of protocol. It was printed out and placed in the file that I put on Stephanie's desk."

The phone clicked, and she was no longer on speaker. "Then how is it that there's another file exactly like it with Stephanie's name in the receiver box?"

Alynne controlled the growl that welled up, and the sky barked it out for her. "I can't say. But I know I received it and have now sent it to you as proof. And I know that I put this deposition into the file that I placed on Stephanie's desk. And that was the last

I saw of it." There, that might very well prove that she hadn't messed up the process.

"I'll look into … wait … how many files did you place in Dropbox?"

"Five." Alynne reflected through them, counting them off. "The deposition, a file of before photographs, and another one of after images, the dictated conversations that I'd had with all concerned as well as their confirmation of the validity of my transcription, and a final file full of testimonials and receipts complete with contact information and paper trails."

"Mmm …" Silence thickened for several seconds. "Don't touch anything in the Dropbox drive, Alynne, but take a look at it."

She slid the thumbnail back onto her screen, popping it fully open. The deposition was on the list as the most recent file loaded. None of the other files showed up at all. "I don't understand."

"Was the deposition the last one you loaded?"

"No. It was the first one." This was crazy. She was sure she'd loaded the others correctly. "Mrs. Oglesby, I know those other files were there."

"I believe you. I saw at least one other appear before I opened the deposition. Someone has deleted them as we've been talking about them." Clicking as though she were typing madly on her keyboard came over the phone. Especially since Alynne was no longer on speaker.

Another roar of thunder exploded overhead.

"Are you there, Mrs. Oglesby?"

"I'm here. I'm not sure what to do about this, though."

"About what?" Alynne suspected that Stephanie had

attempted to discredit her, but she didn't want to make that complete assumption until she heard it from Mrs. Oglesby herself.

The woman sighed. "I hate to do this to you, Alynne …"

The lights went out. "Oh, dear. Wait …" Alynne only had her computer screen and the occasional bolts of lightning to give illumination.

A sound drew her attention to her windows. The drapes on her windows moved several inches into the room and then relaxed back into place.

Mrs. Oglesby had waited, but the hairs on Alynne's neck were tingling. "I'm going to need to call you back."

She hung up, pocketed her phone, and dashed to the side of her window. The only other time she'd seen her curtains move like that, someone had come in the front door. The chime had rung then, but with the electricity off, it wasn't going to ring.

No cars were in the lot except hers and the HPPD cruiser. She couldn't tell with the torrent and the intermittent lightning if the officer was there. Maybe he'd come into the house for safety?

But if that was the case, he would have driven his cruiser closer before dashing in.

A tiny squeak made her gasp. The second step to her room squeaked. Was someone coming up here? She rushed to her door on tiptoes and turned the lock as another burst of thunder covered the sound. But that wouldn't hold anyone for long. Where could she go?

She eyed the window seats under all the windows. Pop had always been such a stickler for safety. Taught her lightning safety, tornado safety, and fire safety. She rushed to one of the window seats and tugged on it. The top flew up revealing a stack of blankets. She tried the next one and found a set of heavy plastic boards connected to two long chains.

Yes.

She pulled open her window and kicked out the screen.

Someone jiggled the doorknob.

She lifted the makeshift ladder from its place. It was anchored fast to the flooring of the room. She tossed the steps out the window.

Someone kicked at the door. No more time.

She climbed onto the sill and stepped down as quickly as she could. The blasting wind swayed her against the side of her little tower, but the steps held up easily under her weight.

The door crashed open in her room about the time she reached the halfway mark.

She missed a step and slipped down the chain. Pain ripped through her hand, but she regained her footing for a few more steps before she could jump off the contraption. She looked up and spotted the head of someone sticking out the window. The faceless person was looking for Alynne on the ladder, but they had missed her. She stood in a bundle of bushes along the edge of the house.

The head disappeared. Whoever it was would head down here and no little bush would hide her. Lightning hit the lake and the air crackled, lighting up her surroundings. Nothing but the woods in this direction and she had no desire to go there in a lightning storm. She could run to the cop, but that would be barefoot through gravel. And she'd be out in the open.

Something broke in the kitchen, spurring her into decision.

She darted lakeside. The kitchen door opened behind her as she bolted around the corner. Her feet slipped out from under her in the mud, catapulting her into a complete somersault down the hill, but she landed feet first and sprinted for the cover of the barn.

She squeezed through the barely opened doorway and sidestepped the ancient tractor. Any number of hiding places offered themselves. Whoever followed her would have their work cut out for them. She raced up the steps to the hayloft as the main door squealed its resistance to opening wider.

Her breathing slowed a little. Why would her tracker come up here with all the downstairs to look through? She let her eyes grow accustomed to the dark. The best hiding place would be on the other side of the boxes that hugged the far wall. But even barefoot, her footsteps would surely be heard if she ran across the center of the room.

A dark corner on the near wall looked promising. Almost looked like a doorway. That would do. It was also close enough for her to move in silence. Even tiptoe. And just to make sure she had some protection—she eyed an ancient rake hanging on the wall. Not much in the way of a weapon, but it had a good stout handle that could do some damage. She pulled it off and the hook it had been hanging from came as well. It clattered onto the wooden floor.

So much for hoping the person downstairs would stay downstairs. She picked up the hook so it wouldn't be an arrow to her hiding place and darted to the blackness of the corner. It was a doorway, leading to a shallow closet full of smaller tools. Tools that would rattle easily if she should bump them. She scooted in soundlessly as boots clumped up the stairs.

This would never do. While she wasn't exposed, she didn't have any room to wield the rake, not that it would give her much protection. Maybe if she could draw whomever over to the boxes in the opposite corner, she could get back down the ladder while he was searching over there.

She took the hook she'd picked up and flung it as hard as she could. It landed exactly where she'd hoped. She ducked back into her place as she felt more than heard the heavy feet reaching the loft flooring.

Wait. Were they coming toward her?

"Well, that didn't work out as you had intended." Ronald Surzchenkov's voice reached her just as his shadow stepped into the dim light of the open hay door.

A gust hit the side of the barn making the entire structure shudder.

"What a dangerous place you've wandered into." He tsked. "So many accidents could happen here." Lightning struck nearby illuminating his hate-filled face. "I'm going to get my inheritance. This is my destiny."

Jason called the inn again, but the phone rang on unanswered. He tried Myra's cell again, but it went straight to voice mail. Why hadn't he gotten Alynne's phone number? He'd thought about asking for it, but he felt too much like a crushing teenager and not enough like an officer of the law.

He turned on his siren. And called Sanchez on the radio again. The man didn't pick up. Concern turned to certainty. He pressed the accelerator. With the wind buffeting his Jeep, his magnetic light would likely blow off. That's if he could get it to attach in the first place. Lightning struck a tree in his rearview mirror and the sky went off like a bomb all around him. He loved storms, but not so much driving in them. He turned onto the creek that the hard rain had made of the oil road leading to the inn. The run-off had cut deep grooves into what had been a fairly smooth surface, but his Jeep muscled through. He turned onto the gravel.

Everything was draped in darkness, but he spotted the cruiser. Sanchez had the shift, but he couldn't see the man in the driver's seat. Maybe he'd moved into the house? He pulled closer and shined his flashlight through the driver's window.

"No."

The man lay across the console and into the passenger seat. Jason got out. The torrential rain blew his hat off and soaked him almost immediately, but he opened the vehicle's door.

Sanchez groaned as Jason pulled him up.

"What happened?"

He groaned again, and Jason noticed a large bruise on his forehead.

"Stay here. That's an order." Jason shut the man's door and climbed back into the Jeep. He roared across the lot, pulling in near where he'd been digging that morning. He put his bright lights on the house. Giving it some illumination.

What was that hanging down … a safety ladder. He glanced up. Yep, from Alynne's room. He backed up and took the drive toward the boathouse. No, she wouldn't go there, not after the other day. Where then? Likely, she was somewhere safe in the woods. He stopped the car and pulled the keys.

Getting out, he scanned the woods, the boathouse, and the grounds. The sky lit up with electricity hopping from cloud to cloud. No movement. No sound except the rumble stampeding across the sky.

Wait. The sound dissipated and something like voices drifted from the lake.

No, from the barn. Jason took off at a run.

Alynne stared through the blackness trying to make out more than just a shadowed outline of the man. Did he actually see her or was he only guessing?

"Come on, princess. Show yourself."

So, he couldn't see her.

"I know you're there. Daddy's little angel. You had everything you always wanted, didn't you? The perfect little family. But I deserve the treasure. I'm the one who studied the family, *my* family, *my* ancestry. I'm the one who visited with Aunt Pearl before she died. You didn't even care."

Momma was right about him doing research on the family.

"Come out!" He screamed and took a step toward her.

She dared not remain where she was, but she wasn't going easily. Yelling at the top of her lungs, she put the rake in front of her and rushed him. He backed up several steps, enough into the room that she could make out his face. She aimed for his eyes with the metal edge of the rake and rushed him again. If he'd move back only a few more steps, she'd try to make a run for the stairs.

"I'll kill you …" He stepped back. She threw the rake at his face and darted for the exit. Wood popped and then a crash shook the flooring. He shrieked. She reached the rail at the top step and grabbed on. Then she looked back and caught sight of Ronald flinging backward into a chasm that hadn't been there a moment before. He disappeared from view, and his shriek cut off with a deadening thump.

She descended a few steps, hearing no sound and seeing no movement from the pile of debris next to the tractor. She clutched at the rail as a flashlight bounced across the lower floor.

"Alynne?" That was Jason's voice.

She lifted her head to answer, but her vocal cords wouldn't obey.

She saw movement at the door. Then he came into view as the sky lit up with another rumble. His flashlight rested atop his gun.

He darted around the tractor and then hesitated at the lump. He stooped and his light caught Ronald's still form. "Alynne, are you in here?"

She tried again to answer, but nothing came except a tiny squeak. She shuffled down the steps and found herself lit up, squinting in the light. She lifted her hands.

"Awe, honey."

She melted into his embrace.

"Are you all right?" His whisper tickled her ear as a weak rumble drifted from miles away. Sirens wailed against the edge of the thunder.

"How did you know?" She could barely shape the words.

"Nerves, I guess, after I learned that Surzchenkov had been released." He leaned back, his eyes searching her face, and he stroked her cheek. "He didn't hurt you?"

She shook her head and glanced at the ceiling. *Thank You, thank You, Lord.*

He went back to the lump in the middle of the room. "Your dad mentioned the rotted flooring in the loft. We hadn't gotten around to fixing it."

"Is he dead?" She hadn't meant for him to fall.

"He's breathing, has a pulse, and doesn't seem to be bleeding much."

The lump groaned as the sirens cut out. Someone called out on Jason's radio. He thumbed the switch and responded, "We're at the barn. Ambulance needed for the suspect."

He slipped his jacket off and pulled it around her. His warmth took the chill out of her shoulders. "Is there anyone else here?"

She shook her head again and caught his eye. This man—this kind, gentle, courageous man—had come for her. Had somehow known that she was in trouble and had come for her.

He took a step closer, and she didn't back away. His eyes dipped to her lips. As much as she longed to feel his kiss, he didn't deserve to be emotionally shackled to all of her baggage. She reached up and brushed a kiss onto his cheek, lingering for a moment until she heard the chief's voice outside the barn.

"Lieutenant Danvers?"

"All clear in here, Chief." He stepped away from her but kept his hand bracing her arm. "Someone needs to take care of Sanchez out in his cruiser."

"Already done. Evans is taking him to the hospital now." The chief rounded the end of the tractor and crossed to the lump that had started moaning. "Good grief. Get her on up to the house. I'll meet you there in a few minutes."

Jason led her out of the barn. Then, his bracing hand at her arm shifted her to his other side, where his other hand rested against her back. "Why are you barefoot?"

BREAKING POINT

Chapter Twenty-Six

Jason silently shredded himself for almost kissing Alynne. And had she not given him that peck on the cheek to shake him out of himself, he would have. Would have drawn her into a kiss that he had no business giving. Would have knocked all chance of any friendship between them out of the water. Not to mention spoiling his professional pursuits.

What had he been thinking? Besides how frightened she looked—how cold and vulnerable—not much else. He ushered her through the dark house and into the parlor again. This room had seen so much action in the last few days. "Blankets." Where had they been? "Here." He reached for the shadowed window seat as she pointed. He lifted out a thick quilt and draped it around her as she seated herself on the couch.

He clicked on his flashlight and set it on its end, to give a dim light to the entire room. "Maybe you should go upstairs and get into some dry clothes first."

"Oh no." She shook her head. "I'm n-not ready to go b-back

up there yet."

Understandable. "Can you tell me what happened?"

"The storm blew out the l-lights. I felt someone c-come into the house."

"You felt someone?"

"Curtains moved. They only do that when the front door opens."

That was a long way for pressure to affect her curtains, but it was certainly possible. "And then?"

"I heard someone on the stairs."

"But you didn't know who it was …"

She tugged the quilt tighter around her. "No. Maybe I had a case of those nerves, too. I knew it wasn't Momma. And anyone simply looking for me, like you or the chief, would've called out. I climbed down the fire ladder."

"Brilliant decision." And seeing it had given him a hint as to where she might be.

She continued to recount her story as Jason took notes on his phone. At least it was something he could see. Headlights roamed across the main hall, catching his eye as she finished her saga. Myra rushed into the room. "Alynne?"

"I'm sure she's fine, dear." The thinner shadow, that would be Bobbie, followed her in.

"An ambulance is pulling in behind us." That was from the thicker shadow, Billie.

As the ladies entered the room, the lights flashed back on in the main hall and the kitchen. Jason flipped up the switch and squinted as the brightness hit his fully dilated pupils.

The three women fussed over Alynne, and she recounted her story. Jason hung to the side, unneeded in the family drama, but unwilling to leave her quite yet. Not until he heard from the chief.

By the time the ambulance had screamed away, the ladies had convinced themselves to make a meal for the officers still on the premises.

Dell came in as they bustled into the kitchen, explaining their plans. "That's not necessary."

"Nonsense. Your men are working so hard."

He sauntered into the room. "And they're all gonna get so fat if we keep having to do duty out here. Did you know she brings full meals with desserts out to the guard in the lot every three hours?" He nodded his head in Myra's direction.

"Here, and I thought she only did that for me." Jason chuckled and patted his stomach.

The chief went down into his baseball catcher pose in front of Alynne. "You okay, Miss Stone? That guy didn't hurt you in any way, did he?"

"He didn't lay a finger on me, but …" She glanced from the chief to Jason and back again. "Is he still alive? I didn't mean for him to fall. I was only trying to distract him enough so I could get back to the first floor."

"He's alive. And with this little trick, he won't be getting out on bond this time. Course he'll likely be in the hospital for a while.

"So, he's the one who killed my … who killed Pop?"

"I don't know." Dell sighed and glanced at Jason. "The facts sure back it up, and the motive is certainly there. But we won't likely ever know exactly what happened.

Her lips pressed together as her eyes swam.

Jason edged his head toward the door and caught the chief's eye.

The man's eyebrow's ruffled in a question.

Jason tilted his head toward the door again, this time repeating the action to make it thoroughly clear.

"Why don't I go see about getting you a cup of tea." Finally, Dell caught his meaning. "Chamomile?"

"Yes, please." Alynne lifted her head and gazed at Jason. No, she was looking past him. "Where did that photo go?"

Alynne hadn't looked at the photos on the wall since the day she'd arrived in Heath's Point. And she had specifically wandered over to that wall and scanned through all of the images while she'd been speaking to Phyllis on the phone. The wall had been filled, no gaps at all.

She got up and the blanket slipped off her shoulders. Instantly, her shoulders chilled, but she stepped past Jason and stood in front of the empty spot, big enough for a wide landscape. "There was a photo here last week."

Jason joined her facing the wall. Rain still dripped off the sleeve of his shirt. "When did you last notice it?"

"I only remember looking at them the first day I got here." Had it been there when they talked with Ronald or with Momma?

"Can you tell what's missing?"

That was a good question. But no. "I would say a landscape,

but there are several up there. It could have been any ..." Wait ... "No. Not anything. The photo of the farm, before the upper floors or the entry hall and porch had been built onto it." She scanned the other images on the wall. "It was the one where the cows were on the hill in front of the house."

He moved to the other end of the wall and scanned the photos as well. "There was a broken frame in Sheila Surzchenkov's car that would've fit this gap."

"What in the world are you doing?" Momma bustled in with a tray of hot tea. She set it down, grabbed Alynne's discarded blanket, and plopped it back over her shoulders. "You've had a shock, sweet girl."

"Momma, do you remember the photo that was here?" Alynne drew her mom's attention to the blank wall.

"When did that thing take a walk?" Myra looked to the floor and pulled back the little table that sat there as well as the wingback chair that was next to it.

"It was the photo of the farmhouse, wasn't it?" Had someone actually taken it?

"Yes, back when it was just a small clapboard, my suite and part of the kitchen were all there was to it. And the barn." Momma took one look at Jason and lifted the edge of the window seat, withdrawing a flannel blanket. "You're going to catch your death of cold," she scolded and handed him the blanket.

With a sheepish look on his face, he unfolded it and slipped it over his shoulders. "What can you tell us about the photo?"

"It was old, and whoever took it would've been standing in what's now the cove." Momma poured a cup of tea and brushed

Alynne back toward the sofa before handing it to her.

"Why do you say that?" Jason settled next to her and Momma handed him a cup as well.

Momma poured a cup for herself. "The view got everything from what is now the drive down to the boathouse to the entire barn and included a garden that was on the west edge of it."

"That must've been a small garden," Jason commented and took a sip.

He got that right. With all the rain they'd received this winter, the lake came right up behind the little rise on which the barn rested.

"Well, Uncle Todd remembered it when he was a child. See the Stone property went from the place next door, right across the cove, and all the way to the highway south of here. It even included most of the scout camp, except for the point. Your father showed me the old property maps when we moved in here. The Kennedale Ranch had been a real ranch back then. It was a lot bigger than the Stone property, but most of it became Lake Grayson. It was just the way the creek ran, I guess."

"I should have thought of that." Jason lifted his gaze to the ceiling for a moment.

Alynne tried to picture it the way it might have been before the lake had eaten up so much of the land. "The photograph was taken before the lake went in. I'm guessing that happened in the 30s?"

"The photo was older than that. The rest of the main house was built before the turn of the century, the Victorian age, you know."

"Wonder if I can find out more about it." Alynne tugged her phone from her pocket.

Momma slipped it from her fingers. "Later, sweet girl."

She resisted the urge to declare her adult status and merely stared at her mom.

"I know. I have no right, but I would do the same thing for Cat. I'd be treating Jason the same way if he weren't a police officer and trained for the trauma you just experienced."

Okay, she could let Momma mother her a bit. "Thank you, but it's only looking up one little thing." She chose to ignore the smug smile on Jason's face as he tried to cover it with a sip from his teacup.

"That will roll into more and more. You need to rest, and I intend to see that you get it. I have a sofa in my suite that makes into a very comfortable bed."

Alynne released a breath she hadn't realized she'd been holding. There was nothing wrong with her suite. She enjoyed her tower and the view it offered, but nothing within her wanted to venture up to the heights tonight. Not after what had happened. She'd wait until full daylight tomorrow to go up there and clean up and dry the floor. She took another sip of the tea and let it drift down, warming and soothing her throat. "That will be fine." And researching the lake could certainly wait. In fact, all she wanted was a warm shower and a soft bed at this point.

"Trust me. We'll look into this again tomorrow."

Jason carried the tea tray back into the kitchen as Myra led Alynne to her suite. For the first time in almost two weeks, he felt the house and all within it were safe.

He hoped he was right.

Helping himself to a couple of roast beef sandwiches Billie and Bobbie had made, he thanked them and made his way out the kitchen door.

Dell was on the steps. "Good timing. I'm heading for the hospital as soon as we wrap this up. I want to question Surzchenkov." The boss had a hardness about his eyes when he said the man's name.

"I need a shower."

"You look like you already had one." The hardness eased and turned into a little laugh line.

He was a mess. "Yeah, but I think I'd rather have a hot one. Can I meet you at Howerton?"

"That'll work." Dell turned to walk along the side of the house toward the barn while Jason withdrew his keys and climbed into the Jeep that still sat on the boathouse drive.

An hour later, refreshed by the shower and the food, Jason nodded at Officer Billings outside a hospital room. "Sanchez doing all right?"

"He took a powerful hit, but he has a pretty hard head." The man shifted his weight and leaned away from the wall. "He'd seen a flare go off in the grass by the parking lot and got out of his car to check it."

"A distraction that let Surzchenkov knock him senseless." The man must've shoved Sanchez back into his cruiser. "Did you find the flare?"

"Exactly where he said it was. He didn't see the person who hit him."

"Shame. I would've liked to add assault on a police officer to what we have on Surzchenkov."

The chief walked up at that moment. "Ready to weed a confession out of this clown?"

Absolutely. Jason merely bobbed his head and followed his boss into the room.

"Well, now, Mr. Surzchenkov. You've been a naughty boy." Dell went to the opposite side of the room from Jason and set his recorder on the rolling table next to the bed in full view of all three of them.

The man between them had one leg with a cast to his thigh hanging outside his blanket, the arm on the same side was wrapped and in a sling. His eyes were blackened, and a large bandage covered his right cheek. Jason picked up a blanket from the chair in the corner and laid it over the man's exposed toes.

Dell continued, "You wanna tell us why you were trying to kill Alynne Stone?"

"I want a lawyer." The man's words came through gritted teeth. Was his jaw wired shut?

"Understandable." Dell sat on the chair next to him. "Especially since we have your prints on the flare that distracted Officer Sanchez and on the door and window of Miss Stone's bedroom. We also have her testimony of the things you said to her. I believe your final words to her were, 'I'll kill you.' Yep, I would definitely get myself a lawyer. Not that he's gonna be able to keep you from going to prison."

"You're not allowed to ask me questions."

"Oh, no. I would never. I haven't asked you anything. Have I asked him anything, Lieutenant?"

"Not since he requested a lawyer. But it's a shame that we'll have to press those murder charges without hearing his side of the story."

"I didn't murder anyone."

"No, no." Dell shook his head and his pointer finger. "We don't want you saying anything without your attorney present. He'll be able to explain why you're facing murder charges."

"You have to listen to me." Still through clenched teeth, but now the man was practically pleading. "I didn't kill anyone. I wasn't even here when Ellis died."

"Anyone claiming such a thing would need to be able to prove it." Dell looked at his fingernails as though contemplating a manicure.

"I've got receipts from restaurants and gas stations all the way from Orlando."

Jason took his cues from Dell. "That may be, but a savvy killer would have had his accomplice collect all of those receipts.

The man's head rested for a minute against the pillow. "I was in New Orleans."

"Strange place to be." But Dell's interest had obviously been piqued.

"Pearl Stone passed away not so long ago." Jason had hit a sweet spot. The man's eyes widened.

"I didn't kill her either. She was already dead."

Dell picked up on the story. "I see. So, you visited the past residence of a distant relative that you'd never met."

"I knew her. I spent part of last summer with her after my mother died. She's the one who told me about the family and the treasure. I was only trying to dig up dirt on Ellis to convince him to give me money."

"Sounds like blackmail." This guy was a peach.

"But I didn't learn anything about him, only about the treasure."

"I get it. You decided to visit the past residence of a distant relative that you had visited once before." Dell shrugged.

Surzchenkov sighed. "I was coming to claim her inheritance."

"Her inheritance, I see." Dell gave the man a quizzical look.

The injured man rocked his head to one side. "I shouldn't say more. But I did speak to an attorney down there. He said that Ellis Stone already claimed it."

Ellis hadn't traveled last summer as far as Jason could remember. But there was no need for Ellis to tell him anything about an inheritance.

Dell picked up on the man's intimation. "That was a big assumption to travel all that way on. It's hard enough to prove you're the closest heir, especially since you weren't, but a woman that old would surely have had a will."

The man didn't respond.

"Ooh. I get it." Dell scratched the side of his mouth and sat back in his chair. "You'd stolen her will when you visited her last summer. You knew she didn't have a will. Or at least, you thought you knew."

"You can't know all of this." The man's dark eyes squinted. "Besides, it's not me you should be grilling. The description that I heard from the attorney's messenger was of a much younger man."

Jason and Dell traded glances. If he believed this guy, then someone pretended to be Ellis last summer and claimed the inheritance.

A nurse walked in and paused the conversation. She checked the monitors. "I've asked the kitchen to put together a liquid dinner for you, Mr. Surzchenkov. Is there anything I can get you while you're waiting?"

The man shook his head.

"Not even an attorney?" A half-smile spread across Dell's face as he arched an eyebrow.

Surzchenkov shot him an evil look.

The nurse didn't reply on her way out the door.

Jason stepped out of her way and waited until the door closed. "We can assume, then, that you no longer want to wait for an attorney. Because we can get one for you if you'd like us to. That's your right."

He cut his eyes at Jason. "Can you swear I won't be accused of murder?"

Dell stood and picked up the recorder. "This is a waste of my time."

"No, wait. I have some things I can tell you."

He stopped halfway to the door. "I'll listen for a few more minutes." He returned and set the recorder on the table.

The man fidgeted. "First swear that I won't go to jail for something I didn't do." His volume rose.

His claim had a ring of truth to it.

"We can't swear to anything like that," Dell stated the obvious.

Jason stepped forward. "But we'll check on your story. You give me the attorney's name down in New Orleans, and I'll talk to the man myself and see if he can give you an alibi."

"He can. I know he can."

Dell crossed his arms. "Okay. We'll give it a shot."

Surzchenkov caved after less than a half-minute of Dell's stare. "I did go to the inn tonight."

"We already know that." Dell leaned back and looked at the man through slitted eyes.

"I only wanted to have the inheritance. All of it. Not only half. I deserve all of it. Not the perfect little princess."

Jason bristled at the man's tone. "You barely even know your sister."

"Half-sister." He spat out the words. "Yet she received family, security, love from two doting parents. And she didn't even care about it. She didn't deserve any of it."

"And you did," Dell suggested.

Surzchenkov turned to him. "I did. And I was going to have it no matter what I had to do."

"Including killing Alynne Stone." Dell brought him to the brink.

His eyes hardened. "The woman doesn't know how to die. She should have died that first night."

"At the grocery store." Jason supplied.

"I had the perfect alibi set up, but she spoiled it all." He turned his empty gaze on Jason. "Or rather you did."

"And poisoning her cereal?" Jason pushed.

He scowled. "That was Sheila's stupid idea when she saw that her car door was unlocked, and the box was just sitting there. We drove into McKinney and bought some rat poison. But that backfired, too."

"So, you tried to run her down?"

The man dropped his gaze to the floor. "Sheila did that while I set up our alibi on the front porch. I told people that she was in the bathroom."

"And the shooting." Dell took over.

"I didn't have anything to do with shooting her." He glared at Dell.

The chief cocked his head to the side and crossed his arms.

"Okay, I bought the wreath. I snuck out the front door early and put it on the chair."

That was why Rose didn't bark.

"I gathered with everyone else in the dining room claiming that Sheila was still asleep. It was a perfect plan."

"Until she was killed."

Surzchenkov straightened. "You never found her phone, did you?"

Jason glanced at Dell who shook his head.

"She'd sent me a text that morning. She'd seen someone in town that she knew." He looked from Dell to Jason. "She was sure it was the man who had been Aunt Pearl's companion. She didn't think he saw her." His face crumpled. "But he must've."

Dell caught Jason's eye. "Did she recognize him from the inn?

One of the cousins?"

"No." His tears raised his tone several pitches. "I met all the cousins. I would have recognized him."

"But you only met him a year ago and for a short time, right?" Jason asked.

"I would have. He hovered over Pearl like a buzzard. And Sheila did recognize him. She even took a photo of him."

"When you were visiting in New Orleans." Dell supplied.

"No, on the street in Heath's Point while she was gassing up the motorcycle."

Dell picked up the recorder and clicked it off without another word. Jason led him from the room.

"Well, Lieutenant, at least you know your friend is finally safe." He stepped to the nurses' station.

Jason cornered Billings. "Did you work the Sheila Surzchenkov murder?"

"You know I did."

"But you followed it through all the way. Until the body left, right?" Jason had left for guard duty.

"Yes, sir."

"And the property of the victim. Who collected all of that?"

"Well, there wasn't much. It went to the county, though if you're looking for the chain of custody." Billings tilted his head with a worried expression.

"I'm not concerned about procedure. I only want to know what besides the rifle was found," Jason explained. "Like maybe a purse or a phone?"

"No. Neither of those. The keys, the sweater, and that broken frame."

The man would know. "Anything else at all?"

"Not on the body, no, sir. And no purse or phone at all. Not even a wallet, but that duffle under the bike did have the makings of a foldable rifle stand."

"Really." He'd expected as much.

"Couple of clamps and some boards with a folding stand. Looks like it could've been attached to one of the trees like the chief thought."

Jason thanked the man.

Dell sidled over. "I'm gonna wait and chat a bit with the doc. Why don't you go home for a change and get a real night's sleep? We can tackle this with fresh eyes and ears tomorrow."

"I thought I'd go through the details of all of these events. See if I can wrap my mind around it." It was unlikely, but maybe something had a clue for him to go on. Especially if Ronald's alibi held up.

"Tomorrow. That's an order. Go home. Sleep. Your halfway to useless." Dell pivoted him away and gave him a little push in the back.

Dell was wrong, though. With the way Jason was feeling, he was all the way to useless.

Chapter Twenty-Seven

Alynne rolled away from the light coming through the curtains.

"Morning, glory," Momma called to her out of the fog of sleepy.

She groaned and ended it with a barely audible, "Hi." She pushed herself up and forced her feet to the floor. "What time is it?"

"Late, I'm afraid. Almost eight. Your aunts have already made a fabulous breakfast. I'm going to so enjoy being in business with them."

Oh, yeah, business. She needed to call Mrs. Oglesby back. What could she say to her? *Some maniac was trying to kill me, and I had to drop your call?* And worse, Mrs. Oglesby had *hated to do* something to Alynne. Was she about to be fired?

If so, would that really be a bad thing? It would make her choice to stay with Momma and her aunts that much easier. But getting fired would also mean that Mrs. Oglesby didn't believe her.

Or Mr. Brevard had lost faith in her. That was the last thing she wanted.

"Breakfast is ready." Aunt Billie called through Momma's closed door.

"Oh, sweet girl, do something about your hair." Momma winked and left, shutting her door again.

Alynne stood and looked in the mirror. "Ick." She bent over double and shook her head, threading her fingers through the unruly waves. Then she flipped her head back up. That was a little better. At least Momma's brush could get through it. She washed her face and changed out of the long T-shirt she'd borrowed. Then she looked in the mirror again. Not stellar, but it would have to do this morning.

She didn't plan to see anyone but her family anyway.

Breakfast was delightful and delicious. Again on the porch, the four of them feasted on Eggs Benedict and miniature cheese soufflés. Aunt Bobbie was a master chef when it came to soufflés. And Aunt Billie's sauce was sheer perfection.

"Do you think you would be all right here for a couple of hours, sweet girl?" Momma's brows were furrowed, and her eyes squinted.

Alynne painted on her best-relaxed face. "Of course. What do you all have planned today?" Maybe Alynne could join them and not have to stay here alone?

"Bobbie's done some research and found a large property up near Sherman that's for sale. We're going to go look at it." Momma patted her hand. "We won't make any decisions without speaking to you about it first, though." Her mom's gaze pierced her. "Do you mind? I mean really?"

She forced a smile across her lips. "No. Not at all. I may take a little jaunt into town. I didn't get to have a good tour, you know. And maybe I can help Cat and Ray with the mission or painting or something at the diner."

"Oh, that would be such fun for you."

The aunts picked up the china from their breakfast while Momma put her arm around Alynne's waist. "It feels so good to finally have you safe again."

Alynne drew in a long breath and released her anxiety with it. Yes, it did, at that.

The aunts made quick work of the dishes. Momma changed into some blue jeans and a sleeveless, flowered top. Looking at her, Alynne could scarcely believe that she'd lost Pop just a couple of weeks ago. Her eyes were lit with possibility and her cheeks flush with excitement.

And she was excited for all of them as well, though she was leaning more and more toward keeping this beautiful old place. Even if it meant she had to be here alone from time to time. When they started taking guests again, she wouldn't be alone much. She wandered into Pop's office and stood at the windows that looked out onto the front porch. This would make a fine office for her. If she stayed.

But for now, she had a phone call to make. She dialed Mrs. Oglesby's extension, and the woman picked up almost immediately.

"Alynne, I had expected to hear back from you yesterday. I have a difficult issue that I'm facing."

"I'm so sorry." What else could she say? "It's rather a long story that can wait for another time."

"Well, about this situation." Mrs. Oglesby began recounting all that they had discussed the day before. Might as well be comfortable while she listened. Alynne turned toward her father's desk to take his chair and froze.

Blayne stood behind the desk, in a corner by Pop's filing cabinets. And he had a handgun pointed at Alynne.

She gasped and almost dropped the phone.

"Did you hear my question?" Her boss had finished her soliloquy.

"I ... I will call you later." She clicked the end button and glanced into the main hall.

"If you want your mom and your aunts to live..." Blayne's voice was a bare whisper. "You'll let them leave. Now."

Alynne swallowed and spun as her mom came into the entry hall. "We'll be back in a few hours." She hustled out the front door with her sisters in her wake. "You're sure you're all right here?"

Alynne followed, but only to the porch. Momma's question opened an opportunity for help. "I'll just do some work in the barn." Momma would never connect with that. Oh! "Or maybe I'll take the boat out."

Momma smiled and nodded as she and her sisters climbed into her white SUV.

Her arm felt as stiff as her smile as she waved while they turned out of the parking lot.

"Wise of you to let them leave." Blayne joined her on the porch, putting his arm around her waist and pressing the gun against her ribs. "And we might just take that boat out as you said. A little boating accident if you don't behave."

"Why are you here, Blayne? What do you want?" For the life of her, she had no idea.

"I. Want. Treasure."

Jason pulled his car into the spot in front of the station. Dell was a pretty smart man, but telling Jason to sleep when things were left undone was wasted effort. Aw, he'd gotten a couple of hours just before sun-up, but he'd spent much of the night on engine searches about Ronald and his wife, Pearl and Todd Stone, and on the property that was now Sunrise Inn.

He'd learned a few tidbits, like the fact that Pearl's assistant, the companion that Ronald had talked about, was a much younger man, probably a handyman. And he was a known gambler by the name of Waylon Johnson. Jason hadn't been able to find anything else about the man, no social media or photos. Not even a record of birth or social security file, so the name was fake. Though why he'd pick up on such a strange name, Jason had no idea.

Maybe the property from the Surzchenkovs could open a few doors.

"Morning, Mrs. Hawkins."

"Good morning to you, Lieutenant. Heard you had an eventful evening." She winked in his direction.

Usually, he would ignore such a look, but maybe he needed to shoot down her hint right away. "I wouldn't call it eventful. It was a crime. They happen. Thankfully, the victim was unhurt, and the suspect was captured and has confessed."

"Sure is a beautiful lady you rescued."

He chuckled. "I didn't do anything. She rescued herself." He started to turn away but thought better of it. "And as for her looks, this county is full of beautiful women that I've haven't been the least bit interested in. There's no story here. Sorry."

Surely, that would quell the rumors that must have been poised to grow today.

He wandered toward the property room. "Evans, would you come check out a box for me."

"Sure." The younger man pulled the clipboard from his top drawer. "Which one?"

"Surzchenkov."

After collecting the box, Jason set it on his desk and removed the lid. Run of the mill stuff in there. A wallet had less than fifty dollars and eight credit cards. His ID checked out. He tossed the fake leather trifold back into the box where it landed next to a knock-off fitness watch and the man's phone.

He picked up the phone and leaned out of his office door. "Hey, was the phone opened?"

"Yeah, the dude didn't even have a passcode on it. Said it was too tiresome."

Jason turned the phone over. It wouldn't have taken a second for the man to have set up a fingerprint lock, but whatever. He opened the phone and checked the call activity. Nothing strange there. And no odd apps.

He opened the text reports. There were several different

people texting him over a variety of topics. From the looks of it, he'd been so sure of finding the treasure that he'd optioned several acres in an exclusive lakefront development.

Jason moved down the list. Sheila. These must be some of the final words with his wife. And part of them might describe the man that had been Waylon Johnson. Jason clicked on the conversation and waited for the file to load. Bingo. A photo. Must have been the one she'd taken while she was gassing up her bike.

The man was looking in the window of the auto parts store across from the Texaco. The hair and shoulders looked a little familiar. Then Jason recognized the reflection of the face in the glass.

Blayne.

He headed for the door. "I'm going to the inn."

"What's wrong?" Evans leaped to his feet. "Need backup?"

He started to shake it off, but his gut twisted. "Yes." He broke into a run for the front door. "And call the chief."

"And you think you can find what people have been hunting for over a century?" Alynne attempted to push away from him, but he held her fast.

"I have intel." Blayne chuckled and prodded her around the corner of the porch. "Looks like someone has already been digging." He pushed her toward the two shovels and the pickax that she and Jason had left in the corner beside the kitchen door. "Grab one of the shovels … easy."

If only Alynne could figure out a way to take the pickax. Though the thought of using such a thing on a person, any person, disgusted her. Still, in a pinch.

But, would Blayne really kill her? "Put the gun away, Blayne. You're scaring me."

"Good." He kept the gun pinned to her ribs. There was no way she could get a good angle to swing any shovel, but she picked one up anyway.

"Now you're going to do a little digging."

"And where will I do that? In one of the hundred places that has already been explored? Or maybe at the bottom of the lake. It wasn't here when the treasure was buried, you know. If there ever was a treasure, to begin with."

"There's treasure all right. Your Aunt Pearl was adamant about that."

"You met my aunt?" Why would Blayne have been speaking to her aunt?

"Of course. Who do you think inherited? Your dad? He didn't even know she died."

He sounded delusional. Alynne couldn't even process all that he'd said. Was this the situation that Pop had written about to his friend in Dallas? "So, you stole from Aunt Pearl?"

He didn't answer right away but pulled a paper out the pocket of his khaki pants. He shoved Alynne downhill from the kitchen door several feet. Then he joined her and turned to face the house, keeping Alynne in front of him. He opened the paper. A photo.

"Is that the picture that was in the parlor? You stole the photo."

"Yes and no. I wasn't the thief. Your big brother swiped it. I simply happened to find it." He smiled as he analyzed the picture.

"Where?"

He glanced at her, a crazy look in his eye. "Why, where they left it, my dear." He walked straight through Momma's herb garden to the edge of the house and turned around. Then again glancing at the photo, he took several paces landing him directly in the center of the herb garden. "At least your digging won't be too hard."

"Don't be ridiculous, Blayne. This area has obviously been dug up. At least a foot deep and probably more."

"Then you'll go deeper." His volume rose with every word. "And you'll keep digging until you find it." He released her.

She began to scrape away the foliage with the edge of the shovel. "What makes you think it's here?"

"The bell is the key." He let out a terrifying sound that was a mixture of maniacal laughter and growling.

Whatever he saw in that picture certainly made him sure of himself. He tucked it back into his back pocket then leveled the gun at her again. "I could make this easier on me and simply shoot you now and do the digging myself."

She lifted a shovelful of Momma's spearmint plants. "So instead, you'll let me do all the digging and, then, shoot me."

"I don't want to kill you, Alynne. This wasn't how it had to be. I was prepared to marry you, remember?"

"So you could have access to the property. Or maybe then kill me and inherit?"

"Access. That was all. I truly cared about you. I even told your father so."

Alynne halted with a load of dirt filling her shovel. "You met my father? When?"

"I was trying to honor the practices of your family. Like you told me. I thought … I was sure that your dad would give his permission for me to marry you."

Alynne tossed the dirt aside. Her spine chilled with what she was hearing. "When was this, Blayne? She took a step toward him. She had room to swing the shovel now.

"Get back to digging," he growled. Then he pointed his gun in the air and fired off a shot. "I'm not afraid to put you in the hole you're making."

She turned back toward her hole and caught a flash of movement in the kitchen window. Momma? Had she returned? Alynne refused to look in the direction of the door, but she'd clearly seen her mom's face. She tossed aside a pile of dirt and went for another, glancing toward Blayne. There was her mom's face again on the other side of the glass, only this time she was looking at Blayne.

Alynne cut into the soil again. "You weren't the one who shot at me, though."

"Why would I want you dead, sweetheart? I believed that I could persuade you to marry me, giving me legal ownership of this land and plenty of time to search it." He swiped his sleeve across his forehead. "But then I found the key."

"A key to a lock?"

"More like a map key. Hanging in plain sight for who knows how long. Pearl told me about a key explaining the treasure's location was hidden somewhere. Shocked me to find the photo laying in the backseat of a car."

"Whose car?"

He waved the gun at her. "You ask too many questions."

She dug for a few minutes to give Momma time to call the police. "Did you kill my father?" She hated the way her voice broke. She'd brought this on Pop. Brought about his death and Momma's pain with her own unrestrained sin.

"I didn't mean to kill him. It was an accident."

"The police said the car was sent off the road somehow."

"Ice."

She paused and looked at him.

He shrugged. "I got mad when your dad said he wouldn't approve of our marriage. I … I hit him, and he stumbled and fell against a big boulder. Well, he was dead already. So, I drove to a truck stop and bought a couple of bags of ice. Then I put him in his car like he was driving and put the ice on his foot against the accelerator. With the engine revving, I only had to shift it into gear and let it roar down the hill. It went over the side instead, but the end result was still effective." He seemed proud of his cleverness.

"Not effective enough. The police realized it wasn't an accident."

Momma appeared at the window again and this time she beckoned Alynne to come inside. She had something planned.

He pointed his gun at her and pointed his finger in the widening hole at her feet. "They have no proof. They only have suspicions. And suspicions without proof are worthless."

She went back to work. Momma clearly wanted her to bring

421

Blayne inside, but that would put Momma at risk as well. Still, if she didn't, Momma would likely put herself in danger some other way. If only she could keep Blayne talking until the police arrived. "Did you kill Sheila because she was shooting at me?"

He laughed. "Don't be so arrogant. Sheila knew me from when I lived with your Aunt Pearl. I'd been so careful to make sure they never saw me here."

Alynne thought back. He was right. The only meals he'd joined were before the pair had arrived. Then he'd been gone, busy, or late to the table, well after everyone else had left. He'd not come inside at the visitation or attended the funeral at all.

"But then she did when I happened to stop in town. I followed her back to the lake but lost her when she took the motorcycle cross-country through the trees. It wasn't a long wait before she came back, though."

He'd killed her in cold blood? Alynne looked up at him horrified. What sort of man was he?

"Don't look at me like that. I couldn't let her report who I was."

She dropped her gaze to the ground. Momma's plan better work. "I'm really thirsty. May I get some water?"

"You've barely been digging for a half-hour."

She loaded her shovel again. "It's hot out here, Blayne. If you want me to keep doing my best, you'll let me get some water. I can even get several bottles from the fridge, so I won't have to go back inside for them."

He seemed to mull that idea while she expanded the hole another foot wider. "Please?" She coughed.

"Fine." He pushed away from where he was leaning against the side of the house. "But don't think you're going to get bathroom breaks, too."

The man's mind was gone. She laid the shovel down, hesitant to leave it behind, but Blayne would never let her bring it with her. Besides, without it, he let her lead the way into the kitchen, staying several steps behind her.

She stepped through the door and caught a movement to her left from her peripheral vision. That had to be Momma. She took another step through the door and then stumbled, rolling to the floor.

Blayne's attention focused on Alynne. He didn't notice the cast iron skillet that caught him across the face. He slammed into the edge of the door and then toppled forward, landing with a thud on the linoleum.

"Are you all right?" Momma kept the pan in her hand as she rushed over.

Alynne snatched Blayne's gun from his open hand. "Why did you come back?" She knelt and checked for a pulse in his neck.

"My purse. I left it over there on the bench. Your aunts wanted to stop at the market anyway, so I dropped them off." She leaned over the man. "Is he alive?"

"I'm not an expert, but I think I can feel a heartbeat." The man's nose was thoroughly broken though, smashed against the side of his face. "Can you call an ambulance?"

"Oh dear, yes. Of course." Her mom toddled toward the counter to use the landline.

Sirens sounded in the distance. "I'm glad you called the

police."

"I didn't at first. I guess I was a little rattled. But when I did, Mrs. Hawkins said that were already on their way."

"God's protection."

Chapter Twenty-Eight

Jason pulled into the lot at the inn. He parked the Jeep on the outskirts, jumped out, and sprinted to the house. He'd already been concerned about Blayne when the 9-1-1 came over the wire about a gunman on the property.

He took the stairs two at a time, gun ready. Sirens sounded in the distance, but he wouldn't wait for them. Not with at least two helpless women in there with a man who might be a murderer.

He glanced through the window beside the door and saw Myra's face. She waved him in.

Holstering his gun, he opened the front door, sending the chimes through the house. All seemed quiet. Though he could hear Myra speaking. "He must've come in through the southside door. It's seldom locked."

Jason entered the kitchen. Myra was standing near the door, looking down.

"That's something that needs to change," Alynne voiced, but she was hidden behind the counter.

His breathing slowed. They were okay. "Ladies, I don't mean to alarm you but … well, your friend …" The words halted as the man came into view, sprawled out on the kitchen floor. Alynne had her fingers pressed to his neck.

"He still has a pulse, but I'm afraid to move him at all," she told him.

A siren cut off. Likely one of the emergency vehicles coming into the parking lot. Hopefully, it was the ambulance. He knelt by the unconscious man. "What happened to him?" Looked like his whole face had been smashed.

Myra picked up the skillet with both hands. Oh, yeah, that would do some damage. Looked like it had. "He was making Alynne dig in the herb garden. Like that spot hadn't been dug up plenty." Myra's face darkened.

"He wanted to go deeper." Alynne stood. "I don't know why, but he was positive we'd find the treasure there. Said Aunt Pearl had directed him to find the key."

"How did he know Pearl?" Her mom asked.

Jason filled them in on what they had learned about Blayne and his multiple identities. "I have no doubt we'll find more names for the man than only these." He glanced from Alynne to her mom. "There's even some suspicion that he had a hand in Pearl's death as well, but we'll probably never know that for sure."

Alynne knelt again and checked the man's pulse as something rattled in the entry hall. Mark Bannister and his partner rushed in.

"I don't mind enjoying your company, Cheesy, but it would be nicer if it wasn't involved in an accident or crime scene."

"My thoughts exactly."

Jason might've misunderstood, but it sure sounded like Bannister had suggested a date with Alynne. He couldn't control the twist that again affected his gut.

Bannister pulled out a neck brace and handed it to his partner. "What can you tell me?"

Myra moved to the front porch to speak to the other officers who had arrived, so Alynne fielded the questions, explaining about the skillet and the continued pulse. His partner slipped the brace around Blayne's neck and then inserted an IV into his arm.

Bannister glanced up at Alynne. "I think I've got all the information I need. Danvers? Your ball."

She stood. "Thanks." She glanced at Jason with a trembly smile. "I assume you want to hear all that happened."

"Yes, ma'am, but I think the porch might be a better choice than the parlor. The breeze is nice."

He followed her to the sitting area and stood leaning against the rail while she sat on the couch.

Before he could ask her the first question, Dell ascended the stairs. "Sheriff followed me in."

He raised his gaze, rolling it across the eaves. Sure enough, a county cruiser roared up to the house. Kindrich opened his door and stepped out. For a change, Deputy Puppy stayed in the car.

Kindrich strode up the steps. "Heard you had some trouble out here again. We were only passing by." He reached for the chief's hand.

Dell shook without reaction, but Jason had to concentrate to keep his mouth shut.

"I appreciate your willingness to help, Beau. I think we have everything under control. And we just might end up with a solution to the murdered woman we found a couple of days ago."

The sheriff's eyes glittered, but he chewed on his back teeth. "You'll keep me updated?"

"Absolutely."

With that, Kindrich returned to his car, and they pulled away.

"What happened?" The sheriff was a different man entirely.

"Maybe he found that I was serious about signing up to run against him. If he ends up losing, he'll want to stay on my good side to get a deputy job and stay close to the department." Dell shrugged. "Or he could be finally changing his mind about working with us."

Nah.

"If I do win the election, you can bet I won't be coming out to all of your crime scenes, Lieutenant." Dell winked.

"Wouldn't mind if you did, Boss."

Alynne proceeded to explain how Blayne had come to be on the kitchen floor. "And he has the photo from the frame in the parlor. It's in his back pocket."

Wait. "He has the photo? Are you sure it was the same one?"

They paused as the EMTs carried the man out of the house. He was alive and stable. That was about all they knew.

Alynne didn't even give the injured man a second look. "He said it was in a frame in the backseat of a car."

"That's enough to put him at the scene of the murder of Sheila Surzchenkov." Jason filled Dell in on what he'd found.

Dell followed the paramedics to the ambulance. "In case there's some sort of confession." He paused and turned back. "I'm glad you're all right, Miss Stone."

"I still can't believe it. And he said that he killed Pop." Her eyes welled up with tears. "Pop's death was all my fault." She lowered her forehead to her knees, shaking with silent sobs.

He knelt and put his hand on her shoulder. "You didn't cause the accident, Alynne. Just because you knew the man, you dated him …"

"I did a lot more than that." She lifted her head, her eyes red and pouring out guilt and regret.

"You don't have to tell me this." Seeing her in such pain broke his heart.

"I do. I should've owned up to my mistake a long time ago. My sin. It wasn't an accident. I knew what I was doing, but I couldn't seem to stop myself. Like running downhill. And I thought marrying Blayne would fix everything."

Marrying the man would've been the worst thing she could have done.

"He thought he was being so good to talk to my father about us." She took a great inhale. "But when he didn't get the answer he wanted, he hit Pop."

"Your dad was already dead when he loaded him in the car."

Alynne nodded. "He used ice on the accelerator to make the car move faster."

Jason let his gaze hit the rafters. That was the puddle in the middle of the headliner. "This isn't your fault."

"How can you say that? If I hadn't … if we … Blayne would never have met my father."

"Blayne already knew about your family. I believe he conned

your aunt's attorney into giving him the bulk of her property. As badly as he wanted to go to Vegas, I bet he gambled it away. Then he set his sights on you in order to gain proximity to the treasure he'd been told about by your Aunt Pearl."

"He said something about that. How did he know Aunt Pearl?"

"I don't know where the connection came in yet, but he was her companion or assistant or handyman. Hard to say what."

Jason stood and tugged a notepad and pencil from his pocket. "So Blayne confessed to killing your dad."

She nodded. "He didn't quite confess to Sheila's murder."

Still, they might be able to swing that conviction if the correct prints were in the right places. "We'll probably get him for that as well."

"So, it's over?" She looked up at him with a hopeful gaze.

He pocketed his notepad and pencil, reached down to take her hands, and lifted her to her feet. "It's over." He stared into her eyes. "You truly are safe now."

Alynne trotted up the steps to her room. She needed to clean up any residual water from the open window, replace the fire ladder into the window seat, and she desperately craved a shower. Now that she was sure her danger had passed, sure that no one would be hiding somewhere to stab her or shoot her, it didn't even bother her to be in her suite.

Blayne, though alive, had sustained life-altering injuries at the hand of her mom. He'd be in the hospital for quite a while and in jail for a lot longer than that once he endured facial reconstructive surgery and a replacement of at least some of his teeth. Nothing the man didn't deserve.

And he was firmly out of her life.

After showering, she dried her hair and dressed in cute, albeit comfortable, blue-jean shorts and a sleeveless button-down top with flowers. She applied some blush to her cheeks and mascara to her eyelashes then slipped on some sandals before going back down the stairs.

Hopefully, Jason would be coming back for dinner.

No, she couldn't be thinking of him. Couldn't allow herself to even consider …

"Anyone home?" Speak of the devil. Jason sauntered into the entry hall and put a crisp, new cowboy hat on the rack at the kitchen entrance. "You look like you're feeling better."

"I am, thanks. Momma and the aunts are cleaning in the south wing."

"We're here." Aunt Bobbie came in with a pile of towels followed by Aunt Billie with a similar load. "I'm glad you chose to join us tonight, Jason."

"Am I early?" He took the pile from Aunt Bobbie's arms and tossed them into the pile next to the kitchen door.

"You're right on time, dear boy." Momma carried in a small tote with cleaning products. She stowed it under the sink. "We're making it an easy night. Ray and Cat will be bringing some barbecue. Not as good as mine, but still delicious."

Aunt Billie picked up a tray of ice-filled cups. "Thought we could have a sort of picnic out on the porch if the June bugs'll cooperate."

"I love that idea." Alynne picked up a stack of paper plates and napkins and followed after the others.

The old blue truck bounced into the lot with Ray at the wheel. When it came to a stop, Cat climbed out. A yellow head peeked out behind her, and then Rose jumped down to the ground.

"Oh." Momma clapped her hands and rushed forward.

"Rose." Alynne followed.

The friendly dog trotted over and licked her hand. She had a shaved place on her head, but otherwise, she looked no worse for the wear.

Cat shut the door. "Dr. Harpavat said she recovered famously. She has a hard head."

"I could have told him that." Momma laughed and scratched the dog underneath her chin.

Ray brought a large box up to the porch and began unpacking brisket, sausage, ribs, and all sorts of sides on the table. "Lots of variety."

"And no people food for the pup," Momma said.

They spent the next couple of hours chatting and laughing. Alynne was thankful they avoided conversation about either Blayne or Ronald. There had been enough hurt from those two men.

Aunt Billie did bring up the Victorian house they still planned to see. "Tomorrow if it works out." The three of them told Cat, Ray, and Jason of their plans to run a bed and breakfast like the Sunrise Inn.

"But you don't want to stay here?" Cat sounded like a

disappointed child. "I thought you liked it here."

"Oh, honey, I love it here. But sometimes things change." Momma patted her hands.

The woman was protecting Alynne. But she needn't have bothered. "Actually, Momma, I've decided that I'd like to stay here and work the place. And I'd like it very much if you and Aunt Billie and Aunt Bobbie would stay here with me and share in the profits."

"Are you sure, dear?" Momma leaned back to look at her evenly. "You're not just doing this for my benefit?" She glanced at her sisters. "Our benefit?"

"No. I like it here. I want to stay."

"What about your job?" Aunt Bobbie asked.

"Funny thing about that." Alynne had finally gotten the full call in with Mrs. Oglesby that afternoon. But she suspected the woman didn't quite believe her when she explained having to hang up on the two other calls. "My boss had to fire the filing clerk and one of the research assistants is taking her place. And they're signing a new partner."

"Is that good?" Momma asked.

"It will mean plenty of job security. But there isn't enough room to make an office for the partner."

"That could be a difficult situation." Ray reached for another spoonful of potato salad. That had to be his third. Where did he put it all?

"The partners have decided to make the researchers' jobs, my job, work-from-home positions to make room for the new partner. I get to keep my job and my benefits, but all of my work will be online."

Momma rushed over and gave her a hug. "That is the best news ever."

"But I don't expect you three to change your plans. I hope you will, and if you stay here, we can set up a financial agreement that divides the money we take in fairly." Alynne looked at all three of them in turn. "But you won't own the property, that's part of Pop's will."

"I can live with that." Aunt Bobbie threw her napkin in the air.

"Yeah," Aunt Billie chimed in. "That means I don't have to foot the bill if the pipes burst or the roof leaks."

"There's that."

"Sunrise Inn continues," Momma declared and gave Alynne another hug.

At least she could bring some joy to them tonight. They deserved it. The three of them started gathering up the plates and trash. Cat helped them, and Ray took the boxes out to the dumpster beside the barn.

Rose padded up to the porch and flopped under one of the chairs as Alynne moved to the swing. "How do you feel about me staying?"

Jason paused then sat beside her. "I'm for it. Can I help you move?"

"Probably…" If he was still interested once she finalized her decision. "And finally dig for that treasure."

He laughed. "Won't get that photo back until after Blayne's trial, but I'll have my work gloves and my shovel ready."

She looked into his eyes. "What I told you before …"

He took her hand in his. "Doesn't matter to me. And it shouldn't matter to you. Clearly, you've repented, and the Father has forgiven you. Why do you still let that past moment define you?"

His words sank in while her gaze shifted to the darkness beyond the rail. "That's a good question. I don't want to be defined by that. Not by my lack of judgment and not by Blayne and his duplicity."

"You aren't. You're smart and kind, beautiful and humble and gracious. You're defined by the attitudes you show from your heart and the Spirit who lives inside you."

Her gaze settled back on his comforting gray eyes. Tears burned hers, but she smiled through them. "I'm so glad the Lord brought me here and brought you into my life."

He reached to embrace her, and she kissed his cheek. He had no idea the healing his presence gave her, and she couldn't thank him enough for all he had done.

But she would try.

Acknowledgments

This book would not have been possible without the Lord's story and without the help of many people. If you want to know how this story came into being, check out "BREAKING POINT: The first ingredient" on my blog: www.MarjiLaine.com/blog. I am so grateful that the Lord has use of the imagination He has given.

Several talented folks helped edit this baby. Thank you, Teri Caldwell, Shirley Crowder, Lill Kohler, Arundhati Goswami, Brittany Clubine, and Fay Lamb! Y'all examined this book with care and precision. I am so blessed to have had your eyes on it!

I also appreciate some folks who have come alongside and encouraged me. Some kept me moving on the story to get it finished and others guided me as I worked through elements of the cover – even teaching me new techniques of photo enhancement. And some did BOTH! Thank you, Jackie Castle, Patricia PacJac Carroll, Sandy Barela, and Chautona Having!

My prayer warriors give me incredible blessings and have held my hand through this process. Thank you, dear ladies: Lori Bryant, Shirley Crowder, Jennifer Ferguson, Cindy Hardy, Julie Hausmann, Fran Williams, Kristi Wilson, and Adriane Young!

And I'm blessed beyond belief with such a patient and generous hubby who lets me do what I love. And grown kids who keep me on task and take care of the little things when I'm focused on the story. I love y'all BIGTIME!

The Lord is good all the time!

About Marji Laine

After seventeen years of homeschooling and eight years teaching in the public-school realm, Marji is still a teacher at heart, nowadays opting for writer meetings, workshops, and conferences as well as teaching a high school Bible study in her home. When she's not writing or publishing the stories of others, she enjoys watching sports (especially NASCAR and Texas Ranger baseball), theatre, and the Hallmark Movies and Mystery channel.

She and her hubby of thirty-two years live in a suburb of Dallas, Texas with two rescue dogs and one precious daughter who keeps them from having to be empty nesters for a little bit longer. She loves game night with her extended family and friends, singing harmonies in worship music, and talking shop with other writers. You can usually find her in her favorite recliner, tapping on her laptop with her fur-babies snoring at her feet. Or at www.MarjiLaine.com.

Learn more about Marji from monthly Crew News. She sends out a brief note every month and also gives away books to her newsletter readers. Sign up at her website.

Other Books by Marji Laine

Book One of Heath's Point Suspense

You've met Cat and Ray in BREAKING POINT, get their whole story in COUNTER POINT.

How does a small-town girl survive when ultimate power wants her dead?

Cat has lost everything except her life and a madman bent on revenge is determined to take that unless Ray, the man who broke her heart, can help her. If Cat can't figure out how to trust him, neither of them will survive.

Marji writes Romance!

Annalee Chambers: Poised, Wealthy, Socially Elite ... Convict?

Annalee floated through life in a pampered shell until she crushed it with a single word. Assigned to community service in the worst part of Dallas, she wonders what a bunch of downtown kids can teach an uptown Texas princess.

CJ Whelen uses his nickname to hide from the prominence that goes with his father's money. When a gorgeous prima donna joins his team, he's faced with open deception or exposing his private life to the world.

Some lessons are learned the hard way, and some seep into the soul unnoticed.

Suspense by Write Integrity

Book 1 of the Imperfect series, IMPERFECT WINGS begins the saga of the Cameron family.

With ties to covert operations in the military, brothers and sisters find a difficult time setting aside their former lives.

Get the entire series at Amazon.

Stacey Weeks delights with a twisted mystery, FATAL HOMECOMING. Her brother was murdered. She's convinced of that even though the people of the town believe he died of a drug overdose. But when an undercover RCMP detective notices attempts on her life, he's inclined to believe her.

Part of the Amazing Grace series, EVERYBODY'S BROKEN delves into the world of a tattered family: a husband who had lived and died in deception. His broken widow, struggling to protect her children from the pain of their father's real life, and survive when that real life begins to get too close.

**Thank you
for reading our books!**

**Look for other books
published by**

Write Integrity Press
www.WriteIntegrity.com